I0553791

Gliders
Of
Enlil

An Adventure Novel

This book is a work of fiction. The names, characters, places and incidents are the product of the author's imagination or are used fictitiously. Any resemblance to actual events, locales, or persons is purely coincidental. Copyright © 2013 by Jeffrey Carl. All rights reserved. In accordance with the US Copyright Act of 1976, the scanning, uploading and electronic sharing of any part of this book without the permission of the author constitute unlawful piracy and theft of the authors intellectual property. If you would like to use material from this book (other than for review purposes), prior written permission must be obtained by contacting the author at jeffreycarlauthor@gmail.com.
ISBN: 0615826334
ISBN-13: 978-0615826332

**Dedicated to my father
Dr. Charles J. Koester**

ACKNOWLEDGMENTS

My first thank you goes out to my mother, Mildred Koester, who tirelessly helped editing and rethinking parts of this book as it was created. Her energy and insight made writing so much easier and fun.

Thanks also to my wife and family for the countless nights and weekends spent writing rather than all the other things we may have been doing.

Thanks to the contributors, especially Jim Stout for his insight into how the Army worked and operated in Iraq. My limited knowledge would have failed miserably to represent the great work and efforts that our troops give in the most difficult of circumstances.

Cover Graphics: Thanks to Joe Keyser at Data Flow in Albany NY for creating cover graphics.

For more information on Iraq's cultural heritage, relations, resource links, and stories that were inspirations for this book, visit my blog at http://jeffreycarlauthor.wordpress.com.

CHAPTER 1

THE BRIDGE AT BAD-ASURIN

From the air, it looks like a dry wasteland. Sand, dunes, and more sand. Crude roads cut across the flat land that is not covered by the drifting sands. Past the desert, a sudden change in geography looks like a rupture in the earth. Barren mountain ranges with ragged edges protrude upward like an exposed spine across the land. Deep valleys fall between the mountains. There is some green, but mostly there are jagged grey rocks with dry river beds. At ground level, the land is harsh and almost colorless. Deep in one of these valleys a US soldier is standing in full uniform, looking up at the sky briefly through sunglasses. A faint hiss is heard from above the ground. A US Air force F15 blisters across the sky. In a split second the sound changes from a hiss to a thundering roar. Right behind are four more. They disappear over the mountain cliffs and streak towards the desert beyond. The thundering engines echo through the canyon walls, down to the soldier and a crowd of people gathered near a bridge across a deep gorge.

Jon looks up again from his position to look at the vapor trails of the F15s overhead. As the echoes fade, the hills seem to shout back to the jets. His checkpoint is at Bad Asurin Bridge over a large gorge that is a key supply route from Turkey to Baghdad and the war theater to the south. This is the only way by ground for hundreds of miles across the treacherous mountains. The US has set up a security post here as they have at many checkpoints, to keep foreign insurgents away, and to keep control of the traffic in and around the country. Jon is on duty, in charge of clearing people to pass. The checkpoint is different from other border crossings you might find because they have a bridge with large wrought iron gates across the north and south entrances.

A long queue of people who want to cross from north to south are waiting to be cleared through the south side to the road beyond the bridge. The queue consists of a mix of cultures and economic classes; shepherds with sheep and goats; a couple of families who are displaced and relocating to another area; a bus overloaded with people and luggage; and a large SUV of people protected by a security escort.

The outpost appears under provisioned. There is just a standard issue temporary army building about one hundred yards from the gate. Running parallel to the building is a dirt road that runs to a steep hillside between the higher hills behind it and the deep ravine that forms the need for the bridge. The gate on the south side of the bridge is a relic from another time. It has ornate ironwork across the top with Arabic writing on it. There are two people working the gate. Jon is an American soldier, and the other man, Hassan, is a paid "Terp", or interpreter who speaks both the local dialects and English. Hassan is the middleman between the Americans and the Iraqis, helping to sort out the issues that come up with every party that is trying to cross. Hassan knows that he is despised by many of his countrymen for aiding the Americans. It's a conflict he faces every day, but while he is working he does his best to aid his fellow Iraqis in the situation they have at hand. He comes from a modest local family but has been fortunate to attend some of the best universities in Qatar, and received a western education, including six years of English.

A goat shepherd has made his way to the front of the line. He knows Hassan, and he is explaining that he is trying to get to the other side to attend his nephews wedding. He speaks in a familiar tone with Hassan, but if he knows him does he doesn't make it obvious to Jon.

He explains in Arabic, "I'm going to my nephew's wedding. The goats are a gift for the family. There will be bad blood between families if I don't get there." He looks down at one of the larger goats which has made its way to the front. "And this one is for the feast!" he proudly proclaims. A cheer rises from several of the others waiting behind him.

"Do you have your identification and paperwork?" Hassan asks him.

"I don't have any identification papers. I have lived here all my life; I have never needed any identification. This is my bridge – in my country! I helped build it. No one has the right to stop me. You must let me pass."

Hassan explains this to Jon, who is clearly distracted and not engaged in the conversation. He looks up at the air for more F15s, then he looks over to the building, hoping for some relief or support from the other troops.

Hassan regains Jon's attention. Jon has his orders; everyone needs paperwork. He tells Hassan loudly in English "He has to go back to his village to get some papers, then he can return and we will let him pass." He waits as Hassan explains the policy in the local dialect.

The shepherd is clearly not pleased with this. He's talking with his hands to Hassan, and the language and tone of his voice don't need much interpretation.

"The office that issues the paperwork is only open three days a week, and they had no power all this week to generate the forms. So, getting any paperwork before my nephew's wedding was impossible! I must get to the wedding for my family! They are just up the road in the hills. In the name of Allah and my family, I must get past the gate!"

Hassan reinterprets for Jon. Jon is clearly annoyed with the situation. He silently considers how long the line is, the absurdity of stopping these people from their own bridge, and how harmless this native seems. There is a depth to this man. There are the lessons of a thousand ages in his eyes. The shepherd continues, even while Hassan is interpreting, and the confusion and tension increases.

Hassan adds, "He says he's an elder from the local town. His family has lived in these hills for generations. Jon, it would be degrading to him if you turn him back in this line. He wishes many blessings on you if you will just allow him to pass."

Jon considers, looks at the man in the eyes for a moment, spits on the ground, and looks at Hassan. Breaking some protocol, he turns his back to the crowd and brings the shepherd close to him. In a minute the shepherd turns around with some miraculously found paperwork in his hand. Jon inspects it and allows the man to pass with his goats. Many of the goats brush Jon as they pass.

"These aren't the droids I'm looking for." He mumbles to himself, to his own amusement. He looks up and chuckles to himself as several more goats brush his uniform as they pass him by.

Maybe he has been soft, but there are many more important things to attend to. As the shepherd and the goats pass, a noise is heard on the other side of the bridge. Jon looks up and sees a pickup and a van barreling towards the bridge. On the side of the van is a red hand print with a crescent on the palm. He can't see him, but a battle-worn Iraqi man is driving the pickup. He's got a scar across his left cheek to his temple, and a disturbed tuft of wild black hair. Jon knows the sound of small arms fire will come any second. He hears the spitting sound of bullets hitting the rocks behind him and across to the security building where his troop is. He hits the dirt and starts yelling a warning. He pulls his radio microphone close to his mouth and starts talking to his commander. He's already on his stomach crawling towards the building as he yells for support. He looks around for Hassan, and he sees he is already running towards the hill on the far side of the road. Just ahead of Hassan is the shepherd.

Jon continues crawling on his stomach towards the command post. Suddenly, there is a streak of red and orange fire from the truck. A rocket launched explosion crashes into the cliffs above the command post.

"They have a rocket launcher." Jon says as he cocks his head to one side, considering the situation. Jon heads faster towards the post. Suddenly, there is a new rocket blast. Jon sees the tracer going directly into the command post, now just a few yards in front of him. The building explodes in a huge fireball of smoke and fire. The compression wave from the explosion throws Jon to the ground again. For a moment he is still. As the scene comes back into focus, he yells into his microphone – "Hello Hello!" but he knows no response will be coming now. The building is destroyed. His ears are deaf from the explosion. He looks up at the building, then back at the bridge, there is nowhere to go now. Just flames on one side, and chaos on the other. His command post is gone. There are some jeeps on the other side, but the keys were in the building. He looks back at the bridge. He sees the van and pickup truck heading for his side. The truck has a turret built in the bed with one or two insurgents firing small arms towards him. He tucks his head down and yells into his microphone again for his commander, but there is no answer. Several moments pass. He feels frozen. It seems like he will have to face the inevitable. He looks around franticly for an escape route. Across the road, heading up a small trail between the crags of rocks, he spots Hassan. He's waving for him to follow him. It's likely no one else is seeing him waving to him, from the position he is standing in. Jon doesn't hesitate any more. He gets up and runs across the road, across a gulch and into the hill. The trail seems barely wide enough for a person to pass through. No one had spotted it before. The trail heads steeply upwards along a wall of stone hiding him from the road. Soon it levels out and turns inward between a crack separating opposing hills. The trail leads upward a hundred feet or more. As he turns another corner, he comes to a small grotto. He's out of breath and now hears himself breathing heavily. In front of him and on both sides, there are imposing walls of jagged rock. There is no exit from here. There is no path forward. The only thing Jon can hear is his own heavy breathing. As he looks at the jagged cliffs, he hears a low moaning from the rocks, but he's not really sure if he heard it or not. He can't see where the trail heads upwards from here. Not sure where to go or how he got there, he stops for a moment, breathing, breathing.

"Jon! – Jon!" He hears Hassan calling him, but he can't see where the sound is coming from. He looks all around him at the walls of rocks. There is no sign of him at all –no visible trace. Suddenly, out of nowhere, Hassan is standing several yards behind and above him on his right. How did he appear so fast?

"This way Jon! This way!"

Jon starts quickly towards him, still not sure how he is going to get up to the point where Hassan is. After a few quick steps, the trail is there, and then just as quickly, Jon is up. He disappears among the rocks. After a few more steps he's at an entrance to a cave. The entrance is formed sideways into to the rocks. Jon quickly ducks down and steps inside the cave. In the grotto, the emptiness returns. The craggy mountains give a low moan, and they return to steadfast silence as if no one had come that way for hundreds of years.

The sound of explosions has disappeared behind them.

Inside the cave a group of Iraqis are sitting against the cave walls. The flickering light of oil -lit lamps throw shadow and light across the walls of the cave. The shadows and light highlight the wrinkles and folds of the aged faces. Most of the people have their heads wrapped in traditional scarves. There is a mixture of smells, of smoke, animals, urine, and food.

Hassan has disappeared. Jon freezes, his training and fear tell him not to go further. This is not a safe place for an American soldier. Hassan and the shepherd have gone deeper into the cave. Jon holds his hands in front of him, palms down, as a gesture of friendship. He moves to sit against a wall. He has his weapon, but he feels sure all of the people around him are much more armed than he is. He has no chance if they want to take him as hostage; this has already gone too far.

Hassan comes back and sits next to him. Jon tenses as he feels the weight of being the uninvited guest in this place. Hassan tries to calm him. "Jon, the shepherd you allowed to pass, Samir, is a town elder. He has called for your safety. If I had not pleaded on his behalf, and if you had not cleared him across the bridge, he would be dead, and these townspeople would have lost another of their elders. For that he owes you your safety."

Jon sighs with relief, at least he won't be killed, or worse, held hostage in this cave.

He considers his situation. He wants to find a radio. He wants to get back to his troops. He wants to radio for help and be picked up. In the worst case he might be accused of deserting his post. He decides to ask Hassan.

"Hassan, what am I doing here? I should be getting back to my outfit, trying to find out what has happened. I need to get out of here!"

Hassan considers this with pause. "I understand, but be patient and consider your situation. Your outpost is no longer there. It has been destroyed, and I'm afraid none of your command post has survived. You will be safe here for now. We will get you back to your troops. For now, feel glad to be safe.

And by staying with me, as a hired agent of the US Army, you are keeping within your guidelines. You cannot be punished for abandoning your command, because you are still with the surviving members."

Jon is skeptical of this logic, "I'm not sure that's how it works, but it's the best I've got right now. Given the situation, I think I'll go with it."

Hassan continues "Jon, this is not a typical family or clan. There are things here older than we know. This family has ties to the beginnings of civilization. We are merely part of the history, for a brief period. There are some secrets that go back to generations, past written history. It's more than tradition. This family is part of a bloodline going back thousands of years. And that bloodline has spread across the world over time. Most people don't know they are part of it. America has the highest population of people native to Mesopotamia outside of the Middle East itself. Before Iraq, there was Persia, and before Persia, there was Assyria. Assyrians have been around since the dawn of man. In fact, Assyria is often considered part of the cradle of civilization. Western, Eastern, and Russian culture has never comprehended the richness and depth of the Assyrian people. They say it probably started from simple needs. As soon as people could farm, they started to do it collectively. And as they worked collectively, they started small markets, and the markets became towns. The towns became cities and history began."

"But now the history of Iraq is hidden by your war and our oil. Some here call oil a false god of civilization. It's as if you look through a lens, and oil is all you can see. While war rages on, the people, the culture, and the history survive. For all its value, oil has never benefitted the millions of Iraqi citizens. The wealth has gone to the fortunate few who pretend they will care for us. But they never do. They use the land and gain their riches. Oil doesn't define us; our culture is who we are. Our history is with us always, and the roots of families are the roots of our civilization here. There once were other gods. And while we live in a world of one God over all our faiths, history shows our ancestors worshipped other gods that once ruled before Him. It is with that, and that alone, that our friend the shepherd invites you to witness an ancient ceremony. This is what we are made of, and part of who we are."

A frail elderly woman walks to Hassan and gives him a familiar embrace.

"Jon, this is Nisaba. Nisaba is one of the most learned women of our clan. She knows more about our history than just about anyone. She has learned the story from her elders, and it is her responsibility to pass it on to the next generations. It will be her daughter Morgiana's responsibility when she is gone. She, more than anyone here, can tell you the story of our family."

Jon is reluctant and confused, but curious. He remembers from school in Oak Brook, Illinois, the legends of the ancient days of Mesopotamia; stories of great Kings, Sheiks, and Sultans. Stories of magic and wonder were read to him by his mother so he could fall asleep on hot summer nights. This gentle old woman in a black tunic dress and head scarf seemed as if she leaped from those pages and appeared in front of him now.

She motioned for them to follow her deeper into the depths of the cave. More elders are there, each staring at him with intensely penetrating eyes as he passes by. Their features are wrinkled and jagged. At times he can't tell shadows on the jagged rock walls from the faces that appear along the way. As he looks closer, there is depth in their aged frames that transcends the time and the place. As if the eyes of ancestors from thousands of years ago are seeing through them. As he passes they look at him, and there is suddenly a familiarity about him within that cannot be explained other than through a sense of belonging.

He walks deeper into the cave. It's dark, cool; he can feel a draft from a cavern off to the left. Nisaba lights several torches on the wall. In the center of the cavern are several cushions to sit on around a large pipe in the center. The small group settles into the cushions. Nisaba settles into one of the cushions near Jon, and Hassan sits between. She sits back into her cushion and starts to tell Jon the wondrous story of their clan. As she quietly speaks, she waits patiently as Hassan interprets for Jon.

CHAPTER 2

TEMPLE IN NIPPUR – ABOUT 3200 BC

The mid-day sun poured down on everything Asif could see or touch as he waited outside the Temple in Nippur with his older brother, Mukhtar. It seemed to burn into his skin and seep into everything exposed to it. As he squints to cut down the burning brightness, he could see waves of heat reflecting off the sandy ground. They danced and blurred into a shiny reflection that looked like floating rivers of heat wherever it was flat enough to capture the light in the right way. The temple was under construction, being built from clay and sun baked bricks from the bed of the river several hundred yards beyond where they stand.

Inside the temple the air was cooler and a breeze always blew near the entrances in the heat of the day. But he and his brother were not allowed inside, per the order of their father. They were told that since they could not behave they would have to wait outside while he conducted his business. More specifically, it was Asif who was told he couldn't behave. Mukhtar hadn't done anything wrong, but as the older brother he bore the burden of making sure his brother didn't get into any more trouble outside. At eight years old, Asif could not help himself from climbing or exploring wherever he could. After his father had brought him and his brother inside the temple, Asif spotted a pedestal under construction which was to be the future place for a shrine to the god of the sun. As soon as his father was distracted talking to the priest and some people from a nearby town, Asif quickly climbed the first blocks of the pedestal. He was delighted to find some bats between two of the bricks. He threw a small rock at them which caused just enough commotion to wake the bats and send them soaring around the chamber. Asif laughed and pointed at the display of the swooping bats. The priest's wife and several women who were busy bringing in some food were much less amused as the bats swooped and darted around them. Several unpleasant words were exchanged, and Asif was ordered to climb down from the pedestal. As he did so, he knocked over a large clay urn, which crashed loudly as it broke into hundreds of pieces. Their father was soon leading Asif, pulling him by the ear, to the outside of the temple with his brother close behind him, where they were to remain until he was done with his business.

Mukhtar wondered just how long that might be. At thirteen years old, he was growing impatient with the constrictions and rules of childhood. He was growing weary of his family. He was growing weary of his friends. And right now, he was very weary of his younger brother. In his mind, they were all holding themselves back by falling into the mind-restricting daily repetition of routines. It seemed as if everything they did was because it was the way it had been done for years. Mukhtar felt the rules needed changed, and when he was older, he was the one who would do it.

Slowly the years passed, and while Mukhtar was bemoaning the stoic rituals of his family and friends, Asif was busy going on adventures, making friends, and learning to enjoy himself.

He met a girl, Rania, through one of his best friends, Rafi. Rafi was the same age as Asif, and his sister was just fifteen months younger than he. She had a simple beauty about her. She had large dark brown eyes and light brown hair. When he first met her she was still too young for boys, so she was always kept close to her mother and her house. Asif would often see her at his house as she did chores or was practicing her music on an oud, a three stringed wooden instrument which made the most beautiful sounds he had ever heard. But after she turned fifteen, she became more visible in social circles. She was often seen as part of their family while out in the town. Asif felt a special closeness to her because he had known her as a child. He knew her beauty, but he had to admire it from afar.

Asif's brother Mukhtar had also noticed Rania. Several times Mukhtar had found a reason to go to Rafi's house with Asif, and it was then that Mukhtar first set his eyes on her as she was playing her instrument. Asif and Mukhtar's parents were friends through the temple and through the friendship of Asif and Rafi, so they were pleased when Mukhtar came to them and spoke to them about Rania. Mukhtar was at the age to take a wife, and Rania was from suitable family and background. When Asif found out what was happening, he ran to his parents.

"What is going on?" He said. "He cannot marry her. She is pure and beautiful and far too good for him. He needs a princess who would be like him! He's cold, unfeeling and vain!" He was hoping to convince his parents she was appropriate for him, not his brother. He knew she had more class and character than any other girl he had ever known. She was spiritual and true, and the truth was he loved her dearly.

"Asif, my son" his father responded. "It's not for you to decide these things. She is young, beautiful, and comes from a good family. That is what we are looking for Mukhtar. And when it is your turn we will find another woman just as beautiful for you."

Asif was infuriated and deeply hurt. "But she is not for him! If anything she is for me when I'm old enough. Don't let this happen, this will be horrible for her, and worse for me!"

But his pleas were in vain. Mukhtar was allowed to court Rania much to the dismay of Asif. He saw his brother at her house, and it made his skin crawl.

On Rania's sixteenth birthday, Mukhtar gave her a necklace with an amber stone. The stone had been given to Mukhtar by his grandmother. She said the stone was good luck and would protect him from any harm that could come from the gods. Mukhtar took the necklace as a courtesy to his grandmother, but thought the superstition was silly and a folly. Asif thought it was the most beautiful stone he had seen. He started to resent his brother. How could he not? Sometimes, when he was at the house while it was just her family and he, he would see her. She would look at him and make eye contact. Her eyes could tear right through him. He saw purity and beauty in her, deeper than anything he had experienced before.

Soon there were wedding plans, and Asif felt he couldn't' stand it anymore. He decided the only way he could cope with his jealousy was to plan one of his adventures. His friend Rafi was also upset. So, they became too busy planning their adventures to worry about the wedding. Just a week before the wedding, they left on a journey into the "*shaky*" mountains with Sabur, another one of their friends. The "*shaky*" mountains were known for their many small earth quakes. They were a favorite destination of Asif, as there were many boulders to scramble on up steep rockslides. They walked off, telling their families that they would be back in a day or two.

The day before the wedding came, and Asif and his friends had not returned. Mukhtar and his father were furious that they would be so irresponsible. Their mother was worried that something had happened to them. Mukhtar felt insulted and embarrassed by his brother's behavior. The wedding proceeded anyway, and they left an empty spots at the wedding dinner where Asif and Rafi would have sat.

But there was a reason they had not returned.

CHAPTER 3

THE CAVE CEREMONY

Hassan stands from the cushioned seats where Nisaba was telling her story and motions for Jon to follow him to a chamber deeper inside the cave. The cave walls come closer around him as he proceeds. The ceiling slants lower so that he has to bend his head, and there is only enough room for one person to move through at a time.

"The next chamber is one of the most sacred in our clan." Hassan explains.

The structure and detail of the next chamber could have been inside a small palace. Soft fire lit torches hang on the wall, providing enough light to see the rich colors in the cloths and ornamental wood that adorn the walls and furniture. Marble columns stand from floor to ceiling. From a distant recess a breeze blows gently through. There is just enough to refresh the air and gently blow the flames on the torches. Most of the stench of the smoke, cave, and staleness is gone. Velvet cushioned furniture from generations long since passed line the walls, and gold leaf and silver adorn many of the pieces of furniture and art.

Samir, the town elder who was crossing the Bad Asurin Bridge with his goats, comes near to Hassan and Jon. At first he is silent. The quiet works to build anticipation to his next talk. Then quietly he begins to tell his family story. Hassan interprets.

"Nisaba started to tell you the story of our family. The responsibility of the people of the Clan of the Boars head is of the highest importance. We are entrusted to protect the people from powers that can bring great evil. There is another clan, the Hand of the Red Fist, which seeks to obtain these powers for their use. Many of their members are kept secret, like ours. They are sworn to destroy us as we are sworn to protect the world from them. Long before Islam, Christianity, and Judaism came into being, our clan was almost destroyed. Many of our family fled for their lives to Turkey to the North or to Egypt in the south. My ancestors that survived went into hiding, working as laborers and house maids in the cities. The Hand of the Red fist hides their destruction and terror by deceiving others into believing they are friends of the people and we are the enemy. Centuries ago they almost destroyed all memory of my family. Our traditions and stories were banned. Houses were burned to the ground. Our possessions were destroyed. It seemed our culture was lost like the drifting sands of the desert, buried with the caves of the mountains. Most of my family were killed or exiled. Even though we were exiled, killed, and robbed of our past, we did not lose the core of our family. Our core is here in these caves. It is a secret of an ancient past, stories forgotten long ago, and of legends that have been forbidden to be spoken for centuries." Samir paused. Jon was somewhat taken aback.

"It's entirely possible, Jon, that some of our exiled family could come back."

Samir turns his attention from Jon and he starts to greet several of the people arriving to attend the ceremony. There are young and old men, mostly silent and stoic. Nisaba arrives with several women, who are pleasant, courteous, and generally more animated than the men. They are clearly highly regarded, but they are busy assisting and preparing for the rituals to happen.

The ritual starts after several minutes. Despite being spoken in Arabic, Jon appreciates the pomp of the ceremonial ritual he is witnessing. Much of their lives are shells of existence, yet here they are as faithful and dedicated to this rite as any ritual Jon has experienced. After thirty minutes Jon starts to lose interest. The adrenalin is wearing off; there is a ringing in his ears from the explosions. He's hungry; his eyes are blurry from the smoke and fatigue.

Slowly the intensity of the ritual rises. The voices become louder. There is a palpable change in the air. The breeze increases and swirls around them. The flames become brighter as if new oxygen were injected into the chamber. Jon is confused but alert. Is this dreaming, or is this reality? From a small antechamber yellow, blue and red lights shine brightly and begin to overtake the room. Samir is chanting louder and higher. The women are chanting or singing an ancient hymn that is as hypnotizing as it is beautiful. Jon rises and looks towards the lights. In the antechamber he sees a nest of stones. In the center of the nest a small crystal glows bright yellow. The stones surrounding the crystal are glowing in red, blue and yellow. The lights rise and fall in intensity as the chanting builds. Jon is mesmerized by the stones, and he looks back at Samir. The congregation is gathering energy from the stones as the stones are gathering energy from the chant. Jon's head is swirling. He's dizzy and confused, as if drugged. He stumbles forward and finds himself being helped forward by Hassan.

The chanting reaches a crescendo. A yellow stream of energy bursts outward from the yellow crystal. It arcs across the chamber and strikes a wall, then arcs back down toward the floor. A bright line in a circle appears in the in the dirt. Inside the ring, a triangle emerges with the light now burning the lines in the dirt. Jon finds himself drawn towards the ring, and Hassan helps him towards the center. They reach the center just as a large burst of energy and light surround them, engulfing them in light. The energy streams reverse their swirling directions and collapse back towards the circle and the triangle in the ground. A loud 'snap' shut is heard as the symbol on the ground disappears. Hassan and Jon are gone. The chanting stops.

Moments later, the circle appears again. The lights within the circle brighten quickly. The triangle symbol burns its shape into the ground as blinding light emits from the edges. An energy stream bursts from the circle, engulfing the chamber. The stream flows around the chamber and collapses back into the circle again. In the center of the circle Hassan lies alone, motionless. One of the women approaches him to stir him. Slowly he rolls to his side. He looks up from his position; the lights and pomp of the ceremony are all gone now. Samir is there at the front of the chamber, looking at Hassan. Hassan, from his position on the ground, slightly turns his head towards Samir, smiling slightly.

Jon is gone.

CHAPTER 4

THE SHAKY MOUNTAINS

The mountains ahead of Asif were beautiful in their majesty and rugged terrain. Asif and his friends climbed along the valley floor along a small river, then turned towards a ravine heading up the valley towards a distant ridge which faced south towards the sun. He was looking up at the hills when he spotted a dark area in the side of the mountain. Suddenly, several birds flew out of the spot, as if flying out of the mountainside. Their wings glinted against the sun and vanished as if a light had been flashed against the stark grey cliffs of the mountain. It was several hundred feet above where they were.

"We need to go up there and see what that is. Those birds seemed to come out of the side of the mountain. We can leave our camping supplies here because we'll be back in an hour or so."

Up they scrambled on the side of the mountain, anxious to find something new and exciting. With no fear in their eyes, they believed no harm could come to them. In an hour they were climbing along the edge of a cliff, barely able to hang on, trying to reach the small spot that Asif had spotted. After several narrow escapes from falling rocks and slippery ascents, they reached the mouth of a small cave. Most likely it had recently been exposed. There was loose rock all around, and it was evident than much more rock had slid from above and continued below where the mouth of the cave was. After proceeding so far, Asif was determined to go in.

Rafi begged him not to enter "You don't know how deep or steep the cave is. There is nothing in there, why go there?"

But Asif convinced them. "Have I ever let you down? Have I ever led you astray?" he asked.

They could think of several times. "There was the time we took the wine in the market, and the time we rolled a huge boulder onto the road from a pass, and ended up blocking a bridge, which took weeks to repair." But their objections did not stop Asif, and soon he was disappeared into the cave. His friends looked on, and soon they followed to the entrance.

As they entered the cave and joined Asif, they felt a cool wind from inside the space below. Then they heard a low groan, as if from the mountain itself. They climbed down several large boulders until they were about thirty feet below the entrance. The light from the cave entrance was at just the right angle so a small sliver of light still came in. They could see a small landing about twenty feet away, but there was a large gap between them and the landing. Some water was next to the landing, and all of them were extremely thirsty. But there was no way across the gap. Not wasting any time, Asif spotted a boulder just above the gap that looked like it could be pushed and might be big enough to allow them to cross. He called for some help and soon the three of them were pushing the boulder over. It started rocking, then rolled with a loud creak and landed with a boom. The rock had filled the gap just as they had hoped. They moved back to the path to use the boulder to cross, but several things then happened very quickly.

First a low moaning sound came up from deep inside the cave, along with a swirling breeze. A loud snap was heard from above near the mouth of the cave. The light seemed to flash from outside, and then there were some brief flashes that came from inside the cave as well. Several rocks and boulders started falling across the path they had come from. Outside the cave, another rock slide started above the cave. It crashed through the small scrub and trees above the cave, then smashed over the opening and covered the entrance completely. Inside, the cave became pitch black.

The three of them sat stunned in the darkness. "Oh no!" they screamed. "What are we going to do now? There was no answer, only silence. The only sound was water cascading into a distant pool; some rocks were still falling down from above. Asif asked "Is everyone all right? Is anyone hurt?"

"I'm not hurt" was the answer. "But I'm not all right either. We're buried alive with no way out. No one knows where we are, and we have no equipment or food. This is not a good situation."

CHAPTER 5

CAMP COURAGE

The US Army Forward Operating Base, or FOB Camp Courage, in Mosul, is in the desert in northern Iraq. It's made up of a Palace owned by Saddam Hussein and used by the US and Iraqi Armies. The buildings of the palace act as a wall to protect the compound, and where there are no buildings the wall continues the fencing. The Americans have added an extra border fence around the entire compound, consisting of large rolls of barbed wire, tank barriers, each shaped like giant jacks in a child's game. There are large trenches in the sand just before the barbed wire as an added deterrent to keep vehicles away. Before light every day, delivery trucks line up along the southern wall of the compound, ready to deliver local supplies into the base.

The security clearance process can be long. Each truck needs to be thoroughly inspected for bombs, and the contents need to be checked.

A strong wind whips across the desert, enough to kick up sand and put it in small drifts across the road and the line of barbed wire outside the compound. The sand pelts everything around it with a constant pinging on the metal and a static hiss sound on just about everything else. The beams of lights from the headlights and haze from the dust create a circled aura around the gate lights. A spotlight beams across the area from the guard tower, and the focus crawls across the sand towards the line of trucks. It reaches the first truck, and then tracks back towards the barbed wire.

Between the wall of the building and the barbed wire fence there is an object, in an area that would be considered a no man's land. The light stays there for a while. The wind and sand have almost covered the object, and for a while the entire area is washed out by the dust and sand. But between the wind gusts, the mysterious object becomes more into focus. There is fabric – army fatigues. And in the front, it appears to be the netting from a standard issue helmet. As the light slowly reveals more and more, it becomes obvious it's a person – or a body, lying in the sand.

The tower guard yells to someone below, "Hey we've got one of our guys outside the wall – he's down! Down soldier outside the wall!"

In a few minutes five soldiers appear through the access gate with a stretcher. Some are armed and clearly acting as security, some are there to do the recovery. They make their way behind the barbed wire to the body. There is a quick and efficient assessment, then they methodically put him on the stretcher.

"It looks like one of our boys" one of the soldiers yells into his radio. He checks his vitals. "And he's alive!"

Quickly they disappear with Jon back into the safety of the army base. Soon afterwards, the process of admitting the supply trucks starts up again.

CHAPTER 6

DARKNESS

Asif asked Rafi and Sabur to join hands together in the darkness. Slowly they moved across the boulder and found their way to the landing. They felt with their hands until they found the water and for lack of anything else to do, drink as much as they could.

Days passed in the darkness. It could have been weeks. Their sense of time was completely diminished. Lack of food added to the confusion of the darkness. They spent hours trying to find the entrance to the cave and pull rocks and boulders away. But their efforts were in vain. Several times they would weep in despair. What were they going to do? They were often feeling delirious and sometimes seemed to hallucinate.

Asif used his spiritual training to try to keep calm and meditate. He tried to teach the others the benefits of meditation, but the timing was not the best for new ideas. He sat in a trance for hours at a time. As he meditated, a strange phenomenon occurred. The walls seemed to glow with a dim light. It would grow somewhat brighter for a while, and then it would dim again. Asif thought his eyes were playing tricks on him. Some lights were a bluish hue, some were a red. There was not enough light to see in the room, but enough to make sense of the shape of the walls of the cavern.

Then Rafi noticed the light also. "Asif," he asked, do you see that light in the walls?"

Asif was deep in meditation and did not hear him. Slowly the light grew brighter, and Rafi stood up to view. He could clearly see the outline of the large cavern they stood in, and he could make out the edge of the water just below the landing they were sleeping on. "Sabur, wake up! Do you see this light? Asif, what is this?"

Sabur woke briefly from his sleep. He was somewhat disturbed he was awakened, as his dreams were his last refuge from this nightmare of darkness they were in. As he awoke, he saw the lights in the caverns. He saw the soft glow that was encompassing them, and he saw Asif, not far away, deep in meditation.

Rafi went to Asif. "Asif, wake up – look at the lights! Asif! Asif!"

But as Asif came out of his meditation the lights suddenly dimmed. "Rafi, what's going on? What happened?"

"The lights Asif, the lights!" Rafi said, "as you were meditating, there were lights in the cave. Sabur saw them too. We could see the cavern walls. We could see the lake and the water. Now they are gone!"

"Your eyes were playing tricks on you. You're hallucinating," Asif said.

"No Asif No – we saw them!" Sabur said.

Asif considered this for a few moments, and then he spoke. "As I was meditating, I thought I was having a dream. I thought I was hallucinating from hunger and thirst. But maybe there was something more to it. As I was mediating, I started to feel as part of the cave. I started to feel the cave was real, in a sense that it was part of me. And I felt as if the lights were there, even if I didn't even really see them myself. I can't explain it, I don't know, I just kind of existed with the cave, and it seemed the lights were building towards something."

"I don't know what it was," Rafi said, "but if we can use it to get out of this cave, let's find a way. If you can make the lights come back, we can climb to the cave entrance. Sabur and I can clear a hole to the outside. We just need enough time to climb the rocks to get to the entrance!"

"Then let's try." Asif replied. "We have to try something, and this is the best we've got right now."

Asif tried several times to meditate while staying conscious. He wanted to see the lights, but every time he tried to stay awake, the lights would not come on. But once he did go into a trance state while meditating, the lights would in fact come on and light up the cavern. Each time it was a little brighter. As

Asif learned how to meditate in such a way to become part of the cavern, he could "feel" the walls. He could feel the water. He could feel the stones and the weight they were holding. As he did, he felt energy through him, and as that energy flowed the lights grew brighter in the cave. As the blue and red lights brightened, Sabur and Rafi would start to scramble up the rock slide towards where the entrance was. It was difficult climbing, but they could eventually make their way towards the top. Once there, it was difficult to see, and the rocks and boulders seemed too big near the entrance to move anything. Each was several times bigger than they were, and many times more heavy.

They returned to the bottom of the rock slide to Asif. This time they returned, the lights were still glowing, and Asif was awake. Although he didn't speak, his eyes were open and they were following them as they came down the final descent to the landing near the water. Rafi and Sabur did what they could near the water to get a drink and the used a cup shaped stone to get some water for Asif before he woke up and they went into darkness again. They approached Asif to wake him up. "Asif, we have been to the entrance of the cave, we can't see how we can get out of here. The rocks are far too big; we would need an army of men to get them out of the way."

The lights quickly extinguished as Asif awoke. Then they slowly started to brighten again. Asif spoke, " I think I can learn how to manipulate the lights. I think I can make them stay on while I'm awake. Watch this!" Asif looked down at the ground, then lifted his arms up in a swooping motion and shook his arms outward. Suddenly a burst of light came forth from the walls, and the darkness was replaced with almost daylight brightness. Asif motioned to his friends to come closer to him, and they did. Asif seemed to grow in his stance as he stood on the floor of the cave. Rafi and Sabur were now standing within arms distance of him, and the light continued to become much brighter. Suddenly, an arc of light shot across the walls just above their head, then seemed to crash against the cavern on the far side of the lake. It burst into an explosion of sparking color and noise, and then it fell silently into the water below.

Asif stood firm with his hands outstretched, but the lights dimmed almost into total darkness. Then slowly the lights grew again across the cavern, this time from even more corners of the space. They grew to a blinding glare, then they slowly concentrated on the wall to Asif's right. Then, in a fireball of light, it moved across the open cavern. It quickly sped up, then arched high across the ceiling. It turned, and headed straight down, slamming into the ground and surrounding Asif in a column of light. After an explosion of energy around Asif, there was darkness in the cave.

"Asif?" Rafi asked, "Sabur?"

"Rafi?" Sabur replied, "are you there?"

"Yes, I'm here, but where is Asif?"

Asif was gone. They were left alone in the darkness.

CHAPTER 7

KUWAIT CITY

Asleep in his hospital bed at a US Army Hospital outside of Kuwait City, Kuwait, Jon's vital signs are quietly being monitored with no indication of trouble. He's in a double room. The patient next to him is under heavy monitoring. He should be in intensive care, but the hospital is overcrowded due to the recent activity related to the surge in Iraq. There are medics coming in and out quite frequently.

Outside his room two army officers are discussing the situation. Sergeant Van Etten, from British Intelligence, is investigating the incident; Sergeant Smith is from Jon's battalion in Iraq.

Sergeant Van Etten is intrigued by this case. "There are really just two possibilities here. One is that Jon made it to the base on his own and collapsed outside the wall of the base. How he survived the attack at the bridge is still a mystery, but obviously he came through it. All his communication equipment was destroyed, his radio, his phone, his watch- everything. The other possibility is that someone dropped him off there. For whatever reason, they must have come in the dead of night and left him outside the gates. What doesn't make sense is how did he make it to the inside of the barbed wire perimeter? Why didn't they signal someone inside the compound that there was someone there, or at least let us know after they dropped him off?"

Sgt. Smith listens accommodatingly, but he doesn't seem convinced or in total agreement with Sgt. Van Etten. "I don't think we can even pretend to know at this point," he comments. "There are too many unanswered questions. How could anyone travel that far on their own without some sort of assistance? It's just not possible. And how could he have assistance?"

Van Etten continues. "We haven't heard from the interpreter Hassan since the incident. Chances are he was killed either at the time of the attack, or soon afterwards. Typically, people we hire like Hassan are treated as the enemy by the insurgents. I doubt if we will be hearing from him again."

"We can't close this out until after we talk with Jon, and according to his doctors that could be any time from a day to a few weeks from now." Smith says.

Sgt. Van Etten considers. "Well, I guess we'll just have to wait this one out a few more days. There are a lot of variables here. I have a lot of questions for Jon. So, if you would, let me know of any change in his condition. I'll come back as soon as I can after he wakes up and can talk to us."

"Sure thing," Sgt. Smith replies to him. He doesn't particularly care for Sgt. Van Etten or the British intelligence he has met, but he's not as bad compared to some of the CIA he has had to deal with. Besides, this gave him the opportunity to get out of Iraq and over to Kuwait City for a few days. How bad could it be?

Smith looks down the hall and sees a general and three sergeants walking briskly towards them. They are walking three abreast past the other rooms and patients. Some of the orderlies have to move out of their way, and they show some of their displeasure with it. General Sampson approaches Sgt. Smith. Smith snaps to attention and salutes, as does Smith. "Sir" he says.

Sampson doesn't waste any time. "This is private Bishop?"

"Yes sir – 23rd battalion," Smith responds.

"Very well," Sampson continues "you may have been notified we would be coming. We'll be taking over his care now. We're with special ops under orders to make sure he has the best care and has due process." Sampson hands Smith a paper – apparently orders. Smith looks at them briefly, then folds them and puts them in his front shirt pocket.

"Sir" Smith interrupts, "I've got orders from our Colonel to find out what happened – I will need to remain stationed here until we resolve our inquiry. I don't have any information about you coming. It would come from our command, and I just checked in with them an hour ago. If you're special ops, can you give us more information on what happened here? If there is any sort of security issue at our base, I have to be informed and report back."

Sampson smiles wryly. "You'll be informed if there is any security issue with your base. Right now this is our baby to figure out. You can check back with your superiors on your process to clear your reports. Right now we will start to secure the room, and we're providing full security. No visitors without Special Ops clearance. We appreciate you gentlemen taking care of this so far, but we'll take it from here. My sergeants here will give you their names if you want to follow up with any questions."

Behind them there is suddenly a lot more activity in Jon's room. His room-mate has flat-lined. Several orderlies are moving quickly, and urgent messages are going out across the PA system. A curtain is drawn and there is no longer direct visibility to their area. At Jon's bed one of the orderlies suddenly appears at his bedside. He peers over Jon's bed – Jon looks at him anxiously. "Jon!" the voice says.

"Hassan!" Jon replies, surprised but not loudly. "How did you get here? What are you doing here?"

"Not now – later!" Hassan says. "We have to get you out of here – NOW. There's no time to talk about it. You have to trust me. We have to leave – for your life, for ours, for your family."

"But how? – I don't understand!" Jon whispers anxiously.

"We'll take care of it" Hassan responds. "Now lie absolutely still."

Hassan removes a needle and syringe from his pocket. He checks the small amount of liquid inside.

Jon's eyes open wide "What are you doing? I don't want to be drugged!"

Hassan turns the syringe upside down and primes the needle with a small pump from the plunger. Then he pushes the rest of the liquid out – squirting into the air. He looks at the syringe, and then he throws it on the floor. "We'll take care of it I said – you lie perfectly still."

There is an urgent call to transport the gurney out of the room – and moments later the gurney leaves from behind the curtain and heads on its way to the intensive care area. Several orderlies are quickly pushing the gurney towards the door of the hospital area. The face of the occupant is inconspicuously concealed.

Sampson and Smith are watching what is going on from several feet away. The orderlies have asked them to step back so they can attend to the emergency situation with Jon's roommate. It's noisy and confusing, but it doesn't look like there is anything out of the ordinary going on.

Smith turns to Sampson and feels a little snarky. "I hope that soldier will make it – he's had some pretty severe problems. As far as Bishop goes, sir – I need to have a report for my superiors. I cannot just hand control over to you without proper paperwork from my side."

"You'll get your paperwork. As of right now consider your responsibility done." Sampson said with some finality to the issue.

The Special ops sergeants pushes past Smith and Van Etten right to the room to start securing the area. They abruptly open the curtain to address Bishop. No one expected to find that Jon had disappeared. In his place lay his roommate. The sergeants look around in disbelief. How could this have happened? They look in the other room – the gurney is gone. They look back at the room-mate.

"Sir!" one of the sergeants yells. "It's Private Bishop – he's gone! They took him on that gurney that just left!"

Sampson runs to the bedside and throws the blankets off the room-mate. He's heavily bandaged, but he seems to be stable. The monitors are blinking away quietly with a steady heart-rate. Sampson's voice starts with a low groan, and then raises his tone to a sharp commanding yell.

"Find Private Bishop and that gurney – Now!"

Outside in the hospital hall Hassan is carefully but deliberately navigating the gurney through the halls. He reaches the elevators where several other gurneys are already waiting. Several awkward seconds pass waiting for the elevator. Hassan moves Jon's gurney to the front of the line. "Sorry – intensive care and it's urgent." Another orderly is waiting for him inside the elevator. Inside the elevator there is a button for urgent care on the seventh floor. Hassan pushes the button for the first floor.

Sampson calls security and demands they lock down the emergency room area and the access to ambulances leaving. In the emergency room area, orderlies and security scurry to secure the doors. Outside the door there is a gurney with a patient on it just being loaded into an ambulance. The door is shut. The driver moves to pull out of the driveway.

"Stop!" an MP yells and runs outside to the ambulance. He shouts and bangs on the side of the van. There is a Middle Eastern driver who looks out of the window in astonishment at the cop. "What the?" He brakes hard enough to squeal the wheels. There is a sound of crashing equipment from inside the ambulance. The MP moves around back and insists the driver opens the door. Technicians from inside open the door. Sampson has just arrived, running to the back of the ambulance, and he jumps in the back cargo area.

He looks at the gurney. Staring back at him is an old man. He's being transported to rehabilitation for therapy after hip replacement surgery. He seems disoriented and surprised at his new visitor.

"Are you my new doctor?" he asks? "You don't look like a doctor. You look like you need some rest though. You shouldn't be so worried. Things can always be worse. You need to relax."

Sampson pauses at the sight. He slowly gets up and exits the back of the ambulance. The attendants quickly go back to attending the old man, shaking their heads. The doors slam shut, and the ambulance leaves. Sampson looks very alone.

On another side of the hospital, Hassan has wheeled Jon's gurney down to the laundry area. Jon looks around. "Where are we? Where are we going?"

"It's too early to say" Hassan says as he looks at Jon, then looks at one of the many laundry bins along the side of the hall. He repeats the look, and motions for Jon to get into one of the laundry bins.

"Really? Is that your plan? Escaping through the laundry bin?"

"It's the best we have, but what we don't have is time. Now get in and you'll be safe. Time is not our friend right now! Get in!"

Jon looks around, looks confused, then concerned. "But they'll think I've gone AWOL! I'll be arrested and get a dishonorable discharge."

"No- you've been kidnapped. They won't think you have left on your own accord. I left the syringe in your room with residue from a sedative. They think you've been drugged. Now get in!" And Hassan motions to the laundry bin.

Jon eases himself out of the gurney. His arms are wobbly from lack of exercise since he's been in the hospital. He does his best to ease himself over the edge of the laundry bin. As soon as his feet and body are inside the edges of the bin, while his arms are still on the sides, Hassan moves the bin quickly and Jon drops like a rock into the bin. Hassan throws a sheet on top of him and moves him through a door to a loading dock where a truck is waiting with the door open.

"Hey – just a second…" Jon says, but his voice is muffled under several layers of linens. Several bins are loaded into the truck, and Hassan jumps into the truck and pounds on the front of the drivers' cabin signaling they are ready to go. The doors are quickly closed and the truck pulls out of the loading bay. As they pass the front of the hospital, Sampson is still standing in the Ambulance loading area cursing his bad fortunes. The laundry truck drives away unchallenged.

CHAPTER 8

SEARCH PARTIES

Outside the temple in Nippur, there was a garden which is tended daily by local farmers. An old farmer was going about his business collecting extra vegetation from the garden areas. As he turned the corner from one section of the garden to another, he found a body lying in the grass. It was covered with debris – loose leaves and vegetation. The farmer pushed the man lying on the ground with the back end of a rake. He pushed on the side of his shoulder that was slouched over his body. The man rolled onto his back. The farmer recognized Asif. He gasped and moved closer to check on Asif's condition. Asif groaned with pain and tried vainly to roll back onto his side. The farmer saw that he was alive and ran back to the temple to call for some assistance.

Asif was brought to a comfortable bed inside the house of his father. They cleaned him up, but his lips were chapped from dehydration, and there were sores across his face and chest. A woman lifted his head and poured water into his mouth. Asif was not fully conscious yet.

Mukhtar approached the room with his mother, Salya, and they stopped outside the door. Mukhtar was concerned, and his mother was trying to defuse the situation.

"Mukhtar," she said, "he almost died. Clearly he ran into some terrible trouble that kept him from your wedding. He's sick and he's dehydrated, it will take days for him to get better. Before you judge him for his insult, you should first find out what happened."

Mukhtar looked at his mother, and then he looked away before he spoke. "I'm glad he's back, but his condition serves him right for the disrespect he has shown me and my wife. He should have known he may not come back in time. He has disgraced our family and insulted me and my wife. He is a disgrace. I will never forgive him for this, and neither should you. I hope he gets better, but he will never be forgiven by me."

Salya looked at her oldest son. "You're becoming older and wiser, and yes you are now a man, but you have not learned compassion for others. You must learn that there are factors beyond your control that will impact others. I understand your anger, but wait until after the anger passes. That is the test of manhood and leadership, like your father. If you still feel the same way, then make judgments. But do not judge in haste."

Mukhtar considered her remarks. "I am in no frame of mind right now to put up with his tricks and his misadventures. He should know he is to pay a price for his actions."

They entered his room. Asif was lying on his back, staring at the ceiling. His mother came to his side and held his hand.

"Asif, can you hear me?" She asked.

Asif lay motionless and distant.

He looked to his left, then he looked directly into his mother's eyes. "Mother!" he said. "How did I get here? Where are Rafi and Sabur?"

"We're hoping you can tell us." She responded. "Their families are worried sick. You came home, and we found you in the garden. But there are no signs of your friends. Where are they?"

Asif looked at his mother, and then he closed his eyes in despair. "They did not get out? They were in the cave with me! Mother – where are they - are you saying they didn't come with me? Mother, they may still be stuck in the cave! I don't know how I got out. How long have I been here? We have to get to them now – it may be too late!"

"I don't understand," she replied, "if you were stuck in a cave with them, how did you get out without them? Are you sure they did not come out with you?"

Asif lay back for a minute. "We were climbing in the Shaky Mountains and we found a cave up on the hillside. We went inside, and then an earthquake happened and a landslide covered the entrance to the cave. We tried to dig our way out; we tried so many times, for days. We had given up – oh my god it was so horrible. Then I don't know what happened. There were lights while I was meditating. We tried to use the lights to get out, but it wasn't' working. I finally figured out how to work with them, but something happened. Then I woke up here in the bed. We have to get them out – but how did I get here?"

"One of the farmers at the temple found you in the garden yesterday morning. Oh, Asif, what happened? Are you sure they are still alive? Where is this place?"

"I think they were alive when I left, but we'll have to get to them fast. Let's get going!" Asif tried to move to leave the bed.

"Just a minute little brother," Mukhtar interrupted. "You aren't going anywhere. I hardly believe your story. You have lied too many times. Now you have disgraced this family and disrespected me and my wife. You will stay here in this house until I say you can leave. If your friends are to be found, you will tell us where they are and we will send a search party out to find them. That is the way it will be."

"No! You will never be able to find them!" Asif explained. "The entrance to the cave has been covered in the landslide, and even I am not sure I can find my way back to the entrance!"

"Well there must be a way out if you got out. Tell us where the cave is and I will make a search party. We will go find them."

"They're in the Shaky Mountains. They are on the sunny side of the hill several hundred feet above the trail. There is a ledge along the side of the hill that will bring them to the entrance to the cave. But I'm afraid it's not there now, because there was a rock slide that sealed it."

"If a rock slide sealed the cave, then how did you get out?" Mukhtar asked accusingly. "You expect us to believe that you got out of the cave somehow with the cave still sealed? What do you take us for?" Mukhtar slowed his tone down. "Where are your friends, Asif – did you agree they would stay behind while you came back so that you could beg for forgiveness? Will we find them still up in the hills fishing and shooting squirrels?"

Asif lay back in anguish and frustration. "I don't know, I don't know! Yes! No! Yes they are still up there; no they are not having a good time. They are near death if not dead. We have to go get them now."

"You will stay right here" his mother replied. "Mukhtar will go with the others to look for them."

His mother and Mukhtar left the room quickly to get organized. Outside, Rania had been standing nearby; close enough to hear the conversation inside.

"Mukhtar" she said, "Where is my brother? Is he alive? We must go and get him!"

Mukhtar looked at his young wife. "Your brother was a fool to follow my brother. If he has found danger then it is of his own doing. You have no concern with this. We will make a search party to find him. But if we can't then it is just his fault for being a fool."

Rania looked at him incredulously, but she knew he was stubborn and tough. "I beg you – we have to find my brother! I can't have peace in my family, our family, without him. You must help him and us!"

The next morning, several hours before sunrise, outside the castle, a lone figure moved out from behind some bushes and towards the road in the darkness. He had an animal skin backpack strapped on his back filled with supplies. He moved around a corner towards a bridge heading out of town. As he approached the bridge, another figure approached him.

"Asif," she whispered. "Asif!" she called louder.

Asif turned around to look at the caller. "Who's there?" he demanded. "Rania – is that you?"

"Yes, it's Rania. I'm going with you. My brother is up in the hills and I have to bring him back. Mukhtar has said its Rafi's problem; he's setting up a search party, but it's only for show. He has no intention of finding him. I knew you would be here. I knew you would be going after him. Your heart is true. Mukhtar's is not. I want to go with you. I can hike with you. I can climb. I can help."

"Rania", Asif replied "I guess I shouldn't be surprised to see you here. You are a good sister and a beautiful woman. But I have to do this on my own. As much as I would have it otherwise, I can't change what is. You cannot help me. You are the wife of my brother now, and you should be at his side. I can't cause more trouble for my family."

"Asif" she said, "I understand, but Rafi is still my brother as much as Mukhtar is my husband. If Rafi is still alive, I have to find him. My god tells me I have to find him, and my god says you will help me. Help me, Asif, help me. And help my brother. My husband will have to understand."

Asif looked into Rania's eyes. "I will find your brother. But you should stay here."

"I can't. Take me with you, and together we will find my brother."

"Come if you must then," said Asif, "but don't hold me back, and you have to listen to me if I give you instructions. I have been there before, and there are many dangers along the way."

From the mist and shadows beneath the bridge their two silhouettes emerged and entered the road. They crossed over the bridge toward the country, not quite knowing the fateful journey they were on.

CHAPTER 9

KUWAIT SAFE HOUSE

At a small stucco brick warehouse in Kuwait city the laundry truck that holds Jon and Hassan is backed up to a loading dock, baking in the hot afternoon sun. On the East side of the building, an industrial overhead door rises, and a black Cadillac Escalade SUV emerges from the building.

Inside the SUV, Jon and Hassan are seated in the back seat. Jon has his full battle rattle uniform on. Hassan is dressed in a dark blue khakis and a light blue short sleeved shirt.

"Where did you get these clothes?" Jon asks.

Hassan is a little distracted looking out the window. "We have access to pretty much any US or ally gear we need– for a price. It's a matter of who you know and how you can influence them."

Jon knows there is widespread corruption in the war. The army has lost millions in weapons and ammunition, let alone clothing and other types of supplies. He's really not surprised that there is access to these types of supplies. He is surprised that Hassan has been this resourceful, that he is this well connected outside of his homeland. He now knows Hassan's organization is much bigger than any group his training has made him aware of. If this group has reach outside of Iraq, to a hospital in Kuwait, and to delivery trucks, they must be a well-organized force indeed. *How have they been kept secret? How have they kept themselves out of US surveillance?*

"Hassan," Jon starts. "I have a lot of questions. And they are important. I can't get any deeper into this without fully understanding what is going on. The entire US Army will be on alert looking for you and me. You have put yourself at great risk by taking me; and I don't even understand why it's so important. How could I possibly be so important?"

"Jon, there's so much you don't know. There's a lot we still don't know. But I will tell you what I know, and I will tell you what is going on. You will understand your role in this, and you will understand why it is so important. Jon, do you know your family ancestry? Do you know where you parents come from?"

"My father is British and my mother is Middle Eastern." Jon replies. "She left the middle east to go to the US for better opportunities. She met my father while he was in the US in college. I think it was in the late seventies or early eighties, just after the Iran hostage crisis. That's about all I know. Why?"

Hassan settles into his seat to tell his story.

"As we started to tell you in the cave, if you remember, this story goes back thousands of years, to the beginning of recorded time. There are things beyond our sensibilities that transcend our rational understanding of the world. These are the things that just are. They bind us to the land. They bind us to each other, and they bind us to our present. We are bound to an ancient order of power that was discovered well before Christianity, well before Judaism, and before the Islamic religions were formed. Some say the power is from God himself, some say it comes from the bond between humans and the land. But how it came to be is beyond the discussion here. You must know that there is a bond between some of us as living souls and the earth. And when combined, things that may otherwise seem unnatural become natural. The world becomes more than a barren landscape we use for our purposes. We actually co-exist and share a sense of existence with it. We are not alone living in the world. The non-living world participates in our living world. You saw the first example of this. When you were in the cave, we awoke the bond between the earth and ourselves. Using that bond, we transported you back to your army base. The energy of the earth combined with your energy to create your transportation. We don't understand how it works, we just know it exists. We call it Ninhursag, after an ancient god."

"Wait – this is crazy," Jon has been trying to give Hassan the benefit of the doubt, but it's not working for him right now.

"What the? Hassan – I don't know what happened in the cave, but this doesn't really make sense. "

"Crazy? Not really that crazy when you think about it. All the major religions have some sort of magic. They have something that connects our existence to an existence beyond. There are holy books, Holy Scriptures, and holy figures or statues. Catholics have holy water. Buddhists have holy shrines. The list goes on and on. When we first hear about other religions traditions that involve magic, it can seem strange. Our clan has a connection to the earth others may find strange at first. But it exists to us. When we first saw you, we knew you had the connection as well. In the cave it was confirmed. Do you remember what was going on in the cave? "

"I remember it was dark and damp, but as I got deeper, it became a little brighter and more colorful. I was less afraid as I went deeper, although I felt I should be more and more afraid."

"Right," Hassan continues. "But you probably didn't notice several things. As you walked through the cave some of the rocks started to glow as you walked by. It wasn't just light from torches as you passed through. There was a physical light emanating from the rocks as you walked by. That was the Ningalite in the rocks. Ningalite is the mineral in rocks that reacts with those of us who have Ninhursag in our blood. This is how we knew you were of our blood. This is how we knew you are part of our family. It's a blessing, and it's a responsibility. You are part of a large and vibrant family in our country. But we have never been more threatened than we are now. It is because of this threat we need your help. And now, since we're sure our enemies know of your existence, you are not safe without us anymore. We're going to a compound in this city where we can show you evidence."

Many of the residential streets of Kuwait city are lined with security walls, most reaching ten feet high. Each is designed to hide whatever is behind them from prying eyes and prevent breaches of security. The occasional breaks in the walls are for security check points. The Cadillac Escalade pulls off to the side of the road near a gate with its turn indicator on. In a moment, the gate opens with a grinding, whining noise, and the SUV pulls into the driveway. Once in, the gate closes behind. Now the SUV is in a secured area, in front of another security checkpoint. There is no way forward, and there is no way back without the anonymous permission of a remote host somewhere in the gated security within. It takes another three of four minutes with Hassan on the phone before the next set of gates opens before them.

Once inside the final gates, Jon can see a well-manicured lawn, shaded in tall palm trees and magnolias. As the car approaches a well-appointed house, the driveway slopes downward into an underground garage.

"Stay here for a minute," Hassan tells Jon once the car is parked. Hassan exits the car and greets two men with whom he has some acquaintance. Hassan turns around to the other side of the SUV and opens the door for Jon to exit.

"Jon, this is Alik and Turkin. They are heads of our security here."

"Pleased to meet you." Jon responds.

The four of them proceed into a windowless room underneath the estate above.

"This office was outfitted during the first gulf war" Hassan tells Jon. "Everything was state of the art in 1993." Jon looks around at the equipment. There are green screens with small blinking cursors on the bottom left of the screen, dot matrix printers loaded with paper and ready for any reports from the mainframe. There are racks of computer equipment with large fans on top blowing cool air into the rack space behind it. At the far end of the equipment racks is a small non-descript table with a plastic scoop-backed chair in front of a terminal screen.

"Yikes," Jon says, "does this stuff still work?"

"It should, the government spent $500K on some contractors for Y2K to make sure it would work. Any way, we don't use any of this stuff. Our good stuff is in the next room."

They proceed to another room, this one deeper into the foundation. Windowless and sealed, flat screen monitors line the walls in a state of the art command center set up. Workstations are set up in small work-island fashion around the room. A woman in a head-scarf is looking at one of the monitors and referring to a book lying on the desk. She turns and politely smiles at Jon.

"This is Morgiana Shilah. She is Nisaba's daughter, who you met in the cave. She is one of the leading historians on ancient Iraq and Mesopotamia. She has been studying both in Iraq and Turkey, with a Doctorate in Ancient Civilizations from Columbia University in New York. She can explain the ancient history better than anyone here."

Morgiana stands and walks over to greet Jon with a well cultured, yet soft handshake. "Jon, we've been looking for you for some time. Our history is now linked to you, and we need your help. It was no accident that Hassan was assigned to your outpost at the bridge. It took a lot of 'influence' on the American military to have him assigned there. What you may not know is the rebels who attacked you were not just trying to kill Americans in your outpost. They were trying to kill our family."

CHAPTER 10

SEARCH IN THE SHAKY MOUNTAINS

When he woke the next morning, Mukhtar found his bed empty next to him. He looked around for his wife. In the early morning darkness, he called her name *"Rania!"* but he got no response. He went outside the bedroom and looked through the house. She was nowhere to be found. He looked for her clothes. Her clothes were gone; her favorite bag to carry daily supplies was gone, as well as her shoes. Sitting alone in the early light, he paused. *What have you done? Where did you go?* His voice became angry. His demeanor changed to rage as he stormed around the house. *Why doesn't she listen to me? Why doesn't she obey? What is wrong with that woman?!*

A short time later ten men gathered in a square near the city temple. They brought ropes and other equipment ready to go out into the hills. It was still early and the light was just changing from the pale colors of morning to a full spectrum of light. The sun was shining on the tops of the hills in the distance, but it had not reached the area where the group has assembled. Mukhtar arrived and gathered the men around for instructions on how they would organize the search party.

"We will head up the valley between the shaky mountains. Asif said they walked less than a day into the hills before finding the cave where they were trapped. We should be able to get there by this afternoon. From there, we will find the cave entrance and rescue Rafi and Sabur from the foolish adventure my brother took them on. Be prepared to spend the night if needed, and you will be rewarded when we return!"

After he was done, several men in the search party joked about Asif coming home without his friends. "He came back and forgot his friends in the hills – a likely story from the town's most mischievous member."

They were still milling about, trying to organize their day, when a servant ran into the square to deliver some news. "Mukhtar, I have some disturbing news. Asif left his house. The other servants found his bed empty this morning. It seems he has disappeared as quickly as he appeared."

Mukhtar was furious. "He's an idiot. He'll pay for this now. He's in no shape for a rescue mission even if he did want to go."

He addressed the search party. "We will find these lost fools. But watch out for my little brother. He is full of trickery. No doubt he will cause more trouble along the way. My brother makes his own destiny, as does anyone who might be with him. I fear that one day he will have to pay a dear price for his mistakes. If you see him in some kind of danger, don't risk your own safety to save him from the foolish decisions he has made."

After he gave his instructions, Mukhtar called the leader of the search party, Kusar, to his side. "My brother is a fool for wandering off in his condition. But now I have more concerns. Keep an eye out for my wife. She may be on a search of her own, or she may be with Asif. She may have some of the same foolish ideas that got into Asif."

Several hours later, Asif and Rania had hiked far up into the hills. The sun had risen and was shining down strongly on the path they are on. Occasional scrub brush was the only vegetation along the way. With no trees and no clouds, there were only the sheer cliffs of the earth and the sky around them. Asif stopped at the base of the cliff that held the cave.

"This is it!" Asif looked up at the place where the entrance to the cave was. There was no sign of it now. There was no shadow of an entrance; there were no birds or bats flying around its entrance. The excitement he had a few days before was replaced with dread and remorse for what he might find once he got up there. He had no idea how he would clear the debris from the front of the cave. He only knew he had to try.

"Rania the entrance is in those cliffs up there," he says. "That's where they are, that's where the cave entrance is. But I don't see it. It looks like it is still covered by the landslide. See the freshly fallen rocks? The entrance is near the top of where they are spread. It will be really difficult to climb up there. It will be even more difficult to uncover the cave entrance. I don't know how we're going to do it."

"I'll help you." Rania said. "I will pull at those rocks until my hands are raw to save my brother. But I don't understand. How did you get out if the cave entrance is blocked? There must be another way out."

"I just don't know," Asif said. "I was in the cave with the others. They were in really bad shape, and so was I. I remember meditating, and sleeping, and at times almost panicking. I felt that through meditation I could wait for help to come, if it would ever come. There was water in the cave. You can survive much longer without food than without water, so it's possible they are still alive if they kept drinking. I don't know how I got out. I know I was meditating, then there was an explosion of light, then it went dark. I think I was in some sort of tunnel. It was like I was gliding through it. There were different passageways to take, but somehow I chose one. The next thing I knew I was in bed back in my father's house. I guess I picked a tunnel that ended outside in the garden. But I don't know what it was, or how I got there to start with."

"Let's start climbing. Mukhtar and the search party will not be far behind us. They would never know where to go, and I need some answers from that cave before I deal with them. Rania, I'm glad you're here with me. I know it comes at a great risk to you, but never the less, it feels right for you to be with me. You remind me of your brother, and I have always loved him as a brother of mine, the type of brother I never had. You are a gift to his family, and I feel like you are a gift in my life."

Rania listened intently. Then she looked away modestly. She shouldn't be hearing these things, but they felt so right. "Asif, I have always cared for you so deeply. Even when you were younger and just a boy, you used to make me laugh. Whenever I was down, I could think of you and I knew I would somehow get through. I thought you were the most wonderful thing. Now you are becoming a man, and I can only imagine how you will be as a husband. I'm so glad I'm part of your family, and you are part of ours."

Asif looked deeply into Rania's eyes. "Yes," he said. But there was so much more that he wanted to say, so much that he wanted for her, how he wanted to be with her. It seemed his burden to suffer his feelings for her in silence. He wasn't sure how much longer he could stand it. He just couldn't bring himself to have his words match his feelings.

"Let's go and save your brother," was all he could say.

They left some of their gear at the bottom of the cliffs, but brought food supplies, torches, and sticks with them. They scrambled up the cliffs towards the place where the cave entrance was. They reached the talus field and had to climb rock by rock towards the top of the land slide. The climbing was made incredibly difficult by the constantly moving boulders as they rocked to and fro. Some would fall quickly below, and since Asif was ahead of Rania, he was always afraid they would fall on top of her as he climbed. They climbed for what seemed like hours in the loose talus field. Each step felt like it could have the direst consequences, and after a while it seemed the path back down would be just as treacherous as the path upwards. As they reached the top of the field, Asif stopped, breathing heavily.

"I can't even tell where the entrance was. With the rocks covering the hill, it's impossible to recognize anything that was here before. Nothing looks as it was." He sat down, anguished and defeated.

Rania reached his side and sat beside him. She was exhausted and had lost much of her energy. "We have to find the entrance. We have to find my brother and his friend. We can't stop now!" She sat beside him and wept. Several minutes went by as they gathered what energy they could. Rania picked up one of the sticks they had brought with them to help move rocks out of the way. She wedged the rock under a nearby boulder and pushed down with all her might. The rock would not move. She moved to another smaller boulder and repositioned the stick. She pushed down. It creaked and scratched against the other rocks, then it tumbled down the mountain. She looked underneath where the displaced rock had just been, but there were just more rocks.

She let out and anguished cry and held her fist up to the mountain. "Rafi!" she cried. "Rafi are you there? We have come to get you out! Let us know if you can hear us!" She paused and listened, but she could only hear the wind across the rocks and in her ears in return. She scrambled up the rocks several boulders beyond where Asif was still resting.

Slowly, a low moaning noise came from the hill. Asif looked up, recognizing the sound. The rocks gave way below Rania. Asif could see her from her mid-body upwards, then she was gone. In a rush of crushing rocks, the boulders gave way and Rania screamed as she fell straight down into the entrance of the cave.

Asif screamed, "No! Rania!" He leapt to his feet and rushed upwards towards where she had been standing. He found a gaping hole in the ground where it had given way.

"Rania!! I'm coming!"

Asif reached the entrance to the rockslide and the cave. Peering over the edge, he could see several feet into the cave, but he couldn't see Rania or any sign of life beyond. He started climbing down. The light behind him was again shining into the cave, but not bright enough or in the right places to see Rania or anyone beyond. After twenty feet or so, he lit one of the torches with a flint. Light brightened the walls, the rubble that had fallen into the entrance, and the floor and the water beyond.

"Rania!" he called. "Where are you? " He scrambled down the rocks to the landing where he had spent so many nights with his friends. "Rania?" He looked back up at the rocks that had slid into the cave. From under one of the rocks he spotted her hand, and part of her arm sticking out from underneath. He ran towards it. "Rania!" he was almost weeping as he touched her hand. He started pulling the rocks away from her. He started slowly then increased in speed in a frantic, urgent pace. She was unconscious and there was blood from her legs and chest area.

"What have I done? What happened?" He pulled away the last rocks to free her still body. He grabbed her from under her arms and lifted her up. He carried her down to the landing near the water. He held his ear to her mouth – she was still breathing. He lifted her head and checked her arms and legs, nothing seemed immediately broken. He held her in his arms, praying.

-

Asif slowly got up and went towards his pack to get a container for some water. He lit two more torches to see better in the cave. He went towards the water, and as he did, he saw Sabur lying on his side. He ran over to him. "Sabur! It's me, I came back. Sabur!" He reached his friend and turned him over. He fell limp onto his back. Asif felt his cheek and neck. It was cold.

Sabur was dead. Asif let out a small wail. "Sabur! No! It can't be. How can this be?" Asif bent over his friend in the dim light of the torches. He wept quietly. As he looked up, he saw Rafi lying several feet away in a darkened corner of the cave.

"Rafi!- Rafi!" he cried. He could barely bring himself to go to Rafi's still body. But he had to find out. He had to know. Rafi was lying on his stomach, and Asif rolled him on his side and held him in his arms. "Rafi – tell me you are not dead, tell me you will be OK." He felt his forehead, and then he felt his neck. He couldn't be sure if he was alive or not. He poured some water from his canteen into his mouth, hoping to get some reaction from him, but Rafi was still. Asif held his head near his mouth trying to hear if he still had a breath. He did! So Asif leaned his head slightly backward into his arms. He opened a container with a mixture of honey and juices he had brought with him. He slowly poured the mixture of liquid nectars into his mouth, slowly dripping it onto his tongue. He knew he could not force too much food or nutrition on him at first; he would have to be brought back slowly. The liquid nectar seemed to work in so far as going into his mouth and down his throat. Asif just sat with him quietly. He looked across the cavern of the cave.

He had not really looked at the interior before; it had been so dark when he first went inside with his friends, and he never really had much time. The cavern seemed to open up high above the underground lake. The large slab of rock that gradually led to the edge of the water appeared almost as a tongue into the water. The roof of the cavern came down sharply on the side of the cave without water, and then it rose again sharply towards the cave entrance. The floor of the cave also rose sharply towards the entrance. The light from the entrance and the low ceiling created a beam of light through the dust of the rubble.

He picked Rafi up from under his arms and carried him towards Rania. He laid him next to her with his back against a slanted rock, which held his head up.

He moved to Rania and talked soothingly to her. He pulled her up with her back against the same slanted rock as Rafi. He slowly poured some water into her mouth, then he poured some of the nectar onto her lips. It glistened against her lips as some of it dripped of the edge of his jar.

"Rania," he whispered, "can you hear me? Can you hear me Rania? I need you. If you can hear me, wake up!"

Suddenly Rania moved slightly. She coughed as the nectar and the water was still stuck in her throat. She coughed again. Asif grabbed her hand and gently squeezed, to try to awaken her.

"Rania, it's me Asif – if you can hear me, please wake up!"

Rania awoke with a start. She opened her eyes, but she couldn't quite speak yet. After resting a while, Rania finally spoke. "Asif, Asif," she said. "What happened? Where are we?"

"Rania, we fell into the cave. Are you OK? Are you hurt anywhere?"

"I think I'm OK, my ankle hurts. I don't think I can stand on it."

"Rania, I found your brother. I found your brother and he's alive. But Rania, Sabur did not make it. He's dead! He's over there by the water. I'm so sorry."

Rania looked around and saw her brother lying a short distance away from her. "Rafi! Rafi can you hear me"? Rafi still lay still and did not respond.

Rania tried to stand to go to Rafi. When she put weight on her right foot, her ankle buckled. She fell to the ground with a small wail.

"Rania, rest here. I will bring them outside. We'll get them back to town."

Rania tried to get up again, but she failed. She laid down where she was, holding her ankle.

Asif moved quickly to attend to Rafi. He gave him more nectar and followed it with some more water. As Rafi lay quietly, Asif moved quickly to move the body of Sabur. He took out a blanket and some rope, and rolled him into the blanket. He tied the rope around Sabur, and then pulled him up onto his back. He started walking towards the entrance, slowly at first, then more quickly. After several stops and near falls, he reached the entrance of the cave. Rania could see his silhouette against the brightness of the sky, with the body of their fallen friend on his back. Then Asif disappeared into the light.

Rania slowly pulled herself next to her brother. She fed him more nectar and water and slowly he began moving his head back and forth, forcing himself out of the fog he was in.

She comforted him with her voice, "We'll be all right. I'm here and Asif will be back soon, we'll rest until Asif comes back."

Rania tended to her ankle. It didn't look broken. She knew an ankle sprain could hurt as bad as or worse than a break. She told her brother "Considering the pain, it must be a sprain and not a broken ankle." They lay back and rested, always concerned that the light may fade and Asif may take a while to return.

Outside, Asif had reached the bottom of the cliffs carrying Sabur to the trail where his other supplies were. He lay Sabur down, wrapped in the blanket he had brought with him. He pulled his equipment out from under the brush where he had hidden it. He got more supplies, including another blanket, food and oil for the torches.

He climbed back up to the entrance of the cave. He climbed down and reached the bottom of the cave just as the light from the entrance was fading. Rafi had woken up, and they were resting quietly. Rafi was in much better shape and was able to talk. "Asif – how can we get out of here?"

Asif looked at his friend, very glad that he had recovered so rapidly. "Can you stand? Are you hurt?"

"I'm not hurt, I'm just very weak. I think I can stand." He replied.

"Great, but let's wait until tomorrow. We can spend the night here and get out in the morning."

"Another night of camping with you?" Rafi replied. "What could go wrong?" Apparently Rafi was feeling good enough to make a joke.

"My father used to tell me," Rafi said in a raspy voice, "The brave man finds a tent everywhere, while the coward knows not where to lay his head." He looked at Asif and smiled.

Asif was very glad to hear his voice stronger now, and it was a great comfort to hear the sound of his best friend's voice once again. He had been so afraid he would never hear him again. Asif set about getting some food and making sure his friends were as comfortable as possible.

-

Outside, Mukhtar continued on his journey up the valley. The terrain changed from ragged cliffs to more rounded and sculpted rock, as if shaped by an ancient river bottom. There was small green brush, and an occasional tree appearing. Mukhtar was looking towards the cliffs. Based on what Asif had said, he knew the cave entrance was less than a day's journey into the mountains. So, as they came to a flat open area they stopped. The sky was slowly losing its light. The sun had gone behind the cliffs on the western side of the ridge of mountains. Now streams of color came from behind the mountains radiating colors across the sky and casting an otherworldly pall of orange and red against the grey and white cliffs of the mountains.

"One night is enough looking for my brother's foolish friends, and enough to keep the peace in my family. Let's break out some food, drink and our favorite pipe for the night."

His men scurried about setting up camp for the night. Soon the camp was set up and they were sitting around a fire under a full canopy of stars, which stretched across the sky until the slate gray of the cliffs interrupted their journey across the heavens.

CHAPTER 11

SHOCK AND AWE

"It started back in 2003 with the US invasion of Iraq. Unknown to Americans, two wars were re-started. Your war was restarted to finish one you started in the 1990s under George Bush Sr. Our war was one that started thousands of years ago. Your invasion awakened ancient powers and two enemy clans that have been biding their time for millenniums and generations."

"Is this an Islamic thing? Like Shia versus Sunni?" Jon asks.

Morgiana explains "No, this pre-dates Shia versus Sunni, before religion, before Christianity, and before Judaism. Even before these, there were thriving civilizations here, but they didn't believe in our form of organized religions with a common single god. They believed in many gods, gods of the sun, the moon, and the air. The most powerful god was the god of the sun. His name was Enlil. He was supremely powerful. The god of earth was called An. The people would build temples in their cities dedicated to a god that represented them; in the same way a Catholic church may be dedicated to a saint. Each believed the temple they created brought favor to them from the god. People believed in good versus evil, but each good or bad event in people's lives was caused by the influence of good and bad gods."

"These ancient times were a time of great human awakening. The first civilizations formed, the first city-states, and the first wars were started. Many of man's greatest innovations started during this time, right on these lands. Writing, money, domesticating animals, the wheel, all were invented in civilizations which started here, long before modern religions. Along with civilization came corruption and greed, power and injustice. It's from these first brushes with evil that your story of

Adam and Eve originates. And it's from these first evil powers that our ancient orders were born."

"Jon, do you remember *Shock and Awe*?" Morgiana asked.

"Sure," Jon said. "That's what Donald Rumsfeld called the original invasion of Baghdad. We lit up the sky with rockets and bombs. It was pretty impressive, and meant to scare away any thought of rising against the American invasion. If we only knew then what we would be up against...." Jon's voice trailed off.

"Right – exactly." Morgiana continued. "It was during that bombing that these ancient powers were exposed, released from their burial after thousands of years. You can even see it. Watch here on the monitor."

Morgiana picked up a remote control and hits play on a DVD connected to a forty inch flat screen TV on the wall. "The Shock and Awe campaign ran for two weeks over Baghdad starting March 21st, 2003. Over 4,800 bombs were dropped on the city during over 1700 air raids. They were supposed to be exclusively on what were called 'military' targets. Those military targets were based on US intelligence, and it's now well documented how intelligent that 'military intelligence' was. Well, not everything was just a military target. In a city built on civilizations that go back over five thousand years, buildings have been built on top of buildings. Any military target has once been more than just a weapons warehouse. Many of Saddam's palaces and key military targets were built on top of old forts, palaces, temples. After two weeks of non-stop bombing, the Republican Guard (Saddam's key security force) had mostly folded. The Americans and allied forces walked in unchallenged for the most part."

The video showed "highlights" of the shock and awe campaign. Bright flashes briefly lit the skyline as sirens blared and the orange glow of open flames illuminated the sky. A thick blanket of smoke rose above the buildings and flashing lights, partially obscuring the view of the districts further away in the skyline.

"Now, Jon, watch here,." Hassan said as he points to a spot along the Euphrates river. "Right about here." Jon watches as a bright flash explodes along the river. There was a small explosion, and a cloud of smoke arises from the area. Then, another light appears from within the burning building. Yellow, red, and blue smoky lights rise and swirl around the smoking area. The smoke continues, but the swirling lights gather strength and grow. They sweep beyond the smoke for a moment, then quickly turn back to the center of the explosion and disappear into the smoke and fire.

Hassan points excitedly to the screen. "There, right there Jon, that was it. That was the crystals, and here's what happened at that moment during Shock and Awe."

Morgiana picked up the story. "The ancient cuneiform writings tell us there are three ancient crystals; one yellow, one red, and one blue. There was a great struggle between two of the most powerful gods, the goddess An and the god Enlil. An created the yellow crystal from the earth as gifts to men. She gave it special power which could transport mortal men to the heavenly fields of Ekru and the temple of the gods. Enlil was furious that she would give the power of the gods to morals. He created the red and blue crystals to show how destructive giving mortal men powers of the gods would be. The red and blue crystals can summon great destructive energy, and when combined, could make a mortal man invisible. But Enlil swore to give the red and blue crystals to mankind, and they would show how destructive they would be with godly power. Men could not be trusted with the power of the crystals. So great was his rage at An that they fought for ages between them. Enlil hid the red and blue crystals deep within the earth, but planned for men to find them. An was furious and forced Enlil into exile in the underworld. Eventually he escaped, but he was forever scarred by his tortured existence in the underworld. While Enlil was in the underworld, An gave the powers of the crystals to the human descendants of Ninhursag as a gift. Enlil became enraged, and threatened to condemn any human he found in the immortal world to the underground."

"In ancient times, there was a fierce warlord who found the crystals and started the clan called The Hand of the Red Fist. But the crystals were returned to the underworld. Descendants of this clan still live today, and they are sworn to regain control of the red and blue crystals. They have been hidden for thousands of years. That is, until the bombings by the Americans and the allies."

CHAPTER 12

MUKHTAR'S SHADOW

The next morning Asif woke early and gathered some food and supplies together. He walked to the water and refilled the canteens. As he returned, Rafi was just waking up. Rafi started to panic as he awoke. His breath was rapid as he realized he was still in the cave. He didn't remember his friend had returned to find him. "Augh! Ah!" He thrashed his body about.

"Rafi" Asif said. "Rafi! I'm here! Rafi"

Rafi looked around at his friend; he paused, and remembered that his friend had come back for him. "Asif – I – I thought I was still alone here."

"I'm here Rafi" Asif said "And we're going to get out of here today. As soon as Rania wakes up we'll start making our way out of the cave. How do you feel? Are you stronger?"

"Yes", Rafi said, I'm feeling stronger. But I'll be much stronger once we're out of here. I don't want to spend another second in here. Rania – Rania! Wake up!"

"We'll see how her ankle feels today." Asif said. "If she can't move yet, I'll have to carry you both out one at a time".

Rafi stood up slowly. Asif watched his progress. He was still weak from hunger and dehydration. His muscles ached with a stiff pain, as if they were hardened into his body. He moved towards the rock slide which he would need to climb to get out. He tried to climb a few steps, but lost his balance and fell against the rocks. Asif knew he would have to help him out of the cave, and then come back for Rania.

Soon Rania was standing on one foot embracing her brother before he started climbing out of the cave with Asif. Rafi wrapped his arm around Asif's shoulder and they started climbing the rocks to the entrance of the cave. As they reached the top, Rania could see them both silhouetted against the light.

Then they were gone, picking their way down the rocks outside the cave. Once they were past the rock slides and on a manageable slope, Asif left Rafi to return to Rania.

Rafi continued to the bottom of the path and found the cache of supplies that Asif and Rania had left along the trail. Asif had told him where he had laid Sabur. He did not expect visitors.

A few minutes later he heard footsteps approaching. Mukhtar rode up to Rafi as he sat.

"Well, well." Mukhtar said, without much compassion for having found him alive. "Look what we have found. And where might your friend be? And have you by chance seen my brother, or my wife?"

Rafi looked up at Mukhtar with hidden contempt. Now was no time to refuse the assistance of anyone. He looked at Mukhtar, "Mukhtar, the cave entrance is just up this trail along the cliffs above. Asif and Rania found me and saved my life. Asif carried me outside to safety. Rania has hurt her ankle, so Asif has just returned to help her. They need our help. My friend Sabur did not make it. Asif carried him out and laid him just up the path," Rafi said pointing up the pathway.

Mukhtar looked up at the cliffs. He motioned towards his entourage to follow him. "You four go with Rafi and find Sabur. You four come with me to find Rania. The rest of you stay here."

Inside the cave Asif returned to Rania. He moistened a cloth and washed her ankle, trying to cool it down to reduce the swelling. Rania bent over towards Asif.

"It's OK Asif, I'll be fine. You can help me out of here and we can go back to Nippur".

"Rania, I can't bear the thought of you returning to my brother. He treats you so badly, and you and I know…"

Rania interrupted him and pulled his face close to hers. "My dear Asif," she said.

Asif couldn't help himself. He pulled her close and kissed her on the lips. It was so wrong, but it felt so right. He pressed his hand against her back to pull her closer to him. It was an embrace that had been waiting to happen for years. At first she resisted, then she responded by holding his hand against her. She moved her hand to touch his face. He closed his eyes and melted into her warmth. The soft light from the cave entrance provided a hushed radiant glow from the small area of the landing they were on. They didn't notice, but many of the rocks on the walls started to glow a soft glow, then they grew brighter as their intimacy increased. Soon there were more colors. Yellow, red, and blue, lights appeared as if lighted from behind the walls by the powers of the gods themselves.

At the entrance to the cave, Mukhtar' shadow appeared across the cave entrance. He stood in the light, shielding his eyes, trying to peer into the cave. The outside brightness and his shadow prevented the light from showing where Asif and Rania were on the floor below. He shifted to one side of the cave as he started to move down into the entrance. Suddenly the mountain groaned again. The floor moved beneath his feet. He stumbled backwards, but as he did, the light passed him and shone on Rania and Asif on the floor of the cave. Mukhtar didn't notice the strange lights in the cave. He saw their embrace. The grounds began to shake more, yet another earthquake happening in this cursed valley. Mukhtar pulled back outside the entrance to the cave as the whole mountain seemed to jump up and down beneath him. Loose stones started falling on him as he looked up the steep slopes above the cave entrance. The low moan of the mountain became a small roar.

Inside the cave, Asif and Rania were being tossed about in the latest earthquake. Large boulders and stalactites were falling from the roof of the cave, crashing into the rocks below, some crashing into the disturbed water of the usually quiet pool. Asif and Rania held each other tight as the world around them collapsed. The moaning sound of the mountain became a roar, with the rocks crashing and splashing around them. Amid the wreckage, the internal lights started to glow more brightly. A white and yellow light dominated the cavernous interior of the cave, coming from the area to the right of the entrance.

Outside, Mukhtar was trying to hold his balance on the rocks as he raged in anger. The rocks continued to rain down from the cliffs above. He took shelter underneath a large boulder below the entrance of the cave. As he looked upwards towards the entrance, he saw a large boulder rocking more and more loosely above the entrance. After several more seconds in the earthquake, the rock gave way and crashed down onto the entrance of the cave. Just before the rock came down, a beam of light burst from the cave and streaked across the sky. Mukhtar watched as the rocks crashed down, and stood in wonder at the lights that were coming from inside the cave. Even against the fading blue sky, the light could be seen in an arc from the cave, then back again. The boulder came crashing down, sealing the entrance as other rocks spilled around it to seal the shape of the opening. Mukhtar stood and looked at the entrance. In a few moments his two companions came into view.

"The rocks fell as I got here. I saw the entrance before, but it's gone now."

From far down below, Rafi was watching the action as closely as he could. He saw the entrance to the cave, he saw Mukhtar fall backwards, and then he saw the rocks fall during the earthquake. He watched as the rocks crashed down, with a puff of dust curling up into the sunlight around the entrance. But he also saw the beacon of light arc just as the rocks were falling. It was a brightly colored beam of lights that shot out from the rocks, swooped back to the cave, and then was gone as quickly as it appeared.

Inside the cave, the earthquake had subsided. Asif and Rania saw the brilliant lights emanating from the side of the cave. White and yellow lights were coming from a small alcove that had been opened during the earthquake. They walked together towards the lights, Rania limping and holding onto Asif, while looking into the crystalline brilliance that appeared to them. As they approached, Asif saw a yellow crystal, about the size of their fist, with yellow lights emanating from it. Rania picked it up. As she did so, a brilliant plume of yellow lights burst from the crystal and swept above their heads. It formed a cloud of light and curled around them, then swooped around the open cavern. It rushed towards the entrance of the cave just as the rocks outside were sealing the entrance and raced back inwards. In a final arc of light and energy, it crashed straight down as a beam onto Asif and Rania where they were standing on the landing. As the light subsided, the cave stayed lit by dim red, blue and orange lights. The yellow lights were no more.

Rania and Asif were gone.

CHAPTER 13

ANTIQUITIES

Morgiana continued her story. "The Clan of the Boars Head held an emergency meeting during Shock and Awe was due to the discovery of new cuneiforms found in an ancient wall uncovered by one of the cruise missile attacks."

"The who? The what?" Jon asked.

"The Clan of the Boars Head is the secret ancient society sworn to keep the red and blue crystals from the hands of men. They have existed as long as the Hand of the Red Fist, trying to counter their goals. A cuneiform is an ancient clay tablet with writing on it. Cuneiforms were the first form of writing. The ancients who invented writing didn't use letters; they used pictures and pointed arrows. Only a few people of the town could read them, usually the local priest and one or two other people that were trained to write them. They were often baked into the clay. There have been thousands found, but only a few that are in good enough shape to be translated. Some of our people were down by the waterfront and found some tucked between two large blocks an ancient wall. They were in pretty bad shape. They brought them back here and contacted me to see if I could interpret the writing. I told them what I could interpret when I addressed the council meeting."

"These cuneiforms told us many new things we didn't know before. The writer focused on telling us the glory of the gods, which is to be expected since it was written in a temple. More importantly, it gives us clues on what we have been looking for over the ages. It talks of strange lights that appear as people approach the Temple. This is similar to what we have seen at the temple of Ezra in the Northeast regions of Iraq. The crystals are most likely to be where these strange lights are. We saw those lights exposed during Shock and Awe. There had long been rumors that an ancient temple existed in the warehouse district by the water. This is the same place where so much of the Shock and Awe bombing had been. There was a good chance the crystals were close to being exposed as we spoke. The cuneiform mentions the ancient temple is several hundred yards south of the bridge over the Euphrates. We researched where the ancient bridge probably was along the Euphrates, and it points to the area near where the ancient temple is supposed to be."

Morgiana unrolled a map and pointed to a location along the Euphrates River. "This is the spot we identified as the most likely place the cuneiform is referring to. We had to get there as quickly as we could to secure the crystals, if they were there."

"Hassan and I were asked to go back out on our motorcycles and search the area where the strange lights had been seen."

Hassan continued. "Outside the hospital ambulances were lined up waiting to get to the emergency room with wounded. I had to weave my motorcycle in and out of the abandoned cars and trucks towards the warehouse district along the waterfront. The closer I got, the higher the fires rose into the sky. Soon I could see open flames in the buildings along the way. Sometimes traffic was backed up right next to the burning buildings. I arrived at the edge of the river just after a cruise missile had left a huge crater only one hundred yards from a petroleum tank farm. I parked my motorcycle just up the street and we walked down the street towards the crater left by the missile."

"There were fires, smoke, and dirt everywhere. Despite our better judgment, we knew we had to go into the crater and see what was there. The missile crater was about fifteen yards across and about ten feet deep. We crawled over the crater wall and down into the cavity. Our feet sank into the soft dirt that made up the area. We made our way over to an exposed wall that had withstood the bombing. We stood there, brushing away dirt and looking anywhere we could for a sign of something unusual, anything that may be of value now exposed."

"I noticed the body of a man lying face down in the rubble on the far side of the crater. We made our way over to him and rolled him over on his back to see if he was alive. I touched his neck and felt a pulse. I checked his breath and he was still barely breathing. His face and body was covered in dirt. If I had only been able to recognize him then I would have been able to take my revenge on him and save us from so much additional hardship."

"What happened next was hard to believe, and if Morgiana had not been there as a witness I may doubt my own story given the extreme circumstances we were in. As we looked over him, a circular black hole appeared in the deepest part of the crater. It was blacker than the night and seemed to spread darkness out from it, in the opposite way that light refracts from its source in the surrounding air. Small wispy clouds of light started to emerge from within it, then a beam of light and energy burst from inside and curved towards the body lying there. It smashed into his body, stiffening and bending his composure into a prone statue position. We stood back several paces. I thought an electrical cable or something of that sort had shorted out and was pouring current through is body. As his body contorted, his face and body morphed into another face and shape. His face became aged, gaunt and more angular. His hair grew thicker and longer, and his hands and arms became thin and stretched over a slight muscular frame. His face became stretched and blackened from the metamorphosis. Suddenly the energy beam stopped. The hole vanished. I have heard of demonic possessions before, but I have never witnessed anything like this. It was as if a spirit was entering the body of the man who had been knocked unconscious from the bomb."

"We looked around for the source of the beam of energy that hit this man's body, mindful that an underground electrical cable or something of that sort may be nearby. As I was walking near the bottom of the crater, I tripped on something in the dirt. I looked down and found a clay box about ten inches long on each side. As I picked it up, I noticed a glow coming from inside the box, around the seams. I knew this is was what we were looking for. I took off my jacket and threw it around the box. I wrapped it up and we headed out of the cratered area, looking for some help for the man struck by the strange beam of energy."

"Just as we climbed over the rim of the impact crater, we found ourselves surrounded by American and British special operations troops, with rifles pointed at us. We were ordered down on the ground with our hands behind our head. I put the box down and did what they told me, there was really no choice. We told them about the injured man inside the crater, but we never heard what had happened to him afterwards. I was arrested for looting and brought to the American army base. We had no idea what happened to the box until you appeared, Jon. You were the last person we knew that held the box."

"How can you be so sure?" Jon asked.

"In those first days of the invasion the US had several priorities. They had to blow the place up, and then put it back together again as soon as they could. Parts of the US orders were to secure some of the national treasures of Iraq. The gold, the art, the historical artifacts. Jon, you were part of one of those details, weren't you?"

"Yeah, I remember those days – we found millions of dollars of gold and art treasures. We couldn't find a good place to keep them. In the end, we secured all of them in the Museum of Antiquities."

"Right, you took the box from me that I had found, and then accused me of looting. It was kind of ironic, if you think about it. Here you are, an invading army, taking our most precious possessions, and arresting me, one its citizens, for looting. We did not know what to do. It took us weeks to find out what happened to the box. It wasn't until several weeks later when this picture came from the media feed to our newsroom. " Hassan displayed a new picture on the video monitor. The picture showed a US Army private holding several treasures he had recovered from one of the bombed out areas. The picture showed Jon holding a clay box, and several other rolled documents. The picture was over exposed with his face and features mostly washed out in the flash. The caption described how the allied forces were saving the nations treasures from thieves and looters.

"This is it, Jon. This is the box. And that's you holding it. This picture was distributed to all the media outlets, but I got a hold of it before it was published in our newspaper. Now, take a close look at your face and that box in this enhanced picture."

Hassan flipped to a new picture on the screen. "I ran Photoshop on the picture and took out most of the flash and over exposure. If you look closely, you can see there are actually lights coming out of the box." Without the washout, one can clearly see light emitting from the box.

"But that's not all of it, Jon. Look at your eyes in this enhanced picture. The light doesn't just seem to be coming from the box. Your eyes are lit also. There is a distinct red light coming from your eyes. This is the picture that first told us you carry Ninhursag. This picture of you was the only clue we had on where the box had gone next. There was nothing in the news feed about who you were or how we could find you. I had to digitally enhance the picture, and there it was. Your name tag showed. 'Bishop.' Next, all we had to do was find you. We don't have much, but we do have some of our own intelligence. All we had to do was to cross reference the US Army list of personnel with the list of soldiers assigned to recovering Iraqi treasures, and we had your name. From there, we found out where your next assignments were, and we found you were assigned to the Bad Asurin Bridge up north. From there it was a simple matter of getting me assigned as a translator for that border crossing."

"And what happened to the man who was electrocuted in the crater?" Jon asked.

"We now think this man gained power somehow by the life force that was in the crater. We know his name is Morabec Mudlarek. He is one of the most notorious and evil rulers in Saddam Hussein's Republican Guard. I have a personal hatred for the man that goes back to my early childhood. We think that the energy in the crater made him even more evil. But we are not sure how he came to be in the crater at that time."

"OK, assuming all that is true, how would he know to come after me?"

"We didn't think he knew your name. That is, until the Bad Asurin Bridge in northern Iraq. If you remember, we had not known each other long. I had just been gaining your trust when that attack happened. It was by pure luck that you and I escaped that attack. It was led by Mudlarek. He must have seen your picture in one of the distributions to other news media. He would have killed us both if he could. As it is he killed five of your troops who were stationed at the outpost. But you may be surprised that he did not go there to kill your American troops. He went there to kill me, and you."

CHAPTER 14

HOMESTEAD BY THE RIVER

An abandoned house stands alongside the Euphrates River as it flows southbound sixty miles away from Mukhtar's kingdom. It's a rural area that was once heavily farmed. Drought had forced the family from this farm. Now, with simple irrigation, this farm and others in this area were viable again. The simple house was built from the local bricks, dug from the mud of the river, and baked in kilns a few miles away.

It is along the river bank, outside the house, where Asif and Rania appeared in the late evening. They lay unconscious and still at first. Asif slowly awoke, and he looked toward Rania. The river was just below them, and the small house was a few steps away. As he came into consciousness, he saw a river snake slowly approaching Rania. He knew many of the river snakes were extremely poisonous. Their venom could kill some of the largest cattle in a few seconds. As he slowly came more into consciousness, he froze. He knew the best thing to do would be to lie completely still, because the snake would react to the vibrations of his movement. The snake came forward towards Rania. Just then she started to stir into consciousness.

"Rania" he whispered loudly, "lie still." But it was too early for Rania to understand what he was saying, or to understand her surroundings. She lifted her head and started to push herself up with her arms. The snake lifted its head to look at its prey and consider its next move. His forked tongue shot out of its mouth, flipping in the air to sense her motion. Rania continued to shift her weight to her arms. Suddenly she saw the snake just inches from her face. She froze. Asif watched intently, then looked around him for something, anything to help. He grabbed a rounded stone near his hand, about the size of his palm. With a sweeping motion he rolled it just past the snake into the grass which headed down towards the river. The snake, as if sensing a rodent running by, quickly redirected its attention and shot after the stone as it disappeared over the embankment towards the water. Asif moved quickly to help Rania. Next to them lay the yellow crystal. They looked around and didn't recognize where they were, but they saw the house standing nearby.

They gathered the crystal and made it to the house. They were not sure how they found the energy to get through their first hours and days. In that simple abandoned house they started their lives together. Within a few days they had made it habitable, but they were not yet sure where they were or how they had arrived there. They had the crystal, and they assumed a power from the gods had saved them. Rania never quite recovered from her ankle injury, and to the end of her days she walked with a slight limp. She rarely complained about the pain. She felt it was the price she paid the gods for her freedom from Mukhtar and the happiness she found with Asif.

Soon, however, another complication arose. Rania was pregnant, and it was with Mukhtar's child. They decided to keep the child as their own. The child was a boy, and they named him Rahid.

The fertile soil was easy to plant, and the other local farmers were eager to help another farm and family start. The droughts of the previous generations seemed to be a story of the old days. They married in the closest town, called Eppru. They told the priest they were exiles from the north; and that they were married there. The people of the North now believed in one god, and they rejected the traditional religion that honored the gods of the sun, the earth, and the moon. Fearing that they would be persecuted for their beliefs, they pilgrimaged south. The priest insisted they be married again in Eppru. That seemed to be a wise move, as it satisfied the social need for association in the town. With a simple ceremony they married, no one knowing that Rania was in fact already married to Asif's brother. They swore they would tell Rahid he was not Asif's natural son when he was older. With the family resemblance already in place, Rahid was a natural fit to pass as Asif's son.

Years passed, Asif and Rania had two more children of their own. Their farm was enough to provide for them and they were able to sell their goods in town. The local temple served both as the religious center and the bank. There was a market outside the temple that grew busier and busier with each year that went by. It was during this time they learned how to use the seven day week for planning at the temple. Rania learned about what the priests were doing with written language. She learned how the pictures and markings represented words, and how the words were put into the clay. They learned to tell stories over and over from the crude writing. Only a select few were taught to read, and even fewer were taught to write.

CHAPTER 15

OPTIONS

"Jon, where are all those treasures and artifacts the allied forces *secured* from the Iraqi people?" Hassan asked with a noticeable sarcasm on the word 'secured'.

"Now wait a minute, if we had not secured all of those things they would have been destroyed or stolen, you know that. We could have had no idea if what you found truly belonged to you. Better safe than sorry and we arrested about two hundred people for looting during that time. You can't tell me that many of them truly had a claim to the TV sets, gold vases, and ancient artwork that we found them with."

"Fair enough, Jon. Regardless, we need to know where that box is, and we need to get it before someone from the Hand of the Red Fist does. Now what exactly did the Allied forces do with all those items?"

"As I was saying, we cataloged and made an inventory of all the items we collected." Jon said. "Because of all the negative publicity of the war and political threat to the allied countries, there were many troops involved that didn't want to take on the hardest parts of the war. We gave the less battle approved troops the responsibility of the more mundane jobs. They did supplies, administration, etc. I think we gave the job of securing and maintaining these assets to the British, if I remember correctly. They are all in a secured location in the Ministry of Antiquities just outside the Green Zone in Baghdad."

"The Green Zone?" Alik asked.

"Yes, that's the area the Army secured for US troops in Baghdad. You know we took over Saddam's palaces. We took the area around the largest one and turned it into a secure area for our troops. We call that the Green Zone. Now it's like a small city in itself, only with a lot more security. At the insistence of the Iraqi government, the national treasures we identified are stored in the basement of the Ministry of Antiquities just outside Green Zone. From a security perspective, it's still considered inside the Green Zone. The bad news is that there is no way we can just walk in there and get the box out of there. The security is just too tight."

"That's why we need you, Jon. You can get the security clearance. If we can get you back into the Green Zone, can you get to the warehouse, and can you find where the box is?" Hassan asked. "By the current regulations, it takes approval from an Army officer and an authorized Iraqi to take something from the Ministry of Antiquities."

"That would be a pretty good trick. First of all, they were holding me for medical observation when you kidnapped me. What makes you think I can just show up again in the Green Zone and have full freedom to move around and get whatever I want?" Jon was confused and a little taken aback at the brash ideas coming from Hassan. Was this guy for real? So far, he had shown he has a lot of resources at his disposal. He "kidnapped" Jon from a secured hospital in Kuwait city. He worked for the communications department of the former Iraqi government. He was able to get himself assigned as a translator at a remote checkpoint in northern Iraq. And, if his story about finding the box in the warehouse district was true, he was part of a secret clan going back thousands of years. Either he was completely legit, or he was completely crazy. For now, Jon would listen to the rest of his plan.

"There is another option if you don't want to go back as you. If we can get you back into the Green Zone, you don't have to go as yourself. Jon, we have plenty of ways of getting you another ID. You're an American, and you said it's the British that are watching the warehouse with the crystals. If we can get you and Morgiana in there, can you find the box?"

"That's way more conjecture than I can deal with right now. I just don't know. I'm not the expert of disguise and deception that you and your clan seem to be. I'm a pretty straight arrow. Let's think about what would happen if I go back. Let's say I make it to the warehouse in the Green Zone, then what?"

"Then we'll use Morgiana to help you remove the crystals from the Ministry. We'll have Morgiana come with you; she is a registered historian and will vouch for your request. You will have the required form as the US approver, and she will have a signed form to remove artifacts. She is a known expert to the people in the Ministry. You will be her military escort to remove the artifacts to be transported to a temple in the south."

Jon was more skeptical than ever. "I can't be part of this. Now you're asking me to become a thief."

"You can say you were just following orders, Jon. If those orders were found to be faked some other time, no one would fault you for carrying out the orders that were given to you. I think you need to understand a little more of the recent history, too. It's as much a part of the story as what happened thousands of years ago."

CHAPTER 16

REUNIONS IN EPPRU

The small town of Eppru was nestled in the lowlands between the Tigris and Euphrates rivers. The town was surrounded by fertile farmland with small houses spread amongst the fields. The fields were often divided by irrigation ditches that brought water to the fields. A single foot path led through the town.

The town consisted of a small temple to the god Nanna, goddess of the moon. Next to the temple was a market, where local people could come to trade and buy goods. Some traders would come from neighboring towns to sell goods from far away cities. One fateful day Rania and Asif brought the children to the market. Mukhtar's son, Rahid, was now twelve years old. He resembled Mukhtar in a striking way. As Rania was looking at some chicken with her other two children, Rahid had wandered over to a leather merchant. It was there that Rafi, who was now selling wares to merchants, was trying to sell leather belts to the merchant. Rafi could not help but notice how much the boy looked like Mukhtar. He took one look at Rahid and stopped in mid-sentence. It was as if Mukhtar had been created again as a boy. Rahid looked at him curiously, since he had many of his mother's characteristics. It was then that his mother came around a corner looking for Rahid. "Rahid – there you are!" We have to get going." As she turned she saw her brother, and he saw her. He recognized her voice.

"Rania?" He called, "Is that you?"

Rania looked down. "My name is Allyra, I'm sorry."

"Rania, it's me- Rafi," Rafi insisted.

"I'm sorry sir, my name is Allyra" she responded. "Come Rahid, we have to get going."

Rahid followed his mother around the corner. But Rafi followed, and it was then that he saw Asif with the other children. "Asif! Asif! It's me Rafi!"

Asif looked at Rafi, looked around at the market to see if others were watching, then gave him a big hug. There was no use trying to hide the truth.

Rania then hugged her brother, but whispered to him that they have to return home, that they should not have a conversation in public. "Can you come to our house later? We are just a mile or so west of town along the river in a brick farm house."

The small farmhouse along the river was a twenty minute walk outside of Eppru. The house was secluded from neighbors, and featured a small garden in the front just before the road. Rafi entered the house and noticed the traditional but simple accommodations inside. There was a small living room area, a kitchen, and some rooms towards the rear. They sat in the warmth of the kitchen to talk.

Rania prepared a simple meal from some of the food she purchased in the market while in town, combined with some fresh vegetables from their garden. There was simple bread, some vegetables, and something that resembled chicken to be cooked over a small earthen stove.

"I thought you both were dead" Rafi began. "I thought we saw you buried alive in the cave, and there was nothing any of us could do about it to free you. How can it be that you are alive? And, you have children! My nieces and nephews! I'm so happy, but I don't understand. There is so much to tell. So many things have happened in Nippur. Mukhtar has started taking over peoples land, their farms, and their money. He has the power of the gods! But let me explain."

"After several months, after the news settled down, Mukhtar brought several slaves to the mountains where the cave entrance is. He uncovered the entrance to the cave. He got inside, but he never found any bodies. He did find the same lights in the walls that we saw. They were even stronger for him. He had the slaves mine the cave for the rocks to bring back to his house. As they were mining, they found two special crystals, each about the size of your hand. One was tinted a faint red, and the other a light blue."

"He brought them back to the temple in Nippur. Mukhtar swore to the priest that he would use the crystals only in peace. But Mukhtar deceived the priest, and forced him to swear allegiance to him. He had the priest declare both of you dead even though your bodies were never found. The priest said the crystals belong to the gods, not men. The blue crystal is of the moon god; red is of fire. They are now held as the most prized possessions in the kingdom. There are powers embodied in the crystals, but it is how Mukhtar has uses them that have made him more powerful than all. The red crystal has the power of the light, and the moon crystal has the power of darkness and the moon. Combined, the power of the darkness crystal shields Mukhtar from the light of the sun, no light will shine upon him. He becomes invisible, as if in the darkness in an eclipse. He walks the fields and roads without being seen. The fire crystal gives the power of lightning and fire. Mukhtar can hide in the light of day with the sun and moon crystals, and he can create fire and lightning with the red fire crystal."

"Mukhtar claims to be the lord of all the land around him. He has used his powers to destroy the houses and barns of his enemies, or anyone that will stand in his way of gaining power over their land. Now all must pay taxes to Mukhtar and his empire. He is reviled by everyone in the kingdom, but no one can challenge him so long as he has the power of the crystals behind him."

"Now tell me, how is it that you have settled here in this town?"

"We told the town elders that we are refugees from the North. We had been forced out of our homes for our religion, and we returned to be near our homeland, although the rest of our family had been killed. We moved into this house and started planting wheat, and we have learned to be farmers ever since. It hasn't been easy, but that is what we had to do to start our lives again. We have kept a simple life, we don't look for problems, and we haven't tried to find news from home, for fear we would be discovered."

"But Rafi, the story you tell us of the crystals is frightening to us. Because when we were trapped in the cave, we found a crystal ourselves. It's how we escaped, and somehow it must be how I escaped the cave the first time. As the cave was tumbling down around us and Mukhtar was outside, we found a yellow crystal. We didn't know there were more of them. It's this crystal that can be used to travel over the earth. It's what we used to get out of the cave, and how I got out the first time, when we were trapped together."

"With the yellow crystal, you can travel through portals in the earth to other locations that are also marked as portals. Each location is marked with a special symbol in the ground, and we noticed each location is near water, and there are more rocks like the crystals nearby that glow with the color of the crystal. At first we only saw the light when I was meditating. But as I learned to use the power of the crystal, I could make the lights glow as I wished. Rania also has the power to make the lights glow, and as her brother, you probably can too, if you are trained. Not everyone can use the power of the crystals, it seems you either have the power as part of your family, or you don't. That's why Mukhtar can use the crystals he has, because as my brother we share the same blood."

"When you're traveling through the portal, there is a swirling light you float above. You can see branches in the swirling energy which direct you to different symbols you can go to. One is back in the cave in the hills. One is at my father's estate. There is one here along this river, and there are several more in areas we haven't explored yet. Rania and I thought of trying more of them, but we decided none was more important than the entrance to the portal near our home here. We have hidden the crystals because they come from the power of the gods, and no good would come from us using them."

Rafi sat back and considered the story he had just heard. He considered the hardship they had in starting a new life as farmers, with no family or friends to depend on. He had both admiration and sympathy at the same time. Admiration for the ability to start anew with the life they wanted, free to love each other as they wanted. He felt sympathy for the work, loneliness, and abandonment they must feel as exiles from their friends and family. As for the crystals, he was amazed and confused. *Should they use it to attack Mukhtar?* What would the consequences be? If mortals play with the power of the gods, what would happen to them?

"Your secret is safe with me. I will not speak a word of your existence. I am happy beyond words to have found you. I will never speak of this to anyone."

"But Asif, Rania, we need to stop Mukhtar. He is spreading terror across the land. There is no stopping him with the power of the crystals that he has. He and his raiders will be here in a few weeks, or even sooner. He has already sent scouts out this far. We must find a way to stop him."

Asif considers his pleas. "Rafi, this would all be unbelievable were it not for what I know of the crystals. I know the power of the yellow crystal of the earth. I can only imagine how he might use the power of the red and blue crystals to destroy our lands. We must find a way to stop him. To stop him in his tracks and return the power of the crystals to the gods."

Rafi, Asif and Rania went outside after their discussions. Rafi got ready to return to his inn for the night. In the darkness of the night they can saw a red glow towards the town. Rafi knew what this meant.

"It may be too late. It looks like Mukhtar has arrived in Eppru."

CHAPTER 17

ALERA'S STORY

After the Gulf War in 1991, the country and citizens of Iraq were in turmoil. Saddam Hussein had been defeated, but not eliminated. The Americans had liberated Kuwait, but they left the Iraqi citizens on their own. Saddam had amassed an army of 250,000 Iraqis and formed the Republican Guard, and the Republican Guard Special Forces. They were charged with defending the country and keeping order in any manner they saw fit, regardless of how they did it. Because the Americans had negotiated their way out of Iraq, the Iraqi troops were free to eliminate anyone opposed to the Saddam's rule. Saddam and his brothers, sons, and sons-in-law spread a reign of terror across the land like no other, to strike fear and obedience into all of Saddam's enemies.

Some still opposed Saddam's rule and wanted to overthrow him. They had hoped for American and Arab assistance in their quest, but those hopes had been dashed when their forces left. A lot of the opposition came from the Kurdish people, who mostly lived in Northern Iraq. They had long been heavily oppressed by Saddam and the minority Ba'ath party that held political control. They saw the Gulf War as their opportunity to rise up against Saddam. Now that Saddam had not been defeated, his wrath against those who opposed him was going to be devastating.

Saddam released un-merciless attacks against them. They were tortured, killed by chemical weapons, raped, and forced to have abortions. Tens of thousands of Kurds were murdered. Those that lived were relocated to "model communities" which were little more than crude slums. There was very little work for the people located in the slums, and very little opportunity for basic needs of food and medicine.

Alera Sinbati lived outside one of the slums that had been set up by Saddam's army. She worked as a nurse outside the Kurd community in Baghdad, called Sadr City. In the hospital, she saw many of the Kurds who had lived through the worst of what Saddam had done to them, and she saw many of them arrive at the morgue. She didn't know everything about what was happening inside the barb-wire fenced in area, but she could tell it must be far worse than anything she could imagine. She saw people come with infections from limbs that had been cut off. She saw a man whose face had been half burned off with acid, and she heard stories of entire neighborhoods wiped out with poisonous gas. She couldn't imagine how a government could do that to its own people, and how the rest of the world could just turn their faces away and not help. But she was not that type of person. She was going to do what she could to help any way she could.

At the end of her shift, she took some of the extra towels and supplies with her in grocery bags to her car. She stopped at the loading dock behind the hospital and found some of the extra bread and food they were throwing out. She loaded a couple of boxes in the trunk of the compact sedan in which her brother drove her home. As they passed the entrance to the Kurd slum, they stopped just past the final gate. She got out of the car and opened her trunk. As the car drove away, three boxes of food were left by the gate, with several bags of supplies alongside them. The next morning as she drove to work, she noticed the boxes and bags were gone, and in their place was a single flower taped to the fence. She knew it was a small but heartfelt gesture of thanks for her work.

Over the next few weeks and months she organized more and more food and supplies for those who were living in the slums. She found others who felt the same way and would help with the cause. She found food merchants and medical suppliers who willingly contributed excess supplies to her cause. She, her brother, and several others would drive around after work picking up extra food, medical supplies, books, blankets, or whatever they could. They left the supplies just inside the walls of the fences of the slums. Sometimes they would see a flower taped to a barbed wire fence as a thank you. Sometimes there would be a drawing from a small child. For Alera Sinbati, these would mean more than any money that could be paid.

Alera's humanitarian operations grew week by week. She started taking her oldest son, Hassan, with her on her collection runs around town. Hassan was just fourteen years old at the time. As he looked out through the small car window, he could see the faces and hear the voices of his mother's accomplices who were giving all they could to people they would never know. As they would drive away from dropping things off at the slum, he would sometimes see the face of small child on the other side of the fence. As they drove away, the child would run along the inside of the fence as long as he could to follow the car. He ran with a stick clinking along the chain link and barbed wire fence. To Hassan's amazement, the child was smiling. He was laughing and waving as he ran to Hassan and his mother. Once Hassan asked his mother if they could talk to the boy, but she just shook her head and said it could not happen. He could never bring himself to cross the cultural barriers on his own; he didn't think he could ever understand the strange and awful forces that could create a world capable of this cruelty.

Late in the summer of 1996, Hassan was in the car with his mother and uncle making their rounds. They came to the back of a mosque which had routinely donated clothing and blankets. Hassan and Alera got out of the car, but were immediately met by six men with guns pointing at them. The leader was a man with a red face and a large scar down his left cheek. The men called him Mudlarek. They were all ordered to the ground. Hassan was bound with his hands behind his back. He turned to look at his mother. A hood was placed over her head, and Mudlarek carried her away and threw her into the back of a truck nearby. Then Mudlarek walked over to his uncle, and in cold blood, put a bullet through his head. The truck took off into the night away from the loading area. Hassan had heard the conversation of some of the men nearby. His mother was being accused of treason against Saddam Hussein. His uncle had just been tried on the street and found guilty. His sentence was carried out immediately. He was shot dead on the street. Hassan could have been tried if he were just a few years older. As it was, he was let go.

Hassan ran all the way back to his house, several miles away. As he passed the fenced area around the slum, he saw a large police operation happening within the confines of the compound. Tanks had rolled in along the small street that led to the center of the community. He could see several troop carriers and soldiers standing in riot gear along the streets. Smoke was rising from several of the houses, and he could hear the distant shouting of male voices. He heard occasional gun shots which were followed by women screaming and more men yelling. Hassan crossed to the other side of the road and ran past the slum as quickly as possible. When he arrived at his home his younger brothers and sisters were waiting for him, worried about where they were and what had caused the delay in their return. They had heard news reports of the "crackdown" in the city.

Hassan, at fourteen years old, was too young to care for his younger brothers and sister. His grandparents lived nearby, and it was they who came to care for the young children as the fate of their mother was decided.

The weeks following that incident were the most painful of Hassan's life. At his young age, there was very little he could do to help his mother. It was a helpless feeling. His grandparents made all the appeals they could to the local authorities, but it was to no avail. Mudlarek was widely known as one of the worst of Saddam's 'social order enforcers'. Stories of his brutality spread from town to town. Although there was very little documented evidence or press on the atrocities he had committed, the rumors were enough to scare anyone who might be in on the receiving end of his twisted forms of justice. After a week they found that Alera had been accused of aiding the enemy, which would result in a trial of sorts. She was charged with conspiring against Saddam Hussein's government by aiding those in the slum who plotted to overthrow him. Hassan was devastated, as were his grandparents and many of the local friends and residents of their neighborhood.

The next days were a series of nightmarish horrors only the darkest imaginations could conjure. Hassan's family was ordered to attend the trial of Alera, to be held in the soccer fields of the local college. As they arrived, there were a thousand or more residents who had been forced to gather to watch the proceedings. About noon, several transport trucks normally used to transport troops rode onto the field. From inside, prisoners were forced onto the ground into the field. Each was bound at their feet and hands, each clothed only in grey hooded robes that barely kept their dignity. Hassan thought he saw his mother's brunette hair from under one of the hoods. In the center of the stadium was a small stage, where Mudlarek had set up a large chair and a table in front of him. One by one each of the prisoners was led in front of him and ordered to kneel. Mudlarek pronounced the sentence on each of the prisoners as they were forced to kneel before him. His voice was broadcast over the poor sound system of the stadium. The audio was full of echo and hiss, his words were mostly in-audible to the audience. After each verdict was read, the prisoner was led or carried away by the troops attending the ceremony.

After most of the prisoners were dispensed with, only four remained. Mudlarek had decided to make the biggest spectacle of dispensing justice on these prisoners. With a hundreds of countrymen watching, he proclaimed the guilty verdict of the prisoners and read their sentencing. The first man was to have his feet cut off, the second, his tongue. The third was to be blinded, and the final was to be stoned to death. With little additional ceremony, the troops were ordered to carry out their orders. The first man was brought forward and bound to a board just longer than his body's length. While screaming and crying for help, a hooded soldier came forward from the crowd with a large axe to carry out his order. Mudlarek watched from his chair with a wild gleam in his eyes.

Hassan couldn't watch any more. He turned to his younger brothers and sister and motioned to them that they were to leave the area right away. Mercifully, the troops were not preventing the crowd from leaving any more. As Hassan and his family were leaving as quickly as they could, they heard the anguished screams of the prisoners behind them. Hassan felt dead inside, and he knew the same feeling must have been felt by the rest of his family.

For three days after the sports field ceremony they heard nothing. On the fourth day, a transport truck drove up to their house. The back door was opened, and from the back a something that looked simply like a sack of cloth was thrown to the ground outside their house. On closer look the sack of cloth contained the shriveled body of their mother. With bloodied bandages and soiled clothing, she appeared to be near death, if not dead already. They carried her into the house, and it was only then that they saw the sentence that had been carried out against her. To keep her from aiding any antigovernment movement, they had severed her hands at her wrists. Her arms lay loose at her side with just loosely bandaged stubs at the end of her forearms.

They carried their mother inside and lay her down on a bed in their house and did their best to tend to her and ease her pain. Her face and skin was an ashen gray from the trauma and malnourishment she had undergone. There were bruises and open sores on her neck and body; it was apparent she was given little if any food or pain reliever. She was too weak to take food or drink. Hassan called one of the doctors she had worked with at the hospital for so many years. He came to the house that afternoon with some rudimentary medicine and equipment to treat her. She was given some intravenous liquids and pain relief to stabilize her.

Hassan did the best he could to help. It was better to be busy than stop to think about the atrocity that the government and Mudlarek had been inflicting on its own people. After Alera had fallen into a drug induced sleep, Hassan stepped outside the house. Tormented and confused, Hassan couldn't process how to move from here. He now knew hatred so deep it felt all consuming. Every part of his being ached with hatred of the man who had sentenced his mother to this fate. The doctor came out of the house and stood next to Hassan in the late afternoon light.

"Hassan, I can't begin to understand the pain you are feeling right now. The world has turned its back on you and your mother. I'm a doctor, and I know there is no way I can heal the pain or remove the hatred you are feeling. I'm not going to try. But what I will tell you can help you change your life when you are ready. Whether it be revenge you seek, or some other sort of retribution, you are wisest to bide your time for action. You're still young, you don't understand the world or how it works. You can work for change, but you can't expect to be able to change things over night. The world did not turn this evil overnight, and it won't be changed back overnight or by the brash lashing out of one boy. We need young people like you to change the world. But to make the change you will have to become bigger than your enemy. More smart, more nimble, more educated. Take your time, study, learn, and bring others with you. Then one day it will be your day to change things, and if revenge is what you seek, you will have it."

Then something unexpected happened to Hassan and his family. Word of Alera's fate had reached around the neighborhood they lived in. People who knew Alera, and many who did not, started to show up at their house with whatever donations they could to keep their family going. Just about every day there would be some sort of food, medicine, clothes, or other donation left outside their house. Hassan continued his tortured search for the meaning of all this; why would such horrible circumstances bring out so much good in people he hardly knew? Why would such horrible things happen without any justice for the criminals?

Hassan, his brothers and sister were now technically orphans. The only thing that kept them from the terrible fate of the Iraqi orphanages was their grandparents who could look after them. Technically Hassan was old enough to work, so in the fall Hassan had to get a job to support his brothers, sister and mother. He got a job with a local delivery company as a courier. He would drive a Vespa from site to site delivering whatever packages and papers needed delivered, or picked up. He quickly learned who the important people in his section of town were. One of the most frequent customers was the newspaper. It was there that he could track news from the rest of the country.

The official news was almost all propaganda from Hussein's media machine, but occasionally he would catch a news story or a picture of Mudlarek. If there was any story about him, it was always about his victories over the enemies of the republic, and never anything negative. A lump would form in Hassan's throat, and he'd want to spit at the mere mention of his name. His connections at the paper grew into his next job, he was hired by the paper, and he started writing copy and doing some journalistic reporting. Most of his stories were not screened by the heavy censorship hand of the Iraqi regime; his stories always appeared too innocuous to be reviewed by the censors. It was here that he learned how to keep his activities under the radar vision of the authorities. There were certain journalistic boundaries to stay in, and if you did, you could often get your point across without the censorship that so many of his colleagues endured.

His job at the newspaper served several purposes. It provided for him and his family, and it allowed him to always keep one eye out for any news of the enemy of his life, Mudlarek.

CHAPTER 18

THE MARKET IN EPPRU

Rafi spoke to Asif in a serious tone. "Asif, I think our meeting was timed by the gods. It's time for you to challenge your brother, and you possess the yellow crystal which can be used against him. Come with me. We must find a way to defeat Mukhtar!"

Asif looked at Rania and then looked at Rafi. "Rafi, I lead a simple life now. I'm not a warrior. I'm a farmer. And I have children, and a wife. Our lives are full, and we're doing OK. You want someone to challenge my brother, but I'm afraid that is not me."

"Asif," Rafi protested, "your simple life won't continue. Mukhtar and his raiders are only a few miles away from here now. Your farm will be taken over, or you will have to give all of your profit to Mukhtar. He will say it is in the name of religion, but everything will go to him. If you want the life you have, you will have to fight for it. I'm sorry to tell you this, but your life is changing no matter what you do. As you have met the challenges in your life before, I'm asking you to meet this challenge in your life with me. I will help you. And there are many more that will help us, but we will need to work together."

Rania had kept silent on the discussion until now. "Asif, listen to what Rafi is saying. I know your heart. You want to keep our simple life, but if what Rafi is saying is true, I think he is right that we will have to fight for our lives once again. Mukhtar must be stopped. I can run the farm; I can take care of the children, and they will help out. Go help my brother. Go help him bring down Mukhtar, and when you do, we will finally have lasting peace."

Rafi looked down at his feet, then he looked up at Rania and Asif. "Mukhtar grows more powerful every day as he learns the power of the crystals. We'll have to get help from more people, and we'll have to learn to use the powers of the yellow crystal to defeat him."

II

In the town of Eppru, the terror of Mukhtar arrived. A red glow hung low over the small buildings near the center of town. Mukhtar's gang of raiders roamed the streets shouting and terrorizing the town. They carried crude torches, lighting everything on fire that they could. Shops, even houses and inns were attacked. The citizens of the town ran in every direction. Confused and terrified, they were not armed to fight against such terror. They were simple farmers who had markets they wanted to run, they were not warriors. They had no idea this terror was coming or why these people would come to their town. Women and children were screaming, and there were loud explosions. People ran through the streets trying to get away from a fear they had never known before.

Mukhtar's gang gathered in front of the temple in the center of town. Surrounding the temple stood the markets where Rafi met Rania just hours before, and the temple stood at the end of the square. The temple was the center of the town's life; it's where most of the commerce would take place, and where most people went for reassurance and steadiness in their difficult lives. At the top of the temple a carved stone is mounted, featuring a simple crescent moon with beams of light streaming out over the land below. Several of the town's folk gathered to watch from a distance as the gang chanted in a small circle in the middle of the square. Asif and Rafi worked their way through the crowd to the front line to see directly into the square. From the smoke between the temple and the market on the south side of the square, a man emerged from the light of the fire and smoke. Mukhtar appeared, out of nowhere, dressed in black and gold robes draped across him. On his head he wore a black hat with two horns gilded in gold, making him look terrifying to the common townspeople. He stood tall facing the temple, and then he turned around to the faces of the terrorized citizens.

"People of Eppru," he shouted. "I take this town in my name – Mukhtar! – With the powers given to me by the gods themselves, I now am your ruler. You now your allegiance to me, and for your allegiance you will be rewarded with the privileges of servants in my kingdom. Those who oppose me will be destroyed, by the powers of the gods themselves."

Mukhtar turned his back to his raiders and the town folk and faced the temple. He raised his arms outward and upwards, his robes flowing down beside him. Soon red swirls of lights appeared above him. On the ground in front of him, a large circle of red appeared in the gravel. In the circle a shape of a crescent moon appeared, outlined in a ring of fire. The fire burned hotter within the ring.

Mukhtar stood near the flames with his arms outspread upward. The swirling lights above him started to swim and curl around him. They outgrew the area above Mukhtar's head and moved over the small crowd and up to, but not against, the temple. They swept back towards Mukhtar, then around the square and back up to the temple again. He moved his arms to the right, and the swirling rings of fire moved right. As the intensity grew, Mukhtar controlled the motion of the fire with his arms. The entire square was encompassed, about twenty feet in the air above the people. Mukhtar suddenly moved left with his arms. He crouched and pointed forward to the left. The swirl moved quickly left, and Mukhtar moved his arms and body in a swooping motion to the right. The swirling lights followed and seem to gain focus. He swept his arms back to the left, as if to pick up the lights.

With a giant swoosh, he slammed his arms down toward the ground, just as the overhead lights reached the left side of the temple. The swirl burst into flames in a cyclonic cone and smashed into the market. The walls of the market building exploded outward and the canopied area around the outside became engulfed in a ball of fire and scattered bricks. The tornado of swirling fire swept across the square and ripped through the roof of the market.

Mukhtar briefly stopped and put his hands into his robe. He pulled out the red and blue crystals from the pockets of the robes. They glowed brighter and brighter as he raised them above his head.

The few people who have stayed scattered in every direction, running away as fast as they could. Mukhtar stood steadfast in the center of the square. He was pleased with his show of power impressed with the power of the red and blue crystal that he has attained. He turned towards where the crowd was and sent out a low laugh across the square. He raised his fist to the sky, and in the red light it glowed against the dark background of the night. The blue lights rose in brilliance around the square. Blue and red streams of energy swirled across the night sky, then came together and combined directly over him. The lights crashed down in a column over Mukhtar, and he disappeared into the vertical beam of light. At first it appears he alone has disappeared from within his robes, and they stood upright as empty shells. Then the robes themselves disappear with a snap, and the blue and red lights went out suddenly.

Asif and Rafi were watching from one of the corners in the square, away from the market which had been destroyed. They looked at each other and ran away from the square with a few others who had remained to watch. Asif was shocked. *Do the crystals carry that much power? Is it truly the power of the gods? Can we find a way to defeat him?* He thinks as he is running away from the red lights of the burning town to the safety of the areas outside the center of town.

Asif and Rafi stopped running outside town along the river. They were out of breath and still feeling the adrenalin through their bodies.

"He's grown much stronger already," Rafi said. "He has learned how to combine the power of the crystals to put on a big show. Now he is really only using the powers in a combination of ways. We have to find a way to take away those powers, so he will lose his grip over the people."

"Rafi, let's go back to my house tonight," Asif says. "We'll figure out what we're going to do in the morning."

As they approach the house, they could still see the low glow of red light coming from the town a few miles away. Rania was sitting outside the house watching the red lights grow and then dim. Smoke was drifting above the lights. They walked into view of Rania.

"Asif, Rafi!" she exclaims, "You're OK! What happened? Did Mukhtar burn down the whole town? What are we going to do?"

Asif gives Rania a hug, then they all proceeded inside the house, as Asif started to tell the story of what they saw. The house was dark and silent from the outside, with just the glow of the fires in the distance illuminating the outline of the house.

CHAPTER 19

OLD FASHIONED ARAB GETAWAY

The afternoon had waned into early evening by the time Morgiana and Hassan's stories started to wind down. Jon was starting to feel the fatigue of the day set in. Alik and Turkin disappeared into another room for a few minutes and then returned with some assorted foods to keep the conversations going. As they were crowding around the table to put food on their plates, there was some activity on two of the security monitors mounted on the wall behind them.

Two white vans had parked just outside the security gates. In black military special operations clothing, nine men appeared outside the vans and spoke to each other briefly before breaking into three groups and splitting out alongside the security fence.

Inside the control room, no one noticed the blinking red lights of the security alarms behind the group of men until some of the audible alarms started to sound. Alik and Turkin turned to look at the monitors and alarms and jumped to their feet to cross the room to assess the situation. There was nothing they could find at first.

"It looks OK," said Turkin.

"No – Look!" Alik replied, and he pointed at the monitor showing the two white vans parked outside the security area. "And there!" Alik pointed to another monitor. Shapes of three men could be seen moving against the brick wall that made up the security fence along one side of the compound.

While looking at that view, two of the monitors went blank. "Cameras are being cut," Alik said. "This is the real deal. We're under attack!"

"What do we do?" Jon asked. "Are there weapons here? OK, that was a stupid question. Where are the weapons here?"

Alik tries a couple more controls to see what he can find on the various alarms and cameras. "Turkin - Drop the stage 4 security barriers."

Turkin navigates a few menu options with his mouse and suddenly a map of the compound appears on the monitor in front of him. He enters a few more commands, and red barriers appear across several of the passageways displayed on the screen. In the room they are in, metal bars drop from the ceiling across the entryway they came through. There are no windows, and no other apparent entryways or exits from the room.

"That should slow them down. This place was designed for highest level government survival during the first Gulf War. Security levels were paid for so even the President of the United States would survive an attack here."

"That's great, why is it that I don't feel comfortable with that? Was it ever tested? Was the money just spent like so many other projects, or was it actually tried? If it's like most of the other Blackwater jobs, someone signed off on it long ago and made off with the money." Jon commented nervously.

"I can't say for sure, I know it was an American contracting company, - I guess we'll find out!"

Alik was trying to tune in some of the other peripheral cameras to see activity outside. One by one, the cameras went dead. "This is one of the most secure compounds in Kuwait. There is no way anyone can touch us here. And if it does get bad, we always have the old fashioned Arab getaway option. Let's hope we don't have to use it."

With that the power went out and everything went black in the room.

"Uh oh." Was all Jon had to say.

"Don't worry. The generators will kick on any second." Alik assured.

A few seconds passed. No generators. No lights. No electricity.

"What exactly was that old fashioned Arab getaway option?" Jon's voice sliced through the darkness.

Fluorescent lights flickered on. That was the good news. The bad news was the visible clouds of gas that started coming through the ventilation system. Hassan was the first to start coughing.

"Tear gas. That won't knock you out. Just annoy the hell out of you. Cover your mouth, shield your eyes and stay low to the ground." Turkin said. He reached into a drawer and pulled out some standard safety goggles to hand out.

"Are you kidding? Safety glasses?" Alik said as he went to a cabinet in a wall, and soon pulled out five gas masks that were stored behind one of the walls.

"Put these on. You'll be able to make it through the gas."

They all put their gas masks on. Alik was last. "Let's go for the old-fashioned Arab getaway. Things are only going to get worse here. And the sooner we leave, the better the chance is that we'll catch them unaware."

"Wait a second – what is the old fashioned Arab getaway plan? I feel like I want to know." Jon comments.

Hassan smiles dryly at Jon. "It's a time-tested Arab way of getting out of trouble. And besides, right now, you're out-voted. Let's go."

Alik heads towards what appears to be a solid wall at the end of the monitoring section. He pushes on a panel, and the panel pushes back to open a crack. He pulls on the panel and a doorway is revealed. He opens it wide for the others to enter. Gas masks in place, they leave the highly secure control room as gas fills the room behind them. Bullets and explosive charges can be heard outside the doors shielded by the metal gates.

The unlikely crew of gas-masked escapees follows a hallway for about twenty yards. Alik stops at a door on the right and listens before turning a knob to enter. "Turkin – see if there is some gasoline on the other side of that door." Alik points to another door across the hall.

Turkin opens the door without hesitating and soon reappears with a forty liter can of gasoline.

Alik opens the opposite door, checks out the surroundings, and motions for the others to follow. They follow him into the room and find themselves in a large room lined with white cinderblock walls. A motion sensor clicks on a bright white overhead light. Inside is a single red Toyota Tundra pickup truck in the middle of the room. The back of the tundra is heavily armed, with two stands of AK -47 machine guns on small turrets in the pickup bed.

Alik starts with the orders. "Jon – you're driving. Hassan – you're shot gun. Morgiana, you ride in the crew cab. We'll drop you off once we get outside. Turkin and I are in back." Turkin is already pouring the forty liters of gasoline into the tank. As the tank empties, Alik continues. "Ditch the gas masks. You won't need them. Let's just hope we're all still breathing when we're done. Get in."

They all climb in and doors slam. Jon is ready to drive. Alik and Turkin mount the turrets and strap in like they are seasoned veterans and pull the machine guns around to be ready for the fight. Hassan is ready on the passenger side. Morgiana is keeping a low profile in the small cab behind the front seats. Jon sees the garage door opener button and pushes it. The white wall in front of the truck falls forward into a dark unseen ramp heading up into daylight ahead.

"Anyone got some keys?" Jon asks.

"Look above the visor!" Alik shouts from the back.

Jon flips down the visor and keys fall into his lap.

At ground level of the compound, outside the building, one of the lead attackers is on a radio talking to his operatives inside. As he talks, he can hear the low rumbling engine of the Tundra coming up a ramp just outside his view. As the Tundra reaches ground level, the leader's mouth falls gaping open as the two AK 47 swing around to point in his general direction. The leader shouts in to the radio and dives to the ground behind a retaining wall as .47mm machine gun bullets paint a stripe of freshly opened mortar in the cement wall behind him. The leader drops to the ground and the bullets paint a stripe across the Cadillac Escalade, shattering the windows. The truck picks up speed as it barrels towards the entrance of the compound, only to find that the entrance is barricaded with the level four intrusion barriers Alik had ordered. Jon swings the truck around to drive along the wall of the compound, not entirely sure where to go. The attackers start emerging from the inside of the building and start engaging small gun fire with the Toyota as it moves around the compound. Alik and Turkin are solidly strapped into the turret seats, pivoting and firing unlimited rounds at will at the attackers.

"How do I get outta here?" Jon asks Hassan.

"I have no idea!" Hassan answers.

Continuing around the perimeter of the compound seems like the only option that Jon has, so he keeps driving until another idea comes up to him. As he pulls around to the third side of the compound, he sees his opportunity in a pile of dirt and stone pushed against the security wall on the north side. Jon pulls into the compound a bit to round the corner, and yells to Alik and Turkin to hold on. The truck sways to the left as he makes the initial turn, then it sways to the right as he adjusts his trajectory track. He guns the accelerator right before he hits the pile of dirt which serves to explode more dirt from the sides of the truck as it is lifted to the top of the security wall. The truck clears the six foot wall and careens outside the secure area of the compound. The Tundra lands on all four wheels with Alik and Turkin demonstrably bounced around in the bed of the truck, while still strapped into their seats. The truck veers into a skid as Jon steers it ninety degrees to move down the highway.

Unknown to Jon and the gang, several other trucks had gathered outside the compound to assist with the operation. Drivers are ready to roll if needed, and as Jon and Hassan start to speed away, the trucks pull out after them. The highway is in a residential neighborhood with stop lights and sidewalks, as the Tundra barrels down the road with six or so pickups in hot pursuit.

"So this is an old fashioned Arab getaway?" Jon asks as he punches the accelerator and swerves around several cars going much slower on the road.

"This is it!" Hassan answers. "It's worked for generations. Just keep headed Northeast on this road – we'll be at the Iraq border and some friendly territory in thirty minutes!"

Alik and Turkin have made quick work of eliminating the trucks following the Tundra as it barrels northeastward. After a quick stop to drop off Morgiana, the truck is headed on Route 80 with no one following; just open road, high tension telephone poles, and jersey barriers lining the road on the way to the border of Iraq..

CHAPTER 20

TIBI

The morning sunrise brought a burning glow that once again validated Asif's belief that the god of the sun can defeat any evil. It defeats the darkness and night every day. The sunrise cast a soft red and orange glow against the white baked bricks of his home.

Rafi came out of the house and saw Asif looking out over the river at the sunrise. Asif had a travelling bag packed draped over his shoulder. They turned from the rising sun and walked out to the edge of the road.

"We need to head back towards Nippur," Rafi said. "It's towards the sunrise about two days walk from here. There we can plan what we are going to do."

Rania came out to wish them well on their way. She gave Rafi a hug, and then turned to her husband.

"Asif, be careful. I know you have to do this, but remember you need to come back to us safely. Rafi, take care of my husband, and Asif, take care of my brother. You are all I have. I'll be fine here, but I'll also be with you as you travel."

Rania hugged Rafi, then turned and hugged Asif. They turned and headed down the path back to town. Rania took a step back, quietly weeping.

-

"I know a man we need on our team," Rafi said as they walked down the road. "Tibi lives on a farm several miles outside of Eppru, on the other side of town. Some people think he's a little crazy, but he's the man we need. He knows animals, and he's good with people, so he can organize as no one else can. Tibi lives with his parents just on the other side of the hill, past Tikrit. He has good connections to some weapons we might need."

The country side around Eppru was filled with small rolling hills filled with wild wheat and grains. In the winter the ground would be mostly brown with only some trees keeping their green leaves. But in the spring, the ground became green with clover, wild mustard, and a wild grass. As Asif and Rafi were walking through the countryside, the sweet smells of clover and mustards filled the air. As they walked, they saw a small cloud of dust in the distance just above the top of a hill.

As the dust was lifted by the wind and blown off to the west, a herd of twenty wild horses appeared over the crest of the hill. Heading straight towards them at first, they turned suddenly and headed towards their right. With another split second adjustment they were directly at them again. As they came within twenty yards of Asif and Rafi, they stopped suddenly. One large horse at the lead had set the pace, and he stomped his front feet and bobbed his head in the afternoon sun. He faced off against Asif and Rafi. He rose on his hind feet, kicking his front feet towards the new intruders on their plain. These horses were a short breed, their heads were not much higher than a man's shoulders. They were mostly chestnut colors, from a light golden red to a dark brown, some with flaxen manes and tails. The leader was a light brown with a golden mane and tail that shimmered as they moved with him.

As Asif and Rafi were watching the next move from the horses, a young man appeared over the crest of the hill. He had long curly hair and loose clothing which flowed with him as he ran. He was carrying a rope in his hand and a small travelling bag over his shoulder. He saw the herd of horses, and then he saw Rafi and Asif facing them directly along the trail.

He stood tall and called to Rafi and Asif. "Stand still, please, this is a special herd of horses to me. Don't scare them!"

Rafi and Asif were happy to comply with his request since they were quite frightened of being trampled by the herd. In a few minutes the man came over to where they were standing.

"Good afternoon gentlemen," he said while regaining his breath. "My name is Tibi. And these are my horses. I have been working with them for months now. We're making great progress, let me show you if I can. The leader with the light hair is named Drendl."

"Drendl," Rafi considered. "You have names for wild horses?"

"These are not just wild horses any more. They are becoming tame, to work with me."

Tibi took the bag off his shoulder and dug in to grab a handful of oats. He walked towards the herd of horses, hands outstretched. Several of the horses backed off, but Drendl stood firm, watching every move that Tibi made. Tibi's movements were barely perceptible as he moved steadily forward. Soon he had come within a few feet of Drendl. Drendl snorted and stomped his feet towards Tibi. Tibi stomped his feet back at him, and held his head down in a submissive manner. The horse sniffed the oats. He took a few steps forward and started to eat the oats out of Tibi's hand. Tibi didn't look at him as he ate. Soon the oats were gone, but the horse was hoping for more. He snorted and nodded towards the bag that Tibi was carrying.

Tibi held the bag towards the nose of the horse. As the horse moved towards the bag, Tibi held it out to his left, which allowed the horse to move alongside him, instead of directly in front of him. As the horse stuck his nose into the bag, Tibi grabbed onto Drendl's golden mane, and with one quick leap he straddled his back in a bareback position.

Drendl pulled away from the bag of oats and reeled onto his hind legs. Tibi was holding on to the mane for his life. Drendl lurched forward, and then bucked his back legs into the air. Tibi was thrown into the air, but he hung onto the mane again. As he came back down onto Drendl's back, Drendl leapt forward into a gallop, with Tibi hanging on to his neck tighter than ever. Drendl took off across the field and the herd of horses followed closely behind him.

Tibi was barely hanging on, having the ride of his life. Faster than he had ever gone before, he was gliding across the plain on the back of the horse he's been trying to break for months. The twelve horses moved across the fields in synchronized waves of thundering hooves. The horses galloped faster and faster through a field of wild wheat, then across a wide shallow stream, which splashed water in a shower of sparkles across the stream and onto the tall grass on the side. They continued on with the tops of the grass just below Tibi's feet at the side of the horse. Drendl pulled to the left, and the herd of horses followed him. He pulled to the right, then he turned back across the plains to the area where Asif and Rafi were standing. Finally he pulled up close to the trail where they started. He stopped as abruptly as he had taken off.

Tibi could not hold on any more. He flew over Drendl's head and landed with a thud in the tall grasses on the far side of the trail. Drendl watched, as if with amusement, and stomped his feet in front of him in protest, as if to say *Never do that again!* Drendl reared up on his hind legs, and gave a front kick salute in the direction of Tibi. Tibi rolled to his side to look at Drendl. With a sudden jump, Drendl galloped off to his left. His herd followed right behind him, making a thunderous exit across the plain. Once again there was a plume of dust rising into the air, then drifting off to the west in the breeze.

Rafi and Asif ran to Tibi's side. "Are you all right?" He was sore and bruised, but he was not seriously injured. They helped him to his feet as he coughed out some dust and dirt.

"That was incredible! I've been trying to ride that horse for months! Did you see how I rode him over the fields, did you see that? These horses have power! This is power we can use!" Tibi's beaming smile lit up his face. He looked at the two travelers who had watched his antics, and he recognized Rafi.

"Rafi! Great to see you! What brings you to these parts?"

Rafi had met Tibi several times at the marketplaces in various towns. Tibi was buying and selling animals, goats, cattle, chickens. Rafi was often selling grains or produce, so they would often meet with the same customers. Several times they talked about the customers, who were successful, and what worked and did not work when selling in the markets.

"My farm is just over those next hills, up the trail. If you help me there, I have food and water, you are welcome there."

Asif and Rafi helped him stand on his feet, and he put his arm around Rafi to shake off a sore ankle as they walked down the trail. Asif picked up the bag of oats. They did not have any other plans for where to spend the night, and they certainly wanted to talk about their plans with Tibi.

They arrived at Tibi's farm an hour later. Tibi, who was about eighteen years old, lived with his parents. Their farm was equipped better than most for the area. They had a brick house and three other buildings. One was for the farm equipment, one was for the food, and one was for the animals themselves. Outside the building area, there were several fields outlined with irrigation ditches. Between the house and the first field was a small river, which flowed from the mountains across the northern horizon towards the south. This time of year the stream was still strong. There was a wooden bridge across the river. The bridge had four large posts on each corner of the bridge, which allowed the bridge to be raised or lowered in the early spring so the floods would not wash it away. The fields had hay and oats growing, about knee high right now. Each of the fields had a grass hut for shelter and a small tower at the end; part of the intricate irrigation equipment. Tibi explained how the towers were used to back up the water at different levels and irrigate the fields during dry spells.

Tibi's father, Salim appeared outside the door of the equipment barn when he saw Tibi coming up the path, being helped by two others. Standing just over five feet tall, Salim was thin and wiry, but tough as nails. His thirty years of farm work had worn him down over the years, and Tibi could see the wear that each season took on him. He had short thick hair with his first grey hair just starting to show around his ears. His hands were small, but strong, with thick fingers and calloused skin like sand paper across his palms.

"You were trying to ride those wild horses again weren't you?" Salim said. "I told you to stop trying! They are wild animals; you can't keep them from being wild! You foolish young kids, you waste your time chasing ideas that get into your head. You're only going to get hurt. When will you listen to your elders? Nothing will come of chasing those horses!"

"Father, you'll see someday. Those animals will do all of your work for you, and you won't have to work so hard in the fields. You'll be able to sit back in your chair while the fields are plowed and then the crop is brought in. You should have seen me today! I rode Drendl, the leader! For at least five minutes I rode on his back while he ran around the open plains. I'm telling you they will belong to us. And we will take care of them while they work for us."

Tibi introduced his friends. Salim offered them his hospitality and invited them inside. Inside the house they worked to prepare a quick meal of fresh poultry, vegetables, and flat bread. Rafi and Asif commented how they felt like they are eating like gods. It all seems so natural and simple at Tibi's house.

After the meal they settled outside the house, sitting in three simple wooden chairs around a roaring fire. Rafi told Tibi about Mukhtar raiding the town of Eppru and the damage he had done.

"I've heard about Mukhtar and the raids he has been making. This is the first I have heard of him going as far as Eppru. And his powers seem to have grown. And yet the news only gets worse for the towns he visits. After he raids the town and takes them for his own, he sends more raiders back to the town afterwards to steal the belongings of the people. He demands they pay taxes for his kingdom. In return they are supposed to get roads and bridges, and safety from enemies, but no one has known anything but what he takes from them. As for our own farm, they came here one day when I wasn't here. My father and mother could do nothing to stop them, so they gave two goats and some water. That seemed to keep them from doing any harm to our farm. But I fear for what they will do when they come back, and I fear for what he has been doing to our towns. Apparently he has heard of me and the story of the tigers of the Sappru farms. The raiders asked for me by name; my father said I was out in the prairie chasing wild horses, which was true, for his part."

Rafi's attention was peaked at the mention of the story of the tigers. He had heard of the story, but he figured it was mostly a fable by now. The chance to hear the real story was a great opportunity for him.

"Tibi, can you tell me the story of the tigers? I have heard of the story, but I need to hear the story from you! Tell us the real story of the tigers of Sappru!"

CHAPTER 21

IRAQ BORDER

Thirty minutes after leaving the compound in Kuwait City Jon and Hassan approach the border into Iraq in their truck. It was obvious the current mode of transportation, with two machine guns loaded in the back of a pickup truck, would not be welcome at the border. About a half mile before the gates, a road runs parallel to the border. Hassan tells Jon to turn right, and they head southeast along the border. Driving past abandoned burned out buildings, cars, buses and trucks, they see several destroyed surface to air missile launchers on the side of the road. The land is flat and dry. There are no living plants anywhere, just sand, power lines, war wreckage, and an occasional camel.

They pull into a warehouse parking lot as the road comes to an end just before a river. Ahead there is another sign to a border crossing to the North, a few kilometers away. To the right is a road south back to Kuwait City. The warehouse looks suspiciously small to be of any help to them. Jon pulls the truck around back and pulls up to the only garage door entrance to the building. Hassan gets out of the truck and walks up to the door.

"Is anyone here?" Jon asks

"I doubt it." Hassan replies. He makes several shaking motions on the lock on the door, then pulls sharply down on a chain, which makes a loud booming noise throughout the building. There is no sign of anyone in the building. With a couple more pulls on the door, it becomes loose and Hassan is able to open the garage door. Jon watches nervously and pulls the pickup truck into to the warehouse. His headlights don't show any features inside the building. In fact, it looks empty. Hassan has moved to another room and soon some sodium lights slowly start to hum to life and bring on their yellow-tinged light into the space.

Alik and Turkin get out of the back of the truck and walk around to the front to meet Jon and Hassan. "There's nothing here! It's completely empty!" Jon says. "I'm not sure how this place is going to help us. We're tired, it's the middle of night, and I don't see any Marriott sign outside!"

"We're not staying here, Jon. We have another place to spend the night. I had hoped to prepare you more when we were in the compound in Kuwait, but obviously our visit was cut a little short with all those people attacking us. You and I are going to use the portal again."

"Now you need to be prepared in how to use it. I'll prepare you now. Once you're inside, you are floating over a river of energy. The only thing separating you from that river of energy is an invisible membrane. It keeps you safe, but it is tricky to navigate. Because you can't see it you don't have your balance. It's tough to stand up or take any steps because you can't tell where the floor is for the next step. The membrane isn't stable. It bounces, it flows, and it moves in waves. The easiest way to move around the tunnel is by lying down and pushing yourself with your own energy. You move by gliding. There is no friction, so you can glide any way you want. Because you're not standing, you won't have to worry about falling."

"I don't remember any of this from time I went through this in the cave."

"I'm not surprised. You were in shock that day, and the ceremony we went through may have knocked you unconscious. But rest assured, I guided you through the tunnel and brought you just outside the Army base in Mosul. This time, you'll be alert, and I'll show you how you can navigate."

"There is no sound in the tunnel, so you won't be able to hear anything. Just follow my lead and don't make any sudden movements. Use hand signals to communicate. We'll be back outside in a few minutes."

"Wait, what's going to happen here? What about the truck? Do we bring it? And what about Alik and Turkin?"

"So many questions! Alik and Turkin are taking the pickup back to a safe place in Kuwait. Only you and I are going to the camp."

"Camp? Wait – a camp – in Iraq? Would that be an Al Qaeda camp? I'm a US soldier –I'm not going to an enemy training camp!"

"It's not what you think. Have I steered you wrong yet?"

"You've got to be kidding! I've almost been killed several times. If you're steering, you should take lessons!"

"OK, fair enough. Not much choice here. We have to go!"

Hassan pulls open his coat and pulls out a small pouch, and from it the yellow crystal emerges. It immediately starts to glow a small yellow light.

"The trick here is to meditate. Concentrate on the crystal, and you'll find how to increase the energy. There will be other times for you to practice. For now, follow my lead."

Hassan lowers his head in quiet contemplation. The lights grow around the crystal. Small swirling wispy clouds of yellow lights spiral upwards above Hassan's head. In a moment the swirling lights are moving around the warehouse, crashing into the corners and spilling back into the center spiral. Jon looks at the center of the floor as a circle of yellow lights starts to burn in the ground, then burn an image from inside the floor. In the center of the circle is a cross. The circle burns brighter as the swirling clouds of energy gain strength and speed around the room. Hassan looks up from his concentration and reaches his hand back to grab Jon. Jon reaches his hand, and Hassan pulls him towards the center of the circle. With a final leap they jump into the center as the swirling energy concentrates into a pillar flowing into the ground. In an instant they disappear into the circle, and the lights and burning circle disappear into the ground with the familiar loud electronic snap!

Hassan and Jon pass into the energy tunnel as the current of energy flows quickly beneath them. Jon has forgotten everything Hassan said in the excitement of the change from an abandoned warehouse to a tunnel of the gods. Hassan lies down on the ground, and catches Jon's eye to get him to lay down as well. Jon looks around and catches on that Hassan is signaling him to lie down. He kneels down and then lies on his stomach. Hassan grabs his hand, and turns them around towards the direction of the energy flow. They move down the tunnel and slowly pick up speed. As they move along, the invisible membrane moves up and down beneath them, creating a rolling, curving slide motion as they move through the tunnel. Jon sees several of the circle symbols as they pass through crossings. After twenty minutes of gliding through, Hassan slows them down. Just ahead is a new sign. A circle with three smaller circles inside, all touching each other. Hassan slows down and changes their direction down the new tunnel. In another minute, Jon can see a black dot in the far distance. As they move faster, the black dot becomes bigger and bigger. Soon Jon can see the black dot has the circle shape with the three internal circles on it. They move faster and faster towards the end of the tunnel, and crash through at full speed.

.

CHAPTER 22

TIGERS OF SAPPRU

Tibi settled back in his chair, and Asif threw another log of wood on the fire. It crackled and spit sparks into the cool dry air of the plains. The three of them sat under a canopy of stars with the Milky Way stretched in an arc from one horizon to the other. Only the sparks, the fire, and their seats broke union of unlimited deep space to the open land.

Tibi started his story. "Now, you know that in our land there are many wild animals. Most are small rodents that occasionally appear across the paths we follow. There are many larger grass eaters that roam the area. Small deer, antelope, and wild horses can be seen in small herds across the plains. The wild boars can be very dangerous when cornered, and occasionally they will attack people. They are smart and strong, and they are especially nasty when they are cornered. Where there are so many plant eaters, there are bound to be meat eaters. Most dangerous are the wild cats, and there are many that roam this area. There are cheetahs, which feed mostly on the wild deer and antelope of the open plains; lions, which will feed on any animal they can prey upon, but most terrifying are the tigers. Their larger body and long fangs are built for killing, and man is no match for them. A tiger is a terrifying sight and an imposing enemy. It can kill a man with one lunge of their claws or a bite of its powerful jaws."

"Recently many towns and farmers have been repeatedly attacked by the tigers. Most often they have preyed on the cattle, sheep and goats that the farmers are raising. But sometimes they will prey on the people themselves, and each town has stories of children, older family members, or others who have met terrible fates at the hands of these beasts."

"After one of these beasts killed a good friend of my father, I became determined to learn how to track and kill the cats that killed people and livestock. Everyone has ideas for how to kill or capture the animals. Some I have learned from the old people of the town. They will tell you if you will spend the time to listen to them."

"Sometimes people think I'm off in my own world, conversing with invisible people or animals. Some people think I'm crazy. But the truth is I listen to the animals as well as the people, and I use common sense. I learn the animal behavior and then I move to capture or kill them. I think my knowledge comes from the land and animals; and not from just people."

"It was only last summer that a tiger was attacking several of the cattle one of the farmers had in a Sappru, several miles away. I was asked to go there and kill the animal, but I told them I would go only if I could do it my way. Tigers are rarely seen hunting in the day, and they generally hunt in small clans of females. They cover a wide range of land, so it is unusual that some would come back over and over to the same fields to kill the same cattle. The farmer was certain it was a tiger, because of the large teeth marks left in the bones of the cattle. The droppings left further away on the hills were much larger, and the paw prints were some seven inches wide, much wider than any of the other cats."

"When I arrived in the town there was a lot of commotion and high expectation among the town's people. Everyone wanted to tell me what to do. All the town elders had to have their say. They said to use poisons, to use prayers and magic spells. But none of that had stopped the tigers that were destroying their cattle. They were all so disappointed with me when I didn't want to listen to them. All I could do was point out that what they were doing wasn't working."

"So here's how I captured the tigers and killed them. It may not be how you have heard the story, but it's the truth. There is no substitute for understanding the cats. For understanding how they hunt. I lived on the farm where they were attacking. I told the farmer he might lose more cattle, but the tigers would be killed. Late at night, under the full moon I lay outside and watched as they came to the fields. They always did the same things. There were two scouts, and there were two attackers.

The scouts would come and watch from outside the field, always down-wind and just far enough to be invisible to the cattle. The attackers would hang back, out of range of the cattle but close enough to see if the scouts would make their move. If the scouts saw an opportunity, they would start at the herd from opposite sides. The herd would bolt away from them, but unknown to them they were running straight at the other attackers. The attackers will wait until the herd is close to them, then they find a target and chase it down. It might be a young cow, or an older or injured one, but their attack was ruthless and quick. One would attack the body, while the other would attack the neck for the kill as soon as she had the opportunity. They can bring an animal down in a matter of seconds. If the cow is lucky, death comes quickly. After the kill, the females feed. First the attackers eat their fill, then the scouts. After a few minutes a male tiger will appear and take his turn feeding."

"What I learned is that there was no way to kill them in the hunt. I had to find another way. So I decided the only way would be to trick them. As smart as they are, they are still animals. Every other night I would get a dead goat carcass from the butcher in town. I left it on a post, in the center of a circle about eight feet across. The circle was covered in grasses and sticks so the tiger would never touch the ground as he crossed the sticks. The first night I only left one carcass in one circle, then over time I expanded it to four carcasses in four circles. The tigresses found the easy meat too good to resist. The first nights, they didn't even take the bait, but then they found that the goat meat was just too irresistible, they didn't even have to work for it."

"This went on for about two weeks. I waited until the moon was new and I knew it would be a dark night. During the final day I had several of the townspeople help me. In each circle we dug a hole eight feet deep all the way around the pole where we put the goat carcasses. At the bottom of the hole, we put thirty sharp spikes facing straight up, each about three feet high. Across the top of the hole we built a small roof, with thatch from the sticks and grasses we used every other day. From a distance, it looked like it had looked every other night."

"That night, we lay in a small grass blind we had made several hundred feet away. We covered ourselves in dirt so our scent couldn't be found, and waited until well past the midnight hour. Finally, we saw the scouts come towards the circles. By now, each knew they had their own carcass to feast on. And just as I had hoped, the attackers came right behind them, just several feet away. The two scouts crossed their thatched roof tops and reached their meal. They started pulling apart their meal right away. The attackers picked their goat hides, and quickly went across their roof tops to the poles."

"Just as they were completely immersed in their feasting, we leapt up from our hiding spot and each of us pulled on two ropes that were buried in the dirt. The ropes spun up a snake of dust as they drew tight. Underneath the thatched roof, the rope pulled away the support for the roofs, and the beasts fell down with a crash onto the upright spikes. All except one of the traps. One of the ropes pulled tight and gave way on a broken stick under the trap. The roof stayed up."

"Three of the cats, the two scouts and one attacker, fell onto the spikes below. With earth shattering shrieks and roars, they met their deaths in the holes we had dug for their graves."

"The fourth cat was the most vicious of the attackers. She saw the other cats drop from site, and she turned to look where the rope lines led her view, back to the blind we were hiding behind. My blood froze. I pulled on the rope again, but it was completely slack. She roared in anger, her oversized fangs shining out in the dim moonlit night. My companion panicked. He started to run away, not realizing this would be no match for a tiger almost twice his size and six times his speed. The chase would be over quickly. My friend had run only several hundred feet before the tiger was almost on him. I instinctively grabbed the spears I had brought with me. I ran after them, but it was not before the tiger made a final leap through the air and brought down my friend with her knife-like claws. She ripped into his back with four inch wounds stretched across his flesh."

"I stopped and steadied myself for a quick moment, positioned my spear, and threw it at her. It hit her in the hind quarters, enough to distract her from my friend, but not enough to knock her down. With another huge roar and a flash of her fangs, she turned and came after me. I had one more spear, and as she leapt at me I thrust it up into her chest. Her claws came down on me and her body crushed me backwards onto the ground. I held onto the spear as it crushed through her chest and her heart. Her body slid down the shaft of the spear, until her head and jaws laid right next to me, her last breath still hot on me. But she was dead. I lay there for several moments before I realized I had killed her."

"After the attack, I was able to bring my friend back to the farm, but he did not make it through the night. The place where the tigers were killed can still be seen outside the town, and many people have gone there just to see the site. The tigress that attacked me is buried with the others, but I carry her fangs with me still."

Tibi reached into his bag, and from the bottom he brought out two large fang teeth, each about six inches long. Asif and Rafi stood and came near him to look at the fangs, lit by the firelight. Their sharp white edges seemed to grow bigger as the shadows of the flames danced across his hands.

CHAPTER 23

TRAINING CAMP

Jon and Hassan lay on an open grassy area, surrounded only by darkness and the night songs of the local insects and birds. Hassan stirs first, looking around as his eyes adjust to the darkness. He can see Jon lying near him, and soon sees a light from a building about thirty yards away. He moves closer to Jon and touches his shoulder to wake him. A breeze blows against Jon's hair as a crescent moon appears low on the horizon from behind a cloud.

Jon stirs into consciousness and finds himself in a very different climate from the desert of Kuwait. It's dark, but he can feel the humidity. He can hear the noises of the night, and he can see the shapes of the vegetation and trees in the darkness.

Hassan whispers quietly to Jon. "We're in Northern Iraq, at a training camp. We have friends in that bunker. We can sleep there, and in the morning you'll see what this whole operation is about."

A motion detector blinks to life as they approach the building. Jon sees a large metal door built into the cinderblock construction. A remote camera turns from under the eave and points at them with a small whir. Hassan gently knocks on the door. He looks directly into the camera, then gestures towards the door. A moment later the door swings open and they enter the darkened area.

"Hassan! It's been a long time! Come in. And who is your guest? Is this the American you were talking about? I'm Uzzi. Please come in. You must be tired."

"Uzzi – this is Jon. Yes, he's the one we were talking about. Jon, this is Uzzi. He's the manager of this camp. For now, just know that he's the man that keeps this place running."

"Come on in. I'll get you each a bed you can sleep in."

Jon checks his watch. 3AM. Once again, Jon thinks to himself, he finds himself in a situation where he has to accept charity from someone he should have nothing to do with.

"Thanks, we're exhausted."

Uzzi proceeds inside where twenty beds are set up like an army Combat Housing Unit, or CHU. Six of the beds are occupied with men soundly sleeping or snoring. Uzzi points out two beds at the end of the room, and Hassan and Jon pick their beds and say their goodnights to Uzzi. As Jon lies down and drifts toward sleep, he wonders if this will be the night this camp could be raided or bombed. And he considers that thought must be on everyone's mind that is sleeping there that night, and every night.

-

The sun is shining through the small window onto his bed when Jon wakes up. The familiar calls to mid-morning prayers are ringing through the air. Everyone else has already risen and gone on their way. Jon checks his watch. It shows 11 AM. How could he have slept so late? Hassan is not in his bed. He stands in his PTs (physical training clothes) to look out the window. Outside he has a partial view of a soccer field. There are orange cones, white sidelines, and goals at either end. Behind the goal within his view are six vertically stacked hay bales set back ten yards from the edge of the field. Jon wonders what they are for. Target practice?

The door at the far end of the bunker opens, and the bright light of the day pours into the darkness. Jon can see Hassan's silhouette against the light. "Good morning Jon." Hassan's figure is blurred by the light from across the expansive room. As he approaches, his image becomes clearer. Soon the details of his clothes come into focus as the light fills his thin frame. Hassan is now dressed in a full Army Uniform, boots to cap, but Jon is not sure what Army he is from. Jon now sees a complete transformation in Hassan from the insecure *Terp* he met a few days ago at the Bad Asurin Bridge. Jon, standing only in his PTs, now feels more than a little vulnerable without his guns, helmet, and the rest of his full battle rattle that is normally worn.

"Good morning Hassan." Jon says as he walks back to his bed to get more of his clothes to put on.

"Good morning Jon. Welcome to the northern base camp. As you can imagine, we keep a very low profile here. But we have the bare necessities. There is a shower and bathroom at the far end. I took the liberty of arranging some fresh clothes for you, I just hope they fit. Why don't you shower and get dressed, I'll meet you afterwards to get something to eat. We have a lot to do, and I'm sure you have a lot more questions after everything we went through yesterday."

Jon is not going to let Hassan go that easily. "Hassan, wait. Where the hell are we? I know we were in that tunnel last night, and we blasted through a portal at the other end. But how can we just *end up* here? Are we safe?"

"First, yes, we're safe. Second, it's best you don't know where you are right now. Third, the reason you're here is because you can glide through the tunnels with me. We have a lot to discuss on what we need to do. But get your shower and we'll talk over lunch. Meanwhile I have to talk to some of the leaders here."

Jon gathers a shirt and heads down the aisle with Hassan towards the other side of the bunker. As Hassan turns to leave, he points Jon to the door that leads to the showers.

"When you're done, just come outside the door here. The mess hall is just on the other side of the field, over there. I have them cooking some decent food for you."

The shower area is cold war era. Just cast-iron pipes across open tiles walls with crude drainage. The toilets stalls are open, no privacy doors. The Hot and Cold valves on the shower are marked in Russian. They must have built this place – so many years ago. As tired and dirty as Jon felt, it looked like a five star Hilton to him. Before getting in, Jon looks at the clothes Hassan arranged for him. "I'm not putting on any uniform made for Saddam Hussein. I'll walk outta here naked as a baby before I do that!" He picks up the pants and looks at the shirt. It's full US ACU – Army Combat Uniform. Up to date, even the most recent version. And they are his size. *How do they do this?* Jon wonders.

After his shower and shave, Jon walks into the sun outside the bunker, looking around at the base camp. It looks more like a park you might take your son or daughter to than a terrorist base camp. There are several buildings, but they are all built within treed areas. He can only see the entrances, and he imagines that from the air, you can hardly tell there is more than a shack or two in the area. There is a large open field area where the soccer field is to his right, complete with a small set of bleacher seats. Surrounding the soccer field is more natural growth area, and beyond are large cliffs which overlook a river. The river bends around the cliffs and borders the field on three sides. As he looks up at the cliffs, several small hawks wing their way along the updrafts of the mid-day. The sun glints off their wings which shine against the dark walls of the sandstone cliffs. In the sky above the cliffs, Jon sees the vapor trails of four allied jets flying in formation. Probably on their way to Baghdad, probably on a spy mission trying to find hidden base camps just like the one he is standing in. "I'm so court-martialed." Jon thinks to himself.

The only obvious choice for the mess hall is directly across the way. There is smoke coming out of the chimney, which is a give-away for food cooking inside. Hassan appears from the side of the building and waves Jon over.

The screen door slams behind them as they enter. There are about twenty men sitting at picnic tables inside the building. All their activity stops as they turn to look at Jon, an American entering their hidden sanctuary; their mess hall. Not only is he American, but he is on-site at one of their most highly secured training camps. Several moments of awkward silence pass; they make whatever assessment they need to and turn their attention back to their meals.

Hassan motions to Jon to proceed to the food-line area. There is not much to choose from, but they've made an effort to accommodate him. Scrambled eggs, potatoes, even something like bacon. He loads some large servings on his plates, and acknowledges the efforts of the cook behind the line. It had never occurred to him that he could have been treated like a prisoner right now. Instead, this group has made every effort to accommodate him; the clothes, the food. He's not sure, but he bets that it is due to the influence of Hassan that he is treated as well as he is.

After the meal Jon is feeling much better about addressing his situation and finding a way out. Hassan is ready to talk, so they approach each other intently across the mess hall table.

Jon starts. "Hassan, I need to get out of here. I am an American soldier. I can't be hiding out in an enemy combatant training camp. I'll be court-martialed. From now on, any discussion we have will be about getting me back to the US Army."

"I know. That is my goal as well. You need to get back to your Army unit. I understand. This camp is not an enemy of the United States. We are the keepers of peace with our order while the bigger war goes on to the south. My plan is to return you to your unit as soon as possible. I'm taking a big gamble with you. Frankly, many of the people don't like you being here. It's a big risk for them. If you don't like what I have to say you can go back to your unit and you will be free from us completely. But, if you choose to help, you can, and still be home with your unit safely when all is said and done. You can have a unique role in this war, and we are ready to take that next step. Let's go over this again."

"There are three Crystals of An we know of. We have the yellow one, called the Utu crystal after the ancient god of the sun. The Blue one is named after Enki, god of fresh water, and the red one is named after Ninurta, a god of war. Legend tells us only the yellow one is made to be possessed by men. The red and blue ones were never meant to be possessed by men, but if they were they would cause great destruction. They will eventually destroy men who try to possess them. The powers of the crystals can only be used under certain conditions. The first condition is location. They can only be used where there water close by. The second condition is there must be Ningalite present. Ningalite is the mineral that lights up as you concentrate near its presence. The last condition is that only the Ninhursag descendants can raise the powers. These descendants have the genetic make-up to interact with the Ningalite contained in the crystals. We can't begin to understand the reasons the Ninhursag can use these powers. The best comparison I can think of is electricity. A copper wire by itself is just copper. But if you combine the copper wire with another force that moves electrons, it becomes much more than a simple metal. And if you attach a light bulb or a motor at the end of the wire, you have a certain type of magic, either light in the light bulb, or movement in a motor. The Crystals of An are like that. By themselves they are just rocks. But if you add the dynamic of someone with Ninhursag in their blood, you have new and different powers that can be used. I'm sure that seems wildly crazy to you, but once you see it working, you accept it like you accept electricity or gravity."

"We call those that can use the powers of the crystals 'Descendants of Ninhursag, god of the earth.' It doesn't make you good or bad, to be one of the descendants. Mudlarek is Ninhursag, and you and I are Ninhursag, because we can summon the powers."

"You're saying that something in my heritage makes me Ninursag. How can that be?"

"How well do you know your family tree?"

"My father is an American but his parents came from Britain. My mother came from Iran in the seventies. She converted to Christianity, but she never talked about her family very much. Do you think that would be enough to have the connection?"

"I would think so. Clearly you have Ninhursag powers from the crystals, as you saw."

Jon has difficulty believing the conjecture Hassan is suggesting about his own origins. But the evidence is intriguing, if not compelling. "If the red and blue crystals are safe in the Ministry of Antiquities, then what is the problem? Aren't they as safe as they can be?"

"Mudlarek and the Hand of the Red Fist know that the crystals have been found. They have seen the pictures in the paper, and they know that they are in the Museum of Antiquities. They will try to get them. We have to expect that. We need to get to the crystals before they do, and secure them someplace unreachable. If they get possession of the crystals, they will bring more destruction than all the insurgent attacks that have occurred so far. Mudlarek has deceived the United States and the allies into believing he is an ally. He will turn on them at his first opportunity. If he has the crystals, that opportunity will be much bigger. The Americans will not be able to stop him. With Enki and Ninurta, he can move about under a cloak of invisibility. With them, he can summon powers of destruction that have no defense. We must keep those crystals from the hand of the Red Fist, and we cannot wait any more."

"We have made arrangements for you to go back to the Green Zone tonight. You will go under another name, one that has access to the Ministry of Antiquities. Once there, you can get the crystals by orders we will give you. There are two requirements needed to retrieve the artifacts. On is a US authorized agent must sign for them in person, along with an authorized authority on antiquities. Morgiana will be the authorized Iraqi agent, and you will be the US authority. Once you have them, you can give them to one of our agents who will be nearby, and you can stay in the Green Zone and report to the Army. There would be a problem if you expose yourself there; there will be too many difficult questions. Where were you all this time? And how did you get inside the Green Zone? Did you impersonate another Army officer?"

"There is another option. You can return here with the crystals. Once we have them, we can "release" you from captivity. You will be exonerated from any wrong doing because you will have the cover of having been in captivity. We will release you outside the Green Zone, in a similar manner to the way we released you in Mosul. You will go back to the US Army, and we will have our crystals to protect you from Mudlarek."

"Nothing has been that simple so far, somehow I doubt this will be as simple as you say. However, once again, I don't see any other way forward. The sooner we make this happen, the better."

CHAPTER 24

RAHID'S FARM

Tibi put the fangs back in his bag. As he turned to sit, he looked across the fields to the horizon. Far to the east, almost to the edge of the horizon, he could see an orange glow interrupting the serenity. Tibi strained to look in that direction. "That looks like a fire!" He exclaimed.

He called to his father in the house not far behind him.

"That's my uncle Tahir's farm over there. There is nothing else in that direction." Tibi's father came out and they looked with concern toward his brother's farm.

"Let's go," he said. They grabbed some supplies, although they weren't really sure what they should bring with them. They decided on a shovel, a scythe, some torches and some buckets.

"It's about an hour if we go by the regular trail," Tibi explained, "but if we cut across the plain we can make it there in thirty to forty minutes." As soon as they were assembled they jogged down the path towards the glow on the horizon.

About thirty minutes later they approached the farm. Two of the four structures were fully engulfed in flames. Tibi's father ran faster towards the buildings, ahead of the group. There was not much left.

"Tahir! Tahir!, where are you?" He ran from building to building, but he couldn't enter into any of them. The flames that shot out belied the nature of the brick structure. *How could there be so many flames when they were built from bricks?* Tibi thought. Tibi had never seen any fire like this before.

After some time, the four of them stood a few yards away from the fiery inferno. There was nothing else they could do. Tibi's father fell to his knees. "My brother, his wife, their children. What could have caused this?"

Across the field, four silhouettes appeared into the light from the darkness. They walked towards the group as they stand in shock at the destruction they see of the farm.

"Uncle, is that you? Tibi? Where have you been?" Ajit, the oldest child, is nearly hysterical.

"They came, and they - they were yelling. I ran outside. I ran outside and hid behind the well." He started to sob and collapsed into his father's arms.

"What happened Ajit? What happened then?"

Ajit could barely stop sobbing. He was a young man who recently turned fourteen years old. At fourteen, a boy becomes a man. He has still been living with his parents, but he has come of age and has gone through a ceremony celebrating his manhood at the local temple. Outside he had grown to be a full size, almost five feet five inches tall. But inside, he was still maturing. He was apprenticed as a carpenter in the town when he was not working on the farm with his father. His talents as a carpenter had become well known both in the town and across the local lands. He was able to craft solutions for farms and houses as they were needed. His master had taught him well, and Ajit often saw new ways to use his craft to solve the problems of his customers.

For now his sorrow cannot be consoled.

Ajit spoke slowly. "They wanted everything. They wanted our tools, our food, and our livestock."

"Who did this? Do you know?"

"I don't know who they were. There were three of them at first. All dressed in black robes with red belts tied around them. They kept saying they were the new rulers of our town. Then another man came. He was dressed in a red robe with a black belt tied around it. He seemed to think he would scare me into giving them everything. I refused, but he swore he would destroy my farm. I told him he could destroy my farm, but he could never own it."

"Then something strange happened. The man with the red robe started yelling and waving his arms. He stood in the middle of the yard, between the house and the barn. As he was swinging his arms around, circles of red appeared moving around his head. They moved around the air near the house, then they moved in bigger and bigger circles. They became brighter and brighter. Finally, they came together, and then crashed into our house. It exploded into flames. Then again the swirling waves appeared and like lightning, crashed into the barn. All of a sudden it was flooded with fire."

Rafi and Asif knew who had done this. "It was Mukhtar and his raiders from Nippur," Rafi explained. "Mukhtar and his gang of raiders have been going from town to town, raiding and burning the towns. He claims supreme ownership of the land, and burns down some of the buildings to scare the townspeople."

Ajit had heard of the terrors of raiders across the land. As the land has not always provided enough for the population of the areas around them, some have turned to raiding other farms and towns, mostly to scare the people and take what they need for their own towns. But Mukhtar and his raiders were different. They have spread far beyond the local area most raiders would venture to. They have raided many towns and farms, and now they have murdered some of them.

"Who is Mukhtar?" Ajit asked.

Asif looked at Ajit. "Ajit, young man, your farm has been burned down by the most notorious raider that has existed in these parts. Only a few days ago we saw him raid Eppru where I live. He destroyed the markets and burned down many of the warehouses the town uses. He and his raiders claimed the town for their own. And he used the power of the swirling energy to start all the fires. Ajit – Mukhtar has some power of the gods that starts these fires. These powers are so strong that no man can match him. He has learned to use them together to scare the town's people and destroy those who go against him."

"Rafi and I have pledged to stop him. We will kill him if we have to. He can't be allowed to continue his raids, and the powers of the gods need to be returned to the gods. We too have some of the power of the gods, but we will only use it to stop him, not to hurt other people."

"Then I will help you." Ajit pledged. "I will go with you and stop Mukhtar. I have nothing here. I can help you. I will have my vengeance, and I can help you in many ways."

Tibi looked at his cousin, and he looks at his father. "Father, I'll go too. I will go and avenge this crime, and I will watch out for Ajit. You can get help on the farm when you need it. I'm sure the neighbors will help, and they will help knowing that we are doing what we have to so they are protected from Mukhtar and his raiders."

Tahir was overwhelmed, as they all were. Slowly he spoke. "This evil must be destroyed. Or else he'll come back. Tonight he has taken from us half our farm. Just days ago he has raided the town of Eppru. If we do nothing he will be back, and he won't stop as long as no one gets in his way. We will have to stop him."

Tibi, Salim, and Ajit knew nothing of the relationship between Asif, Rafi, and Mukhtar. They didn't know everything about Mukhtar's powers. They didn't know about the yellow crystal they possess, and the power they have. But they did know what they needed to know. They knew Mukhtar had to be stopped. They were reluctant to leave but dedicated to their cause. They would rather be at home with their families. They would rather life had not brought them to these unknown, unpleasant tasks. But they knew they had to go forward.

The unhappy group made their way back to Tibi's farm. As they arrived there, they could see daylight breaking across the plains on the eastern horizon. Roosters were crowing for the dawn, bringing a sense of normalcy. As the small group approaches the farm, their footsteps were heavy and tired. They felt anything but normal.

CHAPTER 25

TO THE GREEN ZONE

Hassan and Jon spent the afternoon reviewing the plans for the next few days. Hassan presented Jon full ACU uniform and security pass for the Green Zone. Jon would be going by the name of Corporal Thomas Schwartz. He will be working with an agent Hassan has within the Green Zone whose name is Abdul Khalil. Morgiana and Abdul will meet him. She has official privileges at the Ministry of Antiquities. He has an official looking but forged request for the crystals and several other religious artifacts. The other items are simply collateral, so if there has to be negotiations, the other items could be sacrificed as part of a deal. The forged document says that Jon and Morgiana are bringing the items to a temple in the South that is now in a secured area.

At midnight Jon and Hassan gather outside the bunker. "You'll have to learn how to use the yellow crystal, so you can use it to get to the Green Zone, and later, back here." Hassan advises Jon. "You start by meditating. That's the best way to feel the energy. Once you know how to feel the energy and summon it to you, you can learn to call it more quickly the next time. I'll go with you this time, then you will be on your own next time."

Jon drops his head in meditation as Hassan stands by, watching him. For several minutes Jon stands in silence, looking for the energy to rise about him. He winces and tenses as he tries to contact the energy of the yellow crystal. Nothing happens. Hassan shuffles nervously. After several more minutes, Hassan tries to interrupt Jon.

"Jon – Jon! You're trying too hard. Relax a little bit. Don't try to squeeze it out. It feels more like summoning a breeze than summoning a bowel movement. Really – you are kind of embarrassing."

Jon laughs nervously. "OK OK. I'll do this again." Once again he drops his head in silent concentration, this time without wincing or tensing. After a minute or so, a small glow comes from the yellow crystal which has been laid before them. Jon adjusts his position to a wider stance as he feels the energy rise around him. Swirls of energy start to spiral over his head, twisting and turning around him. Soon the swirls move beyond the borders of the area above Jon's head and they move forward and backward around the open yard. Below them, the glowing circle starts to appear in the ground. The circle grows brighter until the edges are burning, and in the center the ancient symbol of a lightning bolt flames appears. Jon looks up from his trance. Hassan moves to pull him forward to the circle, and together they jump to the middle of the burning circle. The circle collapses around them, and the energy swirls swing sharply downward and suck inside the circle. The electronic Snap! rips the air, and soon the grassy area is back to its original state.

In the tunnel, Jon and Hassan lay down to glide. Yellow streams of energy flow under the invisible membrane that separates them. Hassan points to the symbol on the portal behind them, and they turn to start gliding down the energy flow. Prone on their stomachs, they hit several bumps and curves, going faster and faster. Hassan slows down and shows Jon the different portals as they appear in the flow. At the fourth portal, Hassan points with both hands towards the tunnel that is branching off to the left. The portal sign is three concentric circles. Jon knows this is the portal that will bring him to the Green Zone, but he's not going to enter on this trip. They glide up to the portal slowly, but don't go through. Jon is struck by the stark contrast between the cut stone hardness of the portal against the endless flow of the energy. As they curl around the end of the tunnel and head back into the energy flow, Jon pushes on the membrane to see what would happen. The plasma seems to slow and pool around where he has pressed his fist into the membrane. After he lifts his fist, the plasma below quickly restores the steady flow. Hassan is now far ahead of him down the tunnel. Jon focuses on moving, and soon he's flying down the tunnel towards a plasma yellow horizon.

Once outside the tunnel again and back at the base camp, Hassan wants to go over the plans again. "Our window is from 1:30 to 2:30 to get you into the Green Zone. Abdul Khalil has arranged to have the portal area as clear as possible without raising any suspicion. What you see going through the portal from the outside can be noticeable. There is the small flash of light, and the outline of the portal in the ground. We're doing it in the dead of night for the least chance someone else will notice. Abdul will bring you to the British Ambassador house where you have a bed reserved. Your travel orders say you have come from Kuwait for a meeting on supply safety. You have been asked to pick up the packages from the Ministry of Antiquities and return it to a temple in Basra. Once the package has been returned, the local Iraqis have agreed to increase the number of trucks allowed to travel the highways at night. They were notified ahead of time"

"That sounds simple enough. But then again everything sounds simple when you say it."

The crescent moon is setting low in the west just after 1:30AM. Jon and Hassan are at the grassy area on the edge of the base camp near the river. "This is it Jon. This is the big day. We've been waiting for months to get to this point, now all we have to do is make it happen."

"I'll make it happen, Hassan. Once I'm done and you have all the crystals, all I want is to know they will be secured, and that I will be going back to my unit. Who knows, once this whole mess is over, you and I may get together and talk about exactly what is going on with these "Crystals of An."

"Let's hope so. If you're ready, we're ready. Abdul will be at the other portal waiting for you. Here is the yellow crystal, Utu. We are entrusting this to your care. I hope you understand the deep responsibility and duty we are bestowing on you by giving you this crystal."

"I understand. I'm ready." Jon says as he takes the crystal and bag from Hassan.

Jon drops his head to concentrate. This time wisps appear in a few moments. The wisps of swirling energy appear around his head. They grow stronger very quickly. In a minute or two, the energy has reached the point of inflection when Jon can enter the portal. Jon lifts his head from his concentration. He looks at Hassan, and then he jumps feet first into the center of the portal.

Deep inside the Green Zone, near the Euphrates River, Zawara Lake is a park with an open grassy area and a small lake. It's almost 2AM, so it is about as quiet as it gets in the city of Baghdad. The crescent moon is barely visible, hanging low on the horizon against the soft glow of city lights in the sky. A small breeze picks up and blows a few leaves across the open area. A moment later, a soft circle of light appears in the grass. The circle of light grows brighter, then another circle takes shape inside the first one. The outer rim grows brighter, and a third ring in the middle appears. As the light grows, a man emerges from the shadows, silhouetted by the orange and yellow glow of the light. In a flash of light the circle seems to erupt with beams of light pouring outward. Just as quickly, the flash and the lights are gone. Lying in the middle of the circle is a lone man. The silhouetted man walks to him and prods him with a stick. Jon, lying in full uniform, slowly awakens.
"Mister Jon! Mister Jon!" Abdul whispers as he tries to awaken him.
Jon is unconscious at first. After several seconds, he stirs as if rising from a long deep sleep. As his senses gather around him, once again he can sense the change in his climate. He first notices the city lights and the glow of the sky. Then he hears the noise from traffic along a distant highway, and the piercing sound of sirens moving in the distance. His senses sharpen, and he hears his name. "Mister Jon, Mister Jon!" He turns to look and sees a stranger no more than three feet away, pushing him with a stick. His reflexes kick into action. He rolls to his left, towards the stranger. He grabs the stick from Abdul and swings it around as a club and whacks the knees of the stranger.

"Ahhh! Mister Jon! No! It's me – Abdul! Hassan told you about me! I'm here to help you!"

Jon has rolled to a crouching position holding his stick, not quite sure what he should do next. In the next moment the memory of his mission comes back. He relaxes his grip on the stick and shifts to look at Abdul with sympathy. Abdul is a young man, no more than twenty years old.

"Abdul, I'm sorry. But I was just defending myself. I couldn't tell who you were at first, after just coming out through the portal. Are you OK? I'm sorry I hit you."

"It's OK, it's OK." Abdul responds while holding and rubbing his knees. Abdul's English is not as fluent as Hassan's, or many of the other Iraqis Jon has met on this adventure. Abdul is a student at the University in Baghdad. His schooling had been interrupted several years by the war, and he can barely remember a time when the Americans were not occupying his nation. Abdul knew that speaking English would be the best way for him to get jobs and better opportunities, but this is the first time he has actually been using it to speak directly to an American.

"I have bed for you. Everything is OK mister Jon. We told them you late from traveling, so no one notice you. We go now. It's best. OK?"

"OK, let's go to the bed. We can speak more tomorrow."

"Come this way." Abdul stands and then reaches his hand to lift Jon. They walk across the grassy area and pass through a gated entrance that separates the park from the more traditional city streets. They walk several city blocks of a tree-lined residential area that look as comfortable as any in a well–to-do western city. It's hard to believe they are in the heart of a war-zone. The sodium street lights buzz as they walk along the crooked sidewalks.

They stop at a traditional English design residence, with a gated front and small garden before the entrance. Abdul pushes open the squeaky gate and walks up the four steps to the door. He pushes a doorbell, and in a moment someone is looking through a window peering out at them. Several locks are opened, and an elderly Iraqi gentleman named Behader motions for Jon to come in. Abdul waves to acknowledge the man, the turns to Jon. "I meet you out here at 0-900 hours. There at Bus Stop."

Jon notices that Abdul uses US military time as the way to tell time. "OK. 0-900 hours it is." He speaks out loud. He walks into the house, which has a large foyer and a staircase leading upstairs to the right. "This is truly English traditional." Oriental rugs and pastoral oil paintings decorate the floors and wall.

"Corporal Schwartz, I have your room upstairs." The elderly Iraqi pronounces.

Jon remembers going upstairs and finding his room, but he is sound asleep almost as soon as he hits the down pillow covered by a down blanket.

CHAPTER 26

MUKHTAR'S CRYSTALS

For the next weeks Tibi's farm became a hub of activity. Neighbors stopped by to bring supplies and help reconstruction at Tahir's farm. They wanted to start work rebuilding right away. The plans were organized by Ajit, and work was to begin as soon as they could get supplies. The local priest held ceremonies, and they swore there would be justice against the raiders who burned down Tahir and Ajit's farm. Asif, Rafi, Tibi and Ajit found time to work on plans to destroy Mukhtar. Each one planned in areas they had special knowledge of.

Rafi knew the most about how Mukhtar operated. Ajit knew how to build things, but more than that he knew how to solve problems with the things he built. Tibi knew animals, and he was committed to showing the others how they can use the animals, and mostly the horses, to their advantage. The most exciting training was to come later from Asif. He knew the yellow crystal and how it could help them.

On the evening of the second day, Rafi told the story of what happened with Mukhtar since the disappearance of Rania and Asif.

"After we returned from the mountains, I went home to my family. I was dehydrated, sick, and tired, but those ailments would heal. There were much deeper wounds that would not heal. Rania was gone. My mother and father thought I was dead one day, and when I returned, it was Rania that was gone. The grief was devastating to them. Everyone in the town did what they could to console them, but there is no consolation for the parents of a lost child."

"Mukhtar only made matters worse. He raged for weeks about Rania and blamed my family for her disappearance. Some said he went crazy, and I wouldn't correct them. He slandered us and almost ruined my father's business. If not for the support of the people of the town, we would have been ruined. Everyone knew what Mukhtar said was a lie. Mukhtar fell into a deep depression. He stormed about his family's farm, making wild accusations and declarations. His father couldn't control him anymore. His mother couldn't speak to him at all. Finally his father had the priest come and talk to him. It's not known what the priest said, but Mukhtar emerged from their meeting with a solemn and deeply determined look on his face. He looked as if he had aged ten years in just a few days."

"About a week later Mukhtar put together a team of laborers and set off for the shaky mountains. He didn't remember exactly where the cave was, so he had one of his captains come to me and make me go on the expedition with him. Twenty of us went, including Mukhtar and the priest. We set up camp near at the base of the mountain where our cave was. For days the laborers would travel up the side of the cliff and work where they thought the cave entrance was to try to uncover it. Every time they thought they were close, the mountain would shake again and cover the area they were working with more stone. Finally after weeks of hard labor pulling out rocks, they were able to clear the entrance to the cave. They reinforced the walls of the entrance with trunks of trees. It was as if the mountain had given up trying to stop him. At first Mukhtar refused to go in the cave. He was afraid he would find your bodies, but even more afraid that he would not. He was also afraid of the shaky mountain and another rock slide, so he sent me and some of his laborers in. We spent days inside looking for your bodies, but found nothing. Mukhtar remembered the lights in the cave. He found the courage to enter, and when he did, red, blue and orange lights grew from the walls. He wanted to capture the magic of the walls, so he had the laborers mine them. As they broke away they would continue to shine, but if they were brought outside into the nighttime with Mukhtar, their magic was gone. Mukhtar told them to continue to dig the stones out. After about five days, they made their amazing discovery. I stayed, only in hopes of returning your remains to our families."

"Almost twenty feet into the side of the cave, they found a small rock nest, a nest made of crystals. And in the nest lay the two crystals he has now. One blue and one red. They shone brighter than anything Mukhtar had seen. He held them above in his hands, and as he did red and blue clouds of light started to swirl around his head. Then they clouds swirled around the cave as if they had just been freed after thousands of years of captivity. Finally they crashed into the ground with a burst of fire, setting some wood on fire that had been brought in to work on the mining. At first Mukhtar was frightened, but then he found he was able to control the swirling with his arms. He would wave them around and the energy would sweep back and forth above him. Suddenly it dove down and crashed over his head. It didn't hurt him, but he suddenly disappeared. We thought he was destroyed. At the time, he did not know he had disappeared. It was only after he reappeared several minutes later on the other side of the cave that the laborers that told him he had disappeared."

"He stopped looking for you and Rania, and brought the crystals back to Nippur. He insisted your bodies were at the bottom of the water in the cave, buried forever. The priest insisted the crystals were the power of the gods and must be kept with him in the temple. But Mukhtar was smarter than that. He wanted the crystals for himself. So he went to the temple, and showed that the crystals would not show their power there. As we know now, that is because the temple in Nippur is not near water. So Mukhtar told the priest it was he who had the power, and it was only he who could use the crystals. He brought them to his house and put on a show for the priest. He burned down one of his own barns, and then he disappeared and reappeared on the balcony of his house. The priest assumed it was Mukhtar that controlled all the power, and that maybe he had power of the gods, not just the crystal. The truth was Mukhtar was one of the people that can use the crystals, but it was because he was near the enchanted rocks and water that they would work."

"We knew when we were mining the crystals that others could to make the lights shine. One of the laborers showed Mukhtar that he, too, could control the lights and the crystals.

Mukhtar looked at him with amusement and wonder. The next morning we found the laborer dead. We learned a lesson about Mukhtar then. From that point anyone that thought they could control the crystals kept it to themselves."

"Mukhtar convinced the priest to declare both of you dead, so that he could seek to remarry if he wanted to, and he would try to give his parents some peace in the loss of their son."

CHAPTER 27

THE MINISTRY OF ANTIQUITIES

Baghdad mornings, like all mornings in Islamic cities, start early with a call to prayer at sunrise. The broadcast prayers create a common sense of timing across the city. Not long after the prayers, the noise of city life starts to rise with sirens, horns, and construction vehicles.

Jon walks out of the English house just before 0-900 hours, dressed in the same clothes as the day before, only looking much more refreshed. The garden outside the house is filled with roses, fox-glove, heather, hollyhocks, and other English flowers. Underground sprinklers spray much needed moisture onto the otherwise arid ground. Jon crosses the red brick pathway trying not to get wet and opens the creaky wrought iron fence. His path through the gate is blocked by a delivery man bringing in fresh produce and breads on hand truck. Outside the fence, a red delivery truck is parked with the back loading area open. A large sign on the side of the truck advertises in bright yellow colors which reads "Ahmad and Sons. Fresh Produce and Breads – Since 1978."

"Good morning sir!" The delivery many offers to Jon. "My name is Ahmad. I deliver the fresh produce here and the finest breads in Baghdad. If you will excuse me for one minute, I'll be out of your way in no time."

Jon backs up three steps and waits patiently at the gate as Ahmad negotiates the hand-truck around the gate and onto the brick path leading to the house. As Jon exits the gate area and walks around the red truck, he sees a reflective permit sticker on the bumper with some sort of clearance for the Green Zone.

Abdul isn't at the bus stop yet. There are city maps around the bus stop, even though there's no way to go outside the security of the Green Zone using the buses. Jon thinks to himself that the Arabic writing on the maps looks as confusing to him as the street map. A horn honks behind him. He turns to look, and Abdul is calling him from inside a cab window. Morgiana is in the back seat as well.

"Jon! Jon! Get in! We are going to the warehouse right away."

Jon walks around the cab and sees the same reflective permit sticker on the bumper of the taxi. *This must be what vehicles need to get inside the Green Zone,* he thinks. He gets in on the other side behind the driver. The cab smells of thick old smoke and what may be rotting teeth. Jon almost gags.

"How far is it?"

"It's only about two miles away. It should take about twenty minutes, depending on security and traffic."

The warehouse is housed in the Ministry of Antiquities located several blocks away from the National Museum of Iraq, not far from the Euphrates River. The windowless building is about a half block long, tucked between two other government administrative buildings. There is a small non-descript door identified only with the street number above it. The taxi stops outside, and Jon steps outside on the curb as Abdul pays the driver. Abdul and Morgiana hurry around the back of the taxi onto the curb and escort Jon to the door. Inside there is a small security room lined with wooden panels on the walls. The security desk is in the middle with doors on the right and left of the receptionist area. Abdul approaches the receptionist desk and to announce their names and confirm their appointment. The receptionist, dressed in a formal uniform which Jon assumed was from the British Army, takes Abdul's and Morgiana's credentials and asks for Jon's in English. "Here you are sir." Jon says as he hands Thomas Schultz's paperwork to him. The receptionist checks the paperwork, and speaks to the two men; "I'll be right back."

He leaves the front security area and goes through one of the doors behind him. Several awkward moments pass as Jon and Abdul aren't sure what is going on. There are cameras mounted in three corners of the ceiling. Jon looks at all three cameras, knowing there is probably someone on the other side doing some kind of analysis. After a few more moments, the receptionist returns.

"Thomas Schultz? Your paperwork is missing at least one authorization. You need to have the curator of the National Museum of Iraq sign off on taking these artifacts. Too many artifacts have been leaving without proper authorizations."

Abdul, trying to head off a failure to succeed in their mission, interrupts. "Sir, there is an explanation here. We approached the National Museum, but they assured us we only need two approvals, one must be authorized by the museum, and we have Morgiana Shilah with us who is an approver of the museum. If you check your policy, you will see that Morgiana has the proper authority from the museum to remove items of minor significance without the permission of the curator. The other required authorization is from the US Army, and Thomas Schultz here has that authority. Therefore, we do not need the curator's approval."

"Let me check on that." The guard responds. He recollects the paperwork he has spread out on the counter, and heads back into the room behind the desk. Several more awkward moments pass and soon he returns. "It looks like you are correct that you don't need that approval. However, we're going to do another review once we bring the artifacts up here. There is an escort coming here who will bring you to the storage area. Then you will come back to a room on this floor and we'll do the final inspections."

A few moments later a buzzer buzzes and the receptionist hits a button under the desk. An electronic click releases a door lock, and another guard appears from the opposite door in the room.

"My Lady and Gentlemen, my name is Ludwig. I'll be escorting you today. Please attach these credentials to your clothes."

He hands plastic badge holders containing recently printed name-tags to each of them. After attaching the badges, they follow Ludwig through the door. On the other side is a non-descript industrial hallway with two elevators at the far end. Ludwig leads them to the elevator and selects the down button.

"This warehousing part of this facility has been operational since late 2003. When the Americans invaded, all of the security for the Iraqi museums and temples was abandoned. The Americans avoided bombing the National Museum directly, but they failed to provide adequate security for the artifacts that remained. There was a militia that took over the museum for several days, and many of the most valuable artifacts were looted. The Americans restored security to museum later in 2003." The elevator opens and Ludwig presses the button for four floors below their level as they enter. "At first most people thought the Americans had done the looting, but after a while it became apparent it was not the Americans, but Iraqis who were stealing the treasures. Many of them were stolen for greed, but some were stolen for safekeeping. The citizens were afraid they would be destroyed, and felt they would be safer in their own possession. Many of the items that were taken in this pretense have been returned."

The elevator doors open to a floor considerably more rustic than the floors above.

"I'll have to ask your forgiveness for the unfinished conditions of this floor. It often feels like more of a cave than a warehouse."

The walls consist of solid stone blocks; and exposed wiring runs along the ceiling in trays to serve the various lights in the rooms and hallways. The light bulbs are bare and incandescent. The air is naturally cool, and Jon considers that moisture would likely be a problem for the artifacts, since they are close to the river and probably several feet below it. Contrary to his expectations, it's as dry as a bone.

Ludwig continues his narrative. "There was also the problem of artifacts and religious treasures that were outside the museum. This facility was established by the allies to store and categorize as many of the artifacts and treasures as we could find, in a responsible way. That mission has been going on for several years now. Our mission is not to keep all of the artifacts here, but to record the items and return them to responsible owners if and when they present themselves. Apparently that is the situation you are in now. You will be restoring these items to their rightful owners in a responsible way, as you have stated and signed for on your application."

Jon smiles towards Abdul, surprised that their deception seems to be so simple and complete. Ludwig turns a corner and opens a metal door which has a large sign on it. *Fire door – keep closed at all times.* Beyond the door a large rooms opens before them. Row after row of metal storage shelves make a library type feel, with classification codes printed on paper taped to a shelf at the end of each row.

"These conditions are much less than ideal for antiquities," Morgiana comments. "Although it's cool and normally dry, the moisture is not controlled. These rare artifacts are decaying by the day. We really need to improve the conditions of this storage as soon as possible."

"I'm afraid that won't be happening any time soon." Ludwig explains. "There is so much pressure on the allies to give up security on these artifacts, if there is going to be improvement, it probably will not be from the allies."

Most of the shelves contain bankers' boxes or plastic bins with large numbers on the outside which classify the contents. The items that don't fit in the boxes or bins are displayed in the open. There are hundreds of bowls, plates, statues, and reliefs cut into stones that were taken from the ruins of a temple somewhere. The figures cut into the stone seem to be ancient gods or mythological type creatures. Horses with human heads and wings seemed to be very popular. There are lions, horses, and pictures of warriors. "These are the remnants of ancient civilizations from thousands of years ago. They are all here, categorized and inventoried." Ludwig comments.

Ludwig turns down one of the aisles, and Jon, Morgiana, and Abdul follow him. "These are mostly smaller religious pieces that have been found over the years. Honestly we were surprised someone would be claiming these. But they are on your list of items, so here they are. We store the lighter and smaller items on the top shelves; the heavier items are on the bottom. Oh – here's your items. Please confirm these boxes correspond to the identifying numbers on your paperwork, and then we can find your other items."

Jon, (or Thomas), inspects the items. They seem to be ordinary bowls, and some clay pieces with some type of mythological creatures carved in them. "That looks like what we were looking for." Jon proclaims.

"OK." Ludwig confirms. "Now we have just one more box to collect for you."

After twenty more rows of storage, Ludwig takes a left turn into one of the aisles. Morgiana follows right behind him. It's barely wide enough for one person, so Abdul and Jon wait at the end of the aisle. As Ludwig reaches up to the shelf with the box on it, Jon can see a little bit of potential trouble that he did not quite expect. The stone walls are starting to softly glow. Blue and red lights are slowly shifting in the walls, mixed in with some yellow as well. Jon forgot, he's carrying the yellow crystal now. If the walls contain the element of Ningalite, combination of the red and blue crystals may multiply the effects. So far, the lights are limited to the end of the aisle beyond Ludwig. He is distracted by examining the labeling on the box containing the crystals. Abdul's eyes, looking past Ludwig at the walls, are widening open. He nudges Jon. "Thomas!" he whispers to Jon.

"I see it too. Let's hope it doesn't get noticeable."

Ludwig walks towards the two men carrying the box which has the crystals in it. "Here it is gentlemen. Here is your other box. Please confirm that this box is the one on your paperwork, and we can be on our way."

Jon and Morgiana look into the box and see another metal box with a heavily tarnished cover. There are seams visible in the box, and soon they are emitting red and blue lights quite brightly. There are also two other small items; a small spearhead and something that looks like the handle portion of a staff. There is a white stone embedded in the staff, about the size of a lime. The stone, too, is glowing blue and red light from within. Jon puts the outer cover back on the box as quickly as he can, but Ludwig has clearly seen the lights coming from the inside of the box.

"What is that light coming from sir?" Ludwig asks insistently.

Jon tries to react quickly. "I put a flashlight inside to see the content, that's all. It's nothing at all."

That seemed to satisfy Ludwig for the moment. Jon pushed his hands into the handles on the side of the box so no light would escape through the holes. That action only served to make the energy connection stronger from within the box, and Jon could feel the energy bursting from within and surging through his Ninhursag connection to the crystals inside.

They all turned to walk towards the exit. The heavy concentration of Ningalite in the walls of the vault reacts stronger and stronger with the presence of Jon and the three crystals. Ludwig leads the three men back past the rows of storage. Just behind him and above him small wisps and swirls of light and energy are starting to spread. They don't stay small wisps for long. Small clouds of light appear. A disconcerting wind starts to blow within the confines of the vaulted area. Papers start blowing around, and the classification notes at the end of the aisles become the first papers to blow free from their adhesive. The breeze kicks into a small whoosh that becomes audible as it moves quickly through the racks. Jon pushes Abdul to move faster; if only they can get outside the area with all the Ningalite, maybe the lights and winds will stop. One of the papers blows forward across the visual path of Ludwig.

He stops in his tracks and turns around to see where this paper had come from. He is not ready for the site that is before him. Abdul and Jon are right behind him, but beyond them a micro-storm of swirling dust, light and papers is raging throughout the vault. The lights flicker off, leaving only the brightness of the clouds illuminating the room. Several of the statues and artifacts contain Ningalite, and their features light up, glowing in the darkness and featuring their faces and swords. The pictures carved into the stone relief pictures glow with their original sharp lines and details, each trying to retell their stories not told for thousands of years.

The wind in the room builds to an audible rush as it pushes through the artifacts. Dust from thousands of years ago fills the air, creating beams of lights to carry the stories from the glowing statues and artifacts. Soon the wind starts to dislodge the least balanced bowls and plates, and they start rolling over on the shelves or crashing to the ground in the aisles. Ludwig turned to look at Jon and Abdul. "Thomas, Abdul! What's going on here? Oh my God what is causing this?"

"We don't know!" Jon tries to explain as he turns to look at Ludwig.

Morgiana's long hair has come out of her scarf and blows wildly around as she looks at Ludwig. The light behind her makes her appear to grow in height and dimension as she approaches Ludwig.

Ludwig reels back on his heels as Jon turns towards him. He backs away and collapses against one of the stone statues standing at the end of an aisle. Abdul looks at Jon and backs away as well. Jon's eyes are now glowing bright red, with blue lined edges streaming lights from the sides. His whole head is lit from inside, showing his skeletal frame against a backdrop of glowing blue and red. Jon is aware of the energy, and sees only shadows and fuzzy images of his friends.

Abdul tries to collect himself as he looks at Jon. "Jon! We have to get out of here! Let's go! This is going to destroy everything!"

"Let's go!" Jon yells, but it comes out in a mechanized growl that cuts through the howling wind that is crashing thousands of priceless artifacts and thousands of years of history.

"Not with those treasures, you're not!" Ludwig shouts as he re-establishes himself as a barrier towards the exit. Ludwig pulls out his radio and starts barking into the microphone, trying to alert security upstairs.

"We have to get out of here with these crystals." Abdul says as he pushes towards Ludwig. Ludwig backs away from Jon, still terrified from the transformed look of Jon's face. Ludwig is armed, but hasn't thought of using his weapon since he was left British boot camp. He tugs on his gun, but it's locked in place with a strap. Awkwardly, he looks down at his belt and fumbles to find the way to unlock the strap. As he's looking, Abdul takes advantage of the hesitation. He rushes forward and wrestles Ludwig to the ground, forcing him onto his stomach. He pulls his arms behind his back and pins him to the ground, Ludwig is helpless in his efforts to reach his gun.

"Morgiana, go outside and get the elevator! I'll hold him here until it gets here."

"What are you going to do with him?" She asks.

"Nothing I swear. I'll just hold him off until we can get outside – now go get the elevator!"

"Give me thirty seconds, then head down the hallway."

Morgiana leaps past Hassan and Ludwig. She grabs Jon by the hand and pushes through the fire door. As the sound of their footsteps echo down the hallway, Abdul reaches for Ludwig's gun as he hears a grunt of discomfort from his captive underneath him. Abdul frees the gun from the locked holster, holds it in front of him to look at the safety release, then shoves it into the waistband of his uniform. He grabs a rope from the top of a canvas mail-bag containing several artifacts lying nearby, and ties Ludwig's hands behind his back.

The lights are still off in the room, and the clouds of swirling light are racing up and down the aisles and across the ceiling, dispersing as flames would if the room were completely engulfed in flames. After a few seconds, Abdul stands and runs through the fire door. As he exits, the energy converges at the entrance and exits along with him. The room is left dark and still, with only a small exit sign over the exit door beaming its red light through the darkness.

Abdul runs down the hallway towards the elevator. Morgiana is holding it open for him. Jon enters, carrying the box with the crystals inside. He's already lost his Ningalite glow.

"Where's the other box?" Abdul asks.

"I thought you had it! Oh well, it doesn't matter. We only need this one."

The elevator door shuts, and they press the button for the floor they think is the lobby they came through.

"There are no other exits we can use. We have to go out through the front door."

"We have to get out of here without raising any more suspicion. Chances are the receptionist doesn't even know what happened downstairs yet. We have to make an excuse for Ludwig not being with us, and we have to get out of here cleanly."

The elevator door opens. They walk down hall towards the front entryway. From a side room, the receptionist hears their footsteps coming from a side room and steps into the hallway to get their attention.

"Hello. Bring your boxes in here for inspection, as we discussed."

"Oh, sure, but we did the final inspection with Ludwig downstairs. He stayed down there to pick up some things that had fallen over, but he said we were good to go." Jon assured him.

"Never the less, I need you to bring the items in here and I will inspect them for you."

Jon looks at Abdul as they move towards the conference room where the receptionist is calling from. "Let's do this quickly."

They walk into the room and place the box on the table. Luckily, there are no rock walls, and no streaming beams of lights coming from the box. ``Here's what we could find today. Ludwig said the other items were mis-categorized. He will find them and we'll come back for them next week." Abdul offered.

"Mis-categorized? Nothing is mis-categorized here. There must be some other explanation. Let's wait for Ludwig to come up and explain what happened to your other items."

"No really, this is all we need for today. We have to come back in a few days anyway, so we will pick the other pieces up then. And, our transport is leaving in thirty minutes from the Green Zone gate, so we have to leave if we're going to make it." Jon was trying to sound as convincing and determined as he could.

The receptionist considered his remarks. "This is odd. Your meeting here was scheduled later today. What would have happened if you had kept to your original schedule? The transports run the same time every day. You would have known this."

This insight was followed by several moments of silence that neither Jon, Morgiana, nor Abdul knew how to fill. Abdul stood up to gather the box.

"We really need to go, so if you could be so kind as to escort us out...."

As he stood up the gun he stashed in the waist of his pants fell forward from the front of his khakis. The receptionist's eyes immediately fell to the British insignia on the leather gun holster.

"That's our gun, and you didn't have a gun when you came in here. I need you to give me that gun, and you three stand away from that box, against that wall until this is sorted out."

Jon has no other options; their cards are on the table. He reaches across the table, grabs the gun, and pulls it from the holster. "No, sir, I'm sorry. We'll be leaving now, let's not make any trouble." Abdul grabs the box with the crystals and heads towards the door as Jon aims the gun at the receptionist. Jon and Morgiana follow him. Jon grabs a chair on the way out. Once outside, he wedges the chair back through the handle-shaped door knob and the wall so there is no way out of the conference room. Abdul and Morgiana are already running towards the door leading to the security area; Jon is right behind him. As they reach the door, Abdul turns the knob. It's locked from the other side. The receptionist had to buzz an electronic release to allow Ludwig to go through just a few minutes earlier.

"It's locked from the other side. We have to go out another way!" Abdul says. "Follow me!"

"Where are we going?" Jon asks.

"We have to use the service entrance. Let's go."

Jon rolls his eyes. "Not again...." He thinks out loud.

Abdul runs down the hallway to call the elevator. It seems like it's taking forever to arrive. The door finally opens and they enter. Abdul pushes a button for one floor down. "How do you know that's the service entrance?" Jon asks

"I don't. But it's one floor below street level. That makes sense to me. Any better ideas?"

The doors open one floor down. A long hallway goes to the right, and an equally long hallway goes left. "This way." Abdul says and starts walking to the right.

"How do you know?"

"I don't, but there's an exit sign at the end of this hall, and there's nothing the other way."

Just as they start running, a doorway several feet down the hall the other way opens, and several armed guards start pouring into the hallway. Jon, Morgiana and Abdul are exposed to their line of attack until they reach the end of the hall. "Run!" Jon yells, and they go as fast as they can towards the end of the hall. The guards are yelling for them to stop, and soon there are gunshots ringing down the hall. Jon knows he doesn't have time to stop and return fire; they are almost at the end of the hall. As they reach the door, a bullet ricochets off the door handle just as Abdul is reaching for it, sparks flying in all directions. Abdul's eyes light up as he pushes down on the door handle. They spill into the next room, looking for their next move.

It's a shipping and receiving area as Abdul had hoped. A lone clerk is sitting in an administrative office across the receiving bay. The exterior overhead doors are all closed. Jon looks at the door where the armed guards will be coming through any moment. "Help me Abdul!" He says as he moves towards a large metal cabinet standing near the door they will come through. Abdul turns his back against the far side of the cabinet and pushes with his leg to try to move the cabinet. Jon is lifting and pulling from the other side. The cabinet groans and screeches as it slides across the floor. Soon it is blocking the door way, just as the guards are pounding and knocking at the door. The clerk across the bay has come outside to see what is going on. Jon looks at him, pulls his gun and points in his direction. Then he points at the man and points for him to leave. After eight years of occupation, an Iraqi understands this language without any additional clarifications. He disappears into one of the back rooms.

"How do we get out?" Jon asks.

"I'm not sure," Abdul says. "This wasn't in the job description. Can't you use those fancy powers you've got there in that box?"

"Lets' try it." Jon says. He puts the crystal box on the floor and stands back several feet. He bows his head to concentrate.

"It seems there is not as much Ningalite in the walls here as there was a few floors down." A few wisps of energy puff around his head, and small lights come from the box. Jon seems to focus more, but not much energy is rising around him. Morgiana moves to the other side of the garage bays as Jon gets enough energy for a full circle of light over his head. Several moments pass without much more energy coming. Jon is impatient, and he holds his hands over his head to swing the clouds of energy around the room, then slamming them into the garage doors, trying to force them open. There is no luck, the doors are holding fast. He makes large sweeping motions with his hands as he pulls the energy across the room, then slams he cloud into the metal garage door again. No effect.

Suddenly, the motor starts to turn and the metal garage doors start to open from the bottom, natural daylight is pouring in.

"Got it!" Jon exclaims.

"Not so fast there- Aladdin. Put your magic genie away." Morgiana says. "I just found the switch to open the door in the control room. That's right, I did it. Get over it!"

CHAPTER 28

THE EMERALD BROADS

The morning after Rafi told the story of Mukhtar's discovery of the crystals, Tibi woke up early to prepare for his day to try again with Drendl and the horses. The sun was out, and the crops in the fields around Salim's farm waved in the gentle winds from one horizon to the other. The grains were growing tall now, and waves of golden color were blowing across the fields as the wind blew tall rain clouds off to the east. Asif, Rafi, Tibi and Ajit gathered outside the house getting ready for the day's activities.

Tibi was most excited. "You won't regret this day. This afternoon we will do what I have been trying to do all year. The horses will do as we command, and soon we'll use them doing our work." He could barely contain himself with his excitement. He was sure these horses held part of the future for him; he was thrilled that his new friends were going with him. They left the farm and headed back the way they had come from when Asif and Rafi had just met them.

"They always spend their afternoon at the Emerald Broads, where the river is shallow and broad just a few miles away. We'll each bring some oats and carrots in a bag; they seem to be their favorites. They know me now, I have spent every afternoon I can gaining their trust. They let me walk among them most days, and I always bring them some of their favorite foods."

They walked for an hour or so down the path they used when they met Tibi. They came to a crossing, and turned west, into the afternoon sun. They walked down a small hill from which they could see the river shimmering like green emeralds left in the sun across the flats as it made its way across the plain. On the other side of the river was a small stand of trees extending down to the water. As they came nearer, they could see the horses as they were playing in the protection of the treed area. The four travelers stood still for a while near a cropping of rocks to watch. Soon several horses came out of the trees to the water. First they drank, and then they chased each other playfully, splashing in the cool water. As they returned to the small stand of trees, they stopped and looked towards the woods and the rest of the herd. While two stood nearby on watch, two of them lay down in the water and rolled about to cool themselves off. After they had splashed and rolled around in the cool water, they stood up and shook off the excess moisture in a shower of sparkling water and mud. Then they traded jobs. As the two that were watching took their turn rolling and splashing in the water, the other two stood closely by, watching for any signs of danger.

Tibi had seen this behavior before. "This is how they survive against the predators; the tigers and the lions. They are smart. They take turns. They know me now; sometimes I think they even expect to see me. We will have to see how they react if I bring my friends with me. Follow me, several steps behind, with your bag of treats for them. Once I offer Drendl his treats, maybe the others will come to you. If all goes well, maybe we can all take a ride on their backs this afternoon!"

Tibi hurried ahead of his friends to lead. The others followed in single file down the final slope to the flats that led to the river banks. As Tibi came in to view of the horses, he slowed down considerably so as not to scare them. He held his hand back to his companions to slow them down as well. Asif, Rafi, and Ajit looked toward Tibi with fascination at his strange actions. They followed slowly and quietly. Tibi came to the edge of the water and stood proudly holding the bag of oats in front of him, well in view of the horses hidden in the trees just across the river. "Drendl!" he called "Tck Tck" he uttered gutturally towards the woods. "Tck Tck! Drendl – here are some oats and carrots for you and your friends!"

Drendl pushed his head outside the bank of trees into view. He moved a few steps forward into the water, and then stopped as he eyed the other people with Tibi, as if a trust of some sort had been broken. Tibi called him again

"Drendl, these are my friends." He motioned with his for them to them to hold up their bags of food, and they did, as if to offer something to the gods. Drendl snorted and pawed at the water in a show of protest. Nevertheless, he came forward across the water. As he did, three other horses followed him in a slow progression across the calm waters. The four men stood still as the wild horses crossed the water towards this strange new relationship they were never quite sure of. Drendl stopped just short of Tibi so that he would have to take the final few steps to meet him. Tibi offered a carrot first, which Drendl ate with great pleasure. Tibi put his head close to the side of Drendl's head and started to stroke his cheek, then stroked him along his neck and back. He filled his hand with more oats and allowed Drendl to eat from it as he stroked and spoke quietly to him.

"Drendl, the other day we went for a great ride. Today we'd like to do that with my friends. Do you think we could all ride together?"

Slowly the other three horses approached Asif, Rafi, and Ajit, each with an eye towards the bag of food. Asif and Rafi were frightened beyond words, but they knew they couldn't show it. Ajit was confident and sure of himself, although he wasn't quite sure why. As the horses approached, them, they offered carrots with outstretch arms, then let them each eat oats out of their shaking hands. Their mouths were eager and rough at first. Rafi had to pull his hand away several times before he could be confident allowing his horse to feed.

Tibi talked to Drendl, as he was stroking his back, he jumped gingerly onto Drendl's back. Tibi braced himself for Drendl to try to shake him off, to jump or kick backwards to try and remove him. But it did not happen. Drendl stayed quiet. Tibi loosened his grip and relaxed, just holding on and stroking Drendl's neck. He motioned to Asif, Rafi and Ajit to do the same with their horses.

Rafi was first to try. He held onto the mane of the horse as he tried to throw his leg over his hind quarters. He made it about half way, and then he fell to the ground with a thud. After a small cry of pain and failure from Rafi, the horse jumped away several feet in protest, but then settled down quickly.

Tibi watched and smiled. "Are you OK?"

"I'm fine. "I'm not so sure this is a good idea, but I'll try it again in a few minutes."

Next was Ajit's turn. With his smaller and younger body, he barely seemed to need to grab onto the mane to jump on the horses back. He was on in an instant as if he had done it hundreds of times before. His horse took a few steps to get used to the weight, but then stood still, with an eye towards Drendl to see if this was OK. Ajit leaned forward on his horse. "Good boy," he assured him.

Asif was last to try. After watching Rafi and Ajit, he thought he was an expert. Facing towards the back, with the horse on his left side, he awkwardly reached his left hand out to grab the horses golden mane. With a gallant leap, he swung is right foot up and over the back of the horse. He greatly underestimated his momentum, and he barely touched the back of the horse as his body carried him over his back. He flew completely over the horse and landed on the other side in the mud and grass next to the river. Tibi and Ajit couldn't contain their laughter. They laughed loudly, while the horses seemed to stomp and splash their thoughts on the situation. Asif got up, half covered in mud, which only added to the hilarity for Tibi and Ajit.

Rafi tried again, and soon the four of them were on their horses. Asif pushed the mud away from his face, making it seem almost like a mud helmet. As they stood for a moment quietly in the banks of the stream, they found a moment to relax and consider the profoundness of the situation. It didn't last long, though. Drendl snorted towards the other three horses, then again towards the woods. With near simultaneous motion, the four horses ran towards the plains just beyond the river. Out of the trees poured the rest of the horses to join in the running. In front were the four horses with people riding them, Drendl in the lead.

Tibi's flowing hair over his shirtless back was matched by the golden manes and flowing tails of the horses. Just behind him were Asif, Rafi, and Ajit on their horses. Each had expressions of joyful disbelief as the speed and sound of hundreds of hooves across the open plains filled their senses. Ajit was howling into the wind, Rafi was crouching on his mount talking to his horse. Asif was wide-eyed and scared beyond scared. They rode on up and down the rolling plains in a synchronous motion with the wind blowing the grasses in waves. They crossed the river in shallow areas, creating a fantastic shower of water sparkling in the sun against the dark water beneath them, then back onto the prairie grasses. Tibi held on to Drendl's mane tightly, and lowered his head to hold him even more closely as if to thank him for the ride of his life.

After they returned to the grove of trees, the four new riders stayed on the side of the river banks as the horses mulled about their business near the trees. Tibi talked with great excitement about the greatest ride they had ever taken. Asif moved about in stiff motions, complaining he was sore from head to toe. "It was fun, but could it ever really work? Could these animals, someday, do the work of men for them?" As the sun started to lower over the mountains on the western horizon, they gathered their belongings and headed back to Tibi's house. Asif and Rafi complained of being sore from the ride, and they were walked awkwardly up the slope on the other side of the river.

CHAPTER 29

AHMAD AND SONS DELIVERY SERVICE

The overhead delivery door of the Ministry of Antiquities lifts just enough for Jon, Morgiana and Abdul to crouch under it and exit. They jump down from the loading dock to the ramp below. Jon pulls the smaller box out of the banker's box and carries the crystals under his arm, which is a much more manageable load. Morgiana takes the rest of the contents. They run up the ramp to the alley which connects the road they had entered from to the one-way road back north. They opt to run to the front of the building. As they arrive at the street, their choices become limited. They can go back across the front of the building, in front of the glass entrance, or they can cross the street to a small park which is fenced in along its side with wrought iron. The last choice is to turn right and go down towards the National Museum of Iraq. The large entrance area is filled with mid-day markets setting up shops. There are delivery trucks, tents, and a lot of activity. It looks like a good place to get lost.

As a US soldier, Jon knows he shouldn't be walking around Baghdad without his *Full battle rattle* (full army uniform) and a security detail. He will stick out like a sore thumb as they enter the market. He's an easy target for all kinds of activities; snipers, kidnappers, vigilantes. At least now he's now carrying a gun thanks to Ludwig at the warehouse, but he has no idea if it's loaded, or if it would be of any use to him. He considers his main threats; the guards and security that will be after him from the warehouse; the violent insurgents from the war that are pervasive around the city, and the threat of being kidnapped by opportunistic militias who can get good money for a US soldier. The warehouse guards are his most immediate threat. He knows they will be after them. The other threats are only potential threats right now. So, his primary objective will be to avoid the guards who will be after them and get back to the Green Zone.

Abdul and Morgiana are already ahead of him, thinking less and running more. Jon has to sprint to catch up to them. It's not easy in his standard issue Army boots. Behind them, several guards have entered the street, looking for them. Blue police cars with bubble lights and sirens are coming towards the guards. Jon knows they need to move fast to get out of there. They reach the market area in a few moments and cross the street into the heart of the market place. The chaos of the crowds forces them to slow their pace down.

Morgiana stops Abdul for a moment. "I can leave you here. I can blend in with the other people in the market, no one will know." Abdul looks around the busy market. There are women dressed just like Morgiana everywhere.

"OK, then go. Be safe. We'll see you soon, and thank you for your help."

"Let me keep the other items from the box. I need to do some research on them. They may be useful to us."

Jon looks at the other artifacts Morgiana has. One is an old stone spearhead about the size of a man's wallet, and the other is a twisted, broken old piece of wood with a round white stone embedded in the twisted roots of the end. "OK," he says, "see what you can find out."

Morgiana flips her scarf over her face and disappears into the crowd of men and women in the market.

"Abdul, come over here. See that red van? – it delivers inside the Green Zone." Jon says.

Jon motions for Abdul to follow him. A block down the street Jon has spotted Ahmad and Sons' red produce van parked next to a market. They pick up their pace and run down the street. They turn to the back of the truck, which is open. Ahmad, the delivery man, is outside picking up some merchandise. The guards and policemen are not far behind them now. They climb into the van uninvited, but making themselves comfortable towards the front, between the driver's seat and some sacks of rice. Moments later they can see the guards rushing by the back of the van, looking for traces of Jon and Abdul. Ahmad has arrived with his hand-cart at the bottom of the ramp, which discourages the guards from suspecting anything amiss inside the truck. Jon and Abdul try to hide as best they can against the inner wall of the truck. Ahmad pushes his cart up the ramp and unloads his boxes towards the back of the open area, unsuspecting of any potential intruders. He straps the hand-truck to the metal wall and reaches up to pull the overhead door down. As the door rolls down, the inside turns dark, and the noise of the market lessens. Jon exhales as he hears the rumble of metal bearings while Ahmad pushes the metal walk ramp underneath the bed of the truck. In a few moments, Ahmad climbs into the driver's seat just a foot or so away from Abdul. Ahmad turns the key to start the truck, and soon he is pulling out into traffic away from the marketplace. He turns the radio on for a pleasant distraction, and it is tuned to the Western music station. Bon Jovi is singing his latest hit song. *"Who says you can't go home? There's only one place they call me one of their own."*

Baghdad roads are notoriously bumpy and rough, which proves problematic for the stowaways. The truck lumbers up Nasir Street and turns left onto Qahira Street, pitching left and right. A bag of cumin falls from its stowed position above and lands a few inches from Jon. A small cloud of cumin dust blows into his face, which causes an instant and somewhat loud sneeze. Ahmad whips his head around to look back into the truck.

Jon looks up at Ahmad, as shocked that his cover is blown as Ahmad seems to be that there is a stowaway in the truck with him.

"Ahmad! It's OK! We met earlier today at the English house. I was coming out, and you were bringing in produce to an older man – I think his name was Behader."

"Behader?" Ahmad asks. "I don't know Behader." But Jon knew he did, if only in the way he restated the name with the proper linguistic inflections. Ahmad was furious to find a stowaway on his truck. He braked hard and swerved to the right to pull onto the curb, rocking the truck and causing more of his cargo to fall. A jar of figs falls on Abdul's head.

"Augh!" Abdul yells.

Ahmad stops the truck abruptly and slams it into Park as he pushes the emergence brake down.

"There are two of you here?"

He leaps out of his seat and turns to come back to the cargo area of the truck. "Are there any more? Get out of my truck! What do you think you're doing here?"

Abdul stands into the aisle of the truck and starts to speak Arabic to Ahmad. "Ahmad, we don't want any trouble. We were being chased in the marketplace by some militia men. We had to hide somewhere quickly and your truck was open. We're sorry for any problem we have caused you. We have to get back inside the Green Zone, and this is the American you met this morning at the guest house he was staying in. He knew you would be going back to the Green Zone. We never intended any harm. We have papers to get in."

"Never intended any harm? Do you realize what could happen to me if I was caught with stowaways going into the Green Zone? Do you know what it has taken for me to get the clearance to sell inside the Green Zone? All of that would be ruined. My business, my livelihood would be destroyed. I am not your chariot ride back to the Green Zone." Ahmad switches to English. "GET OUT!"

Jon decides to try to convince Ahmad. "Ahmad, we can pay you well. We just need to get back inside."

This only infuriates Ahmad even more. "Guns are forbidden to be carried into the Green Zone, but I can carry a knife. You will get out of here – Now!"

Ahmad reaches behind the passenger side of the truck and pulls out a thirty inch Arabian machete knife hidden in a leather sleeve along the side of the chair. The edge of the blade flashes in the day light coming through the window as Ahmad swings it menacingly at the two stowaways.

"OK OK!" Jon yells. "Like we said, we don't want any trouble." Jon clenches his box with the crystals closer to him and they move back to the rear of the truck. There is a leather strap used to lift the overhead door, and Abdul pulls up on it. The door panels slide upwards allowing the early afternoon light to fill the truck, temporarily blinding Jon and Abdul.

"GET OUT!" Ahmad affirms.

"We're out! We're out!" Jon said as they jump to the cement sidewalk below.

Ahmad appears in the rear of the truck, brandishing his machete by waving it back and forth in the afternoon sun. He's yelling obscenities in Arabic, which needed no interpretation by Abdul. The overhead door slams closed from within, and in a few seconds the sign on the back "Ahmad and Sons – Fresh Produce and Breads since 1978" is fading into a smaller and smaller spot on the horizon as the truck drives down the road.

"Well, he seemed like such a nice gentleman." Jon remarks as he looks around at the barren cement wasteland they are cast into. The road had a rising arc to it with a cement barricade on the side. Soon they identify it as a bridge.

"I didn't think he was nice at all."

"No, no. – I know. That was just humor. It was a joke. And not a very good one. It doesn't translate well. Let's see where we are. We'll have to find our way out of here now. Once Ahmad gets to the Green Zone, we'll have even more people looking for us and tighter security if he reports us as people trying to get in. Let's go over this rise ahead and see what we can find."

As they walk over the cement bridge it became evident they are walking over railroad tracks, and on the other side is the Main Station in Baghdad.

"Where there is a train station, there will be taxis!" Jon says enthusiastically.

They walk down the other side of the bridge around the escarpment to the train station. As Jon had hoped, there was a taxi stand in front of the station.

"We're outside the Green Zone, so you can only take authorized taxis into the Green Zone from here. Abdul advised. "Do you still have your paperwork? I still have mine tucked away in my pocket. There is no reason to think our paperwork won't get us back in since it was fully authorized both ways when we left. I don't think the Ministry of Antiquities and the Baghdad police will have had enough time to notify the Green Zone security. They just are not that efficient. Also, not every taxi is authorized to enter the Green Zone, so we'll have to find one that is authorized and willing to take us. The Green Zone is only a kilometer or so down the 14th of July Avenue just ahead, but we are much better off to enter by taxi than to try to enter on foot, which might be suspicious."

"I have my paperwork. Can you find the right taxi?"

"Yes Mister Jon. We'll find the right taxi. Come with me."

The Main Station for the Iraq railroad is a majestic transportation center befitting any western city capitol. The domed interior is a hybrid of Iraqi aestheticism mixed with modern transportation needs. After a quick look around the interior, Abdul goes outside to interview several taxi drivers. Soon, Abdul finds a suitable taxi that has authority to go into the Green Zone. Abdul motions for Jon to get into the taxi and they proceed out of the train station, North on Qahira street. They turn left onto 14th of July Avenue, named after the revolution in 1958 that established Iraq as independent state from Britain and the Hashemite monarchy. As they turn the corner they can see the crossed swords over the entrance to the Green Zone in front of them. In a few moments they pull up to the security gate and wait for a guard to approach the car. The driver hands him his papers, and Abdul lowers his window to allow the guard to address him and Jon.

"Good afternoon gentlemen" he starts. May I have your papers please? What was your business out of the Green Zone today?"

Jon hands all their paperwork to the guard. "We just left to go to the Ministry of Antiquities to pick up some religious artifacts. I'm on assignment to transport them back to Basra. We were able to get most of them, and we're returning to base to wait for transportation tomorrow."

The guard disappears for a moment into the guard shack with all the paperwork. Several awkward and uncomfortable moments pass as all their documents, forged or legitimate, are scrutinized. The guard returns soon, with paperwork in hand.

Jon takes this as a good sign. "OK Schultz. Where are the antiquities you collected?"

Jon stops for a moment and picks up the box that contains the crystals and shows it to the guard.

"The box is sealed. There are some sort of religious stones inside that are very valuable to a temple outside of Basra." He doesn't offer any more information than he feels he needs to.

The guard considers the box and looks at the old markings on the side, and is satisfied that is the box referenced in the paperwork. "Very well gentlemen. Have a good rest of the afternoon. Please keep your speed down in the Green Zone."

The taxi pulls ahead. Jon and Abdul sit back in their seats and exhale huge sighs. The relief is palpable. The driver speaks up again, "Now what's the address you want to go to again?"

"The British ambassador's house. It should be just ahead on the left near the British Embassy." As the taxi drives down 14th of July Boulevard, the radio has local Baghdad news on in Arabic. Abdul is listening. The news of a theft at the Ministry of Antiquities has already hit the news. They are reporting several ancient artifacts either destroyed or stolen by thieves dressed as American soldiers and Iraqi security escorts. As they turn onto the road with the ambassador's house, there are several police squad cars outside the house gates. The streets are blocked with the police activity.

Abdul leans forward in the car to speak to the driver. "Let's turn around here. I have another place we need to go." Abdul continues to speak in Arabic with another destination that Jon does not understand. The driver turns his head to look at Abdul and gives a strong reply, as if to suggest he should not go there. Abdul counters and insists on his remarks. The taxi driver turns around as if resigned to drive them to a destination he does not agree with.

Abdul sits back in his seat and speaks in a low voice to Jon. "Jon, it's not safe for you to go back to the ambassador's house. What happened at the antiquities warehouse is already on the news. I just heard it on the radio as we were driving here. We're going to go somewhere else where we can stay low until later tonight."

"Where are we going?" Jon asks.

"You will see, Mister Jon. A place where no one will be looking for us, but still inside the Green Zone."

CHAPTER 30

LEARNING TO GLIDE

The next morning the group of four was up early getting some food prepared for a morning meal. They collected some eggs from the barn and fresh water from the well. There was bread and some grains, vegetables, and some of the leftover poultry from the night before. As they sat down to eat the meal, they talked about what to work on next.

"We have to understand the power of the crystal we have. We have to use the power of the gods and whatever else we have to defeat Mukhtar," Rafi said.

"I know something about the yellow crystal." Asif said. "It can open a doorway in the ground that brings you inside the world of the gods. On the inside there is nothing holding you back from moving around. You can glide in whichever direction you want. As you travel, you can see different destinations go by. Each looks like a different pattern in circles. The pattern looks like the circle in the ground we saw where Mukhtar stood. His circle was blue, but the pattern in the middle looked familiar, I think it was one of the patterns I saw in the gliding tunnels. We need to train with the yellow crystal today and see if we can learn how to use it for our advantage."

"Rafi, if you could make the lights glow in the cave, then you can use the greater power of the crystals, just like me. Ajit and Tibi, we need to know if you can use the crystals. If you can, then we can all travel between the portals very quickly. If you can't, you can contribute other things to make our plans reality."

"And just what are those plans?" Rafi asked. "How are we going to defeat Mukhtar, who has the power of armed gangs of marauders taking over every city he wants? Plus, he has the power of the gods, of fire and lightning."

Asif thought for a moment. He looked down at the table and then started talking slowly. "Here's what I'm thinking. We'll start tomorrow on Ajit's farm."

II

The burned out buildings at Ajit's farm had a deserted emptiness about them after the fires that destroyed them. The stains of smoke painted the bricks black outside every opening of the buildings. The roof of the barn had collapsed. Friends and townspeople had come to help and they piled a lot of the burned equipment behind the barn to see if it could be re-used. The black, twisted and charred remains spoke as a testament to the evil that now roamed the land around it. Where there was once a vibrant, noisy working farm, an eerie quiet blanketed the senses with the same intensity. Ajit started picking through the rubble which was his home just days before. Tibi started to help him.

Asif and Rafi walked past the burned remains in the dimming sunlight, past the remains of the equipment barn, to an open area by the river.

Asif took out the yellow crystal from the satchel he was using to carry it. It looked innocuous in his hands; a simple crystal with a simple beauty about it.

"If Mukhtar could use his blue and red crystals to appear here, I hope we can use the same area with the yellow one. We just need to find exactly where to use it."

Asif placed the crystal on the ground several feet away from the two of them, to the side of the open area where they stood. Asif stood quietly, his head bowed and arms crossed. As he went deeper into his meditation, the crystal began to glow soft yellow. The brightness slowly grew over a minute or so. Rafi looked around to see if any changes were happening outside the immediate area of the crystal. Small yellow wisps of waving energy appeared above Asif. First there was just a hint, then it appeared with certainty and form. It gathered in strength as it undulated around his head, emanating yellow from within. It became a contiguous circular cloud, swirling and gathering energy into itself. A breeze picked up around the area, blowing loose leaves and bending the grassy areas outside the area they were standing. Slowly, in the open area where they stood, a circle appeared emanating yellow light from within. About the diameter of two men, the yellow brightness grew. Soon a shape inside the circle appeared. It was a pentagon with evenly spaced lines around the side of the circle. Rafi watched intently as the brightness of the circle and pentagon grew until it appeared to separate from the firm earth around it.

"Asif – it's here – open your eyes!" Rafi yelled loud enough that he hoped to break Asif out of his meditation.

Asif did not react at first. As if he was carrying a large burden that might break if he moved too quickly, Asif lifted his arms outspread, while he lifted his head. He raised his eyes and turned slightly to look at the circle and pentagon shape within the circle. It stayed brightly lit as he carried the energy from over his head to over the circle. Rafi watched as Asif moved the energy. Asif slowly turned to look at Rafi, and with one sudden motion, swept his arms downward as he flung himself down to the ground. With a sudden flash the yellow lights, the circle and pentagon disappeared with an electronic snap! It crackled the air and sucked the energy and light back into the circle that had appeared.

After several moments, Asif looked up from his side as he lay on the ground. "Rafi, we can control this. I could feel the control. I can feel the energy as it rises, and it responds to my direction. We can do this!"

"This has to be power of the gods. We need to use this to defeat Mukhtar. But once we are done, let's be careful about how this power will be used! We need to make sure it is never used for evil; only for the power of good."

"I don't think any man is divine. That is something only the gods can know. Isn't it an odd twist of fate that we must use the power of the gods to guarantee they are never used again? Maybe that's our destiny in our lives; that is our purpose from the gods themselves. They put me in that cave to find the power of the rocks and the crystals, and they will guide us to keep the power of the gods away from the frailties of humans. I have to believe we will succeed, since the gods have put us here. Let's learn the power that we have and how to use it. Now we have the chance to enter the world of the gods themselves, where no man has gone. Yet it must be our destiny to do so. Let's go to the world of the gods. Let's go through the portal and see what is there. I'm convinced it is part of how we will defeat Mukhtar, but we have to understand what is on the other side."

Rafi agreed "We're on the dawn of a new era. Just look at what Tibi is doing with the horses. Let's do this and see what our destiny brings."

Asif got up from the ground and gathered the crystal and the satchel. He examined it to see if it had changed in any way. The crystal was unchanged. The satchel was burned around the edge He put the crystal back down on the ground on top of the satchel.

Asif lowered his head to meditate again. Rafi lowered his head and meditated also. Soon the yellow glow returned from the crystal and created a swirling storm of energy over Asif's head. Rafi moved toward the open area where the circle appeared and watched as the edges of the circle slowly came to life. Asif slowly raised his arms and turned towards the circle. The circle burned brighter and brighter until there were beams of light shooting into the sky from the outline of the circle and pentagram, and it seemed to separate from the earth around it.

Asif motioned to Rafi to come to his side. Rafi came near him. Asif pulled him close and put his arm around his side. In one smooth motion, he pulled Rafi along with him as he jumped into the center of the circle. As they landed in the middle, the swirling waves of yellow energy swooped down into the center. The energy beam and light was sucked into the circle, and Asif and Rafi were gone. The lights pulled into the circle vanished with a loud snap that echoed across the surrounding sky.

-

Inside the portal, Rafi and Asif were standing on top of an invisible membrane that separated them from a river of streaming energy. The glowing yellow swirls of energy curled and undulated below them. They became the walls, ceiling, and floor of a tunnel. They were floating over the floor, and without a visible footing, they had no solid bearings. They were somewhat out of balance as they tried to stand still. Rafi moved down the tunnel in the direction of the energy. Asif followed, and they simply slid down the tunnel. As they moved, they started to notice changes in the energy stream that ran around them. There were curves in the energy, and there were several branches contributing to the stream as they moved on. The floor felt like tensioned skin or membrane above the energy. It bounced and undulated with the energy flow below it. It became more and more difficult to stand as they gained speed and moved through the tunnel. As they traveled further, the energy sped up around them. They held onto each other as best they could to stand up. The energy increased and it seemed as if the ride became more and more bumpy. Soon they were being tossed about, trying to stay upright, out of control. The bumps increased in frequency, and with a sudden yell they were thrown to the floor on their stomachs.

Rafi and Asif started thrashing about. They were flailing about on their stomachs and backs as they tried to get their bearings and stand up again. Each time they tried to stand they fell, and as they did the floor bounced around them violently. Finally, Rafi stopped trying to stand up. He lay still on his stomach and slowly moved with the energy. He simply stayed on his stomach. He glided with ease down the tunnel, as Asif still struggled to stand. Asif saw him and decided to stop trying to stand. He lay on his stomach and stopped fighting the urge to become upright. He started gliding. In a moment he was gliding towards Rafi, controlled and much less stressed.

After several minutes they understood the first rules of gliding.

First rule: Don't try to stand. Lay down.

Second Rule: You can't hear anything inside the portal. Use hand gestures.

They moved faster and faster, gliding along the tunnels, banking the sides of the tunnels on the curves, then quickly along through the straight areas. Their relative speed was impossible to determine. They couldn't tell if the energy was moving beneath them or if they were moving over it. With no visual cues for bearing, they could only glide onwards, levitated above the ever moving floor of energy, bending through corners, and riding over bumps, then landing on the invisible floor beyond. As they looked down at the floor beneath them, the stream of energy ran in the same direction they were moving. Within the stream, however, there were counter waves and spots moving in the opposite direction, giving a greater perception of speed as they went.

Asif, slightly ahead of Rafi, saw a change in the tunnel ahead. There was an intersection approaching. He raised his right hand towards Rafi to slow him down as the approached. Asif did his best to use his concentration to slow himself down. Rafi did the same. It took a lot longer to slow down than it had to speed up, as if they were going downhill. Their inertia pushed them ahead. As the intersection was approaching, it became apparent it was another tunnel similar to theirs. Asif wanted to see where it might lead. He braked hard with his mind, and held his hands in front of himself to try to slow down. The intersection was coming too quickly for him to stop before turning, so he grabbed onto the corner of the wall on the far side of the left turn he was trying to make. The side of the tunnel gave way a little bit as his fingers grabbed on, but his motion was still too fast and he swung around feet first into the tunnel wall beyond where he was. The walls shook and bounced from where he had grabbed and bounced his feet on the walls. The motion of the energy became severely disrupted. Waves of light and energy crested and came crashing against the membrane as the streams became unhinged from their synchronous flow. As the waves crashed, they were thrown wildly up and down, side to side, bouncing uncontrollably, as if caught in the crashing surf of a twenty foot wave. The bouncing threw them about without signs of slowing down. Rafi tried to reach out to gain some footing, or to lie down, but he was bounced head-first upside down and twisted around in a full spin. Asif was spinning end over end, bouncing from wall to wall as if falling without gravity. With each bounce the walls reacted violently, sending more cresting waves of energy down the line. Slowly, the streaming energy re-appeared within the crushing waves. The violent bouncing started to slow down. The synchronous stream started flowing again. Asif and

Rafi lay prone on the floor of the tunnel, motionless and exhausted, but unhurt.

Third rule: Don't smash into the walls. They bounce back at you.

Fourth rule: Don't go too fast. It takes longer to slow down than it does to speed up.

Slowly they glided back to the intersection. Asif moved slowly and cautiously, trying to make sure not to grab the walls with any sort of force. This time they could see the details of the intersection clearly. There were signs of some sort in the start of each corridor. In the corridor where they came from, they saw the circle with the pentagon sign in it. To their right was a circle with seven small equally sized circles in it. The signs themselves appeared in the energy flow, with the energy flowing over the drawings like water flowing over rocks beneath them. Asif motioned to Rafi to follow him. Soon they were gliding along this new corridor. A few minutes later they could see an apparent end to the tunnel. It was a dark circle. They slowed down, but as they neared the energy flow beneath them started rushing towards the circle faster and faster. They came closer and seemed to pick up speed along the way. Now they could see the circle more clearly – with the same three smaller circles inside the larger one, burning brighter and brighter in the same yellow glow they had seen. They moved faster towards the end and it was clear they were going to collide with the circle at the end of the tunnel. Just as they hit, a blinding light flashed around them. The energy stream was gone, and they could hear the loud snap! behind them.

Asif and Rafi lay on the ground in a brand new area outside the tunnels. Like the other portal areas, there was water nearby. Not far from the water were ruins of a small temple. It had been abandoned many years ago, and now only five or six stone columns stood, some with other stones across their tops, some just standing alone. Rafi got up and looked around. They couldn't tell where they were, but Rafi thought it seemed like an area far to the south east of them, judging by the size of the river and the warmth of the air.

After looking around the area for some time, Rafi wanted to use his meditation to bring the portal back for traveling. Asif agreed. Rafi took the crystal from Asif's satchel and laid it on the ground in front of him. He lowered his head and crossed his arms, deep in thought. Soon a yellow glow came from the crystal and lit the area around the satchel. At times, small wisps of energy appeared above his thick curly black hair, but they never joined together in a continuous motion. After several minutes, Rafi opened his eyes and relaxed his body. The energy stream wouldn't seem to get any stronger for him.

"We'll try again and again." Asif said. "It takes practice and concentration. You have to have intense focus while letting go at the same time. It's a difficult balance. But once you get it, you'll get it forever. It's like when you swim underwater and try to relax. You have to focus, but relax at the same time."

Asif stood up and started his meditation routine. Soon the portal was glowing brightly, and Asif and Rafi jumped simultaneously into the center of the circle that appeared. They spent the rest of the night traveling through the portals. They would glide down the main corridor they had been on, and when they found an intersection they would slow down as best they could. More often than not, they would have to back-track to the intersection and take the other corridor to a new portal. Each corridor was marked with a new circle and drawing in the circle. Rafi noticed that no matter which way they went, the counter current in the energy flow beneath them was showing them how to get back to where they came from, and they followed it several times back to the corridor with the circle and pentagon which would lead them back to Ajit's farm. Rafi tried his meditation at every portal, and each time it grew stronger and soon he was able to control the energy cloud around him. He wasn't quite confident in opening the portal enough to jump through, but he knew that would come in time.

Each portal had a different location, and they guessed they visited ten different locations that day. Most were in remote areas along rivers, but each had some sort of building nearby, as if some ancient group had built shelters or temples near each portal. Some were near market places or temples that were still being used, and they scared more than one person at the market near the temple when the circle appeared, and then the two of them appeared, seemingly out of nowhere. The most upsetting was the portal that led them back to the house where Asif had been raised with Mukhtar. This was the place where Asif had arrived at after being trapped in the cave for days. Asif longed to see his mother in the gardens around the house, but he knew he would have to leave. Rafi was most upset by returning to the cave where he had almost starved to death, and where their friend Sabur had died while with them. The cave was dark and deathly quiet as they entered. Most of the crystal rocks had been mined by Mukhtar, so the only source of light they had was from the crystal they carried with them.

After traveling to many other portals, they returned to their home. The circle in the ground near Ajit's barn started to glow a bright yellow, then burned with the energy from the corridor within. A burst of light exploded from within, and suddenly Asif and Rafi appeared inside the circle, lying on the ground. Ajit spotted them and ran to them to help them recover.

CHAPTER 31

AL SALAM PALACE

The taxi with Jon and Abdul pulls to a stop along a run-down street on the west side of the Green Zone. Outside the taxi is mammoth shell of a building. It has been burned out and hollowed out by fire and bombings.

"This is Al Salam Palace," Abdul announces. "It has been abandoned since Shock and Awe. It is scheduled to be rebuilt and used by the coalition forces, but obviously, not yet. There are bunkers underneath. We can wait in one of them until nightfall, when we will make our way back to Zawara gardens and the portal."

Jon heads towards the palace hesitantly. The huge structure blights the entire block it sits on. Over a million square feet of palace, completely abandoned. Construction trucks and chain link fencing line the outside, a hopeful sign that the loud silence the structure brings to the city block will end one day. They walk to the front atrium and enter, unchallenged. Their footsteps echo down the vacant halls that once hosted lavish affairs for the friends of Saddam Hussein.

Abdul points to a stairway on the south side. "This way. I used to come here when I was young. My sister worked as a servant for Saddam Hussein. She showed me some of the secrets of the palace. The bunkers Saddam had built downstairs should be a good place for us to pass the time without being worried about any visitors."

They walk down a flight of stairs and proceed down a short hallway. The walls are built from stone blocks but Jon notices no sign of Ningalite so far. Abdul stops and opens a metal door on the right, and Jon follows him inside. The bunker is about fifteen feet long by fifteen feet wide. At the far end the roof has collapsed, leaving an open sky overhead. Jon sits in the corner, the first time he has considered relaxing since he left the British Ambassadors home this morning.

"This will do fine for now, Abdul. But what about some food? We haven't had anything to eat all day."

Abdul smiles and takes something out of his pocket. "Will this do Mister Jon? It's not much, but it's better than nothing." Abdul produces some figs and nectarines from his pocket. Jon's eyes light up with excitement.

"Where did you get them?"

"I got them from the delivery truck and our friend Ahmad. I hope he'll forgive me, but I helped myself to some of the produce that was next to us as we were sitting there."

"Well, I hope you are forgiven as well, Abdul. Thank you. Now that we have a moment to ourselves, why don't you tell me a little bit about yourself? Were you raised here in Baghdad? How did you get to know Hassan?"

Abdul looks down and smiles quietly as he thinks about his relationship with Hassan. "When I was a young boy, my family was very poor. We lived in Sadr City, the slums of Baghdad. My father had been killed in the first gulf war, and my mother did everything she could to provide for my sisters and me. But my mother was not well and couldn't work all the time, so we were forced to move into the slums. I was only a child, and my sisters were even younger than me. My uncle lived with us and did his best, but we felt we were barely kept alive."

"My mother became more ill and couldn't care for herself at times, so my uncle and I would try to find what we could for our family. We would beg for what we could and sometimes there would be food that would be brought to us. But medicine for my mother was a fantasy to us. The clinics would only come into the slums once a month or so, and many times it was impossible to get my mother there during the few hours the clinics were open. My uncle heard of some medicine that was being delivered to the slums, so we went with a friend of his to see what we could find. At the gate to the slums, there was a car that would stop and drop many kinds of medicines and supplies every Tuesday night. We went there to see what we could find. A man always drove. A woman would get out of car, open her trunk, and drop bags and boxes off, just inside the gates of the slum. We picked through what she left and sure enough there was some medicine that helped my mother in many ways. I was just a boy, so I loved to go with my uncle and try to catch a glimpse of the angel lady who was bringing us gifts. I remember the car; I thought it was the fanciest car in the world, although now I know it was really just a regular city car."

"I would watch as they drove away, and sometimes I would see that there was a child in the car. I remember running along the fence, trying to keep up with them as they rode away. Even as a child, I wanted to be the type of person she must be. I wanted to help others who were in need and never worry about what was in it for me. I wanted all that, but I knew that to have it, I would have to work with others to take back our country. Not just from the Americans and the allies, but from the corrupt government that was setting up. I'm not one that wants to die trying to expose everything wrong with our new government. I just want to try my best to be true to myself while I work to make the country better."

"Hassan's mother became a local legend to us in the slum after she was arrested and mutilated by Saddam. My mother got much better thanks to a lot of the supplies that she left, and the government finally gave us some money for my father's death. It was enough to get out of the slum, and into an apartment. I got a job when I was thirteen and worked to keep my family fed. I learned English while I was on the job. Sometimes I would go to Hassan's house and leave small tokens of appreciation, and sometimes we could leave some free rice we received from the government. It was there that I first met Hassan, only I was much older than the small boy I was running along the fence. We would talk about our lives, our hopes, and our fears. It was Hassan who taught me not to be afraid of the future. We would talk about how to let go of our anger and hatred, but not to forget. My father died about two years ago, and my mother is still very ill. I have found a woman I love, and we are going to get married as soon as possible so my mother can be at the wedding. Despite all that is happening, the wedding will be in a few weeks. It will be a simple ceremony out in the country with just a few family members. I'll have my mother there, my brother and sister, her family and a few friends. I have a few days off from my job, but if Hassan needs anything, I will always be there."

"After Shock and Awe, Hassan invited me to be part the clan of the Boars Head. He told me how Mudlarek had been responsible for his mother's mutilation, and how Mudlarek was part of the ancient order called the Hand of the Red Fist. It's amazing that two secret societies could remain sworn enemies over thousands of years. We knew that Shock and Awe had uncovered some of the ancient secrets of Iraq, and they were related to the hatred between the clans. These are things that have been buried for thousands of years, and now we face the same dangers our ancestors did all those years ago. It wasn't until today that I truly realized the power that has been unleashed. And now I understand why the power has to be kept from Mudlarek and the rest of the clan."

"Jon, you are part of that ancestry. You could see it today in the Ministry of Antiquities. The power was surrounding you and passing through you. It was surging through you and around you. If Mudlarek or the Hand of the Red Fist was able to get the same power, imagine the destruction they could do. You have a purpose in our history now. You have to bring those crystals back to Hassan and have them hidden again for eternity."

The evening light dimmed, and Jon and Abdul rested in the bunker below the Al Salam Palace. They could hear the distant sounds of city life several blocks away as the noises of the day turned to the noises of the night. A breeze picked up as the sun set, and the evening call to prayer could be heard across the city.

Jon was growing more and more impatient to get back to the base camp with the crystals. He was thrust unwillingly into this adventure. Now the fate of possibly hundreds of Iraqi and American lives was in his hands. If Mudlarek were to get the crystals, he would destroy the Clan of the Boars Head, and he would continue his deceit and destruction of the coalition forces. Jon was determined to keep the crystals from his hands, and expose Mudlarek for what he is. None of that was going to happen from the broken bunker of this shell of a palace. He needed to get back to the base camp quickly. But it wasn't safe to go back to the portal in the Green Zone during the busy afternoon or early evening hours. The portal area was next to the Zawara Lake, which was very popular in the late afternoons and evenings for walking and relaxing. They would have to wait until everyone had gone to bed.

As midnight approached, Abdul wanted to discuss the plans for returning to the Lake.

"Jon, it won't be safe to walk the streets, even at this hour of night. They will be looking for us. I know another way. There are secret tunnels underneath the city that connect many of the main government locations. We can get from here to the Tomb of the Unknown Soldier, and from there it's a short walk to the portal. My sister had told me about the tunnels and after the invasion I did some exploring with friends. As long as you have your flashlight, we will be able to find our way. The secret tunnel entrances are marked with portraits of Saddam and other historical figures. I can show you where the entrance is from this palace."

"Secret tunnels? Under the city? Does the US know?"

"Saddam built them as a spider web around the city to move about undetected. It was partly for easy transportation, partly for defense. I don't know if the US or allies know about them, but I suspect they would no longer be there if they did. They would be a big security risk."

Abdul stands and stretches from his resting spot, and directs Jon in the direction to go.

"Let's go."

Jon stands, stiff from the after-effects of an adrenaline filled morning followed by an afternoon and evening in relative relaxation. Jon finds his flashlight attached to his uniform, and flashes it at Abdul.

"Let's go, but hopefully we won't need the light very much. I don't want to draw attention."

The walk through the tunnels starts uneventfully. The air starts off hot and stuffy, but as they proceed along the stone passageway they felt occasional breezes from the ventilation on the streets above.

"These tunnels were constructed so the politically powerful could travel between locations without the inconvenience of using the public streets. They were ventilated from the street with air ducts disguised as fireplaces, statues or drains. But they are very effective at naturally drawing in air and circulating through the tunnel. They are truly a wonder of engineering."

After walking thirty minutes, Jon was becoming a little anxious.

"The tunnels were going downhill more, and the air is getting so stagnant!"

As they round a corner, Jon can see light up ahead. It is a welcome sight through all the darkness. As they approach the light, it is a mixed blessing. The good news, there is plenty of light. The bad news is that it came from Ningalite. After the incident in the Ministry of Antiquities earlier in the day, Jon wasn't sure at all if the power of the Ningalite combined with the crystals he was carrying was controllable.

"Abdul, what happens if we repeat the energy we generated in the ministry earlier today? How will we be able to control it?"

"I'm not sure we have much choice now, Mister Jon. We should almost be at the Tomb of the Unknown Soldier, so hopefully we can get out of the tunnels before we run into any trouble with the Ningalite."

"Let's pick up our pace, just in case." Jon replies.

The tunnel turns upward slightly. The floor become uneven, to the point where the two travelers are stepping over the separate sections of boulders lay below. The tunnel comes to an end, or at least a junction, several yards ahead. As they approach the junction, they come to a portrait of Saddam Hussein carved into the stone. As Jon approaches, Ningalite from within the stone grows brighter. The edges of Saddam's silhouette glows bright red. Jon wonders how many, if any, people have seen the portrait in this way. *Are they the first to know of the hidden secrets of these portraits? Or were they originally produced this way, left only for the few who carry the Ninhursag gene with them to discover?* They pause and look at the portrait in wonder for a moment. Abdul sees the soft light of the Ninhursag in Jon's eyes.

They exit the tunnels not far from the Tomb of the Unknown Soldier through a panel door and into a street underpass. The streets are quiet. No sign of Ningalite clouds following Jon. They are free to go to the portal unencumbered. Abdul shows Jon the way around the massive Tomb of the Unknown Soldier. After sever blocks they can see the park and the low darkness of Zawara Lake on the horizon. Their step quicken as their determination to use the portal heightens.

The portal access area is thirty yards from the lake, and about twenty yards away from the walkway around the lake. Jon and Abdul consider the significant moment they were living in the history of Iraq. Thousands of years of brotherhood and ancient tradition have persevered without seeing what they have just witnessed in the past few hours. Now, their mission is to make sure it is hidden again for thousands of years more. Their journey will be the heart of stories for generations more.

"It's time to go back," Jon says. "Let's make it happen. I'm sorry you can't come with me. When this is over, I hope we can meet again and tell these stories to your family, and to the rest of the clan."

Abdul smiles. Jon turns and bows his head as he concentrates with the yellow crystal at his side and the container of red and blue crystals under his arm. Soon the yellow clouds of energy are swirling around his head, then swooping across the night sky around the lake. The light dips and swoops into the water, and Abdul swore he could see another similar stream of energy moving through the water of the lake itself, then sweeping upwards and joining the energy in the air. The portal circle burns brightly in yellow lights, then the swirling energy converges above the portal. Jon jumps into the center, and the beams of lights crash down into the ground around him. The snap! at the end is triple the loudness as the sound before, and Abdul is thrown backwards by the compression wave of the energy passing by.

He rises from the ground, his hair displaced and clothes disheveled. "Note to myself- stand a little further back next time!"

CHAPTER 32

GOLDY, LIGHTNING, AND COMET TAIL

While Asif and Rafi were in the portal practicing, Ajit picked through the rubble of his barn to see what he could recover. He found several things he thought he could use, and he packed them in a burned out leather sack he found. Tibi also looked through the mess, and made a collection of things he thought he could use as well. As the light faded in the evening, they lifted what they could onto their backs, and headed back towards Tibi's farm.

The next morning they worked in Tibi's barn to start on their project. Tibi showed Ajit what he thought would work for the horses. He cut leather strands and measured them to various lengths. Ajit watched and worked with his hammer and some of the leftovers from his barn to put his creations together. After an hour or so they had a very crude set of reins they could try on the horses. They weren't so sure the horses would like it, but they had to try. Tibi wanted to try their new invention on Drendl and the other horses; he could hardly wait to go see them again down by the flats of the river.

He gathered more oats and carrots together from the back of their barn, and put them in four separate bags. Then he went back with a smile on his face and added a few extra carrots for his favorite, Drendl. He wanted to be sure all the horses were rewarded, but he was OK rewarding Drendl just a little more. Just before mid-day they slung their bags over their backs and headed down the trail towards the river flats and the herd of horses.

Drendl and the small brood were already standing in the water as Tibi and Ajit approached. Tibi held up the leather bag and called to Drendl.

"Tck tck! Here Drendl, I have come with your treats for today!" Drendl nodded with approval and pawed with his front right hoof in the water. Tibi approached and held some oats and a carrot out for him. Drendl came to him approvingly, apparently very hungry. Ajit came forward with a bag lifted high for the other horses to see. The horse that he rode the other day came forward to him first, and Ajit had oats and a carrot ready for him. His horse ate approvingly, and Ajit stroked the side of his head and neck gently and firmly.

"I'll call you Goldy. Yes, Goldy for the way your hair shines in the sunlight." Goldy nodded with approval as he stuck his muzzle deep into the bag of oats that Ajit had brought.

After Drendl and Goldy were fed, Ajit and Tibi fed the other horses that carried riders the day before. Tibi named Asif's horse "Lightning" for the crooked white spot he had across his forehead, against his chestnut colored hair. Ajit named Rafi's horse "Comet Tail", saying his tail looked like the comet he had seen as a child as it raced across the heavens at night. Tibi worked with Drendl to fit the bridle and reins. Drendl protested profoundly at first. He bucked and pulled back from Tibi. Ajit watched attentively to see how it fit and how he might improve his creation. After Drendl was fitted with the bridle, Tibi jumped on his back and rode him up and down the river bed. This time the ride was not as uncontrolled as the ride the day before. Tibi could direct him to turn right, turn left, go faster, and slow down.

"Tck Tck" Tibi called "Let's go boy!" Tibi shook the reins and he rose up on his heels to allow Drendl to take off down the River.

"Woh!" he called. Drendl slowed down. They rode out to the plains. Drendl was working with Tibi as much as Tibi was working with Drendl. Drendl slowed down to a trot, and together they came back to the grotto where Ajit and Goldy were waiting.

Ajit looked at the bridle and the reins. Everything seemed fine. Tibi took the equipment off, which allowed Ajit to look at it more closely and make some adjustments.

"It worked great!" Tibi said. "It's as if it's made to be between us. With the bridle and reins I can give him directions, and he almost seems to understand by himself. Drendl is such an exceptional horse. He worked with me the whole time, and the bridle made it a natural."

Ajit considered his comments. "With a couple more adjustments, I can make it better, and easier to make. Tonight we can make another set for Goldy." On the way home, Tibi coaxed Drendl to follow him to his house. Ajit led Goldy, and Comet Tail and Lightning followed. They brought them to the barn and gave them hay, oats and carrots to eat. Tibi filled a trough with water to drink, and the horses seemed more than content to spend their time in the comfort of Tibi's barn.

Ajit and Tibi went inside Tibi's barn to work on the bridles and reins. Ajit cut leather strips, and Tibi worked to sew the leather and mold some metal fasteners. After several long candlelit hours they had a new set of reins for Goldy, and they modified Drendl's set. Then they made another two sets for Comet Tail and Lightning. They talked about what they would do the next day.

"For the first time, we'll use horses to defeat our enemies," Tibi said. "But we'll need more riders. Tomorrow we'll ride to Eppru. I know a lot of the young people there, and we can show them how to ride, and we can promise that once we defeat Mukhtar by using the horses, they can return to their families and use the horses to work on their farms."

The next day Tibi and Ajit rose early and prepared for a big day in Eppru. Ajit fit the bridle they had made on Goldy, and as expected it was a perfect fit. He tried the others on Comet Tail and Lightning, and they seemed to work just fine. Ajit put a small pack together with food for the horses and for them. Soon Tibi and Ajit mounted their horses and started a slow trot off into the sun, towards Eppru.

CHAPTER 33

TRAINING CAMP

As he comes into consciousness, one of the first things Jon notices is the dampness of his uniform underneath him. He must have been laying on the grass for some time now for this much dampness to have crept into his clothes. He can taste grass and dirt, mixed with his drool and saliva. He's lying prone on his stomach. He turns his head slightly and opens one eye. The sun is shining brightly, warming his backside. It's strange to him that he would have been left laying outside all night, someone should have been around to find him and help him. Did he return through the wrong portal?.

He opens both eyes and lifts his head slightly to the right to look at the situation. He spits out the dirt and saliva from his mouth. Several yards away from him Uzzi is lying on his side facing him, motionless. Jon looks closer. Blood is dripping from his mouth. He's eyes are locked open; he's holding his abdomen in a final struggle with pain before death. Jon looks to the left. He can see two other bodies outside the bunker where he had slept the night before last. Across the open area, the dining hall is a burnt out shell with small plumes of black smoke rising from two or three places. He lowers his head again, thinking. He's at the base camp. It must have been bombed or raided yesterday or last night while he was in Baghdad.

Hassan! Where's Hassan? Was he killed, or captured? What could have happened here?

Jon instinctively pulls into a crawling position to get a better view of the situation. There is no imminent danger in the area. Still, he's completely exposed in the portal area and very vulnerable if there is anyone left looking for survivors in the area. The bunker windows are blown out from inside, and he can see the hole in the roof where a rocket or bomb was dropped from above. Looking down at the soccer field, the fields look normal and intact. There is a small set of grandstand seats along the home-team side of the field, and the sun is reflecting brightly off some of the metal seating. He rolls to a sitting position, fairly confident his best move will be to head for the bunker and see if there is any shelter inside. He'll have to find some sort of transportation or a way to communicate if he's going to get out of here. Maybe he'll use the portal to go back, but not quite yet.

The decision to move happens quickly. He moves to a crouching position, grabs the satchel with the crystals and runs in a crouch over to the bunker. He's very slow at first; the first steps are painful reminders from his muscles of a long day before and several hours sleeping on the cold ground. From up the road past the dining hall, he can hear a jeep engine start. It's probably not a good thing, he thinks to himself as his feet get their footing and gain speed towards the bunker. He passes the two dead bodies along the way, and now he can spot several more strewn across the open areas.

Once inside the bunker, the stench of death, smoke, and explosives permeates the air. The raid must have been early in the morning, before they would have been getting out of bed. Several men are dead on the floor, apparently shot after having survived the initial impact of a bomb dropping through the roof. There is no indication that anyone got out alive, but some of them lived past the initial bombs. Jon can hear the Jeep stop outside the bunker. Although better than outside, this is no place to hide. He crosses the rest of the bunker and goes out the door on the opposite side, near where he had slept the other night. He can hear someone entering the bunker as he exits. There is no call from a friendly voice, this must be someone he doesn't want to meet. He looks around for his next best escape option. There are trees just to his right; ahead of him and down a small slope is the soccer field. Across the soccer field are the bleachers, they are still reflecting bright lights in the sun. Jon looks at the reflection twice. It's not steady; it seems to be blinking at him. He looks to the side of the bunker. There are no windows all the way back to the front of the building.

Not quite sure what to expect, he doubles back along the outside of the bunker to the front of the building. This wasn't in the Army training manual. Just before turning the corner in the front, he stops to look. The Jeep is an old Willys modified with roll-over bars, the first model of Jeep that made the brand famous in the 50's and 60's. A smile creeps across his face. "My faith in God, once again renewed." He says to himself. The keys are left in the ignition.

Hesitation is not his friend right now. Not a time to think. Jon runs several yards across the front of the building and jumps into the driver's seat of the Jeep. Looking down at the keys, he pushes in the clutch and turns the keys to start. The engine turns but doesn't start. Jon pumps the gas pedal and bangs on the steering wheel for encouragement. The dry cranking continues with no sign of a spark or combustion. He bangs on the steering wheel again and holds the key for a moment to try again. His hesitation is rudely interrupted by a blade pressed across his throat.

Jon pulls back against the seat as his oppressor turns his head towards him. "Not so fast." He says. Jon can feel his thick beard and sweat against his face. His decaying teeth bring forth his breath; rank with unspeakable stench. As he turns his head towards him, he sees a long thick scar along his left cheek. It's Mudlarek, in the flesh. Jon is frozen against the seat.

"I've been waiting for you. I thought you would be here last night, but unfortunately all I found was your friends here. It's unlucky for them that we didn't find you. Now, suddenly, you're lying out in the open. I don't know how it happened, but no matter. Here we are. Now, slowly get out of the Jeep."

Jon turns slightly. His hand is still on the key. He turns it quickly. The engine springs to life and Jon pops the clutch, throwing Mudlarek backwards into the passenger seat behind. Jon lifts his arm and the knife is knocked to the ground in the front seat. It grazes Jon's neck causing a small stream of blood to flow down his skin. Mudlarek tries to regain his balance as Jon drives the Jeep down the small slope towards the soccer field. As Mudlarek rights himself, Jon swerves to the right to throw his balance off. Mudlarek hangs on. Jon hits the brakes hard, smashing Mudlarek into the front dashboard, but he regains his balance. Jon accelerates and swerves hard to the left with dirt and mud flying behind them in a rooster tail as the wheels spin around in the dirt of the field. Mudlarek is flailing about trying to keep his grasp on any part of the Jeep he can.

With one hand Mudlarek grasps the rollover bar to hang on. Jon swerves the other way and Mudlarek's other hand swings to the other side of the rollover bar. The Jeep bounces downward and Mudlarek's body is thrown upwards as he holds on. As the jeep rebounds upwards, Mudlarek puts his knees in front of his swinging body and smashes into Jon. The impact dislodges Jon from his seat and he's thrown from the Willys onto the ground of the soccer field. The bag with the red and blue crystals inside is thrown from his clothes, landing in the passenger side of the Jeep. Mudlarek holds onto the rollover bars, and now swings himself into the Willys' driver's seat. Jon's body rolls to a stop several feet from the Jeep. Mudlarek looks at the crystals lying in the passenger side of the car. He gives a shrieking howl of victory as he gains control of the Willys and turns it around to finish off Jon.

Lying on the ground, Jon is unable to compose himself quickly enough to get up and out of the way of the oncoming vehicle. Suddenly, gunfire rings out. The Jeep turns to the right just before it hits Jon's body and it heads up the slope and toward the road. Jon rolls to look at where the gunfire is coming from. Across the field five men are charging with small arms. Leading the way is Hassan. The Jeep has accelerated to the road exiting the camp, and Hassan pulls to a crouching stance, firing rapidly. The Jeep escapes up the road in a cloud of smoke.

Hassan reaches Jon lying on the field. Jon is inconsolable. "The red and blue crystals – they are in the Jeep."

Hassan looks at the cloud of dust left by the Jeep as it exited. "It's OK Jon, we'll get them back. We'll have to."

Hassan helps Jon to his feet, and Jon throws his arm around his shoulder as they walk towards the bleachers. As they approach, Jon can see a small opening between what looks like a cement pad, likely to be used as a base for a small tower of some sort. But the opening proves to be just big enough for a man to enter, and Jon finds a small ladder going down into an opening below ground level. Once below, the air is cool and still, if not refreshing.

"Jon, we were trying to signal you from here. We were reflecting the sunlight to you as a signal, did you see it? We hoped you would see it as a warning, and hopefully come to us."

"I saw the flashes, yes." Jon responds. " But I had no idea someone was signaling me. If I had only thought about it more!"

"This is one of the caves that you will find scattered around the oldest villages. No one knows who built them, or why, but they have proven to be essential for survival over the past thousands of years. Most likely they were built to hide while ancient warlords raided cities and towns. Maybe they were to store grains and foods after the harvest, or who knows what. Last night, after the first bombs fell, those of us left alive who knew of this cave were able to survive here. Look around. There are all kinds of provisions here. There are places for ammunitions, there are places for food, and there are even places for crude plumbing, thank goodness."

Jon couldn't find the energy to speak more yet. His shirt was covered in blood from his neck wound. He was in full despair. Hassan sat him down in a chair along a wall of canned figs, lemons, and apples. Hassan reached for a cloth to wipe the blood from his neck. He found a bottle of water and held Jon back as he poured some water into his mouth. Jon swallowed appreciatively, then spit the water out on the floor repulsively.

"No, Hassan, you don't understand. I lost them. I lost the crystals. Mudlarek has them. We've failed."

CHAPTER 34

BROK

Eppru was busy repairing the damage Mukhtar had done and preparing for market day, which usually came on the fifth day of the week. Many of the young men and women were busy bringing in food and supplies from their farms and barns to trade with the other families of the communities. The talk about Mukhtar and the damage he had done was everywhere. *When would he strike again? What could be done?* The merchants did their best to set up crude new stalls for selling their wares. The temple was being repaired, but there were black streaks of soot and smoke across the walls.

Nothing prepared the townspeople for the strange arrival of Tibi and Ajit that day. Although they were known in the town, people were amazed as Tibi and Ajit rode slowly on top of their horses into the marketplace. Some people thought they were monsters; that they were part of the horse; and they ran off calling for others to come and see the man-horses that had arrived in town. Others were more curious. They came up to the horses and wanted to touch them, to feel their fur and touch the strange riders who were on top of them.

Tibi and Ajit rode to the center of town and calmly dismounted from their horses. Fifteen or so people crowded around the horses. Tibi knew many of the people that were there. "My friends! Tibi exclaimed. "We have great news for you. We have tamed these wild horses and now they will do work for us. We can ride them, and they take us as fast as the wind. Just this morning we rode from my house. The trip that would have taken two hours took just thirty minutes because we were on the horses and not walking."

"But they are wild animals!" Someone shouted.

"Yes they are, or they were." Tibi replied, "But many of them want to be owned by us now, like your dogs, or your cattle. We can feed them and protect them from the dangers of living in the wild, and some of them will prefer that over living in the wild. There is a whole herd of them that are living further up the river, and we can show you how to ride them, how to take care of them, and how to use them for your farms. Imagine not carrying your food or goods to the marketplace, but having them do it! Imagine riding home to your families instead of the long walk!"

Tibi had captured the attention of the small group of people.

"Let me show you!" He continued. "He mounted Drendl, and Drendl let out a small snort. "Tck Tck Drendl!" And he shook the reins up and down. Drendl started to gallop off down the marketplace road in a rhythmic cadence. The noise faded away as he disappeared, then he returned as he was riding back into the square. Tibi pulled on the reins.

"Woh Drendl!"

Drendl stopped. Tibi dismounted, and walked in front of Drendl to give him a carrot and some oats. The crowd applauded and several of the young men and women came towards Drendl.

"Let me try! Let me do it!" They exclaimed.

Tibi let a few of his friends get on Drendl's back and he led Drendl as they walked around the marketplace square. They held on nervously as if their life could end at any moment. When they got off they jumped and shouted in amazement at the power and the excitement of the event. After a few rides around the square, Tibi had shown enough to get the entire town talking that night, and Drendl did not seem to appreciate some of the inexperienced kicks and pulling of hair that some of the people had inflicted on him.

"Sorry my friends" Ajit said as he stepped forward into the front of the crowd. "This will take some training. And we are here to offer you training and a chance to get your own horse, if one of the wild ones will have you. But there is something we need you to do to earn this chance. Now you all know that the tyrant Mukhtar has been raiding this town and your family farms. Just this week he came to my family's farm and burned it to the ground because we refused to swear our allegiance to him. He burned down the market place here, and he has been a traitor to the temple in Nippur. We have to defeat him and stop him from destroying our farms, our towns, and our crops. He will be back to take whatever he sees fit unless we stop him. Tibi Asif, Rafi, and I will lead you to defeat him and destroy his threat against us forever."

"We need you to work with us. We need you to learn to ride these horses, and with them and the power we have against Mukhtar, we will be free from him forever. Once we are free, you can keep the horses you have tamed and brought for your farms and families. We need you to help us, and you need us to help you. So come with us and we will show you how to defeat him, and we will show you how to tame your own horses for your own families. Go and tell your friends! We need as many people as we can."

"Whoever is ready, we will meet you in ten days, after the market days, at Shepherd's Flat, in the big bend area of the river on the way to our farms. We'll meet you there, and those who are willing to learn to ride, and learn to fight against Mukhtar, will be trained as best they can be."

Tibi and Ajit turned to head back out of town towards their farm. Just as they were leaving, one of Tibi's old friends stopped him. His name was Brok.

"Tibi, give me a minute of your time. We saw some of Mukhtar's scouts near our farm. Three men came and were standing just outside our land, looking at our farm. They were wearing robes like the men who were in the market here in Eppru. I'm sure they were scouts from Mukhtar's raiders. If that's true they will be coming to raid our farm soon. What can we do? Can you help me?"

Brok lived with his family in a house about thirty minutes past Asif's house just above the banks of the same river. His family farm raised goats and sheep, which were known throughout the land as the best and meatiest. He was the eldest child of three living children. There had been two other two children born, but they had died soon after birth from infection.

The farm consisted of a modest brick house and a barn several hundred feet away, alongside the river. The barn was raised several feet above the surrounding ground on a foundation of large rocks. The higher ground was a concession to the spring floods that had destroyed the barn several times since Brok had been born; he could remember his father and grandfather struggling to rebuild the barn several times when he was a boy. Behind the barn was a wooden bridge which crossed a strong creek that flowing to the bigger river. The bridge had four large posts at each corner. This was one of the bridges that Ajit had engineered to raise during the spring floods. The bridge could be raised as needed to allow the flood waters to pass without destroying the bridge.

Brok was a tall lanky young man with short cropped curly hair, about sixteen years old, old enough to start out on his own. He had agreed to work through one more harvest season for his family, then he would start to build his own house. He had picked out some land further down the river from his parents. There was a small hill where he could put the house, high enough to be above the floods, and there were fields nearby where he could start to farm some grains, and maybe have some goats or sheep.

Tibi considered the news that Brok had told him. "Brok, we may be able to help you. But you may be able to help us trap Mukhtar and his raiders. Your farm may be the key to bringing him and his raiders down. Are you willing to help us?"

"Yes, I'll help, but I have to be sure our farm and may family will be protected. Can you assure us it will be safe to trust you?"

"I can't absolutely say nothing bad could happen, Brok." Tibi said honestly. "But I do know you are in grave danger if we don't rid ourselves of this menace on our towns. For now, this is what I want you to do. I want you to be prepared to give him food and water when he arrives. You will have to move your most valuable things away from the house. When he comes, be prepared to swear allegiance to him and give him what we have prepared for him. Tell him you will give him more if he comes back in a week. He'll leave you alone if he gets what he wants now and thinks he can get more when he comes back. In the meantime, we'll get ready for him when he and his raiders come back."

CHAPTER 35

RED BARON

At Camp Victory, the US headquarters base in Baghdad, a communications specialist sees Sergeant Blodget across the room. Sergeant Blodget is a tall man who can take over a room with his booming voice any time he sees fit. As a lead contact for the friendly Iraqi informants, he has to keep a sharp edge on intelligence. It can mean the difference between life and death for the men he might send out into the city, and it may mean the same for the informants involved. He keeps his risks low and expects to get high returns on the actions he takes. He's eating a ham sandwich while walking from a meeting room to his office. He can't remember the last time he had enough time for a proper lunch. A woman approaches him.

"Sir, I have Red Baron on the satellite phone," the communication specialist says.

"I'll take it in my office." Sergeant Blodget says as he turns the corner into his cramped and cluttered office. He puts down his ham sandwich on a military magazine and picks up the wired phone.

"Hello Red Baron," Blodget says. The communications specialist handles the interpretation between the two men. "Your last information on the terrorist training camp was accurate and actionable. I trust we have made suitable arrangements to reward you for your efforts. That is exactly the kind of information that will help us save this country for your people." Blodget took every opportunity he could to reinforce the good intentions he put forward while communicating with his agents.

On the other end of the line, Mudlarek is standing with his satellite phone outside his small apartment in Sadr City, a large slum neighborhood in Baghdad. "Allah was on our side that day, Papa Cicco." Blodget loved the code name he had given for himself. It brought forward an image of an old Italian grandfather. It just made him smile. Mudlarek only knows Blodget by his code name. "I have been in contact with your payment people, and that is going well. Now I have important new information for you that was forced out of the terrorists after we destroyed their training camp. They are consolidating many of the separate factions of the city and they are planning a major attack on one of your bases. I don't have all the information yet, I understand they may still be forming their plans now. But some of my contacts in other towns tell me they have made moves to force some of them to join with them. I will find out as much as I can, but that is all I know for now."

"Thank you Red Baron," Blodget replies. "Keep me informed as often as you can, this may be critical for many reasons."

The conversation ends and Blodget hears the disconnection made by the communications specialists. He looks at his email. He sorts through several of the unopened encrypted messages and finds the one he was looking for.

Subject: Possible VIP visit:

Message: Green Zone Top Secret – Green Zone facilities should be prepared for a potential VIP visit any time from February 28th to March 24th. Timing and location may change according to schedules as needed. Please make all precautions to ensure facility is ready any time, as needed."

Sitting back in his chair, he considers the information that Red Baron has just given him. A bigger attack coming? He'll deal with it when he gets more information.

CHAPTER 36

A VISIT TO RANIA

Tibi and Ajit devised a plan to save Brok's farm from Mukhtar and his raiders. Together, they went to the farmers and merchants in Eppru to gain support for their plan. That afternoon, they loaded several bags of food and supplies over the backs of Drendl and Goldy. They had plenty of oats and carrots for the two horses, and Tibi and Ajit walked ahead of the horses as they carried the food towards Brok's house.

Along the way, they saw the path that led to Asif's and Rania's house. Neither one of them had been to Asif's house, so they were somewhat reluctant to introduce themselves without any invitation. They knew they should stop by and check in with her to make sure she and the children were OK. They knew Asif would want them to talk to her. They followed the path that Asif had described to them, and in a few minutes they were approaching the white brick house of Asif and Rania.

Rania and the children were outside the house, taking in some laundry that had been washed by the river and hung out to dry. Tibi called out to her, as soon as he was within earshot of her.

"Hello! Rania!" He started, hesitating. "I am Tibi, and this is Ajit. We are friends of Asif and Rafi, and therefore, friends of yours, or at least we hope! We just left him yesterday, and our travels brought us this way. So we thought we would stop by his house, it is just as he described it, and you are even more beautiful than he said!"

Rania looked up at the strangers coming down the path with the wild horses behind them, only these horses were carrying some sort of baggage on their backs.

"Hello! You know Asif? If you are friends of his then you are welcome here. But please, can you leave those animals there? I don't want them to harm the children, or me."

"Rania, please don't worry, these horses are now friends of ours, and they help us. This is Drendl, and the other is Goldy. We'll keep them outside, but they could use some water from the river and a quick break from carrying the food and equipment we are bringing. We've already been on adventures with them, and we have even taught Asif to ride on the back of a horse. His horse's name is Comet Tail, and he is a wonder to behold."

Tibi and Ajit led the horses down to the river side for some water, then they took their packages off their backs and put it on the side of the river. Rania invited them inside the house, and they walked in with the children following quickly behind. Since they had heard the name of their father and that these were friends, they were very eager to hear any news of him.

Once inside and seated at the small kitchen table, Tibi told Rania the story of how they met Asif and Rafi, and how Mukhtar had raided Ajit's house and burned their barn to the ground. He told them the story of the horses, and how he gained their trust. He told her about Asif as he tried to get onto his horse, and how he fell into the mud the first time he tried to get on his back. For dramatic effect to the children, Tibi fell to the ground off his chair as if falling off a horse, then he held his hands to his face to show how mud had covered him. He opened his fingers and peeked through at the children who were sitting around the table listening intently. The children screeched with laughter as Tibi imitated their father, covered in mud and determined to get back on top of his horse.

Soon the conversation turned to more serious matters, and Tibi and Ajit told her how it was they came to be traveling by her house. Rania knew Brok's family well. She feared for them if Mukhtar's raiders were to come after them, and she was worried that they might come to her farm as well.

"We have a plan to save their farm and stop Mukhtar and his raiders once and for all. We may need your help, the help of this farm. Can you help us save Brok's farm and his family? If it is OK with Asif and you, we will use this farm as a camp to keep Brok's family safe, and we'll use it as a base to plan our attack on Mukhtar."

"I will do anything to stop Mukhtar. He left me for dead many years ago. Asif and I have started another life without living in fear for our lives, but now he is a threat again. We have sworn we will stop him from hurting more people the way he hurt us." Rania said determinedly. "Brok's family can stay here. And there is another path to their farm that runs by the river. You can take it to their farm if you want. We don't have much here to share, but we can make due while we have to."

Tibi and Ajit stayed for a while longer discussing their plans, but soon it was time to go. They went outside, down by the river with the horses. They split much of the cargo they were carrying and left much of it with Rania. They did not want to take everything for Mukhtar at once.

Rania took them a few hundred feet down stream in the river, past the clearing spot where she and Asif had appeared in the grass so long ago. Just beyond the clearing was a path leading down-river.

"This is the other way to Brok's house. Because of the way the river bends, this is much quicker than if you travel by the other path, but not many people know of this route. You should be able to get there in twenty minutes. Be careful, there are several areas that are muddy, and Asif says there is some quicksand. But this time of year, most of that should be dried up."

"Quicksand?" Ajit asked tentatively. "Most should be dried up?"

"Don't worry, Ajit" Tibi said. "This time of year the quicksand is gone. That's the way it is for our river as well. The only time you will find quicksand this time of year is after a heavy rain."

Tibi and Ajit left Rania and the children as they headed down the path towards Brok's house. The day was getting late, and they hoped to get there by nightfall.

CHAPTER 37

FALLUJAH

The people of Fallujah are no strangers to rumors of mystical powers and powerful enemies. In a city that contradicts itself, the pastoral, idyllic setting of the Euphrates River combined with the calming culture of Islam is offset by gated and guarded houses and wrought iron bars and barbed wire that protect most of the fronts of the businesses. Generations of war have removed the innocence of the region that is often thought of as the original Garden of Eden. In one of the warehouses behind a chain link fence topped with barbed wire, four men in their mid-twenties to early thirties are seated nervously in chairs, facing the inside of the empty warehouse. They have been rounded up and forcibly invited to sit in the chairs. Six armed guards are standing in the shadows against the walls of the ware house, ready to respond to any unacceptable activity.

A man in an militia uniform walks into the light in front of the four men. "Gentlemen" he starts in Arabic, "Thank you for coming here today, forgive us if of our methods of bringing you here were less than formal. You may not have come if we had not insisted. As you know, as Iraqis we have to band together against our common enemies. We bring you here to ask that you use your influence on others to join us, the Hand of the Red Fist. Today we will show you power we have obtained from the most ancient and powerful force in the universe. We have been searching for the source of this power for generations. Only because of the recent bombings in Baghdad have these powers returned to men, and only because of our leader, Mudlarek, do we have possession of them. You will soon see that this unearthly power is unstoppable. With this power we can defeat our enemies and drive them from our homeland. With these powers and your help we can once again bring the balance of power to our people. You can join us, or you can be destroyed."

"Now it is time for you to witness this power. Once we're done, we're sure you will see fit to join us and lend your weapons and supporters to our cause. We are planning big things with this power, but we need your help in weapons and in men. Now, I would like you to meet Morabek Mudlarek, the leader of the Hand of the Red Fist."

In the center of the warehouse, swirling red and blue lights appear fifteen feet above the floor. They swirl and spin, quickly grow brighter, then flash into the ground. Emerging from the blinding light Mudlarek appears, dressed in a black robe and holding a small staff. The four men turn their heads from the bright lights, then look back to the center of the space to see the man that has appeared out of nowhere.

"I am Mudlarek. I have sole possession and power over the ancient crystals of An. Their power comes from the gods, and only I can control them! The power is limitless; I can summon it again and again with never-ending repetition. Watch as I use these amazing powers."

Mudlarek turns his back on the four seated men and points to the darkness of the far left corner of the warehouse. A Sodium light turns on from overhead, and two goats can be seen tied to a post, casually eating some hay. Mudlarek bows his head, then slowly raises his arms outstretched. Clouds of red and blue energy quickly appear around his head. Mudlarek swirls them about into concentric circles, then sends the clouds of light energy across the ceiling of the ware house. The clouds swing sharply around the corners of the warehouse, then head straight on towards the four seated men. As the clouds swoop towards them, they dive from their chairs to take cover. The clouds swing wildly around and accelerate across the floor towards the goats. The men turn to look towards the far side of the warehouse. The energy pauses as it coalesces against the ceiling of the building, then comes crashing down onto the unsuspecting animals. The animals explode into meat shrapnel, flying across the warehouse. A goat leg slams into the wall behind the witnesses, and slides down to the ground just behind them with streaks of blood flowing down the wall.

The energy does not stop after disintegrating the goats. The column of energy stays in formation and travels towards the furthest corner of the warehouse. Along the way, the beam of energy cuts into the ground like a welders flame, exploding a line of dirt in the warehouse floor. In the back corner another light illuminates a small outdoor shack which has been assembled. The line of energy quickly reaches the edge of the shack. Mudlarek pauses his arms and the energy coalesces again above the shack. Mudlarek swings his arms downwards, and the energy explodes into the shack and blows it to pieces across the far side of the warehouse. Smoke, splintered wood and plywood sheets fly in all directions in the far corner.

He's not done yet. The energy continues to the third corner of the warehouse, where a burned out US Humvee transport vehicle has been parked. The energy stops just above the truck and Mudlarek swoops his arms down again, and the truck explodes in the beam. The noise in the warehouse is deafening, and the four men jump out of their seats trying to head towards the exit door.

But Mudlarek still is not done. The beams of energy subside as he turns to his right and faces directly towards the men as they are sitting. He wraps his hands together, forming a ball of blue luminescent energy within them. He opens his stance and hurls the ball of fire towards the area where the men are sitting. The blue fireball explodes against the wall behind them. Dripping remnants of burning energy drip down the walls, igniting small items on fire along the edge of the floor. Several men who were standing along the side of the warehouse grab fire extinguishers and run out to the remains of the burning truck and utility shed.

Mudlarek approaches the terrified four witnesses to his power. "Gentlemen, I have shown you the new powers that I now possess. They speak for themselves. Join us and you will be freed by the power I have. Any who refuse will meet their end with the power you have just seen. Tell your friends and others you have seen the future of this war, and with me you will be the victors."

Mudlarek summons the clouds and swirling energy around him one more time, and he disappears into a cloud of energy before their eyes. The Snap! pushes them back in their seats and echoes through the building.

The militia officer returns to the front of the four men. "You have seen the power we know hold. You will find it in your interest to support our cause. We will be coming to your houses and warehouses to collect the weapons and sign up the men we will need. We will come in three days, so be sure to prepare your people. There are no more planned displays of our power before we use it against our enemies, so make sure you are able to deliver your end of the deal."

CHAPTER 38

BROK'S HOUSE

Brok's house was up on a small hill, just above the flood plain. In comparison to Asif and Rania's house it looked to be a mansion. The house stood almost twice as tall, and had two windows across the front, one on either side of the door. There were also windows on each side of the house. Each was quite a luxury and showed the extra workmanship that went into the construction. Although glamorous in comparison to Asif and Rania's house, it was still a modest home. In the cool of the setting sun on the far side of the river, it took on an orange glow that contrasted sharply against the blue and gray eastern sky.

Brok was inside the house, looking outside from one of the windows. He looked inquisitively at the travelers who were coming along a trail that was rarely used. The two horses were a tell-tale sign of who the travelers were. He came outside and headed over to greet them.

"Hello! Ajit and Tibi! Good to see you. How is it that you came by the river path? That path is not well known in these parts, something tells me you have a story to tell me."

Ajit told Brok about their visit with Rania, and their friendship with Asif. He didn't tell him all the details about the history that Mukhtar, Asif, and Rania have, but he did assure him that Rania was as interested as he was in stopping Mukhtar. Brok invited Ajit and Tibi inside the house to meet his family.

His father was a sturdy and proud man, standing at five feet, seven inches tall; he was taller than most men of this age. He had a greying beard and forward slouch that belied his age of only thirty six years old. His sinewy arms and brick hard hands told of the years of work he had done to build his farm and his family. Behind him was his wife, a slight woman, less than five feet tall. She looked as light as a feather, and she moved with a lightness and quick energy that seemed more suited for a hen in a barnyard than for a mother of four children. As Ajit and Tibi introduced themselves, she moved quickly to direct the children to gather some food.

Although delighted to have visitors, she seemed somewhat burdened that there were two more mouths to feed. She saw the food supplies that Ajit and Tibi had brought, her mood brightened quickly when setting about the chore of getting a meal together.

After dinner Ajit, Tibi and Brok walked outside the house. Brok showed Tibi a small outcrop of rock just behind the house and slightly uphill. From there was a good view of the house and the barn. Tibi could watch Mukhtar and his raiders from there. Then he showed them a pond he had built on the land just above the crest of the hill. He used it to store water for when the dry season came. Tibi said it was a perfect set up. After some discussion, Brok returned to his house, and Tibi and Ajit stayed quietly by the rock outcropping, waiting patiently.

No raiders from Mukhtar appeared that night. Tibi and Ajit returned to Rania's house riding Drendl and Goldy. For the next two nights they returned, keeping Drendl and Goldy out of sight well before the house along the river trail. They arrived an hour or so before sunset ,and they stayed several hours after dark to see if Mukhtar's raiders would return.

Late in the day on the third afternoon they got what they were waiting for. As Ajit and Tibi were watching from the rocks, three strangers in dark red robes appeared along the trail towards Brok's house. Each carried a staff several inches taller than themselves. One couldn't tell if they were merely walking sticks or meant to be used as weapons. They walked down the trail towards the house with a determined walk, and then they stopped several feet away from the front door, looking straight into the house.

"Who's there?" Brok shouted from the window. "What is your business here?"

"I am Qusan. We are men from the Hand of the Red Fist. We come to offer you our protection from evil, and to allow you to join in the support of our cause. We are the protectors of the peace, and we seek your support for our protection. Your contribution of supplies to our cause will be your guarantee of protection. And for that you will be rewarded several times over."

"I don't need your protection." Brok said as he moved into the doorway. He didn't want to sound too conciliatory too fast.

"Oh but you do!" The leader of the robes said. "You do, and you have probably heard why. Didn't you hear of what happened in the market of Eppru when they refused to allow our protection? I'm sure you don't want the same fate for your farm! The Hand of the Red Fist will protect you, but you have to contribute your share. Now let's talk about how you can help."

Brok had rehearsed this many times with Ajit and Tibi. But now that the time was here, and his family was behind him, he didn't know what to do. He wanted these people gone, and Tibi and Ajit said they would protect him.

"Go Away! We don't need your help! You will be destroyed!" Brok was shaking slightly as he moved outside his front door with a torch, as menacing as he could be against the intruders. He was hoping Ajit and Tibi had a plan for this; that they would somehow save him from the danger that was now directly in front of him. But he had walked directly into their trap.

The three intruders split to either side, and a fourth intruder appeared, seemingly out of nowhere. He was dressed in a black robe with a red sash tied around his waist. He carried another larger staff white stone embedded in the end, and he appeared several sizes larger than any man Brok had known, with a boldness and brazen look in his eyes he had never seen before. Brok stood still in front of the new intruder trembling. He was no longer confident that Ajit or Tibi would be helping him.

Mukhtar, dressed in black, raised his staff above his head and grabbed it with both hands. He held the end and swung it around rapidly. As he swung the staff, light glowed from the end of the staff, and soon a red and blue swirling cloud appeared above his head. This is what Brok had seen in Eppru, and he was afraid how this demonstration would end. Mukhtar continued to build the energy of the swirling cloud over his head as he held his arms outstretched. Slowly he moved the cloud of energy from above his head to start swirling outside the area over his head, and the waves of energy started to crash against the front walls of Brok's home. They smashed into the walls, then they returned in waves to the swirling above Mukhtar's head. From within Mukhtar's hooded robe his face seemed to start to glow, with his eyes now emanating red and blue light with their own otherworldly glow. The energy clouds came back and concentrated above Mukhtar's head, then streamed high above Brok's house, ready to come crashing down.

"Wait!" Brok shouted. "Wait! I will help you! Stop now and I will give you what you need!"

Mukhtar stopped the building energy and turned in his robes to look at Brok. His glowing eyes penetrated Brok's mind. Brok fell to his knees, trembling, in front of his house.

"I will give you what you need!" he capitulated.

Mukhtar turned to the side and swung down his staff violently to the ground. The cloud of energy followed his swoop downward and crashed into the ground with a snap! and large burst of dust and steam that rose quickly upwards.

"Now you see!" Mukhtar said. "You see how much better off you will be to help us. You can be on our side, or you can be against us, but we will prevail. You can start tonight. Give your contribution to my commanders here. If your contribution is fit, you will be protected. If not, they will make take any measures necessary to make sure it we have what we need."

Mukhtar lowered his stature slightly as he looked down at Brok. "Those who will support us will be rewarded in the end." Then he turned and held his staff over his head again. The red and blue lights shone brightly for a moment, and then he was gone. He had disappeared into nothingness in a way that Brok had never thought possible. The three robed commanders came forward to Brok, and he motioned to follow him towards the barn, where the supplies that Ajit and Tibi had brought were being stored.

After the three robed commanders left, Brok stood timidly outside the front of his house, still shaking. His family appeared at the door, and they looked at him with a frightened, defeated look.

Tibi appeared from the hill in the fading light with a torch. Ajit was just behind him.

"Are you OK? Each time we see Mukhtar, it seems his power grows, or he has learned more how to use the power that he has to put on a bigger show. Brok, you were a great and brave performer. You were perfect for this. You saved your farm, yet you challenged Mukhtar in a way that he had to show us how he uses his power."

Brok spoke quietly and slowly at first. "I was not pretending with him. I was frightened for my life. I was frightened for my family's lives. I felt I was at the mercy of a god. I never want to feel that feeling again. No man should have such godly powers, and no man should have to feel as powerless as I did. I'm afraid of him, but I know we have to stop him before he takes over. For the first time tonight, I thought I would never see my family again. I thought our house and barn would be destroyed. But somehow, I did what you told me with his commanders. They said they would be back for more contributions. I told them to come on the night of the new moon, and the night of the full moon, and for each I would have more supplies ready for them. Now we know when they will come back, and we can trap this rat."

CHAPTER 39

FALLUJAH

Just after noon, three pickup trucks and a Chrysler minivan pull over the ridge at the base camp and head down the hill towards the soccer field. They stop between the bunker and the canteen. A tall young Iraqi dressed in camouflage gets out of the lead pickup truck and assesses the situation. He checks his cell phone. From the cave across the soccer field, one of the surviving Iraqis comes out from the cave and waves towards him. The Iraqi waves back and gets back into the truck to proceed across the torn up field.He is met outside the cave, and soon several others, including Hassan are outside discussing the situation with him. They talk for several minutes before Hassan returns to the cave while the others go to the bunker and canteen. Hassan orders the others in the cave to be ready to evacuate in twenty minutes.

"We're being evacuated to another safe area. Mudlarek knows there are survivors here, and if he informs the US Allies, they will be back later this afternoon. We'll go in groups of two cars so it doesn't look like a large militia group. The others are going to start collecting the dead and pull out any weapons and ammunitions that were left, if Mudlarek's clan left any at all. Everything else will be burned. We're going in the minivan. You have already been cleared to go, but we'll need to get you cleaned up and into some more appropriate clothes. My suggestion is that you dress like one of us for now. We'll burn this shirt and everything to do with Thomas Schultz. They are starting a fire now outside the canteen. Surprisingly, I think your old clothes were not touched in the firefight or the bombing. I'll have them brought along with us, if you agree. We don't have a lot of time. We're leaving in twenty minutes."

"Every time you offer me options, they always seem to come when I have the least number of good choices. Now you're asking me to dress as part of a militia, and that is probably the only option I have. Let's be sure I have my US clothes available for whenever I can return to my base."

Twenty minutes later, Jon was dressed in a camouflage shirt and cargo shorts like many of the men who were working around the camp. He wondered who they had belonged to. Was it one of the dead? He carried the clothes of Thomas Schultz to the fire near the canteen himself, and he threw them into the yellow flames. He returned to the minivan where Hassan was standing. *Was he turning into an Iraqi enemy combatant? Was he one of those who he was trained to be fighting against?* He knew the war that Hassan and his clan are fighting is not the same war the US is having with Iraq. But would they ever know the difference? If Mudlarek was plotting an attack against the US, then he was fighting on the right side. What was the saying? The enemy of my enemy is my friend. Someone handed him a duffel bag with his old clothes inside. He checked them out quickly, then got into to back seat of the minivan with Hassan.

The 1990s Chrysler minivan belched oily blue smoke as it sped up the road exiting the base camp. Jon wondered how far it would make it. He looked back at the camp as it faded out of view. He was lucky to make it out alive. The road climbed higher and higher out of the valley where the camp was hidden. As they drove ever upward, the climate changed to a hot, dry desert. Inside the minivan, the heat increased, with broken air conditioning. Sand, oil crickets, and electrical lines were all that could be seen for miles in any direction. They passed a small caravan of camels slowly heading back towards the valley. Jon grew sleepy, but if his head nodded the bandages on his neck and the wound below would remind him of his perilous situation.

After two hours of riding, Jon looked forward and saw that the horizon seemed to drop off in front of them. As they drove toward the apparent cliff, the driver slowed down just before a leap into an infinite sky. The car turned left and headed down a steep hill along a cliff. The road was only wide enough for one vehicle as it bumped and swerved along road between the jagged rocks and a thousand feet or so of drop off to the right. They came to a small widening in the road where a make-shift guard shack was assembled. A machine-gun armed guard came out to the car to make sure he knew the driver and look at who was inside. He waved them on and they continued driving until they came to another slightly wider area with several pickup trucks parked against the cliffs.

Jon looked around for signs of a building, but none could be seen. Hassan was moving to get out of the van and motioned for Jon to come out with him. Jon exited the van and looked around. "I thought you said we were staying at the Hilton tonight!" He said to Hassan.

"This is hardly your American Hilton, Jon. Our choices grow slimmer as our operations are squeezed. This is the home of some of the ancient cliff dwellings in Iraq. Thousands of years ago great cities and villages were built among these cliffs. Now all that is left are a few ancient ruins. We have taken what we can. If we had money and time, we could do a lot more. But we can only do the minimum to make it livable here. Someday we'd love to see these ruins restored to their grandeur. But for now, this will be where we make our next plans."

Hassan picked up a duffel bag of supplies they had brought with them and motioned for Jon to do the same and follow him. Jon found a smaller bag he could carry in addition to his own. He threw it over his shoulder and headed to the other side of the road. Hassan made a small leap over the edge and disappeared from view. Jon walked to the edge and saw a steep path leading downward, with Hassan sliding and skidding his way down. There looked to be no easier way. Jon jumped over and found himself sliding, almost skiing down the slope to a landing below. Hassan was waiting there, and they continued along a ledge around a bend in the cliff.

Hassan had not prepared him for what he saw. A deep ravine split the cliffs on two opposite sides. Along the cliffs on the opposing side, walls were built into many of the rough cliff sides. In the walls were small windows looking across the ravine or out into the valley below them. Several of the dwellings had

Many of the people at the table turn to look at Jon. He may be in their local dress right now, but clearly many of them know who he is and where he is from.

"With all of these things we will defeat Mudlarek and the hand of the Red Fist. We will return the red and blue crystals to eternal hiding, we will be rid of this menace from our country, and we will get security in our country once again."

Several of the men present applauded or tapped on the table to show their approval for this part of the presentation. After the meeting ends, Jon, Hassan and Abdul gather near the waterfall.

"Why isn't there a portal here?" Jon asks Hassan.

"Simple," Hassan replies, "There is no Ningalite. The crystals need the Ningalite to generate the energy fields. We know that Ningalite is often located near water, but it is not located near all water. So it's not unusual that we have water, but no Ningalite. We also know that Ningalite is usually near oil as well, and there are no oil fields for miles around this area."

The three men walked outside to the cliffs to head back to their rooms. As they headed along the cliffs the Milky Way arched over them towards the east. In the far distance they could see the twinkling lights of a far off city, probably Fallujah or Baghdad to the south. The crescent moon hung low to the west as it set for the evening. Before they split apart to go to their rooms, Abdul stopped them along the trail.

"Mister Jon and Hassan, it would be my honor if you would attend my Nishan. It's happening just a few days from now. Jon, in case you don't know, the Nishan is a ceremony that happens before a wedding. It's an informal joining of the families. The groom and his family bring gifts to the bride at a celebration place. There is a lot of traditional ceremonies, and of course a lot of celebrating. Hassan, you have been as much a part of my family as anyone the past few years. Mister Jon, you are now welcomed as one of us. Would you do me the honor of coming with me? My wife and I would consider ourselves blessed if you can attend. We don't have much money, so it will be a simple Nishan. We're holding it outside in a field under the blue sky."

"I'd be happy to attend, Abdul." Hassan responded. "I've known you since you were a boy, I'm looking forward to it."

"Abdul," Jon responded, "I'd be honored to be your guest. Your wife is a lucky woman to have found such a wonderful man."

Abdul looked puzzled at this comment, but he appreciated the intent regardless of how it translated into his culture.

-

The morning brought clear fresh air and songbirds singing in the brush and trees that lined the cliff dwellings. Jon and Hassan brought their duffel bags of items to pack out of the cliff town. Abdul carried his equipment in a backpack.

"I'm heading west today to go back to my preparations and family. We have our Nishan next Friday, so there is a lot of preparation and family to attend to. I'm looking forward to seeing you there."

With that the three men headed back on the trail out of the cliff dwellings. They passed the waterfall, the suspended bridges, and many of the dwellings who were hanging laundry out to dry, or cooking in small fires. The trail wound around the cliff and started to rise quickly. Jon looked back as they turned the last corner away from the nestled dwellings, wondering if he would ever see such a sight again.

CHAPTER 40

SHEPHERD'S FLAT

Tibi and Ajit returned to Tibi's farm to prepare for the training of the people of Eppru with the horses. On their way they dropped off Drendl and Goldy at the flats by the river, where they found the other horses enjoying themselves. Before long, Drendl was leading the entire herd across the river in a run across the plains, together once again. Tibi and Ajit continued to Tibi's farm, and there they found Asif and Rafi, talking about how to explore the gliding tunnels and how to best use them.

"We mapped all the portals we could find." Rafi said. Ajit brought out a tray lined with clay they had been working on. With a pointed stick, they had drawn each of the portal designs that they had seen in the clay. All in all they had found twenty one portals, although they did not have time to go through about half of them. "Here's the portal near my house." Asif said as he pointed to the circle with the cross at the top. "Here's the cave where we found the crystals, and here's the portal behind Ajit's house. We found my father's house, and several others that seemed to be further down the river banks. We found that each one had several things in common; each portal is right near a river, and each portal has rocks somewhere nearby with the same rocks that are in the crystals. We found this when we were reentering the portal. As we were bringing out the energy, there were rocks in the area that would start to glow bright yellow, just like in the caves of the shaking mountains."

"I'm going to put this tray of clay in a kiln to keep these pictures. If we include it the next time the kiln is fired to make bricks, it should bake the pictures right into the clay." Asif said.

Ajit and Tibi told them of their visit to Eppru, how they introduced the horses to the people, and the recruiting and training they were going to do. They told them about Brok, and the raiders that were seen near his house. Asif knew of Brok and his family, so he was concerned for Rania. Tibi told him of his visit with Rania and the arrangement that they made to support Brok's family.

"Rania invited Brok's family to stay at your house when Mukhtar's raiders return, and in return they offered to help care for your children if Rania can help you in any way." Ajit offered.

After they caught each other up on their adventures, Tibi and Ajit went out to the barn to make more bridles and reins for training with the horses. Rafi and Asif worked out in the yard, practicing with spears and talking about the best way to trap Mukhtar.

The next morning the four of them headed down to Emerald Flats to see the horses. This time they brought enough oats and carrots for many more horses, and they found that several more were willing to come to them and eat. Tibi and Ajit had ten more bridles and reins ready to try. Rafi and Asif each rode Comet Tail and Lightning with the bridles and reins as they followed Tibi and Ajit. The other horses seemed to be watching and learning as well. As Drendl stood proudly by with the bridle and reins in place, Tibi and Ajit were able to try the equipment on the other horses with only a minimal amount of complaints. With Tibi's soft touch and firm guidance, he was able to mount and ride another six horses. Each one learned quickly on how to hold the rider, and they seemed to talk naturally to Tibi as he gave them commands. Soon all four of them were mounted on horses, and they practiced moving in synchronous motion, only now with Tibi and Drendl in the lead as a team.

They practiced with the team of ten horses for three more days before heading to Eppru to train the other people from the town. Tibi was having the time of his life. He seemed to be able to speak with the horses with his soft touch and gentle motions he used to give directions. Tibi would whistle and talk to them, and they would respond in kind, nodding and pawing. On the last day Asif and Rafi brought spears, and they practiced throwing spears at clumps of hay tied together as they rode past them. Asif and Rafi would often holler and yell as they rode by with their spears, with Lightning and Comet Tail galloping underneath them.

On the morning of the tenth day after Eppru they headed for the training ground they would use called Shepherd's Flat. As the four riders and six rider-less horses approached, they could see bluffs that rose several hundred feet along a bend in the riverbed. The river flowed straight towards the bluffs, only to be turned sharply to the right, in a curve that acknowledged the defeat of the rivers continual assault on the sandstone cliffs. On the inside of the bend in the river was a stone-lined rivers edge. Just above the edge was a flat field, leveled evenly from the progression of floods that returned every spring. On this plain the four riders and horses stopped and waited for the townspeople that would come. They watched the hawks soaring above the cliffs, riding the rising winds as it pushed upwards. A flock of gulls flew across the face of the cliffs, their white wings flashed in synchronous harmony as the sun reflected off their wings as they pulsed across the dark red sandstone. The ten horses grazed peacefully as the four men talked about the plans for training.

"We'll start the training today, but they will need to continue training on their own. We can train some of them to train the others." Ajit said.

"That's only if there are enough that show up!" Rafi said. "I don't think there are enough people in Eppru who will do what we are asking. They have farms to run, families to feed. They live in fear they will be killed if they are found supporting us. What can we expect from them?"

As Rafi was finishing his sentence, three people appeared at the edge of the trail from Eppru.

"Three people!" Rafi said. "We need a lot more than three people!"

Tibi wasn't put off by Rafi's protests. "More will come; they understand what could happen to them if they don't. They understand what happened in the market, and they know what happened at Brok's house. They will come. You'll see."

The three travelers arrived. They were from the farm closest to the big bend. "There will be more." Tibi said, trying to assure everyone. But he sounded like he was trying to convince himself. About thirty minutes later four more people arrived. Asif rose from his seat as he looked towards the horizon. "Rania? Rahid? Is that Rania and Rahid?" Asif started running towards the group that was approaching. As he reached Rania, she gave him a huge embrace that lasted several seconds, then several more seconds. The other travelers and Rahid watched approvingly, but then somewhat awkwardly as they continued their embrace.

"Rania I have missed you so much! What are you doing here?"

Rania draped her arms over his shoulders; she tossed his curly dark hair with an endearing stroke. "I couldn't stay away. You need help, and Brok's family agreed to watch the children while I'm here. They're great helping out, and the children love them. Rahid wants to help, and he wants to try to ride a horse! I couldn't say no. So let's get to work. I can help do this as well as anyone, and you know it's true!"

"But it doesn't look like we have nearly enough people" Asif said, looking around at the six other people who had arrived. "We'll need at least thirty people if we expect to take on Mukhtar's raiders!"

Rania looked at Asif, then she broke away from his embrace. She lifted her arms to point behind her, and just as she did another forty people appeared on the trail. They arrived at the site carrying supplies and food. They were young and old, male and female. Asif stared in open awe as they walked past him towards the plain where the others had gathered. "Who are these people? Where did they come from?" Asif asked Rania.

"All of these people, all of them, believe that we must work together to beat these tyrants. Mukhtar has killed or stolen from many of them. They have lost much, and they know they have to stand up with you. They are here because they believe in you, they won't be held down by a tyrant, and they believe in Tibi and Ajit."

Ajit and Tibi welcomed the visitors with open arms. They gathered in the green fields, surrounded by the dark sandstone cliffs that stood watchfully on the other side of the river. They told stories of what Mukhtar's raiders had done to their farms. Some of the raiders had murdered some of their family. The luckier ones only lost some animals, or food and supplies. Many looked broken and hungry.

The horses grazed nearby. Tibi called Drendl and Goldy with a whistle. Comet Tail and Lightning followed behind, and Tibi fit the bridles onto all of them. The townspeople looked at the beautiful animals and were in awe at the command Tibi had over them. They queued up into four lines. One by one, Tibi, Ajit, Asif and Rafi showed them now to get onto the horses. Rahid was in front of Asif's line, and he wanted to ride Lightning. Asif walked him around the open field.

Rahid rode patiently with a straight back as Asif showed him how to hold the reins. As they were about half way around the field, Rahid sat up and shook the reins. He leaned down to Lightning and said "Let's go boy! Tck Tck!" Lightning galloped towards the far end of the field, then curved around the bend and back to the group of people.

Asif came running after them "Stop Rahid, slow down!" But there was no use. Rahid was having a great time, and he returned to the crowd of people smiling triumphantly.

They got used to the feel of riding on the horse, and how to use the reins to guide them. Rania was busy in the line, encouraging people to try, and not be afraid. Their fears were soon put aside when people saw the excitement of those that had tried before them.

Just as the line was at the end, Tibi was riding with one of the older men who had been very shy about trying his hand at riding one of these "*wild beasts.*" They were trotting on the far side of the fields, when Goldy, who was holding the older man, suddenly reared up on her hind legs, tumbling the man to the ground. Goldy ran off in a flash towards the crowd of people and the other horses. The old man looked around, and he saw what had spooked Goldy away. A wild boar had been feeding in the brush near the river, and it was making threatening grunting noises now as it threatened to charge the old man. Rafi saw that the large boar stood a solid three feet tall and weighed at least two hundred fifty pounds. Tibi, leaned forward and told Comet Tail to stay still as he stroked his neck.

"Stay still!" Rafi called to the old man. "He won't charge if you don't move!"

The old man looked at Rafi, as if to heed his advice, but then he panicked. He started running away, towards the other people as fast as he could. The boar sensed the fear and charged after him, flashing his curled teeth, grunting and snorting along the way. It would not be a match for very long, the boar was much faster than the man, who had about fifty yards ahead of him to run.

"Boar!" Yelled Rafi as he rode from behind, trying to cut the boar off from the man, but he was starting from too far behind. "There is a boar charging!"

Tibi, watching and hearing the action on the other side of the field, did not hesitate. He grabbed one of the spears he had brought with him and whistled for Drendl. Drendl appeared next to him and Tibi jumped on his back while Drendl was still in stride. Tibi gathered the reins and held his spear at his side as Drendl galloped towards the old man. The boar was catching up to the man quickly, his curly horned mouth with sharp teeth and hundreds of pounds of slobbering flesh were only moments from catching up to the ever more panicked man.

Tibi wouldn't make it all the way there in time to save him. He launched his spear, targeting ahead of where the man was now running, and for a moment he feared he would hit the man, not the beast, with his weapon. As the boar made a final leap to attack the man, the spear landed squarely into the side of its chest, right behind its front legs. The beast fell to the ground with an ear piercing shriek-squeal that carried across the field to the far walls of the cliffs. A cloud of dust bellowed above where his body skidded to a stop. Tibi had fallen off Drendl when he threw the spear. He arose to look at what had happened, fearing the worst. He saw the cloud of dust and the old man still running towards the others. A roaring cheer arose from the people who were watching the terrifying episode before them. The man came to a stop after stumbling a few steps, then stood with his arms outstretched towards Tibi. "Ahhh! You have saved me! You and Drendl have saved my life!"

Soon the whole crowd of people came cheering to the site where the wild boar lay dead. Tibi and Rafi made sure that it was dead with a slit of his throat. Asif came to the front of the animal. He raised the head of the beast, and Asif, Rafi, and the others helped him raise the body as he held the head high above him.

"From now on we are the Riders of Utu!" He proclaimed. "We will NOT be afraid of tyranny! We will let any other man claim domain over us! We will protect each other from anyone who would try to take what is ours!"

Soon the smoke from a feast of wild boar was floating in the air above the fields, and those that had brought supplies opened up their satchels and shared whatever they had for the occasion.

CHAPTER 41

THE NISHAN CELEBRATION

Amid an open plain between two mountain ridges there is a small outcropping of loose boulders and rocks. The plain is green; the Iraqi climate is more temperate this time of year. Grass and smaller brush stretch across the horizon. Among the rocks a flurry of activity brings a set of binoculars peering over the rocks. Mudlarek is peering through them. Through the circular magnification, he sees a group of people gathered together. In brightly colored clothing, men, women, and children are carrying tall poles streaming brightly colored fabric. The fabric waves in the wind which creates a fluid motion of color against the fertile plain. A family celebration, a Nishan, is about to take place.

Mudlarek turns away from his view of the gathering celebration, rustling through a small collection of belongings. He lifts a satellite phone and struggles with the buttons to turn it on. Slowly the phone comes to life. He watches impatiently as the phone beeps and blips as it goes through its signal initialization process. Finally it the phone is ready. He touches several numbers and hits the "Dial" button. Soon he speaks quickly and emphatically in Arabic. "They are here. They are meeting in the field as we discussed. There are about thirty of them, and they are here to train prior to launching another attack on your base."

At FOB Courage, the Forward Operating Base in Mosul, an interpreter repeats his words in English. He is surrounded by communication equipment connected by re-transmitters to Camp Victory in Baghdad. In Camp Victory, Sergeant Blodget is conferenced in and listening closely. It's his decision whether or not to send the drones on a deadly attack.

So far, the drones have been used as an emerging technology and a new class of weapons, but rarely used in lethal attacks. Blodget has been leading the effort to coordinate Iraqi informants across the country. It's his intention to show how useful drones can be in attacking enemy combatants, regardless of the risks of introducing such new technology. Mudlarek, code named Red Baron, has been one of his most important and high profile informants. Blodget has high aspirations for the information he will be getting from him.

"Pull in Syracuse." Blodget says. The interpreter looks over to a communications specialist who makes a connection to the drone launch headquarters in Syracuse, NY. Another communication specialist answers the encrypted phone, and hands the headset over to another Sergeant. Just beyond the Sergeant is a row of technicians who fly the drones to their targets. Each station has a series of video monitors, giving the appearance of an airplane cockpit, as if they are actual pilots in an airplane. Next to them sit the weapons experts. They have another set of screens which show radar blips of potential enemies. Above them are monitors from the drone cameras.

Back on the open plains in Iraq, the small group of celebrants has gathered for the Nishan celebration of Abdul and his wife to be. While tasteful and traditional, the ceremony is slightly abbreviated from some of the formalities often used in a concession to the hard realities of life during wartime. Hassan and Jon, as invited guests, sit with the other men of the gathering. The families move about to set up two small shelters from the weather, and the tall poles with streaming colored fabrics are planted into the ground on either side of the shelters.

Samir is acting as the ceremonial leader in the Nishan. In this celebration, the groom and his family give gifts to the family of the bride. Traditional jewelry and precious metals are given, but in consideration of the family wealth and difficulties during war time, simple gifts are being presented. Before gifts are made, the bride, along with the women, is separated from the men and the groom. The father of the bride comes to the groom's side, and the groom will ask for the bride's hand in marriage. The father of the bride will go to the bride's side and ask if she will marry the groom. Assuming she agrees, the father returns to the men and congratulates the groom. The men celebrate with a drink and mark the occasion of joining the families. Then the families come together and gifts are offered to the bride. Children run around the adults in colorful clothes; Hassan's mother and some of the older family members are sitting patiently nearby on folding chairs. There is a simple elegance about the gathering that is both timeless and universally traditional in its intent.

Just beyond the area where the Nishan is taking place, there is an open field, and beyond that, a group of cattle grazing in an open field. A flock of birds is soaring across the plains, breaking higher, then lower, and then splitting in two or three groups across the fields. They settle into the grasses, disappearing from view. The cattle move slowly towards a watering and feeding trough where a small pickup has come into view to feed them.

Back in Syracuse, the interpreter receives an important update from his commander. "We are green light to go." The drone strike has been approved. The interpreter adjusts his headset and speaks to Mudlarek. Behind the rocks, Red Baron is on the phone and receives the news. He pumps his fist in approval and thanks the interpreter on the phone.

"You will have your justice on these attackers of your outpost!"

He has convinced the Americans this is an insurgent training camp, and these people are responsible for the attack at Bad Asurin Bridge. The technicians can't see the actual people, they cannot tell a group of people celebrating from a group of insurgents. They are relying on the information of one of their most prized informants. Mudlarek settles in against the rocks, set to watch the hellfire brought by the lethal attack of drones that will be coming in just a few minutes.

In Syracuse, the commander has activated the drone command center in Iraq. The coordinates have been locked in, and the attendants are closely monitoring their video screens as the drones come to life. There are green blips on the screen in the weapons technician target area.

Twenty miles away from the wedding in Iraq, five US Army drones go through their awakening routines. Their small engines whisper life into their sleek bodies. Lights blink on and off, they whiz, buzz, click, clack, hiss and sputter as they self-check their readiness. Their sleek aerodynamic shape is a marvel of technology of engineering. They have the potential to transform the world of warfare in more ways than any technology since the atomic bomb. They taxi out to a runway in synchronized formations. As the drones pass before several of the larger military aircraft on the runway, they look like small rodents among oversized dinosaurs of a bygone era. As the evolution of technology has progressed, they have inherited much of the military earth that formerly belonged to the fighter jets and giant bombers. They emerge from the shadows of the fighter planes and transport planes they are slowly replacing. They methodically move into positions along the runway. There is a number on the side of each drone, and the number on the drone corresponds to the terminal screen the technicians are viewing in Syracuse. In a cold, machine-like manner, they sit silently awaiting their orders.

In Syracuse, each pilot technician is monitoring the progress of their flock.

"Tiger 1 on its way," one technician announces.

"Tiger 2 on its way," says another.

More follow until five drones are up and away from the runway in Iraqi. The video screens show the landscape as the drones lift into the sky. The monitors in front of the technicians show a radar type blip of the targets on the field in the valley.

Mudlarek hears the commands on the satellite phone. He picks up the binoculars and adjusts his position to watch from the rocks. The satellite phone drops from his shoulder and slips between some rocks to his side. The light blinks off, the call is lost.

In the Nishan, the bride has started the *"Laylit al henna"* ceremony. Traditionally the bride must change dresses seven times; each time there is a progression of colors. The families cheer every time she appears in a new dress. Some of the children grow restless and are running and misbehaving among the seats. Their mother commands them to stop, and they return close to their mothers. They reach out and comfort them with the touch of their hands. The children watch the ceremony with confused amusement.

In Syracuse, the drone commander speaks into his headset.

"Three minutes to target."

The bride appears in another dress. The guests applaud and cheer the colors and beauty.

The drone commander: "Thirty seconds to target."

Abdul walks from his family and approaches his bride. He bends down on one knee to formally ask for her hand in marriage.

"Target is in sight," one of the drone technicians reports. Others repeat – "Targets locked in!"

The drone commander assesses, and then quickly decides. "Fire at will!" he commands. The technicians make final adjustments. "Firing now sir!" they repeat back. The report can be heard up and down the row of technicians. "Firing now! Firing Now!" Rocket tracers streak from the drones across the fields towards their target.

At the Nishan, Abdul waits before proposing to his bride, taking in the moment. He has a beaming smile as he looks up at her. The bride is humble, waiting patiently for the words to come.

Mudlarek watches through his binoculars, there is no time now to worry about the satellite phone he dropped between two crags in the rocky area he is in. No matter now. He knows the attack will come quickly – no warnings. The drones kill with lethal accuracy and uncanny speed. They fly low so no one will know what is happening until it is almost over. He spots something on the horizon – it must be them. They are approach as quickly as he can comprehend what is about to happen. He puts down his binoculars and joyfully anticipates from the edge of the rocks facing towards the Nishan.

Just beyond the Nishan rocket tracers appear. There are explosions, and dust clouds bursting upwards. It's coming from the cattle field. One by one the cows are exploding into the sky. Rocket trails lead like laser lines towards the beasts. White smoke is left in their wake. Cows are blown to pieces by lethal payloads. One after another they are simply wiped out in a matter of seconds. Some are lifted into the air - and cow meat shrapnel, dust and dirt are flying in the air everywhere. The farm boy sent to feed the cattle is sitting safely back in his truck, watching in amazed shock as the cows are obliterated. A cow head smashes against his windshield and slimes down the glass.

As the drones come into view and approach the cattle field, the noise of the drones and the explosions reaches the wedding party. They turn to look towards the fields. They have heard of drone attacks on parties gathering with more than twenty people as a matter of process. But that was only supposed to be nearer to the cities. The guests begin to shriek and scream. There is scrambling, and they take cover in a matter of seconds. The flags and make-shift shelters are flattened, and soon it looks as if no one is there at all.

Abdul covers his fiancé as they dive to the ground. Jon and Hassan take cover. The Nishan party has camouflaged themselves. Tarps cover the celebration area. In only a few moments the area is converted from a colorful celebration area to a flat spot on the open plains, barely noticeable from a distance.

Mudlarek watches from his rocky perch. It takes a moment for him to comprehend the mistake that has been made. He steps down and reaches for the phone between the rocks. It has shut off. He needs to restart it to get in communication with Syracuse. He starts the process, the phone slowly wakes up and then starts its blips and beeps to come alive.

Back in Syracuse the drone technicians announce that the targets have been destroyed. They check their screens – the blips that were on the screen are now eliminated. . A small applause erupts. Behind them, a local delivery man approaches with lunch – hamburgers for all. Blodget smiles a self-congratulatory smile

Mudlarek fails to get his phone started. In Arabic, Mudlarek screams into the dead phone "You missed them entirely! You hit a cattle farm! You incompetent idiots have missed my revenge! You have failed!" His voice trails off in resignation and indignation.

At the Nishan site, Samir slowly rises, looking towards the destruction of the cattle. He stands up while all his guests and family are either hiding or expeditiously gathering things for their journey home. Hassan and Jon stand next to him, surveying the horizon, looking for a clue. The rock out-cropping is the closest point anyone could hide. Hassan points, he thinks he sees an LED light from a phone or electronic equipment in the rocks. He doesn't see Mudlarek, but he senses him. He senses the ancient hate that has been plaguing his family for many generations. He has been lucky this time. He stands, rising tall among his family, and looks towards Mudlarek. This is not the end of this battle. It has been going on for thousands of years, and there is no end in sight.

CHAPTER 42

QUSAN

The full moon was to come in a few days, and Mukhtar's raiders would return to Brok's farm. Brok, Tibi, and Ajit, returned to Brok's house to prepare. Rania returned to her house, where Brok's grandmother had been watching the children while they were working with the horses.

Asif and Rafi go to the marketplace in Eppru to get more supplies to give to the raiders.

One of the farmers asked Asif "Why should we give you supplies, only for you to give them to Mukhtar? He will only use them to attack others!"

"You have to put bait on your line if you want to catch a fish, right? This is what we are doing. We have to gain their trust so we can trap them. And, if we keep him coming to my farm every two weeks, we know he won't bother your farm, or other farms in the area. Be patient, and we will win this in the end. If you don't give us supplies now so we can get rid of this menace, you will have to give ten times the amount when his raiders take over your town." It didn't make Asif feel good to frighten the farmer, but he had to make sure they understood what was at stake.

When Asif and Rafi returned to Brok's farm with his supplies, Brok and his family was there to greet him. His mother and father ran out to greet him, anxious to hear about his adventures.

"The first afternoon we trained everyone how to sit on the horses while they walked around. We thought that would be enough, and that many people would be afraid after trying it. But they loved it! The next afternoon even more people showed up, and we trained them too. In three days we were able to get fifty or so people trained on how to ride a horse. Many of them learned how to carry a spear while they were riding, and we set up targets for them to shoot at. I can't say many are experts, but we will have what we need to attack Mukhtar's raiders."

Tibi and Ajit laid out the plans for Brok's farm. Brok's family, except for Brok and his father, Bardur, would go to Asif and Rania's house on the night of the raiders' return. Tibi and Ajit would hide in the rocks overlooking the farm to observe, and Asif and Rafi would watch further up the road, and signal their approach by releasing a barn pigeon, which would fly to the barn from behind the rocks where they were hiding.

The afternoon of the full moon came. The house and barn stood in an eerie quiet of the afternoon sun. Only the occasional barn pigeon or bird that flew by broke the silence. Tibi and Ajit were at the rock out cropping, keeping as low as they could. Asif and Rafi were further up the trail hiding along a small ridge that ran parallel to the trail just to its west side. For the raiders to look at them they would have to look into the sun at that time of the day, which meant the hiding spot they chose was that much more secure.

About an hour before sunset, the barn pigeon flew down the trail past Ajit and Tibi and perched softly on the ridge of the roof with the other pigeons. A few minutes later four robed raiders appeared on the trail walking towards Brok's house. They stood outside the front door, waiting for Brok to appear. Brok and his Bardur came outside together.

"We're here for the supplies you agreed to. Bring them forward to us and we won't have to burn down your barn!" Qusan bellowed with a self-satisfying laugh. The others shuffled behind him, with low vulgar laughter.

"Over there on the side of the barn." Brok offered. "You can come here and gather them for yourselves." Brok motioned to follow him to the barn, and his father followed him.

As they turned the corner, out of sight of Asif and Rafi, they could see the stock of supplies ahead of them. Two of them ran forward to start collecting the bags and containers.

Just as they did, the leader turned on Brok's father and twisted his arm behind his back. With his other arm he came across his neck with an eight inch blade. He pushed his face right next to his father with a menacing smile. Bardur winced with pain as he braced against the blade and the pain from his arm. Brok swung around to look at him, and realized he had no backup from Asif and Rafi, since they could not see what was going on.

"We have a small change in plans for you." The leader said. "We're going to need more supplies. Our army is growing, and it takes more and more to feed such a strong army. We'll need twice as much next time." He twisted the edge of his knife slightly against Rafi's father's skin and a small bead of blood broke through and streamed down his neck. "I'm sure you wouldn't want to lose anything valuable from your farm, or your family, so we'll expect to see twice as much as this next time we are here. I trust you can give us your word on this."

Brok was taken aback by the lethal threat of the leader. "Yeah- of course. Whatever you need. We'll get it for you. I'm not sure how – we have asked for everything we could, but we will be prepared for you."

"I knew you would come through for us. Mukhtar will be pleased. You have chosen wisely to cooperate with us." He gave a small final twist on Bardur's back and pushed him to the ground.

Bardur hit face first into the dirt, not having enough time to put his hands in front of him. He jumped to his feet, blood starting to drip across his face from his forehead, and started to come after the leader. Brok jumped in front of him and held him back.

"No father! No! We have to cooperate with them. That's the only way we will be able to keep peace with them!"

The leader was in a fighting stance ready to go after Bardur. He stood down as Brok interfered. "You have chosen wisely again." The other raiders gathered the supplies, and stood behind the leader. "We'll be back in two weeks, and we'll need at least twice as much. Make us happy, and no harm will come to you or your farm!"

With that the four robed raiders carried their supplies down the path as Asif and Rafi watched. They were not aware of the confrontation that had happened on the other side of the house.

Rafi, Asif, Tibi and Ajit came to the house when the raiders were far enough away. Brok told them what had happened and what the raiders had demanded. "And whose idea was it to keep the supplies on the far side of the house where you couldn't see how they were threatening us?" Brok asked emphatically.

"Brok, even if we had seen what was going on, we wouldn't have interfered unless they were starting to hurt someone. They were just trying to scare you this time. Next time I wouldn't be sure. They will mean business if we don't have their supplies. We're going to have to put an end to this soon, and we'll need a way to attract them all here at once. If they need twice as many supplies, they will bring twice as many raiders. Next time there will be more, and more after that. We can't keep up with their demands, which put you, your father, and the farm at risk. We'll need to finish this sooner than we thought." Tibi said.

CHAPTER 43

THE INTERROGATION

Abdul spotted the white van used by Mudlarek and his men coming out of the Sadr City neighborhood in Baghdad. While many vans could be mistaken for one another, Mudlarek's was unique because of the decal of the Red Fist in the window of the back door, a cheap replacement bumper that didn't match the original look of the truck, and several rust spots around the wheel wells and bottom trim.

It was now six days past the events at the Nishan. Abdul knew in his heart that Mudlarek was behind the attack on his family and his future bride, and he was going to stop him. He wasn't sure how, but it had to end now. As the van passed by him, he kicked on his motor cycle and pulled into traffic to follow close behind the van. Just behind him, a Baghdad police car rolled out into traffic and followed Abdul, several cars behind him.

The van stopped outside a warehouse on the north side of town. Abdul stopped several buildings before the van stopped. Abdul took his helmet off and pulled out his cell phone to make a call.

"Hassan, I trailed Mudlarek to a warehouse on the North side Sadr City. I'm going to end this now if I can."

Abdul got off his motor cycle pulled out a semi-automatic gun from his side-bag. He checked it and put it in a leather case he could carry. He walked towards the warehouse to get a closer look. He could see Mudlarek and two men exit the van and walk inside the gated area of the warehouse. They were carrying weapons, which could be expected in this part of town. Everyone was out of sight in the warehouse area, so Abdul moved closer to see what he could see or hear.

Inside the warehouse gates Mudlarek stood back as the two men knocked on the warehouse door. There was no answer. Mudlarek nodded to one of the men and pointed two fingers towards the door knob. The men stood back and opened fire on the lock, which gave way in a cloud of bullets and sparks. One of the men kicked in the door, which bounced open back towards the men.

Outside the gate Abdul was watching through a small opening between two fences that made up the wall.

A gun suddenly appeared at his temple. Abdul turned to see two men from the local militia, one of whom was holding a gun to his head. Abdul turned slowly to face them, hands in the air. The other man came in front of him to look at him in the face.

Inside the gates, one of the two men partially entered the warehouse. Warning shots were fired at him, pushing him back. Mudlarek and the other man took positions against the outside wall of the warehouse. Mudlarek bowed his head and started to summon the energy of the red and blue crystals. Even in the daylight, arching beams of light could be seen in the warehouse yard, gaining momentum.

Outside the gates, the men holding Abdul were distracted by the lights inside the gates. They had no warning when two UN Stryker transport vehicles appeared and six British soldiers jumped out into the street and shouted "Freeze!". The man holding a gun on Abdul dropped it and the three of them turned to face the British soldiers. At the warehouse, just twenty yards away, Mudlarek was concentrating the energy to put together a first explosion inside the warehouse. The beam of energy shot downwards and exploded inside.

The British soldiers, reacting to the explosion inside, ordered the three men to get inside transport vehicles. They took their weapons and forced them face-down onto the floor of the six wheeled vehicle. Abdul was loaded into the second van separated from his gun still in the bag. As they raced away from the warehouse, a much larger explosion boomed from the warehouse, and a mushroom cloud of smoke and fire streaked into the sky.

The UN vehicles careened through the streets towards the Green Zone with their captives. Abdul was face down on the carpet with his hands tied behind his back. In the back seat of the van was Van Etten.

Van Etten bent over to talk to the side of Abdul's head. "Abdul, it's a pleasure to finally meet you. We've been following you for some time now. It looks like we picked you up just in time. Those men would have killed you in a few moments. Aren't you aware that just yesterday almost sixty bodies were found around Baghdad, many without heads? Most were killed in situations much less risky than what you were doing. Luckily for you, you are much more valuable to British intelligence alive than dead. The others we captured will be questioned but most likely let go. We probably saved their lives as well. They will go back and find the warehouse and everyone in it is dead. They won't suspect that you were the target of our operation today."

Inside the Green Zone, the transport vehicle pulled into the British Compound. He was led downstairs to an interrogation room, which to Abdul looked as clean as a hospital surgery room compared to the types of interrogation rooms the Iraqis and Americans were known to use. A single table with two chairs was all that was in the room. They untied his hand and sat him down on the chair. Sitting alone in the room, he was left with his thoughts for several hours before an interrogator came in.

The interrogators name was Patrick Hughes. He brought in a manila folder with several papers in it, a pen, and a separate notepad. Van Etten came in separately and paced around, sometimes tapping his fingers on the table.

"We've been watching you for some time, Abdul. British intelligence can sometimes work along with the American intelligence, and sometimes we work without them. In your case, we have mostly been working without them. You have been traveling in some unseemly circles. But what intrigues us most is your relationship with this man." Hughes puts a picture of Jon and Abdul together outside the British boarding house where Jon spent his first night.

"What is your relationship with this man?"

"That's Thomas Schultz." Abdul replied.

"Thomas Schultz? Really?" Asked Hughes. "Does the name Jon Bishop mean anything to you? Because we're pretty sure this man Thomas Schultz is the same man as Private Jon Bishop of the US Army. Do you know him?" Hughes pulls out another picture from his folder. It's a picture of Jon, clearly the same person, in his own uniform with "Bishop" on the name plate of his uniform.

"He sometimes goes by Jon, from what I've heard."

"OK, Abdul, what about this man?" A picture of Mudlarek is presented to Abdul. "You were trailing him today to the warehouse. Why were you following him today?"

"That's Mudlarek." Abdul says, almost unable to control the anger in his voice at seeing his picture. "He tried to kill me and my fiancé a week ago and was using the Americans to do it. You think he's your ally, but you're wrong. He's your enemy, and he will destroy you and anyone else he can to get power. When you are gone, he wants to control this place with his power. We are sworn to stop him." Abdul is surprised he let his guard down this easily. Perhaps he had reached some sort of point of desperation.

Van Etten pulls back in his seat at the confession of this information. "Are you saying Mudlarek is acting as a double agent with the Americans?" He asks.

"Mudlarek is using the Americans to strike at his enemies" Abdul says. "I can prove it to you. Just a couple days ago he tricked them into launching a drone attack into my Nishan- the engagement party we have in Iraq as part of our wedding ceremonies. He barely missed. I have some pictures that were taken, you can check with the Americans on what happened."

"If this is true, Abdul, this could be of grave concern to us. Mudlarek is to be honored in a few days as a model agent of the new Iraqi coalitions the Americans have built. There will be dignitaries there to honor him."

"Hah!" Abdul laughs. "Most likely he will kill them. He can strike at any time. He doesn't need a gun or a weapon. He has power none of you understand to destroy buildings and people. He can blow things up. And he will make it look like it was done by someone else. Just look at the violence all around this town. Most of it is being done by militias and sectarian violence as you know, but a lot of it is also being done by Mudlarek himself. That's why I was trailing him today. I was trying to find out what alliances he has formed, and which of his enemies have remained against him. We need to gather his enemies to fight him, and we only have a couple of days."

"A couple of days before what?" Hughes asks.

"A couple of days, that's all I'm going to say." Abdul replies.

"What about Jon Bishop? The Americans have him listed as MIA, probably kidnapped, but they have not heard of any demands for him. The intelligence they gave me said he disappeared after an explosion at Bad Asurin Bridge in the North. Then he appeared mysteriously outside the FOB Courage in Mosul. They took him to a hospital in Kuwait City, but he was abducted from his room by a known insurgent named Hassan. Do you know that man? Do you know Hassan, and if they took Jon, how did he end up with you in the Green Zone?"

"I don't know anything. All you need to know is that we support the coalition efforts. Any efforts you make to stop me or him only work against you in the long run. Your interest is best served by supporting me and working with me. If I'm not under arrest, you need to let me go."

"We'll be holding you here for a while, so get comfortable with that. We're going to make sure you stay completely out of trouble for the next week or so. When we're comfortable you have let us know everything we need to know, we'll let you go."

"If you release me, I can help you stop Mudlarek. He's going to launch a large attack within a few days. He has scared many of the local militias into supporting him. They will be banding together and attacking in a few days. You can't trust Mudlarek. He will make it look like someone else's fault, but it will be him. It will be Mudlarek."

Van Etten pulls his chair closer to Abdul. "If we had a thousand Dinar for every informant that promised to have attack information, I'd be living in these palaces. We have tried to warn the Americans about Mudlarek before. They have no evidence he is not an ally, and they need allies in the Iraqi citizens right now. In their view, Mudlarek is a friend. And you are an enemy combatant."

Outside in the British compound grounds, a whistle is heard and a small rocket explodes in the open ground between buildings. Almost immediately, sirens sound throughout the compound. Another whistle blares, and a rocket slams into the side of a building. There is no penetration of the wall, the rocket bounces off and explodes into a small fireball and mushroom cloud of smoke from the ground below. Security guards start scrambling around the buildings, yelling to each other and their communications devices.

Inside the interrogation room, Van Etten hears the emergency alarm sounds outside of the room in the hall. He gets up from the table and disappears from the room, locking the door behind him. In a few moments he comes back.

"It looks like we have to get to another room for safety regulations. We're under some sort of rocket attack, and we're required by regulation to go to designated rooms for safety. I'd leave you here in this room, but there are regulations about that. So, come with me and we'll go to the approved safety area until this attack is over."

Van Etten stands and shows Abdul to the door, and then follows him outside into the hall.

"You Brits are very polite people!" Abdul says as he is guided by his arm out the door.

They are one level below ground, and the designated safe area is in the next building. There is a tunnel on their level below ground going to the other building. The connecting hall has two stairways at either end of the hall leading up to ground level lobbies in their respective buildings. As they are passing by the open stair well at the far side of the hall, a rocket smashes through the atrium glass in the stairway and explodes in the stairwell. Abdul and Van Etten are thrown to the ground in the hall. Van Etten looks around, but Abdul has already made his move. He runs directly into the stairwell where the explosion just occurred. The small fireball has just dissipated into a cloud of smoke. Abdul leaps up the stairway three steps at a time, and before he needs to take another breath, he's out the door of the lobby area into the compound courtyard.

Van Etten is still just getting his bearings in the hall way below. He looks out into the stairwell, but the smoke has swelled into a thick shield. He runs back down the hall to the stairwell at the far side of the building. Outside, Abdul runs towards the exit of the compound which is left unguarded by the security forces who are not concerned with attacks from the streets within the Green Zone. The rockets are being launched from outside the secure area. As Van Etten arrives at the ground level of the compound, he sees Abdul disappearing around the corner of the front gate. A security guard sees Van Etten in his British uniform and halts him from leaving the property while there is an attack going on. Van Etten points to the man running away from the building, but the security guard is much more concerned with the safety of all the personnel than he is an individual running outside the gates.

CHAPTER 44

PLANS FOR A CELEBRATION

Two weeks remained to prepare for the return of the raiders. Rania and Asif went to town and worked with the farmers to get supplies and food ready. Rather than finding protests, many people started to offer even more. Word had spread of the terror that Mukhtar was spreading. There were stories from other towns of the raiders destroying entire farms and killing families. Ten miles to the south, one of the elder women told a story that they stormed the market and kidnapped some of the young men; forcing them to join the raiders. They had killed a priest and raped some of the women. Hearing this, and the news of Tibi taming the wild horses and teaching people to ride them, they were excited to help in the cause.

Tibi continued to train those who would come to the fields every afternoon. He couldn't think of anything he enjoyed more. Standing in the field, he looked out on the forty horses he brought from the flats further up river. Several of the townspeople were not quite fit for riding the horses, but they wanted to help. So Tibi had them gather hay and food for the horses, and taught them how to care for them. Many of the people found a sense of purpose they had never experienced before. The bond between horse and man had been established, and both seemed better off for it. The riders were drilling each other and the horses how to gallop, and soon they started practicing drills for attacking. They set up bundles of brush and thatch in the field, and they charged them from a distance with their spears.

Brok was most concerned about the situation, and for good reason. His father had been threatened with death, and the more they heard about the terrors put upon the other towns and farms, the more they realized the magnitude of the threat.

In just a week the moon raised half full above the horizon at sunset. Brok stood outside his front door with Asif in the dimming light.

"I don't want my father here when the raiders return. We need someone who can fight if needed. It's too dangerous for him. I need one of you here with me. The new moon is coming soon. Who knows what it will bring? The gods have been good to my family, but the evil of Mukhtar's gods seem more powerful now. What will happen to us? What have I gotten us into?"

Asif tried to comfort him in his despair. "I will stand with you, Brok. You have been brave beyond your years. Mukhtar is evil beyond anyone any of us has met before. You're young, yet you have found more strength already than you could have imagined. And you will find more of that strength, and we will help you. The Hand of the Red Fist wants you to be afraid. Mukhtar thrives on your fear. But if we take away the fear, we take away their power. If we defeat them and drive them away, they will never bother us again. With the help of the gods, our plan will work."

Seven days later the night of the new moon had come. Asif and Tibi adjusted plans for what they expected to happen that evening. Bardur was to stay with his family at Asif and Rania's house. Rahid had begged to be part of the action. Rania had forbidden it, but Asif swayed her, saying he was to turn thirteen years old that summer, and it was time for him to learn with the other men. Asif would stand with Brok in front of his house when the raiders came. Rahid and Rafi would be in the rock outcropping watching from afar. And Tibi and Ajit would resume their position further down the path, with two other townspeople. They would be ready to let go of the barn pigeon as the raiders approached.

Two hours before nightfall the pigeon appeared from the trail and flew by the house to the roof of the barn. Asif and Brok watched through the front window in the house. Soon, a group of four robed raiders appeared, and soon after that, another four. They stood in two lines outside the front door. Brok and Asif appeared through the door, this time carrying spears at their sides.

Brok didn't wait for them to break the silence. "Who are you? What is your name? Your supplies are over here, on this side of the house. We have brought more food and equipment. This requires a lot of sacrifice from the people of Eppru."

Qusan eyed Brok uneasily. "Your choices to help us have served you well. Mukhtar has spoken favorably of you so far. You will need to continue this service in the name of Mukhtar, who now protects you."

"We'll give you one more shipment of supplies." Brok said. "But we have an idea to make it better. We will make it a celebration of the end of the harvest. We want Mukhtar to come and be present himself, and bring as many of his raiders as he would like. Call it a celebration of his victories and his greatness. We'll talk about his future, and we'll talk about the best way we can support him. We can't give him supplies every two weeks after the harvest is in, but there may be other ways we can work with him. So take the supplies and bring them back to your leader. Come back in two weeks, and we will talk directly to him."

"Hmm, a celebration" Qusan considered. "That might be a good idea. We could all use a chance to celebrate our victories. I'll tell him, and I bet he will welcome your offer. I'll send one of our men back to confirm this with you."

Brok and Asif watched as the raiders gathered the supplies they had laid out for them.

"It's not twice as much as last time" Brok commented. "It's just a little more than half again what we gave them last time. But hopefully with the promise of a celebration when they come back, we are safe for now, and we will have them where we want them."

Two days later Asif and Rafi assembled the Riders of Utu in the fields where they were training on the horses. "At the next full moon, in just about twelve days, we will destroy these raiders. They have never seen the power of the clan of the boars head and our horses. We will convince them they are here for a celebration, and then we will take them on and destroy them!"

CHAPTER 45

VIP INFORMATION

Abdul sprints up the stairwell of the British Embassy and runs around the corner while Van Etten is yelling for him behind to stop behind him. With his hands tied behind his back, he has no chance of out running the guard in a footrace if they choose to race after him. Luckily, the guard chooses to protect the Embassy grounds and Van Etten during the mortar attack instead chasing after Abdul.

Two blocks away, Abdul stops and looks back to see if anyone is following him. There is no sign of the mortar attack going on against the embassy except for some sirens, which occurred so often most people ignored them regularly. He spots a wrought iron fence along the sidewalk in front of an apartment building. Abdul backs up to the fence, and rubs the zip-tie against one of the rusted edges of the iron. After some wincing and stressed strokes against the metal, the plastic zip-tie breaks. Abdul's hands are free.

He looks down at his hands for any scratches and rubs his hands together, glad to be free. He throws the zip-tie over the fence and jogs down the road away from the embassy. *Did the British Ambassador save his life in front of that ware house? Did he tell them too much? What sort of fate or luck was at play that he would escape so that he could get back to Hassan and Jon, unharmed?*

At Camp Victory in Baghdad Sgt. Blodget sits down at his desk with a fresh meal wrapped in paper and a Coca Cola in a paper cup in front of him. On his computer, he opened his email inbox to look at his new messages. Twenty new messages since the last time he opened his email. Looking at the senders, there were several security notifications, several from Amazon.com, and two from his brother back in the United States. He opened the ones from his brother first. He was looking at a new truck for him and had sent some new pictures. The man who was selling the truck was willing to come down another four hundred dollars, but he would need to receive the cash in a couple of days. Blodget didn't want to feel that stress right now, he had enough things to worry about.

He skimmed to some of the security notices. He looks at the subject line of the British intelligence report. "Papa Cicco Security Alert." "Pappa Cicco? He considers the name for a moment. He's heard of it, but it's not any of his top code names, so he's not concerned. Of course, the British are known to have their own code names for their contacts. If they would learn to use the US system, they would all be so much more efficient. He moves the message to his intelligence folder without opening the message.

One of his Corporals comes in for a status meeting on the VIP visit they will be having in a week or so.

"Here's the itinerary we have so far. They arrive at 1300 hours (1pm) at Camp Victory. They are coming from Germany, so the jet lag will not be as bad for them as if they were coming directly from the US. They have two hours to freshen up, then at 1500 hours (3pm) the first reception begins. We are honoring the Iraqi education volunteers who helped re-establish some of the schools after the raids in 2003. At 1600 hours, 4PM, we will be having some appetizers brought in by local restaurants who are trying to establish themselves. It won't be anything too fancy, and KBR (Kellogg, Brown and Root catering) will have some regular food for those that don't want to eat the local foods. At 1700 (5pm) there will be a short presentation outdoors with another group of honorees. This will be to celebrate the progress of the Iraqi security guards and the local intelligence agents. "

"OK", said Blodget, "How are we spinning the success of the Iraqi security? I haven't seen anything that says they are stepping up to their responsibilities so far."

"We're taking care of that. We have invited a few of the men who have completed some of the training, and we will be featuring the successful completion of some of the training programs, not the strength or responsibility of the training team itself. After that, we're going to honor some of the local intelligence agents we have been working with. At this point we will only be inviting a handful. Many of them don't want to risk any sort of publicity of this sort, so we have assured them we are not publicizing or promoting any of their names or photographs. We are just trying to recognize their efforts in a way that is meaningful to them and show the dignitaries that we have an active program engaging local intelligence on the ground."

"How long will that take?" Blodget asks.

"It should only take an hour or so. We'll have the reception outside, and then we will come inside for some dinner. It should wrap up by 20:00 (8pm)."

CHAPTER 46

RIDERS OF UTU

Tibi worked with the horses every day. He picked thirty of the best riders, and thirty of the best horses. He trained them to throw their spears while galloping, and he used bunches of hay dragged by other horses to simulate the raiders running away. As another bale was hit by a spear, he smiled, satisfied in their progress.

Ajit was busy at work in Brok's field just beyond the barn. He and twenty of the townspeople were busy digging trenches around the field, just beyond the edge of the field. The existing irrigation ditches were about four feet wide and two to three feet deep. Ajit had drained the ditches so they could work in them, and now they were six or more feet deep and another foot wider than before. Once they were filled up with water again, no one could tell how deep they had become.

The day of the full moon came quickly. The raiders and Mukhtar would be there in a matter of hours. There was a sense of do or die. The plans had to work. Asif, Rafi, Tibi, Ajit, Rania, and Rahid were discussing the preparations outside Asif's house. "We've done all that we can. We've practiced, we've plotted and we've had just about everyone in the town involved. I can't think of anything left to do," Rafi said.

Asif objected. "I can think of five hundred things to do. We haven't tried everything in the field. We haven't tried all the horses yet here. But I think we could never practice enough. If things go wrong we'll have to adjust."

The afternoon came to an end. They set up tables outside Brok's house with food and drink. There were fires cooking chicken and goat. The smoke rose up into the air around the house and could be smelled for half a mile or more. It was time to take positions. The tow townspeople that had been with Tibi and Ajit along the trail took the barn pigeon to their spot along the trail. There were ten people from the town preparing the feast for the visitors at various spots around the yard.

As the shadows began to grow, the pigeon suddenly flew down the path and landed on the barn roof. The townspeople watched quietly, then went about their business preparing. Soon Qusan, the leader of the raiders appeared from around the corner in the trail with three others. Qusan wore a red stripe around his robe that distinguished him from the other men. Brok wondered about the horrible act that Qusan must have performed to earn him this distinction from Mukhtar. Four more appeared after that, then four more. They continued until at least forty robed raiders had gathered in front of Brok's house. They were looking over the feast that had been prepared for them, and some were starting to drink and eat some of the fruits and meats.

Brok appeared outside the front door, appearing more confident than he had before.

"Welcome to my farm! We have a lot of celebration in store for you. Make yourselves at home here!" Brok exclaimed. "But where is Mukhtar? Where is the man we are here to celebrate?"

"Mukhtar will be here when he gets here." Qusan said.

Suddenly blue and red light burst from the ground between the leader and Brok. A swirling cloud of blue and red light rose above the ground. Mukhtar appeared out from the light in his red robe within twenty feet of Brok. He held his staff with red and blue crystals as he turned to look at Brok.

"Brok! You have served your family and your town well. A feast for our victories. A feast for our future. This is a feast fit for our greatness."

"Mukhtar," Brok spoke loudly, "this feast is a celebration. It's a feast of the future. And we have a surprise for you!"

From within the house Asif's voice was heard. "Mukhtar, my brother. It has been years since you left me for dead in the cave of the shaking mountains."

Mukhtar leaned forward to look at the stranger still in the house. His face twisted in the late afternoon light. "Who's that? Asif? It can't be. You've been gone for years! What kind of magic is this? Show yourself!"

Asif appeared into the light outside the house. "Yes Mukhtar it's me. You left Rania and me for dead all those years ago. Yet we lived. We lived peacefully and quietly. But you have interrupted our lives, and so many others. You weren't happy just destroying our lives. Now you seek to destroy the lives of so many others. We are going to make sure that won't happen. We have some of the same powers you have stolen from the gods for yourself. Yet we have not used them for bad, for greed, for ourselves. You have used them against your own people and towns. You have broken the one trust you have; the trust of all your people. And now you must be stopped."

Mukhtar looked in shock at his brother. "Alive? You, you and Rania are alive? I should have known you would show up somewhere!" he shouted with a bellowing laugh. "And you think you can destroy me and the Hand of the Red Fist? I think you are confused my younger brother! Be gone and hope I decide to spare your life this time!"

The raiders turned to look at the disruption going on at the house, and they moved towards Mukhtar. As they did, a strange new noise started to rise from over the hill. It was a low, thundering noise of pounding hooves galloping from beyond the hills. Several of the raiders turned to look as the first of the horsemen of the clan of the boars head appeared over the horizon, just several hundred feet away from the group. The raiders had never seen men on horses before, and they thought at first they were a new animal consisting of part man, part horse, with two heads but one body. Those raiders who turned to look started to run towards the path they came from, but there were now riders and horses charging at them with spears from the trail. Their only escape was between Brok's house and his barn, over the bridge to the fields beyond. As they ran, spears began to fall between them. Four of them fell dead with spears directly through them. Several of them ran past the house, and one knocked Mukhtar down as they ran. Mukhtar turned his attention to the attack that was coming his way, just as a spear landed only inches away from him. It was too late to pull his magic energy forth.

Asif and Brok had returned to safety inside the house to escape the crossfire from the attack. Mukhtar made his way towards the door of the house. Asif and Brok returned to the entrance with spears in hand. Rahid, on the back of Lightning, saw Mukhtar moving towards the door with Asif and Brok. With a wild yell he came after Mukhtar with Lightning and his spear. Mukhtar turned to look as Rahid approached. Brok took advantage of the distraction and lunged at him with his spear. Mukhtar ducked from Brok's spear, spun around and knocked Brok down, striking him with the broadside of his staff in the back. Turning again towards Rahid, he swung his staff wildly and hit Rahid squarely as he was riding by. Rahid was thrown from his horse and his spear was thrown out of reach from where he landed on the ground in a cloud of dust. Asif was next to attack and he threw his spear directly at Mukhtar's head. Mukhtar ducked his head quickly under the spear as it whizzed just past his left ear. Asif was left without a weapon. Mukhtar swung his staff around and hit Asif broadside on the head with the end of his staff. Asif's head was jarred to the side as blood and spit ejected from his mouth while he fell unconscious to the ground.

Behind the house the Riders of Utu continued to swarm the raiders and forced them onto the fields behind the house. Many of the raiders dropped their weapons and turned to run in fear. Some of the Riders' spears found their mark and the raiders fell dead or wounded to the ground. With all the exits blocked and nowhere else to go, the raiders were forced over the bridge into the field behind Brok's house. When they were all in the field, Ajit called for all the riders and horses to return to the other side of the bridge. As soon as they crossed, Ajit cut two ropes attached to the pulleys which were holding the bridge down. The large rocks that were raised above the bridge crashed down into the water. The bridge was lifted eight feet into the air.

On the hill behind Brok's house, Tibi used Drendl to pull a rope that was attached to a wooden dam on the hillside above. The rope pulled open a latch, and the wooden planks of the dam gave way. A wall of water was released down towards the irrigation ditches. The water roared and tumbled down the hill.

It filled the deep ravines surrounding the field and soon started flooding the field itself. As the water rose, the raiders were forced to pull together in a small group at the highest point of land.

They had no escape. Several of them tried to cross the flooded field to the trench, thinking it was only a few feet deep. As they stepped into the ditch, they found the water well over their heads, and the weight of their robes and the weapons they were carrying pulled them down to the bottom of the water filled trench, mercilessly. They never returned to the surface.

Brok was watching as Mukhtar raised his spear, ready to strike deep into Rahid's chest. As Mukhtar's spear came down toward Rahid, Brok gave a wild yell and came at him from the side. He drove his spear deep into the folds of Mukhtar's red robes.

Mukhtar flipped to his side as Brok's spear came through his robe. The spear grazed his flesh and continued into the satchel carrying the crystals next to his chest. Mukhtar was thrown to the ground from his position over Rahid. The spear ripped open the satchel of crystals and the red and blue crystals fell to the open ground just out of reach from Mukhtar.

Brok fell forward as he lunged with his spear, and hung on to the shaft as he rolled over Mukhtar to take a position just on the other side of him. He gathered his spear and stood ready to attack Mukhtar. Mukhtar rolled to his feet, and took his spear, ready to lunge back at Rahid. Rahid jumped to the side, and then swung around sharply to attack Mukhtar.

Brok saw his chance to escape. He flipped over to a crouching position and ran towards the crystals. In an instant, he picked up the two crystals and the satchel. Staying in stride, he moved from a crouch to a full run, moving away from the house and the barn. He stopped by the barn to yell for Ajit and Tibi, but they were too far to hear him. He turned and saw Rafi with a spear heading around the house and towards Rahid to help. A few seconds later he was past the house and running down the path by the river towards his house. Drendl and the other horses were a hundred yards down the path being watched by a few of the townspeople. Brok whistled for Lightning and he came running up to his side. Brok mounted him. He turned to the people caring for the horses and said "Hide yourselves and all of these horses until you are sure it's our people who are following me on this trail!" With that he clicked his heals into Lightning and they disappeared down the trail.

Mukhtar saw Brok leaving and turned his attention quickly back to Rahid. He took two steps backwards to a defensive position as Rahid reclaimed his spear and repositioned himself. Rahid lunged towards Mukhtar, who swept his spear upwards and knocked Rahid's spear up into the air. As Rahid lost his spear, Mukhtar moved in. He was almost touching Rahid as Rahid's spear came down from above, hitting Mukhtar's shoulder. Mukhtar pulled his spear back and plunged it into Rahid's chest. It penetrated Rahid straight through and exited out the back side of his body. Rahid gasped in agony and fell back onto his knees as he looked into Mukhtar's eyes. Mukhtar looked back at him as he took the spear that was protruding through him and pushed it upwards, forcing Rahid to come face to face with him.

It was then that Mukhtar recognized the stone around Rahid's neck. The stone he had given Rania so many years ago. Rahid's face, writhing in pain, was a still a reflection of Mukhtar's own face at that age. Why would he have the stone that he had given Rania so many years ago? Rahid fell and lay motionless on his side with his arms pulled to his chest.

Asif stirred from his unconsciousness. He felt his jaw, and then looked sideways towards Mukhtar and Rahid.

Mukhtar looked downward at Rahid and fell to his knees, looking at the necklace, contemplating the weight of the knowledge of who he may have just killed. He reached for the stone pendant strung around Rahid's neck. Did he just kill his only son? For a moment the weight felt too much to bear.

Asif stood, crouched over in pain looking at Mukhtar. "He was your son, Mukhtar! He was your son!"

Mukhtar stood there motionless. Rafi appeared at the corner of the house, watching Asif and Mukhtar.

"Asif – we're coming!"

Mukhtar saw Rafi heading towards him and assumed others were right behind. He gathered himself with his staff and ran down the path to follow Brok.

Tibi and Ajit watched as the waters filled the trenches and flooded the fields around the field filled with raiders.

"Where's Mukhtar? Ajit asked. "I don't see him with the others." Ajit and Tibi looked over the field of raiders gathering in the center of the field, looking for the red robes that Mukhtar was wearing that day. They did not see them anywhere. They turned to look around towards the house, where they saw Rafi waving his arms wildly to get their attention.

"Ajit, Tibi, come here quickly!"

They ran toward the house, turning the corner as Rafi was just reaching Rahid lying on the ground. Rahid lay in a fetal position with the spear through him holding him from falling onto his stomach. Asif knelt beside him and pulled back his hair that was covering his face. A pool of blood had formed from his mid-section in the dirt.

"Rahid, Rahid, can you hear me?" He turned Rahid's face slightly towards him, showing his young face, now with a small trickle of blood flowing from the corner of his mouth. Asif held his hand and he held Rahid as closely as he could.

Ajit and Tibi arrived at his side.

Rahid moved slightly, and opened his eyes ever so slightly.

"He's alive!" Rafi said.

They gathered close to his side as Rahid tried to speak. At first no words would come, then he started to speak with a soft whisper. "It was Mukhtar. He was going to kill Brok. Brok got away with the crystals. Brok has them."

His voice faded as he spoke his last words, then his body wrenched with pain and a final spasm. He lay still with his eyes open, facing the river. Asif looked in the direction of his last vision, and saw the orange and blue clouds of sunset over the plains where he had played with him and raised him as a child. With tears in his eyes, he moved Rahid's arm to his side and closed his eyes with his muddy and blood covered fingers.

They stayed for several moments next to Rahid, then rose to their feet. As they turned they saw that most of the Riders of Utu had gathered around them. They were kneeling in quiet respect. Rafi looked among the eyes of those that had gathered, and he saw a family. He saw in their eyes the pain and despair of their existence of living in fear. He saw the torn dreams and broken families from living with tyranny. He raised his spear over his head as Rahid's blood streamed down his arm.

"Riders of Utu" he proclaimed. "We will not let this tyranny hold us down. We will not live in fear. We will not live in the shadows. We must drive this evil from our lands wherever it exists. We are the Riders of Utu! And we will defeat this fear. Anyone who kills one of us kills any of us, and we avenge our dead. Don't despair for the lives of the lost, they are in a better place. But live to defend all of us and make sure those who would try to rule us are defeated!"

CHAPTER 47

AL FAW PALACE

I.

March 22nd – 0200 hours. (2AM) Zawara Lake inside the Green Zone. A small breeze kicks up around the grassy area and rustles the tree leaves nearby. A circular light appears in the grass. The light grows stronger, and wisps of yellow clouds circulate around the ground. A shape appears in the circle, and it forms a triple flower petal shape and grows brighter quickly. The light begins to sear and burn through the ground. There is a burst of light and wind, followed by silence. Jon and Hassan appear, lying on the grassy lawn. From behind some trees nearby, Abdul and Morgiana run towards them. They keep an eye out for any stragglers who may have been walking around the park late at night. Morgiana reaches Jon, and Abdul reaches Hassan. They gently shake them to wake them into consciousness. As soon as they are awake and aware, they move out of the circle and disappear into the trees nearby.

II.

At 0710 hours (7:10AM) Sgt. Blodget reports into his office. He has a cup of coffee and a breakfast sandwich wrapped in paper in one hand, and his freshly cleaned formal Army uniform wrapped in a dry cleaners plastic bag in the other. He navigates his way to place the coffee cup securely on his desk and places the sandwich next to it. He turns and hangs the wire hanger of the dry cleaning onto a coat rack that is already over loaded with various uniform jackets, coats and clothing of all sorts. The hanger sticks, so he turns again and sits down to his breakfast. As he leans his elbows on the table and brings the breakfast sandwich to his mouth, the coat rack leans to the left under the weight of the dry cleaning and crashes to the ground. The noise and the motion of the crash behind him cause him to jump up, popping the sandwich in the air before dropping to the ground. His coffee is knocked over in the process, spreading out like an oil slick across his desk pad calendar.

"Goddammit – son of a *%$#!" Blodget yells.

The words carry outside his office into the common area of the office. The others in the office look up, but coming from Blodget's office, this is nothing new. They carry on with their business.

Blodget finds some paper towel and begins the task of wiping up the coffee and holding papers by the edge to drip excess liquid off. He looks up and finds Colonel Mark Samuels standing in front of him, watching him struggle to clean his desk. Blodget snaps to attention and salutes Colonel Samuels.

"Colonel Samuels, Sir." Blodget stammers as he pulls himself straight up to a salute.

"At ease, Blodget. I don't want you to hurt yourself. I just want to be sure all the final preparations are done. There will be a lot of eyes focused on us today; we just need to make sure everything is one hundred percent."

"Yes Sir," Blodget says. We have been preparing for weeks now. We've run through the schedule several times and all the support people know what they are supposed to do. KBR is handling catering, security, and escorts. They're all set. As you know they have changed the location from the Green Zone to Al Faw Palace, just outside the Airport. We feel more secure transporting the Secretary from the airport, but the Palace is just slightly less secure than what we would have if we hosted them in the Green Zone itself. We've been working with the UN Security team, they have reviewed everything."

"It had better be right for everyone's sake. This country has been a rat's nest for three years now, and the violence is the worst it's ever been. We've got to be able to show the world some real progress. We need the locals to step up and show they will be ready when we leave, some day." Samuels seems like he's trying to convince himself as he speaks.

III

O800 Hours – 8AM. Mudlarek wakes up and jumps out of his bed, punching the sheets away from his sweaty body with clenched fists. His eyes are bulging from his head, yearning wildly for an unseen foe. They are tinged with blue and red in the whites of his eyes and around his eyelids. His scrawny body is tensed up tight as a board from the dream he just escaped from. He looks around at the modest accommodations in his room. The nine foot by nine foot room has only a simple mattress on the floor with loose bed sheets and a pillow. There is a single window above the bed with no curtains on it, and a small table with a lamp on it not far from the bed. Mudlarek stands and gathers his wits as best he can.

Today is his day. Today he will become the bigger man he was meant to be. Standing to look in a mirror, his reflection looks to him like a man ready to assume the powerful stature he was meant to assume. To others who might see him, he is a hollow man being consumed by something inside him much bigger than he can control. His protruding eyes; his wrinkled pasty skin, and the scar on his left cheek reveal the depth his mental obsessions have manifested in his physical being. He pushes back his receding hair, which further reveals how such a hard life has torn at his face. Next to the mirror is a picture of him, much younger, smiling and with no scar, with a beautiful woman next to him. He looks at the picture and looks at himself again. He places the picture face-down on the dresser and moves out of the room towards the bathroom.

IV

1300 hours (1pm) Hassan, Jon and Abdul arrive at the delivery entrance to the Al Faw Palace in a white delivery truck owned by KBR Catering Services. Each has the name tags of employees of the huge private company that services many of the functions the military does not want to do for itself. The actual employees they are replacing have been given the day off. They are three of fifteen employees who have been cleared to work on the job. Each is dressed in white food service pants and shirt. The shirts each have a small logo over left pocket. Their ID tags are in full view and are pinned to their shirts just under the pockets. Each truck is checked at the security gate before being allowed to cross the long flat bridge which connects the palace grounds to the mainland of Baghdad.

Just as they are about to be cleared from the security gate, a red truck pulls up alongside them. *"Ahmad and Sons Produce and More"* sign is on the side. Abdul can hear the radio blasting American classic rock as Ahmad's truck is directly adjacent to the catering truck. The radio is playing a classic rock song by The Clash, "Combat Rock." *"Should I stay or should I go now? If I stay there will be trouble, if I go it will be double."* Jon winces on hearing the familiar chorus in this strange situation.

They watch as Ahmad gets out of the truck and walks to the gate to hand one of the security guards his paperwork. He's only ten feet away from Abdul and Jon, but he hasn't noticed them.

Abdul looks at Jon, Jon looks at Abdul. Hassan watches their curious behavior. He has heard the story of the Iraqi with the machete coming after Abdul and Jon, but he has not made the connection to Ahmad's truck.

Abdul and Jon move quickly to get inside the truck and motion for Abdul to do the same. They take a seat on some equipment and wait for security to finish their clearance. Dogs sniff under the truck for explosives, and security guards hold large mirrors under the truck bed to visually check for any modifications. The driver brings the security team to the back of the truck to validate the IDs of the catering staff inside. After the check, the door is closed with Jon, Abdul, and some of the other employees inside. The driver clicks the truck into gear, and it slowly moves across the bridge to the Palace grounds. The truck bounces back and forth as it navigates the narrow road which separates the Euphrates River from the Palace. There is very little room for vehicle traffic, so parking will be tight.

"What's going on?" Hassan asks as they settle into the back of the truck.

Jon replies. "Hassan – that was Ahmad, the mad Iraqi with the machete who almost killed us outside the Museum of Antiquities! He was right next to us in the other delivery truck!"

"That was Ahmad? The same one, are you sure?"

"I've seen a lot of Iraqis with guns," Jon says, "but I'll never forget the one waving a machete at me and threatening to cut me apart!"

Hassan backs down on his tone of voice. "OK. Then we just make sure we avoid him. I'm sure he's just making a delivery here, then he'll be gone. We just have to make sure you don't run into him."

V

1600 Hours (4pm) Van Etten arrives at the Al Faw Palace security gate dressed in his formal British Military dress along with four other officers. Driving them in a black Mercedes SUV are two men dressed in black suits, which is typical dress for hired security in this type of situation. The visitor security gate is just before a grand entrance across the water to the Palace. Soon the SUV is crossing the two lane road to a grand arch entryway. Van Etten and his entourage get out of the SUV and briskly walk into the front doors to get out of the afternoon heat as quickly as possible. The security guards look warily around them for any signs of disruption. With no signs of trouble, they enter the building.

The grand ballroom of the Palace is a testament to the money and power that Saddam Hussein possessed. Marble columns, six feet across, support a domed central ceiling. Hanging from the center is a crystal chandelier fifteen feet across, which acts as the centerpiece of the room. Surrounding the hanging chandelier are sixteen smaller lights, in concentric circles around the center, creating a floral effect from below. The marble floor has an inlaid octagon shape just wider than the chandelier above it. It is outlined with inlaid marble petals on each side extending from the octagon. The entourage walks across the glossy floor to the opposite wall where a door opens to a large outdoor pool area, where several people have already arrived.

Blodget arrives at the security gate fifteen minutes later. He's driving a Chevy Tahoe SUV as he pulls to the gate. The security guard waits patiently as he fumbles through his paperwork for the invitation and security clearance. In the car with him are Colonel Samuels and two other officers from the Green Zone. The rest of the security staff assigned to this operation has arrived here several hours earlier. Once cleared through security, Blodget drives across the bridge leading to the Palace.

VI

1630 Hours (4:30pm) The secretary general of the United Nations, Ban-Ki Moon has arrived and is socializing through the crowd around the outdoor pool in the Palace. Prime Minister Nouri al-Maliki is with him as he greets many of the invited guests. Mudlarek is mingling through the crowd. Dressed in white traditional robes, Mudlarek is speaking with several of the other honorees. While he is speaking with them, he is remembering each one of their names and faces. These Iraqis are being recognized for their cooperation with the international allies, as he is. However, as a double agent, he is taking notice.

KBR catering has set up several large tables with assorted foods almost fit for a dictator such as the one that was deposed few months before. There is a large table with three tiers of local vegetables and cheeses. Another table is loaded with traditional Iraqi assorted roasted meats. Roasted pork, lamb kebobs on wooden sticks, and sliced beef next to flat bread, so one can easily make a small sandwich. The guests gather around the tables to try the various local food offerings. The food and drink make for a great social lubricant as the guests mix together and exchange stories of homes far away and other pleasantries.

VII

1700 hours, (5pm): an Iraqi official appears on a small stage that has been erected between the Palace and the pool, so that the guests can gather to see and hear from the sides of the pools. Unknown to the guests as they gather around the stage, two servants, who are not from the catering company, work quickly inside the palace to chain shut all the doors that lead into the safe interior of the palace ballroom. The taped background music that has been playing on the sound system is lowered, and the official taps on his microphone to get everyone's attention. Unknown to the security guards around the pool, the doors are now chained shut from inside.

"Good afternoon ladies and gentlemen! Please gather around, we have some short speeches by some of our distinguished guests, then we will move inside to serve dinner."

As he is finishing his last sentence, a large crash is heard from the other side of the pool. Two legs of the table that is holding the three tiered cheese and vegetables collapse and the food crashes to the ground. The top tier of decorative leafy vegetation falls scattered onto the floor. Cherry tomatoes spread out in all directions like a bucket of golf balls dropped on a gym floor. The oils and dressings spill onto the ground. Abdul and Jon are standing closely by behind the table. They run to the table to try to stabilize what they can and recover anything that can be saved. As they run to the side, Ahmad appears with hands over his face.

"What happened? Someone did not set up the table correctly to support the food! Who was in charge of this?" He stops in mid-sentence as he turns to look at Hassan and Jon, who are now trying desperately to pick up one end of a table that has fallen. Ahmad's face changes to bright red as he recognizes the two of them.

"It's you! It's the two of you again who were stowaways on my truck! I should have known you would be trouble!"

Several security guards quickly approach the table.

"Is there a problem here?"

VIII

1709 hours (5:09pm) Mudlarek checks his watch. Looking to the sky, he expects something to happen any time now. From across the pool, Van Etten is watching every move that Mudlarek makes. A faint whistle is heard, then the familiar sound of incoming munitions scares everyone to take cover. An explosion rocks the area just outside the meeting area, sending a small plume of smoke up between the pillars which make the wall between the pool area and the adjacent road.

"Take cover! Get inside!" One of the security guards yells to the crowd.

The security guards talking to Ahmad drop their conversation with him and run towards the commotion around the pool. Another whistle is heard, and another mortar shell drops, this time inside the pool area. It explodes on the far side of the pool behind a palm tree, which shelters the guests from the shrapnel ejected from the bomb. While others are running and screaming from the explosions towards the door, Mudlarek is standing still near the pool, watching with a cool calm. Van Etten is alarmed, but watches Mudlarek closely. Mudlarek bows his head in concentration. The guests run to the doors to get back inside the palace ballroom, but the doors are all chained shut from the other side.

IX

With the security guards gone, Ahmad becomes enraged with anger towards Jon and Abdul. He picks up a long knife used for cutting pineapples and melons, waving it at them violently. Jon and Abdul drop the end of the table they are working on, leaving it and the food that remains on it free to spill onto the floor. Rolling melons, oranges, limes and tomatoes are now all that separates them from the mad man with waving a knife at them at the other end. Hearing the blasts, they run to the pool area to see what is happening. As they approach the open area, strong winds pick up their hair and clothes. Papers and leaves are flying around the pool. At the edge Mudlarek stands with his arms outstretched towards the sky. Swirling clouds of blue and red light are racing across the atrium area, smashing into the walls and spilling back inwards towards the pool area. Mudlarek turns towards the crowd huddled against the doors trying to get inside the ballroom,. He is ready to bring the full power of the fire and wind crystals down onto the crowd. They cower at the door, screaming at the wind and the sight of the light force about to come down onto them.

Jon looks at Abdul, recognizing that Mudlarek's attack is happening now. Just as Mudlarek is about to swoop his arms downward and explode energy all around the pool, Jon charges into Mudlarek's body. He lowers his shoulder and hits him in his mid-section, raising him onto his shoulder. The shock of the disruption to Mudlarek disrupts the energy flow. The clouds of energy snap into oblivion above the quivering crowd at the doors. Jon maneuvers Mudlarek's body onto his shoulder and runs toward the catering entrance of the Palace, away from where the crowds are trying to get in. With Abdul ahead of him, they rush through the kitchen area and through another set of service doors to the inside of the ballroom.

Hassan is standing in the ballroom, focused on the octagon shaped pattern on the floor. With his head hung low, yellow clouds of light are circling above his head.

"Hurry up!" Jon yells. "We only have a few seconds!"

Morgiana is standing nearby. "The marble is two feet thick covering this portal. This may take some time, Jon."

Across the ball room, Van Etten appears with his security staff in one of the alcoves.

"Hold it right there, Jon. Drop Pappa Cicco and step away."

Jon turns slightly to face Van Etten. His eyes are now emanating red beams of light from the sides, blue from the middle. His face is lit, if not burning, from inside his head. His appearance pushes Van Etten backwards a step. He looks around. The stone walls of the ballroom are glowing with red, blue and yellow lights from within. Jon lifts his left hand which is not holding Mudlarek. A fireball of blue energy appears above his hand. Jon hurls it at Van Etten and his team. It explodes on the ground just before them, scattering them across the floor of the ballroom and crashing into the walls.

Jon turns to look at Hassan, whose eyes are now glowing yellow from inside. The marble floor has a large circle in the middle of it with a radiant image of the sun burning brightly through the edges. Yellow streams of light appear above, and then create a plume of energy going straight down into the floor. Morgiana and Abdul are frozen on the side of the ballroom with Van Etten's men recovering from the energy blast. Hassan looks up from his trance and in synchronous motion, Jon and Hassan jump into the center of the flaming bright circle with Mudlarek on Jon's back. They disappear.

The loud snap! that follows the closing of the portal rings through the halls of the Palace ballroom. The yellow lights, the blue, and the red, suddenly disappear. Silence is the most pervasive sound. The crowd outside watches through the glass in astonishment. Van Etten stirs from the other side of the room. Blodget is watching through the doors to the ballroom, with his hands cupped over his face to see better into the room.

"Now the real battle begins." Van Etten says.

CHAPTER 48

RAGE OF ENLIL

Evening was falling on Asif and Rania's house as a single horse approached rapidly from the path by the river. Rania and Brok's family heard the hooves and appeared from inside the house to greet them.

"Brok, how did it go? You're alone. What happened?"

Brok dismounted, almost out of breath.

"We defeated the raiders – they have been surrounded in the fields behind our house. But Mukhtar is still free. I fled when Rahid saved my life. Mukhtar was about to spear me through, but Rahid leapt at him and speared him. Rahid broke the crystals free from Mukhtar. I had no weapon as they were fighting. So, I grabbed the crystals and ran as fast as I could. I have them with me. When I left Rahid was still fighting Mukhtar, and Rafi was on his way to help. Asif was thrown to the ground by Mukhtar, but I don't think he was stabbed. Mukhtar has no power without these crystals. If he survives our house, he'll be looking for them. We could be in danger here, but I had to get them away from him."

Rania looked at Brok, standing tall before her. "Brok, then we have to destroy them. We have to take them where Asif had planned to go. We haven't practiced going through the portal, but I fear if we wait Mukhtar will be close behind us. I'll get the yellow crystal, and let's go to the portal."

Rania ran inside the house as Brok's family looked on with fear and curiosity. Brok took out the torn satchel and pulled the red and blue crystals from the bag. As he did so they a soft glow lit Brok's chest and face in the dimming evening light. He looked up at them as they pulled back in amazement. Rania appeared outside the house carrying the other satchel with the yellow crystal. She looked at Brok and saw the glow that filled his face and hands. It started to shine even more. The glow came from his eyes a well. Deep red surrounded his eyes as he looked upon her.

"Put them away!" She screamed, more alarmed than she wanted to sound. "Put them away now, and let's be on our way!"

Brok, not aware of what they had seen, stashed the crystals back into the satchel. The lights disappeared and his face returned to his normal pleasant demeanor.

"We have no time. We have to get rid of the crystals through the portal now." Rania urged him. She grabbed him and led him towards the open space by the river, where she and Asif had come so many years before.

They arrived at the open area and Rania hastily took out the yellow crystal and laid it on the ground just outside the immediate area.

"Stay near me Brok, and when I pull you, jump with me."

"But we don't know how to destroy the crystals, do we?"

"We can't wait. I don't know how long it's going to take Asif to get here, so you and I should take the crystals into the portal right now and we will find out how to destroy them."

Rania lowered her head in concentration, and soon a glow appeared from the yellow crystal. In a few seconds the yellow swirling clouds appeared above her head, gathering strength and spreading in size and power. As the clouds grew, the circle grew within the open space, with the same cross shape that had appeared when Asif and Rania had traveled there.

Across the circle, a figure appeared, standing in the shadows. As the light grew, the shape took the form of Mukhtar, coming to the edge of the circle. The yellow clouds swirled above Rania and started to arc over her head. As the energy and light started beaming into the ground, Rahid saw another shape coming up just behind Mukhtar. As Rania grabbed Rahid's hand and leapt into the circle, Mukhtar lunged forward. The form behind him leapt after them; it was Asif. The energy beam swept down into the circle and snapped shut with a thunderous Snap! The cloud of energy recoiled into a grey cyclonic cloud that sucked up into the darkening sky above the river.

Inside the portal Rania and Brok looked around as they floated above the invisible membrane. The blinding yellow flow of energy roiled all around them as they struggled to their feet. They tried to stand. They looked at each other and tried to talk, but they couldn't communicate. Asif had told them the tunnel did not transmit any sound. As they stood above the flowing energy, they couldn't tell if they were moving or standing still. Rania pointed to the direction she thought they came from, then she pointed down the tunnel where the energy was flowing. Brok looked at her, then looked upstream in the energy. He spotted something floating in the energy, then it appeared it was coming at them very quickly. It was moving too fast to react any more than falling out of the way. As they fell to the side, they saw it was Mukhtar gliding past them at rapid speed. They looked at each other and watched as he disappeared into the flow downstream. As they struggled again to their feet, they saw another object coming at them in from upstream in the energy. This object was lying down and was slowing down rapidly as it approached them. Asif glided just past them, then slowly returned and stopped just in front of them.

"Asif!" Rania exclaimed, but she could not be heard.

Asif stood up next to them and motioned with his arms to lay flat on the membrane below them. As he lay down he held his hands in front of him to show how they could control their flow with their own energy inside. Asif made fists with his hands and he began to move down stream with his energy. He turned and came back to Rania. Without speaking, he pointed to his head, then to his other hand and made the fist again. Rania held out her arms from prone position and pulled her fist in tightly. She flexed her fists a couple of times, then she concentrated as she did it and started to feel the energy which made her move. Brok was practicing the same thing just behind her. Soon they were moving slowly down the tunnel with some amount of control, although Rania looked as much panicked as she was in control.

They picked up speed, with Asif in front and Rania and Brok behind. Up ahead Asif saw something stopped in the tunnel. He held his hand to slow the others, but it was too late.

They glided right by Mukhtar, who was hanging onto a corner in the tunnel, still trying to stand. The membrane shook rapidly as they went by, because Mukhtar was grabbing onto the walls and trying to use his staff to stand up on the membrane. As they went by Mukhtar saw they were prone on their stomachs. He imitated them by lying on his stomach as well. Asif and the others looked back at him. Asif signaled to keep moving down the tunnel. Not too far behind, Mukhtar started after them.

They moved faster and faster, at times the almost caught up to the speed of the plasma energy beneath them. As Brok looked beneath him, he could see subtle changes in the energy flow. Now there were blue and red streaks of energy mixed into the almost homogeneous yellow flow. He noticed flows joining the main flow from either side of the walls. Some red, some blue, mostly yellow. The energy flow grew in speed and width as they careened along. They banked the sides of several curves and entered a final straightaway towards a small opening they could see at the end.

As they approached the opening their speed accelerated as they glided down a slope. Just before the opening they sloped upwards. As they passed through the opening, they were ejected into a giant open cavern. The three of them arced across the open sky of the cavern so vast they were only small specs of darkness against gilded walls which outlined the cavern. As they flew through the air, the plasma fell away into a pool below.

They landed onto the floor of the cavern, bouncing and skidding several times before coming to a complete stop in a cloud of dust. The floor of the cavern was more defined than the invisible membrane of the tunnels. The ground was amber and yellow, more firm than the plasma and it had gravel and dirt consistency to it. Asif could stand on the ground, and the others followed him to stand. The more fluid plasma from the tunnels was in golden streams and ponds that stretched across the landscape ahead of them. The stones of the cavern walls were glowing with golden edges shaped into peaks ever rising above towards the ceiling. In the distance ahead of them lay the steps of a golden pyramid shaped temple, or ziggurat, that rose several hundred feet high. There was a stairway in the middle leading to the top, with terraces to either side every fifty steps or so. The air in the cavern was different from the tunnels so that Asif could be heard if he spoke loudly.

"We have to bring the crystals to the top of the temple!" he yelled, and he motioned them to follow him. As he did so they could see a small speck of darkness as it was ejected from the mouth of the flow where they had arced across the sky and bounced to a stop several hundred yards beyond where they had landed.

Asif wasted no time running towards the temple, with Rania and Brok right behind him. As they ran, the temple seemed to shrink farther and farther away from them, as if it were some sort of mirage. After what could have been a mile, Rania stopped.

"Wait!" she shouted. "We aren't getting any closer. The more we run, the more the temple moves farther away!"

The others stopped their running. Looking at the temple, and looking around them, they could see the temple kept moving further away.

"She's right," Asif said.

"So what do we do?" Rania asked.

"Look! Over there!" Brok yelled.

As the trio watched across the field, a cyclone of dust and stones formed just above the ground. The cyclone of dust grew into a well-defined rotation, throwing golden dust and gravel high into the air. It started moving towards them.

"Look out!" Asif yelled as the edge of the dust storm approached them.

From within the storm three shapes appeared flying in the rotation. They rotated around and around in the clouds, finally taking shape into winged animals. As they flew through the air, the cyclone clouds started to dissipate. In a few seconds, all that remained were flying animals, circling the small group of people below. Brok crouched to the ground and the others followed his lead. It wasn't until the animals had almost landed that Brok realized what they were.

"They're lions! With wings!" he yelled as the lions landed on the ground one by one, encircling the huddled group back to back on the ground.

"They're griffins!" Asif yelled. "Giant flying lions of the gods. We're done if they want to attack us."

They huddled together, staying as still as possible while the lions walked around them, flexing their wings and roaring to each other. Their wingspan musts have exceeded sixteen feet across to support the flight of their muscular bodies.

After a few rounds of pacing, the lions inexplicably lay down where they were. They relaxed on their haunches and started cleaning themselves with cat-like strokes of their tongues.

Asif relaxed a little. "If they wanted to attack us, we would be dead already."

"Or maybe they just want to play with us like mice when we run." Rania countered.

"I don't think so. These aren't house cats." Brok added.

Brok stood up and took a few steps towards one of the lions.

"Brok! What are you doing?" Rania asked.

"I don't think they are here to kill us. They don't need to hunt here. I think they are here for another reason."

Brok approached the first griffin, which looked at him curiously, but not anxiously. The griffin adjusted his position as Brok approached, as if ready to fly. As Brok reached the side of the animal, he saw how large the animal was. The griffin lying down was almost as tall as Brok was standing. Brok walked fearlessly towards his head. He reached out to stroke it, almost to pet it. The griffin shrugged him off, rejecting his offer with a small snarl. The griffin looked to his back, then looked at Brok as if to say *"What are you waiting for?"*

Brok approached the griffin's back and laid his hand across it. The griffin responded positively. Brok took the bold step and leapt onto its back. The griffin stood up, looked back towards Brok and flexed its wings. With a mighty leap he lunged into the air and took off into flight with Brok on board. Circling around Rania and Asif, he turned and headed towards the temple in the distance.

Rania and Asif stood dumbfounded as they saw the griffin head off into the distance.

"I think we found our ride to the temple." Asif said.

"I think this place is full of surprises." Rania replied.

They approached the other griffins and found they were just as cooperative as Brok's griffin had been. Rania took off first into flight, and Asif followed closely behind, trying to maintain some comfort in knowing he was close behind her.

The griffins landed on the top level of the temple with a smooth, graceful landing. They walked near to each other then lay down just as they had out in the field. Brok, Rania, and Asif got off the animals in silent wonder of their grace and beauty. As they grouped together, the griffins leapt into flight and disappeared quickly over the edge of the temple and across the fields of Enlil.

Brok looked out at the view from the temple. The vast expanse was gilded in golden and amber plasma in every direction. Vast plains spread out below in glorious golden hues. The temple terraces each had gardens and statues looking out towards the horizon. Rania could even see ghost-like silhouetted shapes of people as they walked along the terraces. Their energy seemed mystically restored by the purity of the air and slight breeze.

Their pastoral serenity was cut short as they spotted another griffin headed towards them. It must have Mukhtar on it. It passed the final terrace and landed on the opposite side of the temple grotto.

Mukhtar dismounted onto the top of the temple. Asif wasted no time and ran towards him. He grabbed his staff and pulled him down to the ground of the terrace, just feet from the edge. Mukhtar rose quickly with strength that surprised Asif. He took his staff and swung at Asif, but this time Asif was ready and ducked under the sweeping blow. Asif charged Mukhtar's body and drove him back further onto the terrace, sliding in his robe on his back. Mukhtar slid backwards and skidded to a stop with his robes splayed around him. As he rose, the robes pulled together under him and he seemed to rise above the ground below him.

Rania, Brok and Asif gathered in a semi-circle around him.

"Rania, we meet again after all these years." Mukhtar started. "My dear wife, I thought you had perished all those years ago. I thought you were passed on with the spirits. And now I find before my eyes that you are alive!"

Rania spit at Mukhtar. "I may be alive, but you are dead to me."

As the spit landed near Mukhtar's feet, a swirl of smoke rose above it, then a pool of light emerged in the floor. The center of the pool grew dark. It grew further into a ring of darkness like the darkest of night, with no reflection or shades to belie its depth or severity. Brok and Mudlarek stepped back from the edge as the black ring grew wider and wider.

From within the darkness a low groaning noise was heard. Asif and Rafi recognized the noise from the sounds of the shaky mountains as they stirred and started to quake. Indeed the grounds of the temple started to quake and they all started to toss, holding on as best they could to keep their standing. A roar of wind mixed in with the groaning as a cyclone of air soared from inside the dark circle. Within the swirling cyclone a giant winged lion, much bigger than the others, appeared in the circles of light and clouds that erupted from beneath. The group of people cowered on the ground trying to look up, sheltering as best they could from the wind, the shaking ground, and the deafening noise.

"It's Enlil!" Asif yelled. "He can take many forms, a winged lion, a horse, or a man! Take cover!"

The winged lion broke his flight path from the cyclone and swooped low just over the heads of the group of humans. He let go a thunderous roar that echoed across the temple and plains, deafening the four people below. The wings of the lion almost brushed their arms which were bracing against any impact that may be coming.

Mukhtar fell back on his arms against the ground. Enlil turned in flight and swooped back again across the area where everyone was gathered. He opened his mouth and let out another mighty roar, this one so loud it shook the very air that carried it to the group of people. The lion turned one more time and landed several steps away from Brok. This lion was more than triple the size of any lion that roamed the plains of their home. Brok turned and jumped away towards the edge of the temple.

The lion watched him run away with one eye as a sly curiosity. Then it leapt onto Brok, capturing him between his paws with the ease that a cat would pounce on a mouse. Brok let out a mortal scream of pain as the lion's claws ripped into his flesh. He was picked up into his jaws and shaken about, then thrown across the temple floor, coming to a stop several yards away. Brok lay bloody and motionless.

The lion turned to look at the others. As he turned, his face slowly morphed into that of a man with a long braided beard and curly golden hair falling over his human shoulders and arms that appeared still attached to the lion's body. Asif and Rania looked in amazement at the metamorphosis in front of them.

"What mortals are you to enter into the worlds of the gods?" He roared. "How did you get here? You have no business here!"

He turned to look at Asif.

Asif was not sure how he found the words to speak. "We - we came through the portal of the yellow crystal. We were not sure what would be here. We – we meant to do no wrong and no harm!"

"You presume to have the right to use the power of the crystal? To come here?"

"Yes – we came to return the red and blue crystals to the gods, so that no mortal man would use their power again. That man over there- Mukhtar, he has used the power to spread great evil across our land!"

Enlil looked over at Mukhtar who was now standing straight on his feet.

"I – I can be your servant!" Mukhtar appealed. "I can rule the world of men in your honor and all the humans will honor you above all others! You will see the glory and wonders that all men of the earth can bring you!" Mukhtar's eyes strained wildly open while he waved his arms in large gestures of grandeur. They seemed small and futile in comparison to the size and presence of the man-lion god.

"You have no business making assumptions or meddling in the affairs of the gods! You have no concepts of the eternal struggles or glories that we live in. Ours is world you cannot conceive. How could you dare to make such assumptions?"

Mukhtar decided he must make his bold move now. "Never the less! I will keep these powers for myself and take my place with the power of the gods!" With that he lunged forward at Enlil with his staff, stabbing into his flank with the end of the staff. Mukhtar withdrew the staff and swung it around wildly to strike him in the head with the blunt end.

Enlil reeled back from the stab wound of the staff. His head flung around sideways as he leaped into the air. His body instantly changed back to the lions head and winged body, which took immediately into flight. The lion roared in pain and anger, which echoed through the cavern walls. Already in flight, he pulled his front paws in front of him, descending downward, claws ready to rip Mukhtar apart. Mukhtar avoided the direct hit of his wrath by falling to the side. One of Enlil's claws ripped at his face from his eye to his chin. Enlil landed just to his side.

With a mighty swipe of his paw, Enlil swiped across Mukhtar and his staff, shattering it into pieces. The end of the staff spiraled around and around and landed at Rania's feet. He swiped again, this time hitting Mukhtar's body directly. The force threw Mukhtar over the edge of the black circular abyss from which he came. Mukhtar held onto the side of his face as he screamed in pain, fading as he fell endlessly downward.

"So you want to know the powers of the gods? You will learn of them! You will learn of them for an eternity in the underworld! How dare you presume to be of importance to us!" Enlil screamed as he watched Mukhtar fall into the eternity of the underworld.

Asif looked at Rania, who was just rising from her crouched position. They ran over to Brok, who was lying on his side, holding his body.

"Brok! Brok! How badly are you hurt?"

They rolled Brok over on his back. He was gravely injured. His gut was sliced open across his stomach, and his chest was pierced from Enlil's teeth through his ribs into his lungs. Rania pulled him close so he could speak.

His breath wheezed as he tried to speak.

He whispered. "Hold me one last time. End this. Tell my family I love them."

Rania held him close as his life faded and his body fell limp.

Asif stood from where Brok lay and faced Enlil, who now stood with human face from afar.

"We came in peace. And you have taken from us someone who can't be replaced. We come reluctantly to the world of the gods! Take your crystals and power and never give them to mankind again!" With that, Asif removed the satchel with the red and blue crystal and threw it into the abyss of the underworld.

Enlil watched the bag fly through the air as it entered into the black circle. With his cat-like reflexes, he leaped into the air and grabbed the satchel as he flew down into the abyss below. As he passed the entrance, the temple shook. The golden luster disappeared. The gilded edges vanished, the cavern walls vanished into wisps of dust, blown away in the wind and replaced with stars. The god-like world disappeared and transformed into the terra-forma of earth. The darkness of night surrounded the stones of the temple under construction. Asif and Rania were dropped onto the cold hardness of the mud-brick top of the temple under construction. A cool wind blew across the temple, rustling some leaves and dust surrounding Asif and Rania.

CHAPTER 49

EKRU – THE TEMPLE OF ENLIL

I

Jon and Hassan circle around Mudlarek as he calibrates his balance inside the portal. Sensing that he was about to gather his senses enough to move away from them, Jon moves in to attack him. He has no weapon, so he moves to take Mudlarek's white staff away from him. His move is too late. Mudlarek moves to his side but falls onto the membrane, avoiding Jon's approach. Jon lurches at the staff and loses his balance on the membrane, falling to the surface. Mudlarek looks back at Jon from his prone position, only a few feet away. He adjusts his position and swings his staff over his body to strike Jon. Jon rolls out of the way, and the staff strikes the membrane with a furious force. The membrane bends down in to the energy stream and rebounds upwards sharply, throwing Jon and Mudlarek bouncing into the air in opposite directions, striking the top of the portal, then back down against waves of energy tumbling through the portal. Hassan is thrown from his position onto the ground.

Mudlarek is shaken but recovers from the tossing and tumbling of the portal almost as quickly as it subsides. He slowly stands on the membrane, but sees that both Jon and Hassan are now maneuvering better while lying prone. He waits until both Jon and Hassan are turned upstream in the flow, and then he leaps headlong horizontally downstream. The membrane reverberates once again as he hits it, bouncing Jon and Hassan as they are turning around to go after him.

Mudlarek holds his hands in front of himself as he pushes as fast as he can through the tunnels. The lights fly by underneath him. He's not sure where he's going, but his clan has told him of this portal, and that there are many ways out of it. As his speed increases, the small bumps and curves of the tunnel toss him closer and closer to bouncing between the walls. He is paying no heed to the speed control; he goes faster and faster. Jon and Hassan follow behind, catching glimpses of him ahead of them once in a while where there is a straight portion of the tunnel.

The tunnel takes a sharp drop downward, and Mudlarek is going too fast to control his descent. He crashes into the ceiling of the membrane, then bounces downward, hitting the bottom membrane hard with his hand. The energy flow bounces violently against the side of the membrane which separates them. Mudlarek is crushed between the membranes and tossed about like a stick tossed into a twenty foot high ocean wave. Mudlarek is pushed, stretched, and crushed beneath the weight of the energy. Far behind him, Jon and Hassan can see the disruption ahead. They slow down as fast as they can, but find themselves being tossed about, sometimes directly into each other. Slowly the energy flow re-establishes itself. Mudlarek lies on top of the membrane, exhausted. Jon and Hassan are quicker to recover. They see their opportunity to catch up to Mudlarek, and they accelerate downstream together.

As Mudlarek slowly recovers from his violent shaking, he sees Hassan and Jon bearing down on him. He turns to go further downstream, just as Jon and Hassan catch up to him with their arms stretched out between them. Mudlarek is caught between them as the energy flow picks them up and starts to carry them all downstream. Hassan and Jon see the change in the energy stream below them. The yellow, blue and red are mixing and swirling together, pulling the trio forward. In the distance, Jon can see the final portal where all the streams empty into a space beyond. There is no chance to grab onto the side of the tunnels this time. They are bound to head through the large portal ahead of them.

The energy dips, then throws the trio upward as they burst through the portal. The flow of energy drops off below them precipitously, but they are ejected across a great open area below them. They have entered the large great cavern of Ekru; the same cavern of the gods that Asif and Rafi entered thousands of years ago.

Their trajectory arcs across the cavern rooftop of Ekru like a shooting star across the heavens. They crash into the soft ground below them, unhurt but gliding and bouncing hundreds of feet across the open plains below. As they land, they are separated from each other, tumbling and rolling as they come to a stop.

Mudlarek is the first to regain his composure. Hassan and Jon are just starting to twist and turn to stand up as Mudlarek has already started to run across the plain towards the large temple before him.

Jon stumbles to one knee as he looks at Hassan. "Hassan, can you hear me here? Are you hurt? We have to go after him!"

Hassan turns to look at Jon. "I'm OK, Jon. I can hear you. But where are we?"

"This must be the Ekru – the Temple of Enlil that Morgiana was telling us about. It's the world as the gods themselves see it, like the other temple we visited. But this is the pantheon of their gods. Except for the power of Ninhursag, we have no business being here. We have to assume that if we are here, we are here for a reason. And that reason is to get the crystals back from Mudlarek and return them to the gods. Come on. Let's go."

II

Jon and Hassan start jogging across the legendary plains of Ekru towards the temple. The ground below them crackles as they run across gilded rocks and grass. The leaves, the rocks, and the streams are golden replicas of their earthen mates. Even the sky is a pale amber color which blends into to the varied shades of the cavern walls.

"What are we going to use for weapons? " Jon asks.

"I'm not sure, Hassan replies. "Perhaps, if this is the cavern of the gods, there are weapons here we can use."

"If you're right, if this is the land of the gods, there is more to this place than meets the eye. Let's look around and see what this place has going for it. Let's go over to that palm tree."

They jog over to the palm tree just a few yards away from them.

"There is nothing here." Hassan says in despair. "This place is barren. In the land of the gods, things are rarely simply what they appear to be. Every feature may have more to it than what meets the eye. This is the Ekru, the Temple of Enlil; the favorite Temple of the gods. I heard stories of this place as a child. Now we may find if any of those stories are true."

Looking out over the plains, Jon could see the silvery mirror of heat waves rising, just like heat waves across the sands of the deserts. Yet these waves were not from the heat, they were from the energy of the plains themselves. For a moment he wondered, "Is the reflection we see in heat waves coming from the heat itself, or is it really the small part of the temple of Enlil that mortal men can see?"

"Let's try something," Jon says. "We're not in Baghdad anymore. Break off that palm frond and hand it to me."

Hassan walks over to the tree pulls on a frond, knowing that they hold very tightly onto palm trees. To his surprise, the frond came right off into his hand.

"Here's one." Hassan offers.

Jon looks at it inquisitively. He holds his hands around the stalk of the frond, studying it intently. Slowly he moves his hands apart along the shaft. The palm frond transforms between his fingers into a shaft of wood. As Jon spread his hands out further towards the end, he expands his grip right at the end. From within his hand appears a spear with a sharpened stone at the end.

"Not in Baghdad anymore is right!" Hassan exclaims. He walks over to the palm tree and pulls off another frond. This time he pulls off each individual palm leaf and holds it between his hands. As he pulled his fingers apart, an arrow appears from each palm frond. When he was done with the fronds, he folds the barren stem from the palm fronds in two. After stretching it out, it folds into a perfect bow. He clasps his hands together at the top of the bow, and it seals together between the folds of the frond.

In five minutes they have two spears, two swords, two bows, two shields, and forty or more arrows each.

"Not bad!" Hassan says. "I could get used to this place. I wonder what other surprises are here!"

"We don't have time to find out." Jon replies. "We have to get going to find Mudlarek."

III

Mudlarek sprints across the plains of Ekru towards the towering temple in front of him. *"There must be a portal out of here in that temple,"* he thinks. For all the running he has been doing, he is not any closer to the temple then when he started. He's out of breath and starting to slow his pace down. In a few more steps he stops to look around, breathing heavily. There is no one behind him, and yet it seems he has barely begun to cross the plains. Looking at the temple, he it is just as far as when he started. He takes a knee to rest and think about this strange situation he has found himself in.

As he kneels, he grabs some of the golden grains of sand from the ground and lets them slip through his fingers. How he wished for a camel right now. But as the wish was passing through his brain, the sand gathered together in the shape of a camel hoof beneath his fingers. Mudlarek stared in disbelief. *"Am I hallucinating?"* He grabs another handful of golden sand and lets it fall from his waist as he wishes for a camel. An entire leg appears in silhouette of the sand. Then it disappears as the sand runs out of his hand. Mudlarek becomes giddy. He grabs handfuls of golden sand and throws them into the air. As the sand reaches its peak before falling, it transforms into the part of a camel where the sand would have hit. Mudlarek moves in a circular motion and throws sand wildly, making a small dust storm of golden sand, visible across the plain. As the sand dust settles down, a fully saddled golden camel emerges from the cloud of dust. Mudlarek sits on his knees before the camel in humbled awe.

Camels are known to run at fast speeds in the open, but not when carrying men.

J

IV

Jon and Hassan pick up their sprint across the plains, but now they are burdened much more with the weight of the weaponry they have created. After several minutes, they stop for a rest.

"This is too heavy, we can't go fast enough." Hassan says.

"You're right. We'll never catch up to Mudlarek at this pace."

"Time for a rest. Let's think about this some more."

"Right – if we could use the palm tree to make weapons, there must be something we could do to reach him faster. Any ideas?"

"Let me think for a minute. We need to wish for something that the gods of Ancient Mesopotamia would understand for speed. Something they created, not a creation of man. Otherwise we'd have a helicopter here in a flash. "

"So what can you think of?" Jon asks.

"Stay there. Let's try this." Hassan says. He stands still and inhales as much air into his lungs as he possibly can. He exhales into the air, with golden streams of wind blowing outward from his mouth. As they cross the area in front of them, they grow into a large sail, with a catamaran boat waiting underneath them."

"Great! This is just what we need!" Jon exclaims. "A boat stuck in the middle of a desert, with nothing but land around to be seen in any direction!"

"Now you're not thinking!" Hassan says. "Get in! but hurry up, the wind is picking up!"

Jon looks at Hassan like he's crazy, but he throws his gear onto the sailboat and jumps on. As Hassan jumps in with his gear, the boat turns quickly into the wind, gliding swiftly along as if on one of the lakes of Iraq. Hassan grabs the rudder and the guide rope, pulling it taut. The sail catches the wind, and the boat speeds forward into the open plain towards the temple. The golden ground below them parts like water on a lake. The wind from their port side of the boat pushes them forward faster and faster.

"You were thinking of the ground of the earth. This is the ground of the gods. It becomes what they need it to be. We need something as fast as a sailboat, so the ground acts as water beneath us. What a great day for sailing!" Hassan smirks as he pulls tighter on the rope.

V

Jon sits forward in the catamaran, looking towards the temple coming up before them. He can see a spot on the plains, looking like it is also heading towards the temple.

"What's that?" He asks Hassan as he points to it. "Is that Mudlarek? It looks too big!"

"Let's see" says Hassan. As they get closer, they can see the four legs and distinctive shape of the camel moving towards the temple.

"It looks like Mudlarek conjured up himself a camel" Hassan says.

"Well, we're gaining on him. We should make it to the temple soon after he does, if not just as quickly."

The Temple is a sprawling complex five city blocks long on each side and four levels high. There is a stairway in the middle of each side that rises through the four terraced levels. The structure is in its full glory as it was intended to be built, even though it was never completed by the Ancient Mesopotamians who worked on it from 3400 BC to 3000 BC. In this world, however, it is completed and remains in its intended grandeur. The golden walls, floors and statues glisten above the horizon as Jon and Hassan arrive in alongside it in their boat. Mudlarek has arrived several minutes before and has already moved to the grand stairway to start his ascension to the top of the temple.

Jon helps Hassan out of the boat. They walk onto the first golden terrace, which is lined with palm trees in large planters all dispersed around the open pedestrian area. Standing nearby in the open area the camel that Mudlarek rode to the temple is sniffing a golden palm tree. The camel turns to look at Jon and Hassan, then freezes momentarily. The pointed ears disintegrate into grains of sand, followed by the head and body. The grains of golden sand burst into curtains of dust to the ground. Jon looks at Hassan, they look back to look at their boat. The sails and masts disintegrate into wisps of wind and blow away across the plain. The boat turns into grains of sand and drops to the open plain, dissolving into the surrounding grounds.

"They appeared only as long as we needed them." Hassan comments.

"What do you think Mudlarek is up to?" Jon asks.

"I think he's looking for a way out. He knows we have him cornered here. He wants to get back outside. The crystals he has are not meant for mankind to possess. Here we are in the halls of the gods, and he knows we want to return them to the gods"

"What's at the top of the temple?"

"I'm not sure, but chances are if there is a portal here, it's at the top of the temple. That's probably why he is going there. We need to get up there and put an end to this. "

"Then let's go. We're wasting time talking."

VI

Mudlarek reaches the top of the Temple and looks out over the land below. Before him he sees a panorama of idyllic golden plains as far as the eye can see. The top of the temple is about fifty square yards. Its surface is flat except for benches that sit across the corners in L shapes. On the stairs below, he can see Hassan and Jon coming up, just minutes away. He needs to find the portal to get out of here, and he needs to find it fast. Looking around the surface, there is nothing apparent that could be a portal. He clasps the crystals close to his body. Looking down, he concentrates, trying to summon a power from within the temple. There is nothing at first. Mudlarek gives one look to the edge of the stairs, where Hassan and Jon could appear at any minute. He looks back down, and there are faint hints of red and blue lights appearing within the golden hues. He stands quietly to summon them more..

Jon is the first to reach the top of the stairs by several seconds. He's winded, but not as out of breath as Hassan, almost a full flight behind him. Those are the benefits of army training.

He looks up to see Mudlarek several yards away in deep concentration. Jon has his sword slung across his back. He pulls the sword forward and considers his next move.

The red and blue lights within the golden mezzanine which Mudlarek is summoning grow brighter, but there is no portal appearing. Mudlarek looks up to see Jon crossing the open area between him and the next set of stairs. The edge of Jon's sword is glowing a golden yellow. Mudlarek lowers his hands to the ground and throws at Jon as if throwing a coconut. Nothing projects immediately from his hands. But in the invisible trajectory of his throw, a blue fireball of energy appears and picks up speed as it heads towards Jon. Jon barely has a moment to react to the oncoming fireball. He rolls to his left as the fireball hits just behind where he had been standing. A small explosion throws Jon several feet more to his left. Regaining his footing, Jon looks again for his next move.

Mudlarek looks down again and turns to throw another fireball at Jon. He hurls it, swinging his robed clothes around. This one is bigger, stronger, and red and blue. Jon runs to his left again, but this time the fireball curves towards him as tries to run. Jon leaps to the right as the fireball explodes just below him. The compression field throws him up into the air, tossed upward like a limp pillow. He is blown into the air ten feet high, then lands on his side with a thud. His sword lands five feet away from him with a metallic clank. Mudlarek turns towards him to send another fireball.

As he turns, an arrow flies by him and lands onto the floor. Another one flies by, this one penetrating his robe, but not hitting his body directly. Mudlarek turns to see Hassan with another arrow loaded and ready to fire. The arrow flies towards Mudlarek. Mudlarek doesn't have enough time to react and the arrow hits its mark in Mudlarek's side. He winces at the pain and looks at the arrow sticking out through his robes. A small red spot of blood appears around his white robes. His turns to glare at Hassan, his eyes glowing red and blue, his veins stretched across his arms and forehead. Reaching down with his right hand, he pulls the arrow from his side with another wince of pain.

Hassan's attack has given Jon the opportunity he needed. Scrambling to his feet, he lurches for his sword and picks it up as he charges Mudlarek. Just as he is upon him, Mudlarek turns and faces him. Stretching out his hand in an underhand thrust, he throws a lightning bolt of energy directly into Jon, only a few feet away from him. The impact of the blow throws Jon backwards through the air and over the edge of the temple wall. Mudlarek grimaces a smile towards the wall, relishing his small victory.

"No!" Hassan yells towards Jon. But Jon is gone. Hassan turns back to Mudlarek. He swings his shield that has been slung around his back and gathers one of the spears that he has brought with him. Mudlarek slings a fireball at him. Hassan's shield, created by the gods, deflects the fireball and it is sent flying off to the far side of the temple floor in a shower of blue and red sparks floating to the floor. Hassan repositions himself, prepared for Mudlarek's next throw. The next one comes quickly. Hassan raises his shield and lowers his body as the fireball is directed high into the sky. The fireball explodes above the temple, showering blue and red sparks over the temple landing and temporarily changing the landscape from the golden hue to a darker setting with red and blue lights streaming down.

Hassan wastes no more time. Pulling back his first spear, he throws it directly at Mudlarek. Instinctively Mudlarek dodges the spear and it falls harmlessly beyond him. Hassan only has one more spear; so he will have to attack in a hand to hand combat. Rushing at Mudlarek, he holds his shield as he lunges his second sword into him. Mudlarek reels backward, avoiding the penetration from the spear. He spins to the ground. With his right hand, he reaches directly into the ground of the blue and red lights below him, which allow his hand to smoothly enter. From within the ground his arm emerges pulling an electric string of energy. He pulls more and a series of electric blue fireballs emerge connected to the string. Mudlarek stands, grasping the weapon by the electric lightning between the balls. He swings them around his head and releases them towards Hassan. The electric fireballs swoop in a circular motion, making a whooping noise as they rotate around each other flying towards Hassan. Hassan picks up his shield and deflects one, but the electric string between them pulls the other fireball around the shield and directly into Hassan. The explosion throws him across the floor sliding across his back. Mudlarek springs upon him immediately. Grabbing Hassan's second spear, he peers over Hassan as he is struggling to regains his composure. With his eyes glowing blue and red, Mudlarek's face is contorted by the inner lights and his blue veins popping from his skin. Hassan wakes up just enough to see the end coming. Mudlarek plunges the spear into Hassan's chest. Hassan screams in pain as the spear passes through his body, then succumbs to the attack.

Mudlarek looks down at his victim with his wild eyes beaming. Dropping his grip on his spear, he kneels down on one knee and reaches inside Hassan's clothes. From inside, he pulls the satchel with the yellow crystal. He pulls the crystal from out from the satchel and cups it in his hand. Now, with the three crystals in his possession, no one will be able to stop him.

VII

Mudlarek rises from Hassan's body with the yellow crystal in his grasp. He slowly walks across the top of the temple contemplating the weight of the victory he has just achieved. Walking across the floor, he considers all of those who have gone before him waiting for this day. Waiting for the day when the Hand of the Red Fist would have all of the crystals, and never be able to be challenged again. Looking out over the cavernous opening of the Temple of Enlil, he has achieved something the gods had never anticipated. He is as one of them. The sting of the Hassan's arrow is now gone. He stretches out his arms triumphantly. "I'm invincible!"

"Not so fast." A voice is heard from across the temple. Mudlarek looks up. Across the temple a young woman is walking toward him. Behind her, a young man is following.

"Morgiana, Abdul, how did you ever get here?" he asks with more amusement than concern.

"We jumped into the portal behind the three of you." Abdul responds. "We were about to be shot by the Brit. We had no choice."

"Well, you should have stayed where you were. You have no power here. Leave now and I may let you live. You can tell people of the great victory I have achieved. They will all bow to me from now on."

"Maybe not." Morgiana added. From behind her back she produced the old wooden spear, now fully restored from the remnant taken from the Ministry of Antiquities. "This is the spear that defeated the enemy thousands of years ago in this very same spot. It has been preserved all these years in Baghdad and now the power of the gods has restored it."

"And this is the staff that sealed the crystals for the ages, thousands of years ago." Abdul brought forward Mukhtar's staff with the white stone inserted into the wood from thousands of years ago.

"Impossible! Mudlarek says. "No one can stop me now. I have the red and blue crystals!"

"Except in the land of the gods!" Morgiana corrects him.

Morgiana moves in to attack Mudlarek with the spear. Mudlarek dodges her attack and momentarily grabs the shaft of the spear, swinging her around. To his surprise, she hangs on and plants her feet firmly on the ground. She swings him around and pushes the spear against his side with strength fit for a man more than three times her size. Mudlarek is swung wildly around as Morgiana gives a push and forces him to slide across the floor of the temple to the far side.

"Do it now!" She yells to Abdul.

Abdul grabs the shaft of the staff and raises it above his head. He plunges it down sharply into the floor of the temple. The temple floor vibrates violently, shaking them about. They are tossed about like pebbles on the shore. The floor of the temple under Mudlarek disintegrates, shattering into shards of sharp rocks. He falls, spiraling downward into an endless chasm towards the underworld. Many of the stones in the walls of the Temple fall into the chasm on top of Mudlarek in the infinity below. The rest of the temple disintegrates around Abdul and Morgiana, and they are dropped onto the mortal earth below.

CHAPTER 50

HOMEWARD

As the sun rose over the eastern valley of the Euphrates
River, the temple of Enlil rose above a thin blanket of fog
over the valley. Fertile fields were spotted with occasional palm
trees peeking through the fogged landscape. Asif and Rania
started to stir after sleeping one level below the top of the
terrace. As they awoke in the mortal world they looked out over
the valley with a new perspective of the world they saw. They
decided to climb as far up the stairs and see in the daylight what
had happened the night before. They could climb almost to the
top, but several of the stairs near the top were missing. As they
peered over the edge, they saw a deep abyss that had opened up
in the middle of the temple. The sides and top of the temple had
caved in and were scrambled in a heap at the bottom of the
abyss.

"This is the temple of Enlil," Asif said. "They have been
building this temple for twenty years. Rafi and I visited here
when we were exploring the yellow crystal, and we knew this
would be a good place to capture Mukhtar, if we could get him
to the top."

"But why did he fall?" Rania asked.

"Enlil had once been condemned to the underworld. It was
there that his wife bore his sons. In the world of Enlil, the
gateway to the underworld still exists. In the mortal world, it's a
deep hole in the ground. When we were in the tunnel, we saw
the world as the gods would see the world, only through our
eyes. The membrane we could stand on was only held up by the
energy of the gods. It was like water holds up a flower, or how
the tide is brought in by the sea. This temple was not
completed. When I threw the crystals to the center of the terrace,
Mukhtar had to go directly over where the gateway to the

underworld was. We stood above this rock terrace that had been built. When I took his staff and penetrated the membrane, I disrupted the flow of energy from the gods which separated the godly and the mortal world. The flow stopped, and dropped Mukhtar into the underworld. We were dropped back into the mortal world as the energy flow retreated to the gods like the tide retreats from the shore, or like water disappears from a flower. It will come back with time, as the tide returns and the rain returns, all in its time. Mukhtar is buried into the underworld of the gods. He and the red and blue crystals will be sealed for eternity under this temple, and we must guarantee that the power of the crystals is not put into the hands of men again."

"How do we know he's gone forever?" Rahid asked.

"There is no way to return to the mortal world from the underworld." Asif replied.

"And how will we get home?" asked Rania.

"We'll follow the river to the west and the north. We'll find the branch that leads us back to Eppru, and in a few days' time we will be back with our friends. I sure wish we had one of those griffins now!"

CHAPTER 51

BAGHDAD AIRPORT

From the tarmac of the Baghdad airport, a low hiss is heard as the C40 cargo plane approaches the runway. The hiss turns into a roar and the plane engulfs the tarmac with wind and noise. The wheels touch down, with smoke swirling into a cyclone as the wheels spin up to meet the ground. As the plane roars down the runway, it flashes past four bodies lying in the burnt out grass on the side of the runway. The pilot doesn't see it. One of the co-pilots does.

"What was that? That looked like some bodies lying in the grass back there."

"I didn't see anything. You'd better report it, just in case."

Jon lay across the tarmac of the landing strip, face down. As the C40 roared overhead, he was shaken into consciousness by the noise and wind. Looking up at the belly of the plane, he freezes as the landing gear smokes to life around him. He looks around. Abdul is several yards away on the north side, just starting to roll over into consciousness. Hassan's body is lying in the grass on the south side of the runway. Morgiana is lying directly on the tarmac, several feet closer to danger than Jon. He rises unsteadily, looking behind him to see when the next plane is coming in. He reaches Morgiana as he spots another cargo plane headed for them. He stumbles as he picks her up, still unconscious. He carries her to the side of the grassy area on the north side of the runway next to Abdul.

Jon collapses in the grass next to Morgiana as the next cargo plane roars onto the tarmac just yards away.

Thirty minutes later, four ambulances have scrambled out on the tarmac.

The radio tower calls one of the first responders.

"We've got four bodies here, sir. Three are still alive and appear to be in stable but serious condition. One may be an American. We have one dead, who appears to be an Iraqi civilian. We'll clean it up for ya and you should be able to get your runway back open about thirty minutes."

"Roger that," the tower says.

II

At the Army hospital in Baghdad, Jon Bishop lays on his back in a hospital bed. A heart rate monitor is blinking by his side, with an intravenous bag dripping slowly into a plastic tube leading to his body.

Jon squints his eyes as he opens them. The sleep in his eyes distorts his first view.

Outside the room Sergeant Van Etten is sitting on a chair looking at his new iPhone. A nurse comes out of his room.

"I think he's waking up, Sergeant."

Van Etten turns and looks at the nurse. "Oh thank you. I'll be right in."

Inside the room Jon is staring at the ceiling. Van Etten approaches his bed.

"Jon. You're safe now. You're in a US Army hospital in Baghdad. We think you're a hero of sorts, but we have lots of questions for you."

"Honestly Sir," Jon replies. "I don't think I can remember anything just now. Maybe it will come to me later. But right now, I remember nothing."

III

Two weeks later Jon passes his ticket to the airline ticket checker at the gate at the Baghdad airport. He's booked on the military flight from Baghdad to Kuwait City. From there he will go to the US base in Munich, Germany on a commercial flight; and from there back to Chicago, before heading home to Oak Brook. With his duffel bag in hand and his casual Khakis on, he's got his pass home. He takes his seat over the wing and checks his paperwork. Discharge papers – check, Doctors diagnosis – PTSD, Post Traumatic Stress Disorder – check.

Medication, check. Looking out the small airplane window over the airport grounds he can see sand, and more sand. It's everywhere. He can't wait to get out back home where he belongs. Looking further out, he can see the lights on the buildings of Baghdad. A spire from a mosque, some warehouses, and the lights from a bridge over the Euphrates make up the skyline.

As the Boeing 747 taxis down the runway to take off, the pilot comes over the speaker. "Right now we're number two for takeoff. We should be on our way shortly." Jon's arms tense up as the anticipation builds. He never liked flying. He likes it less now.

Underneath the plane the landing lights under the wing light the way as the plane taxis. At the final turn to the takeoff runway, the plane rotates around counter clockwise. The plane is over the area of the runway where Jon, Morgiana, Abdul and Hassan were found. Alongside the plane and along the side of the tarmac, yellow, blue and red lights emerge from the rocks and stone under the runway. Jon stiffens his arms and looks up toward the flight attendant walking by. His eyes are glowing yellow from inside. Luckily, the attendant and his seat mate are looking the other way. The plane completes the turn and accelerates down the runway, wheels lifting into the sky. Jon's eyes return to normal. The engines roar as the plane thrusts upward into the night sky over Baghdad.

ABOUT THE AUTHOR

Jeffrey Carl lives with his wife and family in upstate New York. When not working or writing, he enjoys hiking or sailing in the Adirondack Mountains. He would love to hear from you at http://jeffreycarlauthor.wordpress.com/. Latest update January 2014.

www.ingramcontent.com/pod-product-compliance
Lightning Source LLC
Chambersburg PA
CBHW070810180626
46818CB00001B/192